"I_____" Shouted.

Grimaldi eased off the accelerator, falling back a few yards. Behind him Bolan powered down his window and leaned out, rattling off a diversionary burst. The ploy worked. The Stony Man warriors heard the faint throttle of the AK-47, but the rounds flew wide of their mark.

Kissinger had ducked below the dash, but righted himself, clutching his pistol, his eyes fixed on the rear of the panel truck in front of them.

"Looks like the guy's reloading," Grimaldi warned, putting the pedal to the metal. "Hang on. I'm going to ram them!" The Stony Man pilot was executing a last-ditch play. If they didn't stop the truck, Franklin Colt was as good as dead.

Don Pendleton's Mack Bolan®

Blood Play

A GOLD EAGLE BOOK FROM

WORLDWIDE®

TORONTO • NEW YORK • LONDON
AMSTERDAM • PARIS • SYDNEY • HAMBURG
STOCKHOLM • ATHENS • TOKYO • MILAN
MADRID • WARSAW • BUDAPEST • AUCKLAND

Recycling programs
for this product may
not exist in your area.

First edition July 2010

ISBN-13: 978-0-373-61538-4

Special thanks and acknowledgment to
Ron Renauld for his contribution to this work.

BLOOD PLAY

Printed in U.S.A.

When a friend is in trouble, don't annoy him by asking if there is anything you can do. Think up something appropriate and do it.

—Edgar Watson Howe
1853–1937

What's appropriate is direct action against perpetrators who commit atrocities for their own profit. Law-abiding people have no chance against these predators. That's where I come in.

—Mack Bolan

PROLOGUE

Taos, New Mexico

Walter Upshaw stared noncommitally at the elaborate architectural drawings laid out on the table of his modest two-bedroom home. It was situated atop Pueblo Peak, which afforded a panoramic view of the one-hundred-thousand-acre tribal reservation he helped administer as seven-time president of the Taos Pueblo Governing Council. One set of drawings illustrated a proposed sixty-thousand-square-foot casino with an attached four-story, four-hundred-room hotel. Another rendering transposed the designated site for the gaming facility onto a topographical map that included several circled areas set deep in the Taos Mountains. There were no markings to explain the intended use of the latter areas, but Upshaw knew they indicated long-abandoned uranium mines. Resting next to the topo map was a manila file filled with documentation as to various means by which to carry on an environmental cleanup of the sites.

"You've certainly put a lot of effort into this presentation," Upshaw finally told the two men who'd made the arduous four-mile drive up a winding mountain road to confer with the tribal leader. He'd already met Freddy McHale, a bald, barrel-chested man of roughly the same age, several times during the past few months. McHale's colleague, a younger, rusty-haired man who'd been introduced as Pete Trammell, was noticeably shorter than his companion and had said only a few words since Upshaw had invited them into his house. McHale, on behalf of Global Holdings Corporation, ran the gambling operations at the Roaming Bison Casino, a co-venture with the Rosqui Tribal Council located an hour's drive south of Taos on the outskirts of Santa Fe. McHale had told Upshaw that Trammell was GHC's Ancillary Project Manager. The widowed tribal leader hadn't bothered to ask for a translation as to what such a job might entail.

McHale smiled amicably. "I know we've already hashed out most of this a few times and gone over some crude drawings," he said, his voice tinged with what seemed to Upshaw more of an Eastern European accent than the Irish brogue his name would suggest. "But I thought maybe if you had a clearer picture of what we had in mind you'd see this as a win-win deal. We're not only offering you a way to increase your pueblo's per capita income by at least a hundred percent, we're also committed to cleaning up uranium sites that, if they existed outside the reservation, would likely be declared EPA supersites due to the risk of toxic exposure."

"I can't help thinking there has to be some kind of ulterior motive on your part," Upshaw replied. "All this altruism about cleaning up the uranium sites… I'm sorry, but something about it doesn't ring true."

"It's not just altruism," McHale explained. "As you know, we don't just run the casino at Rosqui, we're also in charge of the nuclear waste site there. We have a sound track record on that front, and it'd be easy enough for us to secure funding to add facilities for dealing with your uranium."

"It's business," Trammell piped in.

"And a successful one," McHale went on. "If you don't believe us, ask any of your colleagues at Rosqui. They get a cut of both ventures, just as you would here."

"You've presented this same argument every time we've met," Upshaw said, "and when I counter with my position, I can almost see the words going in one ear and out the other."

"I'm sorry you feel that way." McHale's voice had begun to lose its tone of cordiality. The shift was not lost on Upshaw, but he pretended not to notice.

"Rosqui Pueblo is a bit fonder of Red Capitalism than we are here in Taos," the tribal president went on. "Here, we're already a bit uncomfortable with what little gambling we offer at our small casino. We have, if you'll pardon the pun, certain reservations about expanding things any further. As for the uranium mines, they're located far from any inhabited areas, and we've already conducted tests to confirm that the tailings are in no danger of leaching into the watershed. The way I see it, it's a case of 'let sleeping dogs lie.'"

"Are you sure you speak for the majority of your people?" McHale asked. "Not to mention your fellow members of the tribal council?"

Upshaw narrowed his eyes and stared hard at the businessmen.

"I'm in charge of this pueblo," he said coldly. "I hope I'm wrong in sensing that you've been trying to wheel and deal behind my back."

"We've requested all along that we be allowed to make a presentation to the entire council," McHale countered. "You keep refusing. Why is that?"

"I have my reasons."

"It's because you know they'd probably back our offer."

"I think you're mistaken."

"There's one way to find out."

"If this were a poker game, I'd call your bluff," Upshaw said. "As it is, however, I'll merely advise you that if I find out you're trying to make an end run around my authority, there will be consequences."

"Are you threatening me?" McHale asked.

"I'm a man of action," Upshaw replied. "I don't bother with threats."

"Neither do we," Trammell snapped.

McHale shot Trammell an angry glance. Chastened, the shorter man diverted his gaze and fell silent. McHale turned back to Upshaw.

"Seats on the governing council are elected positions," he said. "As is the council presidency."

"I've been reelected by a landslide every time I've run for another term," Upshaw said. "I don't see that changing."

"Times have changed, Walter, and not for the better. Your people are struggling to make ends meet like everyone else. If they see a way to better their lot, are you certain they'll be willing to stick with the status quo?"

"I'll thank you not to address me by my first name, Mr. McHale," Upshaw said. "We're getting nowhere here and I have some other matters to attend to, so I would suggest that we call it a day."

McHale stared at Upshaw a moment, then sighed and began to gather up his presentation materials. Trammell grabbed a large leather portfolio propped next to the table and held it open so McHale could slip the materials inside.

"I have computer copies of all this," McHale told Upshaw. "I'll send them to you and maybe once you've had a chance to look everything over more thoroughly—"

"There's no need for that," Upshaw interrupted. "I've already committed to a small expansion of our existing casino with our current partners. That's as far as I intend to see things go."

McHale stopped what he was doing. His neck flushed crimson and the rage in his eyes was matched by the coldness in his voice. "What did you just say?"

"You heard me," Upshaw said evenly. "I'd prefer to stick with the people I'm already working with. Nothing personal."

"If you've already made up your mind," McHale said, "then why did you have us come all the way out here to the middle of nowhere and make a presentation?"

"I wanted to see your reaction," Upshaw said calmly. "You really need to work on your poker face, Mr. McHale."

McHale checked himself and slowly continued putting away the drawings and files. By the time he'd finished, he'd regained his composure. He took the portfolio from Trammell and tucked it under one arm, then extended the other to Upshaw.

"I'm sorry we couldn't do business, Mr. Upshaw, but thank you for your time."

Upshaw stared at McHale's hand but refused to shake it. "Good day, gentlemen," he said. "I'm sure you can find your way out."

McHale pulled his hand back. Trammell was already headed for the door. McHale followed him. A few minutes later they were back in McHale's customized Hummer, heading back down the long service road linking Upshaw's home with the existing casino, a small converted lodge visible two miles below on a plain at the foot of the mountain.

"He knows something," Trammell said, speaking, not in English but in his native Russian. McHale nodded, then responded in the same language.

"We've had our suspicions he might."

"We need to consider our contingency plan, then," Trammell said.

McHale nodded again as he navigated a turn in the road. "We need to step up surveillance on him," he said. "Tap his phone, hack his computer, tail him. Whatever it takes to find out who tipped him off."

"It has to be somebody at Rosqui."

"More than likely," McHale said. "Keep an eye on his son, too. He'll factor into this."

"Orson, too?"

"Absolutely," McHale replied. "There has to be a way we can kill two birds with one stone here."

"More than just two," Trammell said ominously. "And I have a feeling we'll be killing more than just birds."

CHAPTER ONE

Stony Man Farm, Virginia

Mack Bolan was twenty minutes into his jog on one of the gymnasium treadmills facing a floor-to-ceiling window that overlooked the eastern perimeter of Stony Man Farm. Through the window he could see the bare-limbed, regimentally planted poplars surrounding the distant Annex as well as the tip of that building's storage silo, which outsiders were led to believe contained nothing but wood chips ground up as a byproduct of the Farm's timber-harvesting venture. In fact, the uppermost cavity of the silo contained not only a concealed array of antiaircraft ordnance but also a bevy of communications antennae and data-link transmitters servicing the cybernetic team operating out of the subterranean bunker facility located one floor down from the lumber mill. Two blacksuits stationed amid the poplars were equally discreet, busying themselves with farm chores, their firearms concealed beneath coveralls and lightweight shirts so as to not give away their primary function, which was to safeguard this, the clandestine headquarters for America's foremost covert task force. Bolan himself was a key player for the Sensitive Operations Group, having helped found the organization years ago when his War Everlasting had expanded from forays against organized crime to tackling the global threat posed by terrorists, drug cartels and other entities hell-bent on subverting U.S. interests in pursuit of their own self-serving agendas. For the moment, the warrior who'd come to be known as the Executioner was between assignments, but there was already another mission in the offing, and within the hour Bolan expected to be en route to the West Coast to engage once more with the enemy. As always, he planned to be ready for the challenge.

"I figured I might find you here."

Bolan continued to jog in place as he glanced over at the attractive, blond-haired woman approaching the treadmills. Barbara Price was SOG's mission controller, but she and Bolan shared a bond that went far beyond their mutual commitment to the Farm's top-secret charter. A few short hours ago, they'd been in each other's arms back in Price's bedroom at the farmhouse, a gentrified structure that helped the Farm present itself outwardly as just another of many upwardly mobile country estates dotting this remote sprawl of Virginia's Blue Ridge Mountains.

"I thought I gave you enough exercise for one day, soldier," Price teased.

Bolan grinned faintly. "I figured I'd tire myself out a little more so I can sleep on the flight," he replied. They both spoke quietly, barely above a whisper, mindful of several off-duty blacksuits working out with free weights on the other side of the exercise room.

"They're still refueling the jet," Price responded. "I just heard from Ironman, though. They're bogged down on logistics and don't figure to have their ducks in a row until sometime late tomorrow. So you have the option of laying over in Albuquerque for that convention Cowboy's attending."

Ironman was Carl Lyons, field leader for Able Team, SOG's go-to commando squad for countermanding threats to the U.S. usually on American soil. The three-man team had been deployed a few days ago to Seattle, where it was now closing in on a smuggling ring purported to be running arms across the border in nearby Vancouver. The smugglers were linked to a survivalist sect on file in the Farm databases for actively abetting several purported al Qaeda sleeper cells throughout the Northwest. Able Team was concerned about spreading itself too thin in pursuit of the various leads that had turned up since its arrival, prompting Bolan's offer to fly out and lend a hand. Intent as he was on tackling the assignment, the Executioner also saw merit in the notion of spending an extra half-day in Albuquerque with John "Cowboy" Kissinger, the Farm's resident weaponsmith. Kissinger would be attending a three-day trade show focused on the latest advancements in weaponry and combat gear, and Bolan was intrigued by some of the breakthroughs Kissinger had told him about. Anything that would help give him and his fellow commandos an edge over the enemy, Bolan felt, was always worth a firsthand look.

He switched off the treadmill and slowed his jogging in time with the decreasing churn of the rubberized belt beneath his feet.

"Let's play it by ear," he told Price. "It'll be a good eight hours before we're in New Mexico. A lot could happen between now and then."

Price smiled faintly. "The voice of experience."

Bolan nodded. "One thing I've learned about the enemy is that their game plan can change on a dime," he said. "We need to be able to do the same."

CHAPTER TWO

Taos, New Mexico

An early-evening spring breeze rustled the leaves as Petenka Tramelik, aka Pete Trammell, stole his way through a stand of cottonwoods surrounding the estate of Alan Orson. With him was Vladik Barad, a fellow member of Vympel, the special-operations arm of Russia's Foreign Intelligence Service, SVR. There was a faint chill in-air thanks to an approaching storm front that was already soaking central New Mexico. Tramelik figured they had time to carry out their mission before the rain came. Afterward, he would welcome the downpour, as it would help to obscure any boot prints he and Barad might leave along the dirt trail leading to Orson's spread, a five-acre parcel located north of Taos near the small New Mexico town's municipal airport.

Both men had staked out the property the three previous nights, establishing Orson's routine as well as that of Walter Upshaw's estranged thirty-year-old son, Donny, who served as Orson's groundskeeper and lived in a one-room guest cottage located near the converted horse stables Orson used as his primary work space. If he stuck to his routine, Orson would be in the stables for another few minutes before retiring to the main house. Donny, on the other hand, had once again gone to bed shortly after sundown and, even though the cottage was dark, Tramelik could see that Upshaw had closed only the screen door on his front porch. The Russian figured the door would be unlocked; if it wasn't, he knew it would be an easy matter to jimmy it open and still have time to get to Donny before the other man could respond.

A commuter jet had just lifted off from the airfield's lone runway and Tramelik watched through the trees as it droned its way into the night sky. Within moments the plane disappeared into the same thick, swollen clouds that had already snuffed out the moon and all but a handful of stars. The darker the better, Tramelik thought as he slipped on a pair of purple latex gloves and pulled up the collar of his black jacket. His straggly reddish hair, uncut since he and Frederik Mikhaylov had met with Upshaw's father the previous week on behalf of Global Holdings Corporation, was tucked beneath a dark stocking cap, but a few loose strands dangled to his shoulders. Barad, a shorter, stone-faced man with short-cropped light brown hair, was dressed similarly to Tramelik. As he donned his gloves, he whispered, "Ready?"

Tramelik nodded, thumbing open his cell phone. He quickly text-messaged two more SVR agents waiting in a Dodge Caravan parked back on the dirt road linking Orson's property with a handful of other estates scattered between the airport and Rio Grande Gorge. It was a short message, two asterisks indicating that he and Barad were in position and about to make their move.

Once they cleared the trees, the two operatives split up. While Barad stole his way toward the stables, Tramelik circled a long-abandoned horse track and approached the guest cottage, nestled beneath a cottonwood less than forty yards from his colleague's target destination. The sound of their footsteps was masked not only by the breeze stirring through trees but also the melodic tingling of several wind chimes hanging from the eaves above the bungalow's front porch. As he drew closer, Tramelik reached into his jacket and removed a secondhand police sap he'd bought two days ago at a pawnshop in Espanola. A flat steel bar and lead-weighted striking head were encased by heavily stitched black leather, making the weapon as potent as it was compact. Tramelik also had a Glock 17 9 mm pistol tucked in a web holster beneath his coat, but he had no plans to use it. For the moment, he only wanted to render Upshaw unconscious.

Tramelik was within ten feet of the bungalow when there was a sudden commotion next to the garage. When he reached the porch, the Russian crouched alongside its wooden steps and stared across the grounds. Barad had taken similar cover behind a water well near the stables. Fifty yards beyond the well a trio of coyotes had emerged through brush on the far side of the driveway and staged a raid of their own on a large garbage Dumpster heaped high with refuse. One of the creatures had already leaped up into the bin and begun tearing at a half-filled plastic trash bag. When a second coyote made the same leap and joined in the foraging, the smallest predator circled the Dumpster, yipping in frustration at its inability to join the festivities.

Tramelik was trying to figure a way to deal with the situation when he was startled by the rattling of a doorknob directly behind him. Glancing up, he saw Donny Upshaw storm onto the porch in his boxer shorts, brandishing a Mossberg 930 shotgun. The thin, long-haired Native American had apparently been roused by the coyotes and seemed equally taken aback by the sight of Tramelik crouched directly in front of him.

Tramelik was the first to react. Acting on reflex, he swung upward with the sap, striking the shotgun's barrel and diverting a 12-gauge round that would have otherwise turned his head into chowder. Half-deafened by the rifle blast, Tramelik lunged forward, clipping the other man below the waist with enough force to buckle Donny's knees and send him stumbling headlong down the porch steps. The Mossberg went flying from Upshaw's grasp and clattered to the ground as he landed hard on his right arm. Before Upshaw could reclaim the weapon, Tramelik pivoted on the steps and swung one leg outward, connecting the steel-toed tip of his right boot with the other man's jaw. Upshaw slumped to the ground, dazed. Off in the distance, the coyotes had already bounded from the garbage Dumpster and were racing off down the driveway.

Tramelik sprang from the porch, his mind racing. His well-orchestrated plan may have gone awry, but there was still a chance he and Barad could carry out their mission. When Upshaw began to stir, Tramelik rushed over and clippped him across the skull with his sap. Upshaw slumped back to the ground, blood oozing through his scalp where he'd been struck. Tramelik cursed under his breath and dropped the sap, putting a finger to his victim's wrist. The man still had a pulse.

"Good," Tramelik murmured. He fished through his pockets and withdrew a penlight, a shoestring and a syringe enclosed in a protective sheath. Once he'd tied the string around Donny's left biceps, he snapped open the sheath and tested the syringe, squirting a few drops into the night air, then shone the light on Upshaw's well-scarred inner right elbow. Once he pinpointed a vein, he inserted the needle, injecting enough heroin to ensure that it would be some time before the groundskeeper regained consciousness.

Now it was all up to Barad.

ALAN ORSON WAS SEALING the last of four cardboard shipping boxes set near the doorway leading out of the stables when a call came in on his cell phone. He tapped his transceiver and took the call as he applied a final strip of packing tape. Nearby, Orson's pet terrier lazed on a foam pad tucked beneath one of several work benches vying for space with storage cabinets and an industrial lathe inside the modified building. All the benches were strewn with tools and various half-built prototypes that Orson hoped would soon add to his list of patented inventions. The Taos native specialized in gadgets for the military and had made millions in recent years off contracts with the Department of Defense. Once he closed a deal for the items he'd just packed in the cardboard boxes, Orson calculated that his fortunes would quadruple, if not more, giving him the option to retire early and enjoy a life of travel and leisure.

"'Lo, Alan," the caller drawled in Orson's ear. "It's Franklin."

"Hey, Frank."

Franklin Colt was one of Orson's longtime poker buddies. They played twice a month, usually at the home of a mutual friend in Santa Fe. It was a long drive for a low-stakes game, but Orson liked the action as well as the camaraderie.

Colt was calling for another reason, however.

"Are we still on for tonight?"

"Sure thing," Orson said. "I just need to load the truck and take Ranger for a walk and I'll be on my way. Your friend's due in at midnight, right?"

"Thereabouts. Turns out he's got a couple friends flying in with him."

"I'll meet you at the airport," Orson said. "You think those guys might be into playing a little Hold 'Em?"

"Dunno," Colt told him. "I'll ask when they get in."

"Great." Orson wrapped up the call, then walked over to scratch his terrier behind its ears. "What say, Ranger? A quick lap around the track so you can do your business?"

Ranger seemed in no hurry to leave his bed. Before Orson could try any further coaxing, however, the dog suddenly turned its head and growled low as it stared past the boxes stacked near the door.

"I hear 'em, too," Orson said. "Easy, boy. Shh."

Orson flicked off the main overhead lights and moved to the nearest window overlooking the driveway. He parted the blinds and peered out.

"Good, they fell for it," he whispered.

Orson moved from the window and grabbed a shotgun racked on a wall illuminated by the dull glow of a nearby bench lamp. It was another Mossberg, identical to the one he'd bought for his groundskeeper a few days earlier after coyotes had killed his other terrier.

"Payback time, Ranger," Orson told his dog.

The inventor was thumbing the rifle's safety when he heard the other Mossberg fire. Ranger bounded from his bed and began to yelp. Orson ventured back for another look out the window. The coyotes had fled the Dumpster and were scurrying down the driveway. None of them appeared to have been hit.

"He missed 'em!"

Orson headed for the doorway. Ranger beat him there, still barking,

"Sit!" Orson commanded. When the dog obeyed, he gently pulled it back from the door. "Don't worry, if I get those critters in my sights they're toast."

The bespectacled inventor slipped outside and was closing the door behind him when he detected movement to his immediate right. Turning, he caught a brief glimpse of someone pointing a gun at his head. It was an image he would take with him to his grave.

THE MOMENT HE SAW Orson drop at Vladik Barad's feet, Petenka Tramelik made a quick call on his cell phone.

"It's done," he whispered. "Get up here, quick!"

Tramelik was slipping the phone back in his pocket when Barad jogged over, holding the small Raven Arms MP-25 he'd just used on Orson. "Those damn coyotes almost ruined things."

"Never mind that," Tramelik said. "Give me a hand."

Barad stuffed the handgun in his waistband, then took hold of Donny Upshaw's ankles. Tramelik grabbed the groundskeeper by the armpits and together they hauled him across the grounds to the stables. Ranger was barking wildly behind the closed door. Once they'd set Upshaw on the ground a few yards from Orson, Barad drew the Raven again and threw the stable door open. The terrier backed away momentarily, then was about to charge when Barad put a bullet through its chest, dropping the dog in its tracks.

"There's been enough racket here without having to listen to that," he told Tramelik.

Tramelik nodded. "It'll be a nice touch once we're finished. Let's do it."

Upshaw had begun to groan slightly but was still unconscious when Barad crouched beside him and put the Raven in the groundskeeper's right hand, then clasped his own hand over it and guided Upshaw's index finger onto the trigger. Tramelik helped Barad aim the weapon at Orson, who lay on his side facing them, blood draining from his left temple where he'd been shot.

"Okay, Donny," Tramelik whispered to Upshaw. "Put one through his heart for good measure."

Barad gently pressed his index finger against Upshaw's and the Raven fired once again. Orson's body stirred slightly as it absorbed the round.

Far down the driveway the men heard the crunch of tires on gravel. It was the Dodge Caravan, heading up toward the garage with its lights out.

"I already got his keys," Tramelik told Barad. "Get Orson's, then we'll wrap things up here so we can go take care of the chief."

CHAPTER THREE

Antwerp, Belgium

Evgenii Danilov thanked his valet for bringing him the evening edition of the *International Tribune* and took the paper to his study, a lavish room that, like much of the small centuries-old castle, had been painstakingly restored to its medieval origins. Through the large stained-glass window he could see night falling over his secluded upscale neighborhood. It had snowed earlier, and downhill from Danilov's two-acre front lawn there was still a light frosting on Grote Steenweg, the ancient Great Stone Road that had once been the main thoroughfare linking Antwerp and Brussels. This stretch of the road had been historically preseverved every bit as much as Danilov's home and strategically planted trees blocked his view of neighboring homes as well as any other sign of modern civilization.

There were times, like now, when Danilov could stare out the window and imagine himself transported back to the age of his forefathers, specifically Prince Eugene of Savoy-Carignan, one of Europe's greatest military commanders and mentor to Frederick the Great, whose Prussian Empire included the land upon which this, one of Danilov's six homes, stood. Over the past fifty years the silver-haired St. Petersburg native had carved out a financial empire of his own that was impressive in its own right. But for all his success, to Danilov the world of commerce, in the end, didn't hold quite the same allure as military or political conquest. Yes, he'd made a lifetime of negotiating shrewd investments, but how could that compare with the visceral passion his ancestral hero had to have taken with him to the battlefield when crushing Ottoman Turks in the Battle of Zenta? If he had it all to do over, Danilov wouldn't have bought his way out of military service, because in the years since, in his heart of hearts, he'd come to know that his greatest yearning was to be more like his namesake: a true warrior.

Little wonder, then, that while known to the world as the billionaire founder and CEO of Global Holdings Corporation, Danilov's preferred renown was that of a covert financial backer of Russia's Foreign Intelligence Service. It was a position that allowed him, without fanfare, to be a party to decisions geared toward returning his motherland to a state of global prominence surpassing even that of Frederick the Great's empire or the once-formidable juggernaut that had been the Soviet Union.

It was in this warrior's state of mind that Danilov turned from the window and eased into his favorite chair facing the fiery hearth that staged a battle of its own, fending off the unseasonal chill outside the castle. The financier read with fervor the *Tribune*'s front-page headlines, many of them devoted to America's ongoing preoccupation with the forces of radical Islam. The U.S. was still bogged down in Iraq and was repeating Russia's grand mistake of thinking it could impose its influence in Afghanistan. And these were just two fronts on which Washington was distracting itself. There were also headlines about threats posed by North Korea, Iran and China. Danilov had to turn to the fourth page before he came across any mention of U.S. concern over Russia, and that was with regards to Moscow targeting missiles at Eastern

Europe. As it had been for some time, there was no mention in the entire paper that America so much as considered the idea that its one-time greatest rival might be silently working on the means by which to launch a preemptive strike that would make the horrors of 9/11 seem tame by comparison. And the notion that such a blow might be dealt from within the United States's own boundaries rather than by way of long-range missiles? Danilov felt certain the powers-that-be in Washington were far more wary such an attack would be instigated by al Qaeda than on orders from Moscow.

Next to Danilov's chair was a large antique globe resting on a pivot stand that allowed it to be spun or tilted at a variety of angles. When purchasing it, the selling point for the Russian, besides its exacting geographic detail, was the fact that it was not divided into countries in a way that would have made it obsolete every time some fledgling nation won its independence or borders were redrawn by some existing power. As such, when he slowly rotated the globe until the United States came into view, he had to guess as to the exact whereabouts of New Mexico, where he and the SVR had elected to carry out their long-range plan to do what the latest economic downturn had failed to do: bring America to its knees. To some, the desert sprawl of the Southwest may have seemed an unlikely place from which to stage such a grand scheme, but Danilov found the location not only ideal, but fitting. After all, it was in New Mexico that the U.S. had finalized tests for the Manhattan Project and ushered the world into the age of nuclear weapons. What better place for Russia to create a trove of warheads that could be put to use without having to contend with the multibillion-dollar measures the U.S. was committing itself to as a defense against long-range attacks.

The groundwork had already been laid when Danilov, with the help of SVR agents, had fabricated the scandal that had led to the removal of the Rosqui Tribal Council's previous partners at the Roaming Bison Casino as well as the reservation's long-running nuclear waste facility. When Global Holdings had subsequently moved in to fill the void, Danilov had taken care to orchestrate things so that it appeared that his corporation was interested primarily in gaming operations and would be taking over the waste facility with some reluctance. In the years since, GHC's public-relations arm had followed this cue and shone a bright light on the casino and its resort amenities while steering focus away from the storage of spent fuel rods and other radioactive waste. Likewise, the late-night construction of ancillary bunkers in the mountains flanking the waste plant had been every bit as secretive as the intended use of the new structures. The new sites would be completed within the year, at which point all that would be needed was a more viable source of uranium than that coming from the fuel rods to carry out what Danilov had convinced SVR to call Operation Zenta, in honor of the battle in which his famed namesake had lost only five hundred men while slaying thirty thousand Turks.

All had gone well with the project until the past week, when the SVR team in New Mexico had faced a string of setbacks. First had been Taos Pueblo President Walter Upshaw's refusal to accept a partnership with GHC, thereby foiling—at least temporarily—the SVR's hope to secure uranium from the tribe's long-abandoned mines. Then there had been the matter of Alan Orson, the Taos geophysicist they'd been lobbying to help develop a quicker means by which to process mined uranium into weapons-grade plutonium. Orson had been courted with the understanding he would be helping GHC conduct a feasibility study for using the uranium as a nuclear power source, but the inventor had balked, ironically out of fear that his work might somehow fall into the wrong hands.

At the time he turned down GHC's offer, there had been no indication that he had any suspicions about the organization, but over the past few days it had come to light that he was friends with Roaming Bison security officer Franklin Colt, who had apparently come upon some as-yet-unknown evidence of GHC's ulterior agenda at the reservation. Colt had gone to Upshaw with his findings and the fear was that Orson had been brought into the loop, as well. Left unchecked, it was a security breach that could well undermine Operation Zenta, but Danilov had been assured by his point man in New Mexico, Frederik Mikhaylov, that all three men—Upshaw, Orson and Colt—were about to be taken out of the equation, with the bonus of the SVR getting its hands on not only Orson's research data on uranium processing but also a handful of invention prototypes, some of which could be put to good use by the Russian army as well as its intelligentsia. In fact, before retiring for the evening Danilov expected to receive confirmation that the mission had been carried out. Once he got the call, he would breathe a little easier, but, on the whole, he remained optimistic that destiny was on his side and that in the end he and the SVR would prevail.

As he waited for the phone to ring, Danilov stared into the fireplace a moment, then glanced up at the oil portrait of Eugene of Savoy-Carignan hanging over his mantelpiece. In the portrait, the wild-haired military strategist stared out with a look that Danilov normally found to be expressionless. This night, however, he fancied that in his forefather's eyes he could see a glimmer of approval. Moreover, he wanted to think that if the portrait could talk, Eugene would be telling him, *Well done, Evgenii.*

CHAPTER FOUR

Albuquerque, New Mexico

"Any luck?" John Kissinger asked his friend Franklin Colt.

Colt shook his head as he slipped his cell phone back in his pocket.

"He's still not picking up," he said. "Must be all this rain has things backed up on the highway."

"I guess we can stick around awhile and wait for him." Kissinger glanced over at Jack Grimaldi, the Stony Man pilot who'd flown him to Albuquerque along with Mack Bolan. The Executioner stood a few yards away, his back turned to the others, cell phone pressed to his ear.

"Fine by me," Grimaldi said, adjusting the brim of his baseball cap in preparation for stepping out into the rain. The four men stood outside the main terminal at Albuquerque International, an overhang shielding them from the drizzling remains of a downpour that had left pools of water on the sidewalk and out in the traffic lanes separating the airport from the outdoor parking lot. The Stony Man warriors had arrived nearly an hour earlier and deplaned on the runway, where, thanks to arrangements made by Barbara Price, an airport police officer had picked them up in a shuttle cart and brought them around to the front of the terminal, allowing them to bypass security screenings that would have turned up the small cache of weaponry and ammunition they'd brought with them. Colt had been out on the sidewalk waiting for them.

"No, let's go ahead and get you guys checked in," Franklin told the others. "I left a message for Al to catch up with us at the hotel. It's just down the road and he's got a room there, too."

"Works for me," Kissinger said.

Bolan rejoined the others once he was off the phone. After Kissinger filled him in, the Executioner replied, "There's been a change in plans on our end, too. Seattle's off. I'll give you the details later."

Colt grinned knowingly. "I've got a better idea," he suggested. "Why don't I go get the car and swing by to pick you up? That'll give you time to debrief...or whatever it is you guys call it."

"Appreciate it," Bolan told Colt.

"I told John I've got a little intrigue of my own going on at the reservation," Colt countered. "Maybe at some point we can swap stories."

The crossing light changed before the Stony Men could reply. As Colt headed out into the rain and sidestepped puddles on his way to the parking lot, Kissinger turned to his colleagues.

"He was kidding," he told them. "He knows what I do, and who I do it with, isn't up for discussion."

"I figured as much," Bolan said.

"Any idea what he meant about the reservation?" Grimaldi asked.

"Not sure," Kissinger said. "He mentioned it when we first spoke but all he said was that things were a little hinky there. Probably something at the casino."

"He seems like a straight-up guy," Bolan said.

"Franklin's the best," Kissinger said. "I still can't believe we fell out of touch for so long."

Years ago, Kissinger and Colt, a full-blooded Rosqui Indian, had worked together as field agents for the DEA and forged a strong friendship. Kissinger had saved Colt's life during a drug raid a few months after they'd partnered up, and Colt had returned the favor less than a year later, taking a few rounds while shoving his colleague out of the line of fire during a botched undercover operation.

The wounds had been severe enough to place Colt on extended medical leave, and though Kissinger had initially made a point to keep tabs on the other man's recuperation, as time passed and Kissinger's shift into covert operations demanded more secrecy, their contact had become sporadically and, as often happened with even the best of friends, eventually the men had drifted apart. More than a dozen years had slipped away before Kissinger sought to reestablish contact. With help from Stony Man's cybercrew he'd been able to track Colt down to the Rosqui reservation north of Santa Fe, where he worked graveyard shift as a security officer for Roaming Bison Casino, one of several tribal-owned resorts located just off the major interstates running through New Mexico.

After a two-hour long-distance phone conversation, Colt had suggested a face-to-face reunion. Kissinger had been all for it and volunteered to fly out to Albuquerque, where he figured he could squeeze in some business for the Farm by attending the city's annual New Military Technologies Expo. Kissinger had mentioned that his present government work was classified, but Colt had assumed it had something to do with Cowboy's fascination with firearms and weapons systems. He'd suggested that Kissinger meet his poker buddy Alan Orson, who was driving in from Taos to run an NMT booth featuring several of his latest inventions. Kissinger was already familiar with some of Orson's patents and looked forward to seeing what else the inventor had up his sleeve. Should Orson have something worth adding to the Farm's arsenal, Kissinger knew SOG had the funding—and clout—to get first crack at putting any invention to use. For the moment, however, those considerations would have to wait on Orson's arrival from Taos.

As they waited for Colt to pick them up, Grimaldi asked Bolan, "So, what's up with Seattle?"

"Canada beat us to the punch," Bolan explained. "I didn't get the details, but apparently CSIS staged a couple preemptive raids across the border. They turned up grenade launchers and plastic explosives in a shipment of machinery parts earmarked for some retrofitting business in Takoma." CSIS was the Canadian Security Intelligence Service.

"'Retrofitting' my ass," Kissinger said.

Bolan and Grimaldi had their backs to the airport traffic lanes but Cowboy was facing the other way and, glancing over their shoulders, he could see Colt cross the street to the outdoor parking area. When they'd spoken on the phone, Franklin had boasted about the restoration work he'd done on a vintage 1969 Chevy Nova, and Kissinger could see the muscle car out in the parking lot, its yellow, laquered coat almost gleaming in the rain.

"Sounds like they shut down the suppliers," Grimaldi told Bolan, "but what about the guys that stuff was being sent to?"

"That's still on Able's plate," Bolan said. "They were already working the Takoma angle and figure they can follow through on their own."

"If that's the case, it sounds like we've got ourselves a minivacation," Grimaldi said. "Sweet. Maybe we can get in that card game Colt was talking about."

"Hang on, guys," Kissinger murmured, eyes on the parking lot. "Something's not right."

Across the roadway, Colt had made his way past a handful of parked cars and was circling around his Nova when he was intercepted by two men bounding out of an unmarked black panel truck parked next to him. Kissinger's first thought had been that one of the men was probably Alan Orson, but as he watched on, a sudden scuffle broke out between Colt and the others. Bolan and Grimaldi tracked Kissinger's gaze to the altercation, just in time to see Colt being overpowered and dragged into the panel truck. Even as the other two assailants were clambering aboard, the truck was already backing out of its parking space.

Bolan and Kissinger were on the move. They sprinted into the pickup lane, their eyes on the truck as they signaled for oncoming traffic to stop. A cabbie was slow to respond and had to veer at the last second to avoid running the men down. Slamming on his brakes, the driver fishtailed to a stop, splashing water up past the curb and nearly drenching Grimaldi.

Bolan yanked a 9 mm Beretta 3-R from the shoulder holster concealed beneath his jacket. Kissinger already had his pistol out and both men braced themselves in the middle of the thoroughfare, drawing bead on the panel truck as it crossed the parking lot. There were too many innocent bystanders in the way, however, forcing the men to hold their fire. As traffic backed up in front of them, a number of motorists began pounding their horns. Bolan ignored the bleating as well as the cursing of the cab driver. He shouted to Grimaldi, "Get us some wheels!"

"On it!"

As Bolan and Kissinger broke their firing positions and crossed the roadway, Grimaldi slammed his fist on the taxi's hood before its driver could pull away. The cabbie turned and glared when the Stony Man pilot tugged open the front passenger door.

"I need to borrow this," Grimaldi said.

"Like hell," the cabbie snapped.

Grimaldi produced his M1911 pistol and aimed it at the driver.

"I don't have time to argue," he said. "Get out! Now!"

The cabbie's anger quickly morphed into fear. He put the taxi in Park and bailed out into the rain. Grimaldi tossed in his overnight bag, along with the totes Bolan and Kissinger had left on the curb. He was circling around to the driver's side when a security officer raced out of the baggage terminal, his gun drawn. It wasn't the cop who'd picked them up on the runway, and he had obviously quickly jumped to the wrong conclusion.

"Hold it right there!" he shouted at Grimaldi.

"Federal agent!" Grimaldi shouted back, taking the risk of reaching into his shirt pocket for the certified Justice Department badge he and his fellow commandos routinely carried while on assignment. SOG Director Hal Brognola was officially entrenched with Justice, ensuring that even though the badges were issued under aliases they would hold up under scrutiny. Given the circumstances, however, Grimaldi wasn't about to wait around for clearance. He pointed at the racing panel truck and bellowed, "We've got a hostage situation!"

The officer paused, which was all the time Grimaldi needed to scramble behind the wheel and slam the taxi into gear. Raising a rainwater fantail, the pilot veered into traffic, nearly sideswiping a slow-moving Honda as he crossed lanes and plowed his way through a gap between two of several sand-filled steel drums separating northbound traffic from vehicles heading south, away from the airport. A shuttle bus in the oncoming lane swerved to one side to avoid colliding head-on with Grimaldi as he wrestled the taxi's steering wheel, foot still on the gas, bounding over the far curb before completing a U-turn and aligning himself with southbound traffic. Up ahead, Bolan and Kissinger had reached the sidewalk and were firing at the panel truck, which had just smashed through a swing arm at the pay station and burst out of the parking lot. The truck clipped a passing Cadillac and forced the luxury car off the road into a curbside planter. Bolan and Kissinger aimed low for the truck's tires but the getaway vehicle veered wildly on the rain-slicked asphalt and proved an elusive target.

Grimaldi sped forward, then pulled to a stop alongside his colleagues. Bolan and Kissinger piled in, slamming fresh cartridges into their weapons.

"Stay on 'em!" Kissinger shouted.

"I aim to," Grimaldi replied. "Fasten your seat belts, boys and girls!"

The Stony Man pilot floored the accelerator. The taxi's wheels spun in place a moment, then gained traction and hauled the vehicle forward, past the disabled Cadillac.

The chase was on.

BY THE TIME THE panel truck had left the parking lot, Franklin Colt's abductors had already stripped him of his cell phone and hog-tied him by the wrists and ankles with duct tape. There were no seats in the rear of the truck, and Colt lay pinned against the cold metal floor, his captors kneeling on either side of him. They'd pulled a stocking cap down over his head, as well, and there was little he could see through the tight-woven fabric. He assumed the men were hoping to conceal their identities, but during the brief skirmish in the parking lot he'd gotten a good look at them. He didn't know them by name, but he recognized them from the casino. They were regulars who spent most of their time at the roulette and blackjack tables. Franklin suspected they were more than mere players, however, given their burly physiques and the frequency with which they would wander off to the main bar to meet with one of the pit bosses whenever they went on break. Judging from their accents, he figured the thugs, like most of the casino's executive personnel, were either from Eastern Europe or Russia. He had a good idea, as well, as to why they'd taken him hostage.

"Who are those other men?" one of the captors bellowed at him over the drone of the truck's engine.

"Friends," Colt muttered, wincing as he spoke. He'd been struck in the face several times and his jaw was throbbing. He could taste blood in his mouth and traced the source to a split on his lower lip.

"Friends with guns!" the captor shouted. "Who are they working for?"

"I don't know!"

Colt groaned as his interrogator kneed him sharply in the ribs.

"What did you tell them?"

"What would I tell them?" Colt countered, feigning ignorance. "What's this all about anyway? What do you want with me?"

"You know!" his captor shouted. "Don't pretend you don't!"

"I'm just a res Indian who minds his own business," Colt protested.

"We know better! If you know what's good for you you'll start—"

The interrogation was cut short when one of the truck's tinted rear windows imploded, shattered by a 9 mm slug that lodged itself in the headrest of the front passenger seat. The driver responded by jerking the steering wheel, throwing Colt's abductors off balance. One of them caromed off the side of the truck while Colt's inquisitor fell sprawling alongside him.

"We can worry about him later!" the other man shouted. "We need to take care of these people, whoever they are! They're after us in a goddamn taxi!"

The inside of the truck suddenly reverberated with the deafening reports of an assault rifle. Colt assumed that Kissinger and his friends were the ones being fired at. His concern for their safety was mixed with no small measure of admiration at how quickly they'd responded to his abduction.

Cowboy hasn't lost his chops, Franklin thought to himself.

The second thug let loose with another autoburst, then cursed.

"Where's our backup?" he roared.

WHEN COLT HAD BEEN taken captive, his abductors had made a point to take his car keys and kick them just beneath the Nova's chassis near the left front wheel. Moments after the panel truck had pulled out and sped toward the pay station, SVR operative Viktor Cherkow had abandoned his surveillance post outside the baggage claim area across the street and jogged past stalled traffic to the parking lot. When he reached the Chevy he stopped and crouched in the rain, pretending to tie his shoes. Once the panel truck had crashed through the barrier and sped into the street, Cherkow grabbed the stray keys and let himself into Colt's Nova. The plan had been for him to go through the vehicle for evidence Colt might have brought along with him, but when he saw Bolan and Kissinger fire at the panel truck and then take up chase in a passing taxi, the Russian decided the search would have to wait.

The moment he keyed the ignition and heard the Nova's rebuilt V-8 rumble to life, Cherkow smiled to himself. He wasn't sure how much horsepower Colt had harnessed under the hood, but he suspected it was a lot more than whatever would be powering the taxi.

"I'll catch up soon enough," he vowed as he revved the engine and shifted into Reverse.

In his haste, Cherkow squealed out of his parking space just as a Mercedes GLK was pulling forward from the space directly behind him. Cherkow cursed as he rammed the SUV, crumpling its front end. The Nova hadn't been retrofitted with air bags, and the impact threw Cherkow against the hard plastic of the steering wheel. Dazed, the Russian groped at his bruised ribs. Behind him, the other driver rocketed from his vehicle and stormed forward, kicking the Nova.

"Look where you're going!" he roared. "I just bought this car!"

The man had nearly reached Cherkow when the Russian threw open his door and pointed the MP-446 Viking combat pistol he'd just yanked from his shoulder holster. He fired a single 9 mm round into the other man's forehead, then slammed the door shut and threw the Nova into first gear. His rear bumper was still snagged to the Mercedes and when the Chevy screeched forward, the steel strip pulled loose and clanged to the asphalt a few feet from where the owner of the Mercedes had fallen, spilling his blood into a growing puddle of rainwater.

Cherkow sped toward the pay station, reaching it just as the parking attendant had charged out to inspect the damage caused by the panel truck. The man dived to one side to avoid being run down when Cherkow raced past the pay booth and quickly veered past the disabled Cadillac so that he could take up pursuit of the taxi. There were no cars between them, and as he eased down on the accelerator, Cherkow quickly began to gain ground. Given the rain-slicked surface, the mobster was forced to toss his gun on the seat beside him and keep both hands on the steering wheel.

"That's all right," Cherkow told himself, "I won't need a gun to take care of them."

ONE EXIT BEFORE INTERSTATE 25, the panel truck abruptly cut across two lanes of traffic and shot down the ramp leading to University Boulevard. Grimaldi followed suit in the taxi. It would have been a dangerous enough maneuver on dry ashpalt and both vehicles nearly hydroplaned off the road as they took the sharp turn. The taxi, its front hood already scarred by AK-47 rounds, took on more damage as it swerved onto the shoulder and brushed against a guardrail before Grimaldi corrected course and eased back onto the roadway.

"Nice save," Kissinger told him.

"Yeah, well, I'd stay buckled up if I were you," Grimaldi responded, keeping an eye on the truck. "I'm sure they'll keep trying to shake us."

Bolan was in the backseat, pensive, Beretta at the ready. He'd only fired at the truck once since getting into the taxi, but if Grimaldi could get within closer range, he hoped to get off a few more shots.

At the end of the ramp, the panel truck turned left, heading away from the city. By the time Grimaldi made the same turn, there was nearly a hundred-yard gap between the two vehicles. The rain had begun to pick up, forcing him to peer through the mad thrashing of the windshield wipers. A streak of lightning lit their way briefly as the pursuit continued southward, past an industrial park and the University of New Mexico's Championship Golf Course. By the time they passed the Rio Bravo intersection, the center median had widened and there was no longer any other traffic to contend with. Grimaldi gave the taxi more gas, quickly gaining on the truck. A quick look in his rearview mirror revealed the flashing lights of a police cruiser turning onto University Boulevard far behind them.

"No guarantee they know we're the good guys," Kissinger said.

"Hopefully we'll get to the truck before they catch up with us," Grimaldi said. He'd reached an incline leading to a barren stretch of flatland and coaxed the speedometer another ten miles per hour. He was now pushing eighty, and once he crossed over a bridge spanning a railroad trestle he slowly began to close in on the panel truck. They were within thirty yards of it when a face appeared ahead in the rear window Bolan had shot out earlier. Once again, one of Franklin Colt's abductors raised his assault rifle and pointed it through the opening.

"Incoming!" Kissinger shouted, ducking in the front seat.

Grimaldi eased off the accelerator and tapped his brakes, falling back a few yards. Behind him, Bolan powered down his window and leaned out, rattling off a diversionary burst. The ploy worked. The Stony Man warriors heard the faint throttle of the AK-47, but its rounds flew wide of their mark.

Kissinger righted himself and clenched his pistol, his eyes fixed on the rear of the truck before them. The shooter had pulled away from the shattered window.

"Looks like he's reloading," Grimaldi said, flooring the accelerator. "Hang on, I'm going to try to ram them."

As THE TAXI BORE down on the truck, another jagged shaft of lightning brightened the desolate terrain. Glancing behind him, Bolan, for the first time, caught a glimpse of Franklin Colt's Chevy Nova. The muscle car had been traveling with its lights off and had managed to sneak up to within less than twenty yards of the taxi. The police cruiser, by contrast, was still more than a mile away.

"We've got company," Bolan called out to Grimaldi. "Give it all you got!"

Grimaldi spied the Nova in his rearview mirror and cursed. His words were drowned out by the Executioner's Beretta. Bolan fired through the rear windshield of the taxi, clearing the way for a better shot at the Nova's driver. Before he could draw bead, however, Viktor Cherkow suddenly flashed on his brights. The raised beams half blinded Bolan and startled Grimaldi, as well. The Stony Man wheelman had closed in to within a few yards of the panel truck, but the Nova had already caught up with him.

There was a sickening crunch as Cherkow beat Grimaldi at his own game plan and slammed into the rear of the taxi. He'd made a point to strike at a slight angle, and the cab immediately began to swerve out of control despite Grimaldi's best efforts to compensate.

"Not good," he murmured.

CHAPTER FIVE

The taxi had spun completely by the time it left the road and crashed into a guardrail. Unlike earlier, this time the car didn't merely glance off the barrier. Instead, it snapped the wooden supports and left the railing in twisted shards as it flipped and went briefly airborne before landing upright on a steep-pitched dirt incline leading to Tijeras Arroyo, a normally dry flood channel that was now swollen with runoff from the day's rain. The taxi was still turned around and momentum carried it backward downhill into the raging current. For a moment the vehicle bobbed on the surface, surrounded by clots of tumbleweed and other brush dislodged by floodwaters. Then, as water surged through the opened windows and shattered windshield, the taxi slowly sank and had soon disappeared from view.

Back on the roadway the Chevy Nova had also spun completely before coming to a stop. Cherkow groaned in the driver's seat, his rib cage throbbing from yet another collision with the steering wheel. His right knee had slammed into the dashboard and throbbed with pain, as well. The engine had died and the right front headlight had been crushed, leaving a single beam shining through the rain, illuminating the stretch of road Cherkow had sped along moments before. Far up the hill leading back to the airport, a police cruiser raced downhill toward him, its rooftop lights flashing.

Cherkow grimaced as he retrieved his MP-446 and staggered out into the rain. Behind him, the panel truck had stopped in the middle of the road and was backing up.

"Nice work!" one of his cohorts called out through the shattered rear window.

"It's not over yet!" Cherkow shouted through the rain. Favoring his sore knee, he hobbled to the break in the guardrail. He was staring down into the arroyo when lightning shone on the brownish floodwaters. Cherkow watched intently as the cab slowly disappeared beneath the floodwaters. He took aim with his autopistol, on the lookout for any trace of the men who'd been inside the vehicle. When no one surfaced, he scanned the dirt slope to see if anyone had been thrown clear. All he could see were the taxi's tire tracks and a few pieces of sodden litter bogged down in the mud.

Behind Cherkow, the police cruiser reached the flat stretch of the roadway, and its siren shrieked to life above the thunder and harsh patter of rain. The Russian crouched behind the mangled guardrail and waited for the squad car to draw closer. When it came to a stop twenty yards shy of the Chevy, he raised his gun and lined his sights on the officer riding shotgun in the front seat. Behind Cherkow, the gunman in the panel truck took aim as well and let loose with his Kalashnikov.

The cruiser's front windshield disintegrated and a stream of 7.62 mm NATO rounds took out the cop behind the wheel, obliterating his neck and jaw. The officer riding alongside him, already bloodied by flying glass, was next to die, struck down by a volley from Cherkow's Viking. The man had partially opened his door and tumbled out of the car, landing on the gleaming asphalt.

Cherkow made certain there was no one else inside the vehicle, then broke from cover and limped back toward the

Chevy. Before he could reach the muscle car, the rear doors of the panel truck swung open and the gunman with the AK-47 shouted, "Get in!"

"I want to check for evidence!" Cherkow shouted back.

"There's no time!" the other man retorted. "There'll be more cops here any minute!"

Cherkow hesitated, then changed course and staggered to the truck. His comrade helped him aboard, then pulled the doors closed and yelled to the driver, "Let's go!"

Slowly the truck began to pick up speed. Cherkow dropped to the floor and sat, wheezing slightly as he ran one hand along his right side, trying to pinpoint which of his ribs had been cracked. Franklin Colt lay nearby, still bound and hooded.

"Has he talked yet?" Cherkow asked.

"No," one of the abductors responded, giving Colt a fierce shove. "But we'll loosen his tongue once we get to the safe house."

Cherkow grinned at Colt. "Nice job souping up that car of yours," he told the prisoner. "You gave me a chance to catch up with your friends. Too bad they won't be able to help you."

MACK BOLAN WAS DISORIENTED when he first came to and found himself immersed in the cold, murky water of the flood channel. He was still in the rear of the taxi, secured by his seat belt, slouched at an odd angle. The taxi had tipped onto its side as it dropped below the waterline and, though it had come to a rest at the base of the culvert, the vehicle continued to wobble slightly, jostled by the swift-moving current.

Air, Bolan thought to himself, closing his mouth to keep from taking in any more water. Need more air.

Reaching for his waist, he clawed open his seat belt then let himself float upward to the driver's side of the taxi, which now lay closest to the surface and had yet to fill with water. When he reached the air pocket, the Executioner gasped, spitting brackish fluid from his lungs. He drew in a few deep breaths and submerged himself once more. There was no partition between the front and back seat, and he was able to quickly reach his fellow commandos. Grimaldi was still out cold behind the steering wheel, but Kissinger had come to and was freeing himself from his seat belt. Bolan reached through the water and tapped him to get his attention, then gestured, first at the air pocket above him, then at Grimaldi. Kissinger nodded and lunged upward as Bolan reached around the Stony Man pilot and unclipped his seat belt, then pulled him clear of the steering wheel.

Kissinger was coughing when Bolan returned to the ever-shrinking pocket of air and hoisted Grimaldi's head above the waterline. He turned the pilot's head to one side and expelled water from his mouth, then gently clenched an arm around the other man's chest and squeezed him, just below the diaphragm. Grimaldi convulsed slightly and sputtered, involuntarily ridding himself of still more ingested water.

"Where are we?" he gasped.

"I'd say hell, only it's a little wet for that," Kissinger said, slapping away a small clot of debris floating near his face.

"We're in some kind of flood channel," Bolan guessed.

"More like a river," Kissinger said.

A flash of lightning gave the men a brief glimpse of the water's surface, which lay only a few yards above them.

"We can get out through the back windshield," Bolan said. He turned to Grimaldi. "Think you can manage it?"

"I'll sure as hell try," Grimaldi said, coughing out the words.

Bolan went first. He drew in another breath, then dropped below the waterline and twisted his body so that when he kicked against the driver's headrest he could propel himself through the windshield he'd shot out earlier. Once clear of the taxi, he extended his arms and swam to the surface. There, surrounded by floating bits of tumbleweed, he treaded water and fought the current as he looked around him. Uphill to his right was a small bridge spanning the arroyo. He spotted the section of guardrail they'd crashed through and, beyond that, the roadway and the flashing lights of what he assumed was a patrol car. His ears were clogged and a faint din resonated through his skull, but he could also hear the incessant wailing of a siren. By the time Kissinger and Grimaldi had rejoined him, two more sirens were competing with the peals of thunder. Bolan saw a squad car speed across the bridge, heading southward, while yet another cruiser was making its way down the incline leading away from the airport.

"Cavalry to the rescue," Kissinger muttered as he swam close to Bolan.

Rather than fight the current, the men conserved their strength and allowed the water to carry them away from the road. Slowly they made their way to the culvert's edge. Bolan's legs were going numb by the time he reached a point where he could touch bottom. He lumbered up out of the water and collapsed on the muddy embankment, exhausted. Kissinger and Grimaldi straggled ashore soon after, shivering in the rain.

"What now?" Grimaldi asked.

As if in response, the beam of a high-powered searchlight cut a swath through the darkness and fell on the men. Squinting, Bolan glanced uphill and traced the light to a squad car that had pulled to a stop near the break in the guardrail. Two officers had already begun to climb down the embankment, guns drawn. With their weapons still back in the taxi, the Executioner realized they were no longer in a position to give chase to Franklin Colt's abductors, much less take them on.

"For now," he told his colleagues, "it looks like we're going to have to play ball with the locals."

CHAPTER SIX

Taos, New Mexico

One night every week for eighteen years Walter Upshaw had taught an extension course on Native American Heritage at the University of New Mexico's Taos facility on Civic Plaza Drive. The tribal leader charged nothing for his services, and the class enrollment fee was underwritten by the Pueblo. The class was always full, made up of local residents as well as tribal members, and there were those cynics who derided Upshaw as using the teacher's pulpit as a blatant effort to bolster his political clout and presence in the community. Upshaw always denied the claims, insisting that he felt it was important for both his people and the locals to cultivate a better understanding of native customs. Anyone who took the class would have backed him up as they invariably came away with the sense that Upshaw was truly passionate about the history and traditions of his forefathers.

Another part of the TPGC president's weekly ritual for most of those eighteen years was the short trek to Taos Plaza, where he would settle in at his favorite booth at Ogilvie's Bar and hold court with fellow teachers, students and anyone else who struck his fancy and would accept an invitation to join in on what would usually be a few hours of lively debate and raconteuring. This particular night, even the torrential downpour and a preoccupation with other matters couldn't keep Upshaw making his usual after-class visit to the local watering hole. Only two colleagues from the university had decided to brave the elements with him and the bar was less than half-full, but Upshaw still managed to drum up a festive air among the small gathering.

As was his custom, the tribal elder offered to pick up the tab for anyone drinking something other than alcohol. A steadfast teetotaler, all his life Upshaw had bristled at the stereotype of "drunken Indians." He frowned as well on most other forms of substance abuse, a hard-line stance that had led to an ongoing estrangement from his only son after Donny's rebellious adolescence had led him to alcoholism and two prison stints, one for DUI and the other for heroin possession. Donny had gone through rehab as a means of shortening his second sentence and had been clean for over five months, but Upshaw had thus far refused to reconcile with his son. There was a part of him that regretted his recalcitrance, especially on nights like this, his son's fortieth birthday. The sentiment, however, was always dwarfed by Upshaw's grim memory of the day, almost ten years ago, when his beloved wife, Paulina, had been killed in a head-on collision while riding home from the annual Taos Solar Music Festival. Donny had been behind the wheel and had suffered bruises that were only minor compared to those administered by his father shortly after Upshaw had bailed him out of jail, where Donny had been incarcerated with a blood alcohol level three times the legal limit. Taos being the small town it was, the two men had crossed paths countless times in the years since, but in every instance Upshaw had refused to meet his son's gaze. During that time, Donny had e-mailed his father even more frequently, begging for forgiveness and making overtures for a renewed relationship, but, as he had with the message

Donny had sent him earlier that day, Upshaw's response had always been to delete the communiqués without so much as reading them.

While this matter weighed somewhat on Upshaw's mind during the two hours he spent at Ogilvie's, there was another, more pressing concern lurking behind his convivial facade, and once he'd paid his bill and started to drive home through the remnants of the storm, Upshaw dropped all pretense and brooded about his predicament with the Tribal Governing Council. Over the past few days he'd casually brought up the matter of expanding the casino with other council members and found, much to his dismay, that the majority of them were, at best, lukewarm to his small-scale plans. He'd avoided confronting anyone directly, but the response had confirmed his suspicions that Freddy McHale had indeed been lobbying under the table to secure support for GHC's proposal to replace the existing structure with a larger facility and allow for a cleanup of the old uranium mines, a move that would entail sharing the land's mineral rights. Worse yet, there now seemed a good chance that McHale was also right about the ground shifting beneath Upshaw's political feet. The way things stood, Upshaw feared that if he were to run for reelection this time he might well be defeated. The prospect daunted him, and he was determined to do all he could to avoid such an ignominy.

There was plenty of time before the election, and in his battle to turn the council tide back in his favor Upshaw still had one potent ace up his sleeve.

Franklin Colt.

Upshaw knew Colt from the latter's periodic speaking tours throughout the state where, as a former DEA agent, Franklin spoke at local high schools and reservations about the dangers of drug abuse. It wasn't in this capacity, however, that Upshaw saw Colt as an invaluable ally but rather the Rosqui native's position as an officer with the Roaming Bison Casino's security force. Colt had, over the past few weeks, been

privy to a handful of incidents involving suspicious activity
at both the casino and the reservation's controversial nuclear
waste facility. Looked at separately, the incidents may have
appeared isolated exceptions to GHC's overall management
practices. Placed together, however, there seemed evidence of
a pattern of covert activity that went far beyond the realm of
profit-skimming and money laundering—alleged crimes that
had led to the outster of Global Holdings' predecessors. Much
as he'd been tempted to go to his council members with these
suspicions, Upshaw had held back, wary they'd be dismissed
as the desperate innuendos of a man who'd do anything to
hold on to power. What he needed from Colt was corrobora-
tion; hard, solid evidence that would convince the council that
GHC was every bit as corrupt as the mafioso figures that had
ruled Las Vegas during its early years as a gambling mecca.
Earlier in the day Colt had called Upshaw saying he'd finally
secured just such evidence and would forward it once he'd run
it past a friend working for the government to get his opinion
on its viability as a proverbial "smoking gun."

Much as he looked forward to the revelation, Upshaw
was concerned over the one possible concession Colt might
demand in exchange for it. In a rueful twist of fate similar
to those that drove some of the more compelling tribal leg-
ends Upshaw taught in his extension class, Franklin Colt had
come to know the tribal leader's son by virtue of the fact that
Donny lived on the property of Alan Orson, one of Colt's
longtime friends. Insofar as the importance of family support had always been a cornerstone to Colt's speeches about
dealing with drug abuse, he'd taken Donny's side and was
insistent that Walter's forgiveness and support was crucial to
his son's long-term recovery.

Upshaw had given lip service to those pleas, telling Colt he'd
consider the advice, but deep in his heart he doubted that he
would ever bring himself to take such a step. The way he saw
it, nothing he said to his son would bring his wife back from
the grave, and Donny's responsibility for the woman's death

wasn't something he felt he could sweep under the rug as if it were some small transgression. Colt could name just about any other terms he might want in terms of compensation for divulging what he'd found out about skeletons in GHC's closet, but for Upshaw, embracing Donny as a prodigal son was a favor he couldn't willingly oblige.

These thoughts were still sifting through Upshaw's troubled mind when he turned off the main road leading out of Taos and drove through the reservation, his wipers squeaking across the windshield. Two side roads later he turned a final time and slowed to a stop next to the mailbox situated near the wrought-iron gate guarding the long driveway leading uphill to his mountain home. He pushed the remote clipped to his visor, and the gate began to slowly creak open as he rolled down his window and reached out through the rain to get his mail. He was withdrawing a handful of bills and other correspondence when there was a stirring in the tall bushes growing up just behind the mailbox. Upshaw's eyes widened with disbelief as the man he knew as Pete Trammell emerged through the shrubbery, drenched from the rain.

"What are you doing here?" Upshaw demanded.

"Your son's upset that you didn't send him a birthday card," Petenka Tramelik replied. "He wanted me to send you a little message."

With that, Tramelik raised his gloved hand and calmly fired a round from his Raven Arms MP-25, the same weapon Vladik Barad had used to kill Alan Orson.

Upshaw's head lolled from the impact and the mail fell from his hand. Dead, the tribal leader slipped his foot off the brake and his car slowly eased forward, just missing the still-opening gate. As Tramelik watched on, the sedan continued up the driveway another twenty yards before failing to negotiate the first turn leading into the mountains. Mature cottonwoods grew up along both sides of the road, and the car came to an abrupt stop once it left the driveway and crashed into one of them. The engine died, but Tremalik could still hear its wipers trying to fend off the rain.

The Russian operative jogged to the car and leaned in through the window. Reaching past Upshaw, he ran his hand beneath the dashboard and removed the dime-size homing bug he and Barad had been using to track Upshaw's movements, as well as any conversations made in the vehicle. Next, Tramelik carefully frisked his victim until he came across the dead man's cell phone. Pocketing both items, he strode back through the rain to the shrubs he'd been hiding behind and retrieved a small backpack containing a laptop and several other valuables he'd stolen from Upshaw's mountain home hours ago, before he and Barad had laid seige to Alan Orson's estate. He tossed in the cell phone, then trampled over the dead man's mail and made his way back to the turnoff. Farther up the road, Donny Upshaw's run-down Buick LeSabre was parked on the shoulder just in front of a hedge that had shielded it from his father's view. Barad was behind the wheel. Donny was still out cold in the backseat.

Tramelik got in front and nodded to Barad, who then started the Buick and pulled back onto the road. Tramelik turned in his seat and reached over, nudging Donny with the Raven's barrel.

"First Orson and his dog, and now your own father," Tramelik said disapprovingly. "That's quite a killing spree, Donny. Something tells me that when you come down off the smack and realize what you've done the shame is going to be too much for you."

CHAPTER SEVEN

Albuquerque, New Mexico

Less than an hour had passed since the Stony Man trio had escaped from the submerged taxi. The three men were back up on the main road, sitting in the rear of a paramedic van that had arrived a few minutes earlier. They'd already had their vitals checked and had changed into dry clothes the EMTs had been instructed to bring along. Miraculously, aside from bruises and a wrenched shoulder suffered by Bolan, the men had been come through their ordeal unscathed. Now, shrouded in thermal blankets, they were waiting for their Justice Department credentials to be verified by the Albuquerque police.

Bolan had warmed up sufficiently. Shedding his blanket, he told the others, "I'm going to see what the holdup is."

"If they're passing out hot cocoa I'll have a double," Grimaldi said, his teeth chattering.

"Same here," Kissinger added.

"I'll see what I can do," Bolan said.

Outside the van, University Drive had been officially closed off and officers had already taped off a crime-scene area nearly half the size of a football field. The officer standing closest to the van quickly blocked Bolan's way the moment he stepped down onto the tarmac.

"Sorry, but you need to stay put."

"We've got a friend missing out there," Bolan countered. "We'd like to do something about it."

"And we've got two dead cops along with another body back at the airport," the officer said. "Cool your heels."

Bolan didn't care for the officer's attitude but wasn't about to take issue with it. He remained near the truck, slowly flexing his shoulder. It was stiff and he had a limited range of motion, but he doubted the injury would compromise his ability to resume what he now saw as a bona fide mission. Perhaps the plight of Franklin Colt had little bearing on national security, but given the man's friendship with a fellow Stony Man warrior, Bolan felt a personal stake in Colt's fate. And, too, there was the matter of him and his two colleagues barely escaping the grim fate of the two police officers now lying in body bags inside a second paramedic van parked near the squad car that had come under assault while the Executioner was struggling for his life beneath the cold waters of Tijeras Arroyo.

The rain had let up and, although Bolan could see lightning far to the north, the storm had passed Albuquerque. Any thunder accompanying the flashes was muted by the commotion out on the roadway and up overhead, where a police chopper rumbled its way southward, no doubt in pursuit of Colt's abductors.

Twenty yards from Bolan, homicide detective David Lowe stood next to an unmarked Ford Taurus, a cell phone pressed to one ear. As he wrapped up his call, someone inside the vehicle handed the tall, sallow-faced man the three JD badge IDs belonging to Bolan, Kissinger and Grimaldi. Lowe exchanged a few words with the other man, then strode past the bullet-riddled squad car, issuing instructions to the forensics team going over the vehicle. As he approached Bolan, the detective waved aside the cop guarding the van, then handed over the badges.

"You checked out," Lowe said. "Sorry for the inconvenience."

"No offense taken."

"What exactly is it that a special agent does?" Lowe asked.

"That's classified," Bolan said.

Lowe shrugged and let a thin smile play across his equally thin lips. "That's the party line we got from Washington, too. But we just lost two men on account of whoever it is you're up against, so I was hoping you could unzip it a little."

"If I had some information on who killed your men I'd share it," Bolan replied. "All we know so far is they grabbed a friend of ours at the airport and made a run for it."

"You've already told me that," Lowe said. "Any idea why they grabbed him?"

Bolan shook his head. "He said there was something going on at the reservation where he works, but at this point there's no way of knowing if that's why he was kidnapped."

"Which reservation?" Lowe asked. "Rosqui?"

"I think that's the one."

"There's definitely a connection, then," Lowe said.

"Why's that?"

"One of our units just came across the panel truck you described," Lowe said. "It was parked just off the road near the interstate. No one in it."

"They switched vehicles," Bolan guessed.

"Most likely," Lowe said. "Anyway, the truck was reported stolen earlier tonight from a warehouse three miles from the Roaming Bison Casino. The casino was its last stop, and the driver's thinking someone must've snuck aboard while he was making a delivery."

"Safe assumption," Bolan said.

"I'll make another assumption." Lowe fixed Bolan with a straightforward gaze. "Since you guys have a finger in the pie, you'll likely have the option of pulling rank and outflanking us on the investigation front."

"If the situation dictates."

"Well, here's *my* situation." Lowe gestured at the second paramedic van. "I knew the men gunned down here tonight. I knew their families, too, and I'll likely be the one passing along word to the next of kin. Now, if something turns up here that you feel you need to keep off our radar, suit yourself, but anything that involves bringing in the perps that pulled the trigger on those men, I'd like that to be another matter. I want in on that."

"Understood," Bolan said, "and if it can be arranged, I'll see to it."

"Is that a promise?"

Bolan extended a hand to Lowe. "You have my word."

Lowe shook Bolan's hand and told him, "I guess that'll have to do."

Glorieta, New Mexico

FRANKLIN COLT SAT IN stony silence as he was driven through the night in what he presumed to be the backseat of some kind of sedan. His kidnappers had transferred him into the vehicle shortly after the exchange of gunfire near Tijeras Arroyo. His sense of time was uncertain, but he felt as if they'd been on the road for at least an hour, and judging from their speed he knew most of that time had been spent on one of the interstates. Even with the stocking cap pulled over his eyes he'd been able to detect city lights for the first twenty minutes, after which the ambient light outside the car had decreased, leading him to believe they were heading north on 1-25 along the largely undeveloped corridor between Albuquerque and Santa Fe. A few minutes earlier he'd sensed the car following a bend in the highway. If his assumption was right, it most likely meant they'd veered away from the capital and were now skirting the southern fringe of Santa Fe National Forest.

As he struggled to remain attuned to his surroundings, Colt found himself distracted by feelings of grief and dread. For most of the ride his captors had been speaking to one another in a foreign tongue, but immediately after the shoot-out they'd made a point to make sure he understood that the men he'd met at the airport had been slain while attempting to come to his rescue. There seemed little reason to doubt their word, and Colt was filled with remorse at the thought that he was responsible for their deaths. What a cruel twist of fate it was to have reestablished contact with John Kissinger only to have their reunion result in his friend's slaying. Colt hoped for a chance to extract revenge, but given his dire circumstances he knew there was a greater likelihood that he would be the next to die. It seemed equally probable that his death wouldn't come swiftly. Given the way he'd been questioned moments after his abduction, he knew that his captors had somehow learned that he was looking into illegal activity taking place on the reservation. There would likely be further interrogation once they reached their destination and Colt suspected that torture would likely be involved. If it came to that, he could only hope for a chance to force a struggle that would lead to him being killed outright. More importantly, he hoped that after silencing him his abductors would let the matter go. The last thing Colt wanted was for these savages to turn their sights on his family.

Colt was still mulling over his dilemma when the car turned off the highway onto the first of what turned out to be a series of side roads. For several miles the ride was smooth, but after a series of sharp turns, the car slowed to a crawl and Colt could hear the crunch of gravel under the tires as they made their way along a winding stretch of unpaved roadway. Several times the driver cursed as the car bounded roughly across deep chuckholes concealed by the recent rain. At one point the

sedan veered sharply to one side and Colt was thrown against
the man sitting beside him in the backseat. The man let out a
pained cry and brusquely shoved Colt away, then jabbed him
in the side with what felt like the butt of a pistol.

"Watch it!" Viktor Cherkow snarled, speaking in English
for the first time in nearly an hour. "I've got cracked ribs
thanks to that steering wheel of yours!"

During the verbal exchanges between his captors, Colt
had gotten the sense that Cherkow was the most short-
tempered of the group, and he saw in the Russian's outburst
a chance to bring things to a head before they even reached
their destination.

"It's that idiot driving who knocked me into you!" Colt
retorted, leaning back across the seat and elbowing Cherkow
in the ribs. "If you want to blame somebody, blame *him!*"

The Russian howled in agony. Colt was hoping the man
would shoot him, but instead Cherkow made do with the
butt of his Viking pistol, slamming it against the side of his
prisoner's head, just above the ear. It wasn't the fatal blow
Colt was hoping for. It did, however, flood his field of vision
with a bright, sudden flash of light that, just as quickly, gave
way to the black void of unconsciousness.

CHAPTER EIGHT

Mack Bolan stepped off the elevator on the fifth floor of Albuquerque's El Dorado Hotel and made his way down the hall to room 547. He opened the door with his keycard and entered the two-bedroom suite that had been booked for him and his Stony Man colleagues under their Justice Department aliases. Kissinger and Grimaldi had already checked in and were seated at a table in the dining alcove, half watching cable news on a television set wedged inside a light pine entertainment unit that also included a stereo system and mini-refrigerator stocked with overpriced provisions. The two men had already gone through several packets of mixed nuts and crackers and were now snacking on packaged cookies.

"Orson still hasn't checked in," Bolan told them.

Grimaldi grabbed the remote and switched off the television. "Not a good sign," he said.

"No, it isn't." Bolan joined the men and handed out toiletry kits he'd bought at the lobby gift shop to replace those lost to the roaring floodwaters of Tijeras Arroyo. He then gave Grimaldi and Kissinger each a bare-bones replacement cell phone.

"Mine shorted out under water," he told them. "I figure yours did, too."

"Thanks," Kissinger said. "I was going to try mine again once the SIM card dried, but that usually doesn't work."

"Any other news?" Grimaldi asked.

"Lowe put out an APB for Orson's car and has the Taos police on their way to check out his place."

"There's still a chance he was just waylaid and'll show up here," Kissinger offered.

"True," Bolan said, "but given what's happened, we have to consider that he's somehow tied into all of this."

"As a target of one of the perps?" Grimaldi wondered.

"I'm sure we'll find out soon enough," Bolan said. "There's something else. While they were searching the panel truck, they came across a map of the reservation. Colt's place out in the mountains was marked off."

"Their next stop?"

"Could be," Bolan said, "but I think it was more a backup plan in case they didn't get him at the airport."

"If they're looking for something and Colt didn't have it on him," Kissinger suggested, "they still might show up there."

"If that's the case, I want to be there."

"Good idea," Kissinger said. "Colt's got a wife and kid."

Bolan nodded. "Lowe's already called and told her to be on the lookout. She has some neighbors coming by until I get there. I want to see if she can shed any light on things, then I want to get her to a safe house. Lowe's off tracking down the families of the cops that were killed, but he's arranged for the tribal police to chip in."

"The reservation's probably out of his jurisdiction anyway, right?" Grimaldi said. "They usually have some kind of sovereignty thing going on."

"That, too," Bolan said.

"Well, we're cleaned up and ready to roll," Kissinger offered. "I don't know Colt's wife, but I'd like to come along."

"We've got a lot going on," Bolan countered. "It might be better if we split up for now."

"What did you have in mind?" Kissinger asked.

"Once I change, one of Lowe's men will take me to the reservation," Bolan said. "I think somebody should stay here on the chance Orson shows up."

"Got it," Kissinger said.

"Good." Bolan turned to Grimaldi. "Lowe's also got a crew on the way to the arroyo to fish out the taxi. We're already cleared to get our things back, no questions asked, but it'd be best if you could be there to keep an eye on things."

"Will do," Grimaldi said. "We can probably salvage the guns and ammo but the notebook's not going to be of much use."

"We can worry about that later."

"About Franklin's wife," Kissinger interjected. "How much detail did Lowe go into when he talked to her? Does she know the kind of people we're dealing with?"

Bolan nodded.

"What happened at the airport had already been on the news before Lowe called," he said. "Some of these neighbors coming over are war vets. They'll be armed, but I'll still be glad when I get there."

"Let's just hope you get there in time," Kissinger responded.

Bolan nodded gravely. "Don't think that hasn't crossed my mind."

Glorieta, New Mexico

WHEN HE CAME TO, Franklin Colt found himself bound to a straight-backed wooden chair set in the middle of a small, cold room bare of any other furnishings other than a dim lightbulb shining in a wall sconce near the only doorway. The stocking cap had been removed from his head and through the gaps in the shuttered windows he could see it was still dark outside, but he had no idea how long he'd been out. His skull throbbed where he'd been struck, and he could feel that both his wrists and ankles had been chafed by the duct tape. He was now bound by thick lengths of rope tethering him to the chair. He could also feel a dull pain in his right biceps and figured this captors had to have injected him with something to keep him unconscious. One of the men was in the room with him, a pistol tucked into the waistband of his trousers. When he spoke, Colt recognized the voice of the man who'd knocked him out back in the car.

"It's about time," Viktor Cherkow complained when he noticed that Colt had come to. "That tranq dose wasn't all that strong."

The cut on Colt's lip had scabbed over but all it took was a faint grimace to reopen the wound and give him a fresh taste of his own blood. He spit it out and demanded, "Where am I?"

Cherkow laughed. "Do you really think I'm about to tell you?"

"Where am I?" Colt repeated.

"What are you, a parrot?" Cherkow squawked derisively and flapped his arms as if they were wings. "Bwawk, bwak! Polly want a cracker?"

Colt fell silent. When he took a deep breath, he felt suddenly nauseous, overcome by a cloying, musklike smell that permeated the stark room. It was a vaguely familiar odor, and Colt soon placed it as the scent of javelinas, boarlike creatures that roamed the outer edges of the pueblo as well as other parts of the state. It wasn't much of a clue as to his whereabouts, but moments later Colt heard the mournful howl of a train engine as well as the rhythmic clatter of steel wheels rolling across a stretch of rail tracks. The sound was close, less than a mile away. Colt knew there was a train line that paralleled most of the eastern leg of Interstate 25 between Santa Fe and Blanchard. It seemed likely, then, that he was being held somewhere along that fifty-mile route. He had doubts that he would be able to put the information to use, but the knowledge gave him some small sense of empowerment.

Steam rose from a cup of coffee Cherkow held in one hand as he paced the room. As with the others, Colt recognized the Russian from the casino. He was tall and lean, wearing denim jeans and a matching lined jacket. His complexion was pasty, and his jaw was outlined with a thin, well-groomed beard the same dark shade of brown as his close-cropped hair. An equally thin red scar trailed down his right cheek. Colt had seen his share of knife fights over the years and suspected the Russian's scar had come from a similar skirmish.

Outside, the sound of the train faded, only to be replaced by the persistent drone of an approaching helicopter. Cherkow went to the window and glanced out a moment through the shutters, then turned and ambled back toward Colt.

"We both know you're going to talk eventually," he told his prisoner. "Why not save us all a lot of trouble and do it now?"

"I already told your friends," Colt responded. "I live on the reservation and work at the casino. I just do my job and don't ask questions, so I don't know what it is that—"

Cherkow cut Colt off, dashing the scalding contents of his cup into the bound man's face. Colt let out a cry as the coffee burned his skin and stung his eyes. The Russian wasn't finished. He took a quick step forward and raised his right leg, planting his foot against Colt's chest. With all his might, he thrust the leg outward. Colt's feet swung up into the air as the chair tipped and fell backward, taking him with it. His head struck the hardwood floor and he saw once more a cluster of fast-moving stars, but this time he remained conscious. The pain inside his skull magnified, however, brimming his eyes with involuntary tears. The floorboards beneath him shuddered faintly as the helicopter set down, seemingly less than a few dozen yards away. A few seconds later, the copter's rotors fell silent and the floor went still.

Looming over Colt, Cherkow withdrew the Viking pistol from his waistband. He leaned over and pressed the gun's cold barrel against Colt's forehead.

"Here's something for you to think about," Cherkow said coldly. "We know where you live. We know your wife is at home with that new baby of yours. If you won't talk, maybe she will."

Colt froze in terror, his worst fear realized.

"Leave my family out of this!" he said. Staring past the barrel into Cherkow's cold gray eyes, Colt could see that he was appealing to the conscience of someone who had none.

"That's up to you, now, isn't it?" Cherkow said. "Which kind of hero do you want to be? The kind who thinks there's something noble about keeping silent or the kind that puts his family first?"

Colt was coming to grips with Cherkow's ultimatum when the door swung inward and another of his captors entered. The other man shouted angrily at Cherkow, again in a language with which Colt was unfamilar. Cherkow shouted back but pulled the gun from Colt's head and stood upright, facing off with the other man. They continued to argue briefly, but Colt had no way of knowing what they were talking about. Several times, however, he heard a word that was all too familiar.

A name.

Orson.

Colt's heart sank anew as he realized something far more ominous than heavy rain or slow traffic may have prevented his friend from showing up at the airport. Had these men killed Orson the same way they'd killed Kissinger and the others? Or had the inventor been taken hostage, as well? If so, why? What could possibly be Orson's connection to what he suspected was going on at the reservation? It made no sense.

Once the Russians had finished arguing, Cherkow turned to Colt.

"As long as you're laying down, you might as well get some sleep. We have a little surprise in store for you when you wake up."

Cherkow followed the other man out of the room. They left the door ajar, allowing Colt his first glimpse of what looked to be an adjacent living room. All he could see was a table, two chairs and a sun-faded, overstuffed sofa. Several cardboard boxes rested on the latter's cushions. Standing beside the sofa was a short, thin man dressed in black. He had long red hair and a matching goatee. Colt had never seen him before.

Thinking back to his last conversation with Orson, Colt remembered the inventor mentioning that he would be leaving Taos for Albuquerque once he finished packing the things he planned to bring to the New Military Technologies Expo. Colt couldn't be certain, but he felt there was a good chance he was looking the boxes that contained those items.

Lying on the cold floor, Colt tried to piece it together. What did it all mean? What had he gotten himself into?

Moments later, Colt heard the front door open. A cold draft swept its way toward him, carrying the pungent stench of javelinas. Franklin's stomach clenched and he retched, bringing up little more than saliva mixed with more blood from his cracked lip. Out in the living room, the front door slammed shut and there was renewed arguing among his captors. Soon a fourth man strode into Colt's view, wearing a knee-length black leather trench coat over his well-tailored suit. He was bald, thick-chested and carried himself with an air of authority.

If there had been any doubt that his abduction was linked to what was going on at the reservation, those doubts quickly vanished, for Colt found himself staring at the Roaming Bison Casino's Director of Operations, Freddy McHale. When

McHale glanced his way and the two men shared a look of mutual recognition, Colt realized as well that there was no way he would be allowed to live now that he knew who was behind his abduction.

CHAPTER NINE

The Roaming Bison Casino was not Frederik "the Butcher" Mikhaylov's first foray into the wagering industry.

Following the collapse of the Soviet Union in the late 1980s, gambling establishments had sprung up in nearly every major city throughout Russia, and, as was the case in many of America's early casino ventures, organized crime had been quick to latch on to the phenomenon and turn it into one of its primary cash cows. Mikhaylov had been a thirty-year-old low-level goon for freelance mobsters in the suburb of Dolgoprud-niy when the first casinos opened down the road in Moscow. His reputation as a brutal enforcer for loan sharks made him a natural choice when several small, competing mobs merged into the dreaded Dolgoprudnenskaya and muscled its way into the capital city's more upscale gaming halls. Over the next dozen years, Mikhaylov specialized in "negotiating" the payment of gambling debts incurred by high rollers, and in those rare cases when physical assault and torture failed to produce desired results, the one-time slaughterhouse employee had no qualms about putting his butchering skills to good use, killing debtors in ways gruesome enough to earn press coverage that helped serve as a deterrent to anyone thinking they could welsh on monies owed the mob without dire consequence. By his own count, during his years as an enforcer, the Butcher settled over sixty million dollars' worth of gambling debts and executed at least fifty individuals who were either unable or unwilling to honor their markers.

There came a point, however, at which Mikhaylov tired of what, for him, had become mere drudgery. He yearned for advancement within the ranks and a chance to set foot in the casinos for reasons other than targeting his next victim. He liked the idea of wearing a well-tailored suit and consorting with Moscow's upper crust at the tables instead of in dark, back alleys, and in 2000 he carried out the vicious execution of a rival gang lord in exchange for an opportunity to become pit boss at Dolgoprudnenskaya's crown jewel, the Regal Splendor Casino, located only a few blocks from the Kremlin. He flourished in the position, quickly becoming fluent in five languages and developing a personalized sense of savoir faire that combined a newfound cosmopolitan sensibility with the rakish charm that drew on his lower-middle-class upbringing. On the side, Mikhaylov ran a high-price escort service that allowed him to freely indulge in the sexual favors of some of Moscow's most comely women. As his stature rose, the Russian forsook his modest apartment in Dolgoprudniy for a lavish penthouse suite at the Regal and began to dine regularly at the casino's five-star restaurant, Nostrovia, where he would often use a private booth to entertain valued guests and conduct the sort of business negotiations that couldn't be discussed out on the gambling floor. With a personal tailor at his disposal and no less than five customized luxury vehicles stored at a private garage adjacent to the casino, Mikhaylov, on the whole, had enjoyed an extravagant, privileged lifestyle that he couldn't have even imagined in his youth.

Of course, part of Mikhaylov's job at the tables required that he continue to deal with gamblers prone to wagering beyond their means, but the Russian had an uncanny knack for judging people and, unlike his predecessors, he routinely made a point not to extend credit in cases where he felt it would become necessary to execute the debtor and write off his or her debt. Yes, there had still been the frequent need for back alley "persuasion," but Mikhaylov was now in a position to delegate the dirty work to others. He trained his own crew of goons, including Petenka Tramelik and Viktor Cherkow, and he trained them well. Over the next eight years, there were barely a dozen instances in which torture or blackmail failed and his men were forced to commit murder.

All seemed right with Mikhaylov's world when, in 2008, the Russian president decried the proliferation of gambling in Russia and pushed through legislation banning casinos from urban centers throughout the country. Over the next two years, the Regal Splendor, as well as its illustrious counterparts in Moscow, St. Petersburg and other major cities were closed down, leaving the Russian populace with the daunting proposition of traveling to Siberia or some other godforsaken hinterland to indulge in any form of wagering other than the national lottery. Some crime syndicates rolled with the punch and reluctantly set up shop in these remote wastelands, but Mikhaylov was among those who decided to leave Russia in pursuit of greener pastures. With Tramelik and Cherkow in tow, the Butcher pulled stakes and moved to Bolivia, where Dolgoprudnenskaya, through a shadow company, had poured nearly three hundred million dollars into the Andean Splendor, a gambling mecca modeled after the Moscow casino where Mikhaylov had reinvented himself. The resort was slow to catch on, however, and felt too much like a step down in the world to leave him satisfied. He continued to go through the motions as a duteous pit boss, but all the while kept his eye open for other, better opportunities.

He didn't have long to wait.

Fourteen months into his Bolivian tenure, by which time he'd been promoted to Chief Officer of Gaming Operations, Mikhaylov was approached by seventy-year-old Evgenii Danilov, whose global renown as an eccentric billionaire was little more than a well-orchestrated front for his allegiance to the Russian Foreign Intelligence Service, which in 1991 had replaced the notorious KGB. Danilov, with SVR's blessing, had bought a stake in the Bolivian casino to help keep it afloat but he'd also chosen what he considered to be a more promising—and lucrative—gambling frontier to infiltrate: reservation casinos in the United States. Danilov's various American enterprises were all affiliates of Global Holdings Corporation, which the elderly financier had painstakingly created as an Antwerp-based entity supposedly made up solely of investors from the European Union. GHC had recently won a bid to take over operations of the Roaming Bison as well as the nuclear waste facility located at Rosqui Pueblo. Mikhaylov was presented with an offer to come to America and help oversee the casino's table action. It was, for Mikhaylov, the proverbial offer he couldn't refuse. That offer was gilded even further when Danilov arranged for The Butcher, Tramelik and Cherkow to be sworn in as agents for SVR's special operations force, Vympel.

Following several months of training and SVR debriefing at GHC's Belgian headquarters, Mikhaylov and Tramelik were given forged identity papers along with extensively fabricated personal backstories and put on an international flight bound for the U.S., where, as Freddy McHale and Pete Trammell, both men spent the next two years slowly establishing themselves as an influential presence at both Roaming Bison and the nuclear waste facility. As much as the casino was a perennial moneymaker, for Danilov and SVR a stake in tribal gambling profits wasn't an end in and of itself, but rather a means to help finance clandestine activity at the waste plant. The activity there served a long-standing agenda dating back more than fifty years to the height of the cold war, when Russia had squared off with the United States as the one country most capable of thwarting its aspirations for world domination. Part of that covert agenda was dependent upon securing access to a ready source of uranium beyond that contained in the nuclear fuel rods stored at the waste facility, hence Mikhaylov's fervent lobbying with Taos Pueblo's tribal leader Walter Upshaw and the decision to put Upshaw under increased surveillance when he balked at partnering with GHC. It was a bugged phone call carried out as part of that surveillance that had pinpointed Franklin Colt as the informant who'd aroused Upshaw's suspicions about GHC's ulterior motives for wanting to place the Taos reservation under its umbrella. Given what was at stake, the Butcher had made a point to be flown to Glorieta so that he could personally ensure that Colt would divulge the information he'd only alluded to in the cryptic phone message he'd left with Upshaw earlier in the day.

There was a second reason for Mikhaylov venturing this far from his duties at the casino, and it was the other matter the Russian chose to first deal with once he'd entered the modest five-room farmhouse that served as a base of operations for more than two dozen lower-tier SVR agents charged with dealings that fell beyond the scope of debt-collecting at the casino.

After confirming that Colt was still alive, Mikhaylov briefly chastised Viktor Cherkow and the other three SVR agents for having caused so much disruption in the course of abducting the security officer. Afterward he sent them to prepare for their next assignment, raiding Colt's house to look for the evidence he'd collected against GHC. Once he and Tramelik were alone Mikhaylov told his red-haired colleague, "I hope you managed things a little better on your end."

"Everything went smoothly," Tramelik replied. "Upshaw and Orson are both dead, and it'll be pinned on Upshaw's kid. We took care of him, too. Vladik stayed behind to monitor things and keep an eye on the safe house."

"What about Upshaw's cell phone?"

"I got that, too," Tramelik reported, "but there's only one call between him and Colt and that was two weeks ago, before we visited him."

"That doesn't make sense," Mikhaylov said. "You said Colt called him while he was in his car just this morning."

"I know," Tremalik said. "He must have deleted the call afterward."

"I'm not so sure," the other Russian said. "Ilyin took Colt's cell phone right after they grabbed him at the airport, and the only call to Upshaw was the same one from two weeks ago."

Tramelik frowned. There seemed only one likely explanation. "They must've each gotten separate phones for when they called each other."

"Smart move if that's what they did," Mikhaylov said. "Upshaw didn't have a second phone on him?"

Tramelik shook his head. "It's not like I had time to search through the whole car," he said. "Besides, when I found the one phone I figured it was the one we were looking for."

"You'll need to get back to Barad and have him sniff around a little more," Mikhaylov said. "If Colt and Upshaw were exchanging text messages or attachments, that other phone might have the proof we're looking for."

"The car will end up at the police impound yard," Tramelik said. "If they haven't gone through it, maybe Barad can beat them to it."

"It's worth a try," Mikhaylov said. "And when Cherkow gets to Colt's place he'll need to look for his other phone, too."

"What if Colt kept it in his car?" Tramelik suggested. "We should probably try to get to the impound yard in Albuquerque, too."

"Let's wait and see what Cherkow can come up with," Mikhaylov said. "Now back to Orson. Did you get hold of his inventions?"

Tramelik gestured at the cardboard boxes on the nearby sofa. "We obviously couldn't get to his helicopter, but we took everything from his workshop except his computer."

"Why not the computer?" Mikhaylov asked. "There had to be something we could use on it."

"I got all that." Tramelik fished through his pocket and withdrew a key chain loaded with pinky-size flash drives. "I copied everything off the hard drive. I left the computer because I used it to make sure the kid gets blamed."

Mikhaylov's radar went up immediately. "You didn't plant the heroin?"

"Yes, along with the kit and syringe, but—"

"The plan was to make it look like he stole the inventions to buy smack," Mikhaylov reminded the other man. "You were supposed to shoot him up so everyone would think he went off on a rampage."

"That's still the way it'll look," Tramelik insisted. "I just figured it'd be better to underline everything in case the police there are idiots."

"What exactly did you do?"

"Let's go to the barn," Tramelik said. "I'll show you on the computer there."

"WHY DIDN'T YOU TELL him about the map?" Ivan Nesterov asked Viktar Cherkow as the two men headed past a large, walk-in freezer resting next to the barn and made their way to a small outbuilding twenty yards past the farmhouse. The building had once seen use as a milk shed but the SVR operatives had turned most of the structure into a makeshift weapons depot.

"Tell him it got left behind in the truck?" Cherkow snapped at the wheelman who'd driven the stolen vehicle they'd used to abduct Franklin Colt. "After the way he chewed us out? Are you crazy? He'd probably shoot us!"

"Good point," Nesterov conceded, unlocking the door to the shed.

"What he doesn't know won't hurt him," Cherkow said. "Besides, we already know where we're going. We don't need a map!"

The men entered the shed, where a shelving unit lined the far wall, stocked top to bottom with an assortment of weapons and ammunition.

"I'm just concerned the police might find it and figure out what we're up to," Nesterov said.

"They don't have jurisdiction on the reservation," Cherkow reminded his colleague. "By the time they go through all the red tape to get the tribal police involved, we'll have been there and left already."

"I hope you're right," Nesterov said.

Cherkow detected the other man's skepticism and gestured at the weapons cache. "Look, if you're worried we can just load up more firepower and bring along a few more men."

"I think that'd be a good idea."

"Let's do it, then," Cherkow said. He grabbed a wheelbarrow next to the shelving unit and began to fill it with firearms and grenades. "I'll take care of this. Go round up some more men and get the chopper started. If anybody gets in our way at Colt's place, they won't know what hit them."

Stony Man Farm, Virginia

"BARBARA," AARON "THE BEAR" Kurtzman said as Barbara Price strode into the Computer Room, "what's Striker's status?"

Striker was Mack Bolan's in-house handle.

"He's on his way to check on this Franklin Colt's wife," she replied.

"Sounds like he and the boys had a close call in that flood channel."

Price nodded. "It could have been a lot worse."

"I hear you." Kurtzman shook his head wearily. "Two cops dead along with a civilian. And we still don't know about Colt. Or this Orson guy, for that matter."

"Let's hope the crews come up with something," Price said.

Inside the large dimly lit chamber, Kurtzman's three associates were seated at their respective workstations, eyes fixed on their computer screens as they diligently combed through cyberspace for data that would allow them to lend support to Stony Man field teams. The older two—former FBI agent Carmen Delahunt and one-time Berkeley cybernetics professor Huntington Wethers—were so engrossed in their tasks they didn't realize Price had entered the room. Akira Tokaido, a young computer hacker extraordinaire, glanced up from his keyboard, however, and nodded a greeting as he dislodged the earbud trailing down to his ever-running MP3 player.

"Orson's still MIA," he reported, "but I cobbled together a little more background on him so we can at least have a better idea who we're dealing with."

"Fire away." Kurtzman eased into his workstation and set down his mug. There were other seats available throughout the large room but Price remained standing, preferring to pace off some of her nervous energy.

"Orson came out of Stanford with a Ph.D. in geophysics and tried his hand at think tanks for a few years," Tokaido reported, glancing at the work file he'd cobbled together on his computer screen. "He tinkered with inventions on the side and registered a handful of minor patents, but nothing caught on. About four years ago he switched gears and signed on with an R & D outfit based out of Chicago. Must've been the jump start he needed because after a couple years he went freelance and wound up getting the Defense Department to cough up big-time for a couple of his inventions involving depleted uranium."

"Like the tank armor," Price interjected.

"That was the biggie all right," Tokaido said, "but there were a couple others, and he's got a booth at that expo in Albuquerque and is supposed to be showing off a new batch of gizmos."

"Provided he shows up," Kurtzman said. "What's he been working on?"

Tokaido scrolled down his screen. "I don't have a lot of details, but among other things he's taken the armor thing a little further and adapted it for battle gear."

"Some new generation flak jacket?" Kurtzman asked.

"That'd be my guess," Tokaido said. "If it takes after the tank armor, we're talking something lighter but stronger with some kind of embedded solar capacity."

"Sounds like something out of one of those superhero movies," Price commented.

"Sure does," Tokaido said. "Anyway, along with that he's built a prototype high-speed armored helicopter and is doing some kind of work with redox batteries."

"Redox?"

Tokaido nodded. "I think it's another uranium application. Something about a backup power source."

Kurtzman mulled over the information as he took another sip of his coffee. "Cowboy's right. That flak jacket sounds like something we could make use of. Maybe the chopper and battery, too."

"Hold the fort, gang," Carmen Delahunt suddenly called out.

"You got something?" Kurtzman said.

Delahunt ran a hand through her red hair as she glanced up from her computer screen.

"I've been running Orson's name through the search engines and came across his blog," she told the others. "Check out his last entry. Monitor three."

Delahunt moved her cursor and moments later her computer-screen image was duplicated on one of the large flat-screen monitors mounted to the east wall. Kurtzman and the others turned their attention to the display and Price wandered toward the wall for a closer look.

Orson's blog page featured his photograph along with a series of entries logged over the past week. Delahunt had highlighted one entered a few hours earlier.

I've been betrayed! the post read. I just came back from running errands and my workshop's been cleaned out. Everything! My life's work! Gone! It could only be one person. I gave him the benefit of the doubt and a chance at a new life, and this is how he repays me? By playing me for a fool? A word to the wise out there: never trust a drug addict, no matter how clean they claim to be.

"Whoa," Tokaido muttered once he'd read the dispatch.

"This would certainly explain why he didn't show up at the airport," Huntington Wethers said.

"Maybe," Kurtzman replied, his brow furrowed. "Maybe not."

"What do you mean?"

"I don't know," Kurtzman said. "Something about it doesn't smell right."

"I skimmed a few of the earlier blogs," Delahunt said. "If it's the ranting that throws you, he's gone off a few other times about other things."

Kurtzman shook his head. "No, I don't think it's that. It all just seems a little too pat. And I'm not just talking about why the guy felt he had to go blabbing to the world about this. Me? Something like that happens, I'd skip the 'press conference' and just take care of business."

"I'm thinking the same thing," Price said. She turned to Delahunt and Tokaido. "Is there anything in either the blogs or background check that could give us an idea who this drug addict might be?"

"Nothing in the background," Tokaido said, "but I'll go back over everything."

"I don't think you need to bother," Delahunt said. "There's mention in some of the earlier blogs about him taking in one of the tribal members. The son of the guy who runs the pueblo as a matter of fact. He's got him living in a guest house on the property and doing work on the grounds to help pay his rent."

"There's opportunity," Kurtzman said. "What about motive? Does this groundskeeper have a drug record?"

"Affirmative," Delahunt replied, glancing back over the data. "His name's Donny Upshaw. According to the blogs, he's cleaned up his act but used to have problems with alcohol and did some time for heroin possession."

"It looks like he might've had a relapse," Tokaido observed.

"It would appear that way," Price conceded. "Still, I'm with Bear. There's something a little off-kilter." She flipped through a few pages of notes on her clipboard then glanced back up at the screen. "I think I found it. Take another look at the entry time for the blog."

"What about it?" Delahunt said.

"When Striker checked in after that whole chase incident," Price explained, "he said Colt had spoken with Orson on the phone at around the same time as this posting. Orson had said he was just packing up the things he was going to bring to the expo."

"Which would mean he still had the stuff," Delahunt said.

"Exactly," Price said. "There wasn't time for him to have run any errands and come back to find the stuff missing."

"Not to mention the fact that he told Colt he was heading out right after he got off the phone," Kurtzman added.

"Maybe Colt had the time wrong," Wethers suggested. "Maybe the call was earlier."

"It'll be easy enough to check Colt's phone records," Kurtzman said. "Somebody want to take it?"

"Yeah, sure," Tokaido said.

"Let's touch base with Taos, too," Price suggested. "Striker said something about the authorities up there heading out to Orson's place. Hopefully they're already there and'll be able to shed some light on this."

CHAPTER TEN

Rosqui Pueblo, New Mexico

Franklin Colt lived in a remote corner of Rosqui Pueblo, far removed from the casino and the new housing development paid for largely out of proceeds from the gambling resort. His modest, four-room adobe home sat on a small knoll at the base of Mt. McCray, overlooking a fourteen-acre parcel comprised of rolling hills surrounding a wide meadow bisected by a deep, mountain-fed river. The river powered the gristmill Colt used to mash corn harvested from a large field that bordered grazing land for the four hundred roaming bison after which the resort had been named. It had been a good harvest, but Colt had yet to clear the field and endless rows of dry stalks rustled faintly in the cold night air, some sagging under the weight of the earlier rain. A mile-long gravel driveway wound from the house to the service road Colt took each day for his commute to the casino. Four vehicles had traveled up the driveway twenty minutes earlier and were now parked in front of the house next to Colt's other car, a weather-beaten Volvo station wagon half as old as his impounded '69 Nova.

One of the vehicles was a well-traveled 1993 Toyota Camry owned by Jeffrey Eppard, a Gulf War veteran who lived three miles away but was the Colts' closest neighbor. Colt's wife had called Eppard immediately after speaking with David Lowe, and the vet had arrived soon after along with his nephew and two close friends from the reservation, safeguarding the woman and her two-year-old son while awaiting backup. The other vehicles were clearly marked as belonging to the Rosqui Pueblo Police Department.

Mack Bolan stood alongside the Camry, holding open one of the rear doors while Colt's wife leaned in and secured the car seat holding her dozing young son, Frankie. Gwenyth Colt was an attractive woman in her early thirties, her large brown eyes red from tears.

"I'm sorry it has to be like this," Bolan told the woman once she slid into the seat next to her son.

"I understand." Gwen drew in a breath and looked up at the Executioner. "It's only temporary. Until Franklin is freed."

Bolan nodded.

"Why did they do this?" Gwen wondered. "We're not rich. What kind of ransom could they be looking for?"

"We don't know their motives at this point," Bolan admitted. He was reluctant to question Gwen further regarding her husband, but given the circumstances he felt it necessary. "You're certain he never mentioned anything abnormal going on at the casino or elsewhere around the reservation?"

"Positive. He doesn't like to talk about work. The only thing he's ever told me is how he hates watching people throw their money away gambling."

"He plays some poker himself, though, right?"

"A couple times a month with some friends," Gwen confessed. "There was a game just last night, actually. There's not a lot of money involved. For Franklin it was always more about socializing."

Bolan could sense that Gwen was telling the truth, at least what she saw it to be. He couldn't help wondering, however, if there might be something more to Colt's gambling, especially to the extent that it involved Alan Orson, who, according to

Kissinger's latest update, still had yet to check into his hotel room back in Albuquerque. That the men played cards together and were now both missing after a game the previous night was something that, lacking any other leads, needed to be considered as something more than mere coincidence.

Gwen took Bolan's momentary silence the wrong way and fought back a fresh flow of tears.

"My husband's still alive, isn't he?" she whispered. "You'd tell me if he wasn't, right?"

"We're all hoping for the best," Bolan answered tactfully.

"But you don't know," Gwen said flatly. "He could already be…"

Her voice trailed off.

"We're doing all we can," Bolan told her. "Take care of your son and try to keep your hopes up."

Gwen tightened her lips and nodded, then turned and busied herself bundling a small blanket around her dozing son. Bolan looked toward the front seat, where Jeffrey Eppard had already started the engine and was waiting to pull out. Beside him sat his nephew Leeland. The other two men he'd driven to the property would be staying behind to assist Bolan and the tribal police in their stakeout.

"Don't worry, she's in good hands," Eppard assured the Executioner.

"Just call the number I gave you once you have her checked in," Bolan responded.

"Will do."

Bolan quietly closed the door and stepped back from the vehicle. Eppard slowly backed up, then turned the sedan and started back down the long driveway. Bolan watched the car until it disappeared around the first bend, then turned and headed past the police's Yamaha ATVs to the Crown Victoria. Tribal Police Sergeant Cecil Farris, a tall, broad-shouldered man with a retro crew cut, stood hunched alongside the vehicle, leaning across the front seat to make use of the dispatch transceiver. As he waited for Farris to finish his call, Bolan tested his sore shoulder and glanced into the night sky. The cloud cover had long since moved out of the area, leaving the heavens dotted with as many bright, shining stars as Bolan could ever remember seeing. He could also see a jetliner streaking through the sky far to the south, and just a few miles away a helicopter drifted high above the hills, its rotors barely audible. Bolan was still watching the chopper and working his shoulder when Farris approached him.

"Shuttle chopper from the airport," Farris explained. "Lots of high rollers can't wait to get here and start losing."

"I know the type," Bolan said.

"Shoulder acting up?" Farris asked.

"Not that much."

"Glad to hear it," Farris said. "That taxi plunge sounds like it was one hell of a ride."

Bolan gestured at the dispatch radio. "Any news?"

Farris nodded. "That was Taos. A black-and-white just showed up at Orson's place. They've got some kind of situation up there, but they aren't sure what to make of it yet."

"What'd they find?"

"For starters, Orson's dead," Farris said. "Taken out at close range with two rounds from a .25 caliber."

"I was afraid of that," Bolan said. His hopes for Franklin Colt had just diminished, as well.

"Whoever did it took out Orson's dog, too," Farris went on. "Male terrier inside his work lab. They say it looks like the lab was ransacked, but there's no way of knowing at this point what was taken."

"Colt told us Orson was loading some things to bring down to the tech expo."

"Well, DMV has him registered with a Chevy Silverado pickup," Farris said. "No sign of it on the property. You gotta figure it's gone along with whatever he was planning to bring."

"What about clues?" Bolan asked.

"Nothing but shell casings so far," Farris said. "They're getting walloped by the same storm we got, so there's not going to be much chance of finding footprints. Right now they're searching the other structures on the property to see what else they can come up with."

Bolan absorbed the news. He didn't like the way things were adding up.

"I don't see how Orson ties into Colt being kidnapped," he told Farris, "but there has to be a link. And they sent at least four guys after Colt."

"Which means we'll likely have our hands full if they wind up here," Farris said. "Of course, there's a chance we're wrong about this. They might not show."

"True," Bolan said, "but all we've got to go on is that map they found in the panel truck. I like the odds."

"I hope you're right. I like the odds better, too, when they come to us instead of the other way around."

"We'd better finish setting up."

Farris nodded again. "I'll get our wheels behind that gristmill over there so it'll look like it's just the wife here."

"Good idea," Bolan said.

"You want to take the house?" Farris suggested. "I can keep an eye on things out here."

"Done."

As Farris wandered over to speak with three tribal police officers standing alongside the ATVs, Bolan surveyed the grounds. Eppard's two other friends had already stationed themselves out in the darkness, one near the gristmill's massive water wheel, the other a few rows out into the cornfield. Once the tribal officers took up their positions, Bolan felt certain they'd have set an adequate trap should Colt's abductors send men after his wife, but he knew better than to figure the game was already won. Whatever stakes the kidnappers were playing for, it was clear they were high enough to kill for, and when lives were considered expendable, it had always been the Executioner's experience that there would be no end to the bloodshed until the enemy got what it was after or was put down. Either way, he knew it was unlikely that things would resolved without a fight.

THE TOYOTA CAMRY CARRYING Gwenyth Colt and her young son slowed to a stop as it reached the end of the mile-long driveway leading from their home. The property was fenced off and the main gate was drawn closed.

"Franklin's been meaning to fix the tension spring," Gwen told Jeffrey Eppard. "It slams shut automatically."

"Yeah, we noticed that when we came in," Eppard's nephew said. "I'll get it."

Leeland got out of the Camry and closed the door behind him before heading toward the gate. In the backseat, Frankie stirred and opened his eyes. Gwen turned to him and stroked his forehead.

"Hey, sweetie," she said. "We're going for a little ride, okay? Go back to sleep."

"Where are we going?" the boy asked.

Before Gwen could respond, the front side passenger door suddenly swung open. Gwen was confused, as was Eppard; his nephew was still out on the driveway, drawing the gate open.

Pffftttt.

Eppard's head snapped to one side and Gwen let out a scream as she felt herself being spattered by blood. The front door closed again, and she caught a glimpse of the gunman quickly circling around the front of the Toyota. It was a man dressed in dark clothes, a full-face ski mask drawn over his head. Gwen watched with horror as the man fired at Leeland. Eppard's nephew had a gun on him but he crumpled to the ground without having a chance to draw it.

"Mommy?" Frankie called out, frightened by his mother's screams.

Gwen instinctively drew closer to her son and leaned across him as the gunman yanked open the driver's door and poked his head into the vehicle.

"Shut him up or I will!" he commanded, aiming his sound-suppressor-equipped pistol at Frankie as he reached under the dashboard, triggering the latch release for the rear trunk.

"Mommy?" Franklin cried out again.

"Shh." Gwen placed a finger over her son's lips and did her best to sound calm, even as her heart raced with fear. "Shh, just be quiet, okay? Be a brave little boy."

Frankie nodded but began to whimper softly, tears coming to his eyes.

By now five more men had materialized out of the darkness. Two of them hunched over Leeland then hoisted the young man's body between them and carried it toward the car. Another man circled to the rear of the vehicle and popped open the trunk. The shooter who'd killed both men, meanwhile, grabbed Eppard by the armpits and dragged him from the driver's seat. The two remaining men closed in and took charge of the body, carrying it back to the rear of the car as the gunman took Eppard's place behind the wheel. Moments later, the Camry jostled slightly and Gwen flinched at the sound of the two slain men being unceremoniously dumped into the trunk.

This can't be happening, she thought to herself.

Once the trunk slammed shut, one of the other men circled the vehicle and got into the backseat next to Frankie. Gwen was on the other side. The second man, like the driver, wore a full-face ski mask. He grinned malevolently at Frankie and said, "Boo!"

Gwen had to hold herself back from lashing out at the man.

"Where are you taking us?" she whispered, barely able to get the words out.

"Good news," the man beside her replied as his cohort shifted the sedan into gear and passed through the opened gateway. "We're taking you to a little family reunion."

Frankie could no longer control himself. He let out a deep sob and began to scream.

"Hey, hey," the man beside him said with icy calm. "We're going to see your daddy. Do you want him to think you're a big crybaby?"

As HE WATCHED THE Camry head down the service road leading toward the distant, gleaming lights of the Roaming Bison Casino, Viktor Cherkow shed his ski mask and led the remaining men back to a wide gully where, in a clearing surrounded by narrow-leafed cottonwoods, Ivan Nesterov sat at the controls of the Sikorsky S-76 helicopter that had brought them to the reservation from Glorieta. The twelve-passenger chopper was part of an aerial fleet belonging to MidState Air Charter Services, a subsidiary of Evgenii Danilov's Global Holdings Corporation. The Sikorsky, as Sergeant Farris had pointed out to Bolan, was normally used as a shuttle service for high rollers looking to beeline to the casino from Albuquerque International, but this night it had been pressed into duty of quite another nature.

"So far, so good," Cherkow told the pilot while two of his colleagues hurriedly raided the aircraft's storage compartment for an assortment of assault rifles, grenades and incendiary devices. "Now's when things get a little tricky."

"We saw them spreading out around the house," Nesterov replied. "Are you sure you don't want to just come in by air?"

Cherkow shook his head, holstering his Viking pistol in favor of a Russian-made PP-2000 submachine gun handed to him by one of the other men. As with the pistols used in the gateway ambush, the subgun had been outfitted with a sound suppressor.

"We'll have a better element of surprise if we sneak up on them," he said. Tapping his earbud transceiver, he quickly added, "If we need backup, though, you'll hear about it. Otherwise, just stay put and wait for a pickup order."

"Understood," the pilot said.

Cherkow moved away from the chopper and led the others back up the service road. Once they'd passed through the gate he told them, "All right. Everyone spread out and make your approach the way we discussed. Do your best to take everyone down before they can get any shots off. If we can take the house without incident, we'll search it top to bottom, then move out."

"And if there are problems?" one of the men asked.

Cherkow grinned, patting the incendiary grenade he'd just clipped to his ammo belt. "If we can't get inside the house, we'll destroy it along with any evidence Colt might have stashed there."

CHAPTER ELEVEN

The interior of the Colt home was as modest and inauspicious as the exterior. Paver tiles lined the floor of the sparsely furnished main room, and the walls were white and unadorned except for a large oil family portrait hung proudly over the fireplace. There were Native American artifacts—three ancient Anasazi pots and a ceremonial Kokopelli doll—displayed on the mantel, and a simple wrought-iron chandelier hung suspended over the dining-room table. The chandelier worked off a dimmer switch, and Bolan had its lights turned low so that as he maintained his vigil he could see his way around without casting a silhouette against the closed drapes. The house was eerily quiet except for the dull murmur of the refrigerator and an occasional creaking of the exposed rafters spanning the raised ceiling.

There was a flashlight on the hearth next to a fire extinguisher and an antique kindling box. Bolan took the light with him to a darkened alcove adjacent to the living room. A small writing desk faced a shuttered window overlooking the backyard. It was covered with paperwork, a handful of books, a deck of cards and an old cigar box filled with toy soldiers. There were a series of drawers as well, but much as he was tempted to search through them in hopes of finding some possible clue to Colt's abduction, Bolan wasn't about to violate the man's privacy any more than he already had by entering the house without a warrant.

Bolan spotted a small, framed black-and-white photo propped in front of the shutters on the recessed windowsill. He shone the flashlight on it and found himself staring at a much younger Franklin Colt sitting across from John Kissinger in what looked to be some kind of country bar. They were lofting their beer glasses and grinning with a carefree ease that suggested the photograph was taken before the gunshot injury that cut short Colt's tenure with DEA. Bolan wondered if Colt had recently taken the photo out of storage or if he'd had it on display all these years.

The Executioner's ruminations were interrupted by the sound of gunfire on the property. He quickly set down the photograph and switched off the flashlight. Assault rifle in hand, he strode back to the main room. He'd made it as far as the dining-room table when the front door swung open. Bolan held his fire when Sergeant Farris lurched inside, one hand clutched to his chest. Blood seeped between his fingers, turning them red. In his other hand was his service pistol. Another shot thumped into the door as he was slamming it shut.

"So much for wondering if they'd show up," he muttered, sagging against the doorjamb. "I don't know how many of them there are but—"

Farris's voice was drowned out by a tinkling of glass. Bolan whirled in the direction of the living-room picture window. The curtains rustled where something had just struck them and a second later a projectile dropped into view on the paver tiles.

Grenade, Bolan thought. He was already in motion, diving instinctively to his right. He made it halfway behind a large sofa before the incendiary device went off, filling the room with light and smoke. The thunderous blast shattered more of the windows and echoed loudly through the house, triggering a sensor alarm mounted to one of the overhead rafters. A light began to blink on and off at regular intervals, punctuated by a shrill, staccato bleeping.

The smoke stung Bolan's eyes and lungs as he drew himself up behind the sofa. Through the noxious cloud he could see flames eating away at the front curtains and spreading across the tiles toward the dining area. Leaving his rifle behind, he held his breath, charged to the window and yanked down the curtains, then dropped them onto the pavers and stomped out the flames. The danger wasn't over yet, however. Behind him, a throw rug as well as the dining-room tablecloth had caught fire. The alarm continued its torturous bleating as Bolan bolted to the hearth and grabbed the fire extinguisher. He yanked off the safety ring and directed the nozzle at the spreading fire. He doused the rug until the flames died, then took aim at the table, scattering the jigsaw puzzle on its top with a foamy jet of fire retardant. The flames were snuffed out but the tablecloth smoldered, adding to the smoke.

Bolan couldn't hold his breath any longer. Casting aside the extinguisher, he rushed to the kitchen area, hacking from the acrid smoke. He ran the faucet and held a dishcloth under the running water, then clutched the cloth to his face and ventured back into the living room. The alarm continued to shriek and throw off its spastic light. Bolan retrieved his rifle and peered up through the smoke, then took aim and put a slug through the alarm's plastic shell, obliterating it as well as the wiring inside. The house went dark, and there was a moment of silence before a hail of gunfire sang through the exposed window and whisked past Bolan, slamming into the wall behind him. He threw himself onto the floor and crawled toward the door, carrying his AR-15 with him. Farris had collapsed onto the tiles, as well. The officer coughed as he stared through the smoke. Bolan saw the all too familiar look of a man who sensed his wounds might be fatal.

"I'll be all right," he gasped. "Go give 'em hell."

"And just leave you?" Bolan said. "Sorry, I don't work that way."

AFTER FIRING THE SHOT that struck Farris and lobbing his incendiary grenade through Franklin Colt's front window, Viktor Cherkow had crouched back behind the cover of a ramshackle toolshed in the front yard. It was from this position that he'd subsequently unleashed the shots that had just missed Bolan. Cherkow was an expert marksman and it had been more than the sudden darkness inside the house that had thrown off his aim.

"It can't be!" the Russian whispered incredulously as he stared at the shattered window. He'd only had a fleeting glimpse of his target and he knew there was a chance the smoke and fire alarm's strobe light had deceived him, but in the split second before Bolan had shot out the alarm, Cherkow had hesitated with his trigger, dumbfounded to realize he was staring at one of the men Colt had been speaking with outside the terminal at Albuquerque International. It didn't seem possible. Cherkow himself had rear-ended the taxi the man had leaped into prior to giving chase to Nesterov and the other men who'd abducted Colt. He'd watched the taxi go off the road and plunge into Tijeras Arroyo. With his own eyes he'd seen the cab sink beneath the current without any survivors coming to the surface. And yet there he was: the same man! If he could manage it, Cherkow now wanted the man taken alive so he could be questioned, not only about what Colt might have told him, but also about how he'd managed to cheat death in the storm channel.

At least one of the other SVR agents had been taken out in the first moments of the seige. Cherkow was about to call out for the others to leave the mystery man to him when an incoming round pulverized one of the shed's planks, stinging his face with shrapnel. Cherkow cursed and spun to his right, tracing the shot to the gristmill. He spotted one of Jeffrey Eppard's friends crouched near the water wheel and quickly returned fire, dropping the other shooter with a burst of Parabellum rounds to the chest.

"See you in hell!" he taunted his victim as he wiped at the fresh blood trickling alongside the scar on his cheek. "But not tonight."

THE SMOKY HAZE BEGAN to dissipate slightly as it drifted through the house, but even with the dampened washcloth Bolan still found it difficult to breathe. Reaching up, he threw open the front door. He could hear gunfire outside but none of the shots were being directed his way. Rising to a squat, he cast aside the cloth and grabbed Farris under the arms then slowly dragged him outside. The tribal cop tried to wave him off, but he was too weak to put up much resistance.

"I don't need a babysitter!" Farris groaned.

"Can it!" Bolan snapped back. "Save your strength!"

Just outside the doorway two rectangular, waist-high redwood planters flanked a small porch. The containers were heavy, but Bolan was able to shift them until they were touching up against each other, creating a V-like barrier that would hopefully shield Farris from any further incoming rounds.

"Stay low and keep pressure on the wound," he told the cop.

"I know the drill," Farris snapped. "Now go! Do what you have to!"

Bolan picked up his carbine and peered out past the planters. There was no sign of the enemy, but he could see that Eppard's friend had been downed near the gristmill where the squad car and ATVs had been parked. The man didn't appear to be moving, but he was an open target and on the chance he was still alive, Bolan was determined to get him out of the line of fire. Rising to one knee, the Executioner drew in a deep breath and prepared to hurtle himself over the planters, hoping to make it at least as far as Gwen's station wagon before drawing fire. Before he could make his move, however, he was stopped short by a trembling sensation beneath him. The feeling slowly intensified and soon there there was thunderlike rumbling in the night air around him.

"Earthquake," Bolan murmured.

"This is New Mexico," Farris gasped. "We don't have earthquakes!"

Bolan's eyes had adjusted to the darkness and he once again glanced out past the planters, trying to account for the trembling, which continued unabated. As the sound grew louder, Bolan placed it and stared out at the distant cornfield. There he could see the stalks being parted and flattened by what looked to be some dark, approaching flow of lava. By now the gunfire had ceased and there was only the growing rumble, which soon enough distinguished itself as the pounding of hooves. Seconds later, the front wave of the dark force broke clear of the cornfield and Bolan realized it was no single entity, but rather a collective mass of two-ton beasts driven to flight by the sound of gunfire and the explosion of the incendiary grenade.

Bison stampede!

CHAPTER TWELVE

Cherkow was in disbelief when he saw the first wave of bison emerge through the cornfield. And the beasts weren't alone. Another of Jeffrey Eppard's friends had cast aside his sniper rifle and bolted clear of the dry stalks a few steps ahead of the creatures. He had no chance of outrunning them, however, and the man went down and was quickly trampled underhoof as the herd continued its manic charge. The bison were in a tight formation, shoulder to shoulder, racing toward Colt's house with no sign of slowing. Cherkow was directly in their path. He knew his subgun would be of little use against them and he had doubts the rickety toolshed would provide much in the way of protection were the beasts to barrel into it. Breaking from cover, the Russian bolted toward the house, hoping to reach it before the stampede caught up with him.

As he crossed the grounds, Cherkow saw Bolan leap over the planters and race past the station wagon toward the gristmill. Cherkow fired on the run but his aim was errant and his rounds flew wide, taking out the Volvo's windshield. The Russian wasn't about to waste time lining up another shot; the bison were gaining on him. He tossed the weapon aside and lengthened his stride, running like a man possessed toward the window he'd tossed the grenade through. Once he was within a few yards of it, he raised his forearms in front of his face and dived headlong through the opening. There were still shards of glass clinging to the window frame and they drew blood from Cherkow's forearms as they shattered under his weight.

Cherkow cleared the window and landed hard on the living-room floor. His right shoulder absorbed most of the blow, but his already sore knee struck the tiles as well and added to the searing pain in his rib cage. He groaned and slowly rose to his feet, hacking from the still-lingering smoke as he pulled out his Viking pistol. The thundering of the stampede rattled the house as he staggered across the room like a man half-drunk. He was halfway to the doorway when a shot rang out, and he felt a stabbing sensation in his right hip. Spewing obscenties, the Russian quickly traced the shot to Sergeant Farris, who lay out on the front doorstep where Bolan had left him. Before the tribal officer could get off another shot, Cherkow cut loose with his Viking, stitching Farris across the chest. The gun fell from the sergeant's hand as he slumped lifelessly to the concrete. Staring past his victim, Cherkow saw a handful of bison abruptly change course and veer away from the planters. Relieved, Cherkow slumped onto the sofa and tore at the bullet hole in his bloodied jeans. It looked as if the slug had passed through cleanly. Still, the man's entire body now throbbed from the cumulative toll of his wounds.

Grimacing, the Russian hauled himself over the back of the sofa and dropped behind it. From there he figured he'd be in a position to take on any enemy that chose to enter into the house. A part of him hoped the man from the airport would return. Much as he'd earlier wanted to take the man alive for questioning, Cherkow was now in a killing mood, and if the bison didn't finish the man off the Russian was determined to do the job himself.

ONE OF CECIL FARRIS'S colleagues had been the first victim of Cherkow's goon squad, struck in the back by a silenced round while staking out the grounds from behind a cord of firewood forty yards from the house. With Eppard's friends already downed, that left two surviving members of the tactical force Bolan had helped assemble. One of them, tribal police veteran Louis Thon, had managed to take out two of the Russian assailants before the bison had begun their charge through the cornfield. He'd made it as far as one of the large shade trees behind the house before the creatures reached the grounds and began to split off into smaller groups, all of which were still at least thirty strong and rampaging out of control.

With no other cover within reach, Thon circled behind the tree and pressed himself against the rough bark. A group of more than twenty bison charged by, still in mad flight, brushing close enough that their smell clung to the officer even after they'd passed. As they neared the boulder-strewn base of the mountainside behind the house, the creatures slowed momentarily, then began to scatter, some heading left toward the long driveway, others to the right, where within a hundred yards they would find their way blocked by the river. A dozen of the beasts chose a third course, doubling back toward the house and the tree where Thon now stood facing them. The officer was about to circle to the other side when someone called out to him from directly overhead.

"Up here!" shouted Officer James Lynwood, who had fortuitously set up a sniper post in the lower boughs of the tree before all hell had broken loose. He'd already claimed one of Cherkow's men with his scope-mounted DPMS Panther and had just seen another trampled by the bison while trying to flee down the driveway.

Thon reached up to the hand Lynwood extended his way. They grabbed hold of each other's wrists and as Lynwood pulled, his counterpart stabbed his boots at the trunk's bark and half climbed up the side of the tree. Thon reached Lynwood's side just as the bison charged past.

"This is insane!" Thon muttered.

Lynwood nodded solemnly, staring at the herd. He figured there were at least three hundred of them, of which fewer than twenty had ceased stampeding. "We'll have to wait for them to run themselves out."

"Fine with me," Thon said. "No way am I going back down there and playing matador with them."

Intent as they were on watching the bison, neither man took notice of movement out on the rocky mountainside behind them. Cherkow's lone surviving accomplice, Cheslav Abramowicz, had reached the safety of the rocks well before the stampede, but it wasn't until he saw Thon being hauled up into the tree that he spotted Lynwood's sniper post. Both officers were partially concealed by the thick boughs branching out from the trunk, but Abramowicz felt he had a clear enough target. Ignoring the commotion of the herd, he calmly drew aim with his PP-2000. The lightweight subgun was far inferior to Lynwood's Panther as a sniper weapon, but the Russian compensated by strafing his target with half his 44-round box magazine. Enough of the rounds found flesh to drop both Lynwood and Thon from the tree like pieces of overripe fruit, adding to the already grim body toll.

BOLAN HAD DIVED TO the ground briefly when Cherkow's errant shots had taken out the Volvo's windshield. With the bison racing headlong toward him, however, he had no intention of staying down for long. He crawled around the station wagon, then sprang to his feet and charged toward the man lying near the gristmill. The man's eyes were open, but Bolan could see there was no life in them. There was no time to try to drag the body to safety; several of the bison were already bearing down on him. It was all he could do to veer to one side to avoid being struck head-on. As it was, one of the beasts clipped Bolan's right thigh with so much force the AR-15 went flying from his grasp as he was propelled backward into the gristmill's eight-foot-high waterwheel, which rested in the muddy channel where the river would normally be diverted to operate the mill. Colt had taken the wheel off its axle for refurbishing, however, and when Bolan struck it there was enough give for him to realize it was merely propped against the side of the building. Still, he hoped it was wedged securely in the mud because he saw it as his only chance of not falling victim to the stampede. Scrambling as best he could, he used the wheel's horizontal paddles as ladder rungs and began to climb upward, hoping to reach a point from which he could lift himself onto the mill's roof.

It wasn't to be.

Bolan had reached the top of the wheel and was trying to stand up when a two-ton bull, foaming at its bearded muzzle, veered from the herd, trampling Eppard's slain friend and charging the wheel. The recessed channel forced him to strike at an angle, but the bison's massive, fur-lined skull carried the force of a wrecking ball and there was a splintering of crushed paddles as the wheel was jarred free of the mud and began to roll clear of the mill. Thrown off balance, Bolan dropped flat against the curvature of the wheel and held on to its sides as it began to carry him backward down the channel toward the river. A few yards along, the wheel abruptly slammed to a stop against the channel lock, throwing Bolan clear. He landed on a muddy embankment, which surged with a noisy fury that drowned out the thundering of the stampede.

By now, the handful of bison detoured by the rock formations behind the house had looped around and were heading back toward Bolan along the side of the river. Fortunately for Bolan they gave the embankment a wide berth, buying him enough time to clear his senses and stagger back to his feet. When the creatures converged upon the waterwheel, several of them joined the bull in butting their heads against the exposed paddles. Bolan welcomed the diversion. To his left, he could see the police cruiser and Yamaha ATVs parked behind the gristmill, next to an open doorway that beckoned as a possible safe haven until the stampede had run its course.

As with his plan to reach the roof, however, the bison, in their frenzy, once again proved the Executioner's undoing. He had made it only a few yards along the slick embankment before the beasts managed to collectively butt the waterwheel with enough force to roll it over the channel lock. Bolan heard the splintering of more paddles and barely had time to glance up before the wheel teetered to one side and began to tumble into the river. Bolan stood directly in the wheel's path, and there was no way he could get the necessary footing to move clear.

One second Bolan was bracing himself on the embankment; the next he found himself knocked into the river by the wheel's weight and momentum. For the second time that evening, an icy New Mexico current seemed destined to claim him as a sacrifice to its unchecked power.

CHAPTER THIRTEEN

Glorieta, New Mexico

The javelina farm serving as Frederik Mikhaylov's SVR base was roughly the same size as Alan Orson's Taos estate and, as with the inventor's work space, the largest structure on the property—in this case a dilapidated dairy barn dating back to World War I—had been gutted from within and rebuilt to serve a function other than storing hay and providing stalls for livestock. The stalls had been converted to bunk quarters for the Butcher's minions, and the upper hayloft now served as work space replete with drafting tables, benches, laboratory facilities and an array of machinist's tools. It was to these elevated quarters that Petenka Tramelik had taken the boxed items Orson had intended to display at the New Military Technologies Expo in Albuquerque.

While Tramelik busied himself with inventorying the plunder, Mikhaylov paced the ground floor near the barn door, watching Hedeon Barad—Vladik Barad's brother, as well as the mechanic who'd taken care of Mikhaylov's fleet of luxury cars back at Moscow's Royal Splendor—carefully peel away taped sheets of paper covering the windows of Orson's stolen Chevy Silverado. Hedeon had already spray painted the pickup's formerly white chassis a shade of forest green. Even with the windows and main door cracked open to allow for cross-ventilation, the aerosol fumes still lingered in the air, holding their own with the omnipresent scent of the javelinas. Mikhaylov wandered to the rear of the vehicle and inspected the license plate, which had been lifted from a similar Silverado gathering rust in a Santa Fe salvage yard owned by yet another of Evgenii Danilov's GHC shadow companies. The plates, front and back, were both well scuffed and dented.

"Well?" Hedeon asked as he peeled away the last strips of paper. "What do you think?"

While impressed by the paint job, Mikhaylov wasn't the kind of person who lavished praise on subordinates. He looked over the pickup noncommitally then told the other man, "Once the paint dries you'll need to drive through the hills and get some dirt on it."

"Of course," Hedeon responded. "I'll see to it first thing in the morning."

"After you've done that, drive to Santa Fe and buy a used camper shell for the back," Mikhaylov went on. "Then stop by a few places and get some decals and bumper stickers. Something innocuous. Don't put them on until you're away from the stores you bought them from. Once that's all taken care of, bring the truck back and drive through the hills some more. I want it to look like it's gone weeks without being washed."

"You've thought it all through," Hedeon said.

"It's what I do," Mikhaylov responded coldly. "It's why I'm the one giving the orders and you're the one following them."

"I understand."

"Let me make sure you do," Mikhaylov said. "Repeat the instructions back to me."

Hedeon was used to the other man's condescension. He suppressed his annoyance and obliged Mikhalov. He'd nearly finished when another of the Butcher's men opened the barn door wider and poked his head in, admitting a cold draft of air.

"The trench is ready," he reported. "And Ilyin just showed up with the woman and her kid."

"Perfect timing," Mikhaylov said. "I'm on my way."

"He wonders if you've heard back from Cherkow."

Mikhaylov shook his head. "Not yet. Go ahead and open the door wider so I can drive out."

Parked a few yards behind the Silverado was a small, battery-operated utility cart. Mikhaylov was halfway to the vehicle when Tramelik called down to him from the railing of the converted hayloft.

"As far as I can tell it's all here," he said. "And it looks like all the matching specs and schematics are on the flash drives."

"We'll get a better idea once Diaz shows up," Mikhaylov responded, glancing up at the red-haired man.

H e was referring to Melido Diaz, a Bolivian scientist and avid roulette player Mikhaylov had come to know during his brief time at the Andean Splendor. Diaz's credentials weren't as impressive as Alan Orson's in terms of dealing with uranium, but he, like Orson, was also an inventor. The hope was that he would be able to help the SVR make use of the plunder from Orson's laboratory. One thing Mikhaylov knew for certain—he preferred Diaz to the only other likely candidate, Dmitri Vishnevsky, the SVR agent who'd replaced him at the Bolivian casino. Vishnevsky was an intellectual with two Ph.D.s and a high-tech background who'd made millions for the SVR as a card-counting blackjack player at rival casinos back in Russia. He'd been in the running for the position Mikhaylov now held at Roaming Bison but had been passed over by Danilov, who preferred the Butcher's harder edge. Mikhaylov hated Vishnevsky's pretentious elitism, and the two men had often quarreled back at Moscow's Regal.

During one particularly heated argument, the men had come to blows, requiring the intervention of casino security to keep Mikhaylov from beating the other man to a pulp.

"There's another matter we need to attend to," Tramelik reminded Mikhaylov.

"Upshaw's other cell phone? Has Vladik been able to get to the impound yard to look for it?"

"He says they haven't brought in Upshaw's car yet, but it looks too well guarded for him to sneak in anyway," Tramelik said.

"Then what's the other problem?" Mikhaylov asked. "As if we don't have enough to worry about."

"We need to replace the heroin I planted in Taos and then some," Tramelik said. "We have three dealers with standing orders. Four kilos total."

"You handle it," Mikhaylov said as he started up the cart. "I have some damage control to attend to."

Mikhaylov powered the cart past the Silverado and out of the barn. Jeffrey Eppard's hijacked Toyota Camry was idling thirty yards away near the main gate to the javelina pen. The car's headlights were directed toward the pen, illuminating the eyes of a dozen swinish creatures foraging off clumps of mesquite and plant scraps piled in a large heap next to a long, shallow water trough. By the time Mikhaylov reached the vehicle, Zhenya Ilyin had gotten out of the backseat and circled to the other side to open the door for Gwenyth Colt. The woman, like her husband, had been driven to the farm with a stocking cap pulled down over her eyes. There had been no need to bind her by the wrists or ankles; the mere threat of harming young Frankie had made her compliant for the duration of the trip.

"All right," Ilyin told the woman as he removed the stocking cap. "We're here. Get out."

Gwen's hair was disheveled, but she made no effort to straighten it. She eased out of the backseat, then leaned back in and unfastened Frankie's seat belt. The young boy stirred and opened his eyes.

"C'mon, sweetie," Gwen told him quietly. "We're going to go see Paparoni and show him how brave we are, okay?"

"Okay," Frankie repeated with dubious conviction. He climbed out of his car seat and bounded from the car, wrinkling his nose. "What stinks?"

"It's not so bad once you get used to it," Mikhaylov told the boy. He remained in the cart and left it idling.

Gwen stared at the Butcher, first in anger, then with a glimmer of recognition.

"I've seen you before," she said.

Mikhaylov smiled in a way that was devoid of warmth. "What's that saying, 'Let's not go there'?"

"This is your doing, isn't it?" Gwen persisted. "You're behind this."

"It would probably be better if you didn't ask so many questions," Mikhaylov warned her. "When the time comes, that will be my job."

"I've already told your men. I know nothing that could possibly interest you."

"But your husband does," Mikhaylov told her. "You and your son...you're what we could call 'bargaining chips.'"

"You'll threaten us to make him talk, is that it?"

"Again with the questions." Mikhaylov turned to Ilyin. "Take them inside so they can have a little family time with 'Paparoni.'"

"Paparoni's here?" Frankie said.

"He's our guest," Mikhaylov told the child. "And now you and your mother are guests, too. Guests know how to behave themselves. I'm sure you were taught that."

Frankie nodded.

"We'll do our best," Mikhaylov promised. He gestured to Ilyin. Ilyin moved in and began to escort Gwen and Frankie across the grounds to the main house, located fifty yards past the barn.

Mikhaylov turned his attention back to the javelina pen. Another worker had already opened the gate and the stolen Camry was proceeding through. Mikhaylov followed close behind in the cart. Out in the pen, the nearest javelinas took flight in the other direction, disappearing beyond range of the Toyota's headlights to the far end of the compound, where at least another two hundred of the creatures were cloaked by darkness. The two-vehicle procession made its way through the muddy turf for another fifty yards before coming upon a freshly dug trench and the backhoe-equipped Bobcat 963 that had performed the digging. The trench was more than six feet deep and nearly as wide as the cart Mikhaylov was driving. He parked alongside the opening and left the cart running as he got out.

"Let's do this quickly," he told the driver of the Camry, who'd already gotten out and was opening the trunk. With him was the man who'd operated the backhoe.

It took two trips for the men to dump the bodies of Jeffrey and Leeland Eppard. There was nothing ceremonial to their burials. One after the other, they were flung down into the trench.

"Fill it back up and pack it down," Mikhaylov told the Bobcat operator. "Once you finish, cover it with a load of feed, then do the same with all the tire tracks on your way out. Shovel and rake as much as you can, then spread around more feed so the javelinas will come over and finish the job."

"Yes, sir."

Mikhaylov turned to the driver of the stolen Camry. "Get the car in the barn and tell Hedeon to get started on it. He'll know what to do."

The Russian waited by the grave while the driver got back in the Toyota and turned, then started back toward the gate.

After he'd watched the Bobcat operator shovel the first load of dirt onto the bodies, Mikhaylov returned to his cart and pulled away, his mood darkening. All this work, all this manpower… none of it would have been necessary if Franklin Colt had been more corruptible. When they found out he was Walter Upshaw's informant it would have been much easier to have just lured him into the fold. Mikhaylov knew that most men would cross over to his side without a second thought if the price was right. But in the time he'd worked with Colt at the casino, he'd come to know the man as one of that other breed; the ones high on principle and morally steadfast. And Colt was too smart, as well. It never would have been possible to bribe him into switching loyalties. He would have smelled the trap and realized his acceptance into the ranks would have ended, along with his life, the moment he disclosed all he knew and revealed who else had been given the information besides Upshaw. And so it had come to this: a half-bungled abduction and a trail of dead bodies that now meant they had to go about their business while avoiding what was sure to be a statewide manhunt. And, after all this, there was still no guarantee Colt would talk, although Mikhaylov felt confident that, one way or another, he would get the man to cooperate. Colt had been been able to hold his tongue while dealing with lesser means of persuasion, but come morning the security officer would learn that dealing with the Butcher was another matter entirely.

Mikhaylov's grim disposition was about to darken further. Halfway back to the gate, his black-market cell phone vibrated in his shirt pocket. He stopped the cart and took the call.

It was Viktor Cherkow.

As he listened to Cherkow's account of the debacle at Colt's property, Mikhaylov's countenance hardened. A bison stampede? All but two of his men killed? And, for all that, none of the evidence they were hoping to find?

"You checked everywhere?" Mikhaylov asked.

"I've checked the house top to bottom," Cherkow told him. "I'll try the gristmill next, but first there's something else I need to deal with."

"What?" Mikhaylov demanded. "The buffalo are still there?"

"A few of them, but they've calmed down," Cherkow said. "It's one of the men who was in that taxi that went into the flood channel. There's a chance he didn't drown there like we thought."

"Like *you* thought," Mikhaylov corrected. "Are you saying he was at the property?"

"I'm still not positive it was him," Cherkow said. "We managed to kill all the rest of them, but he's still unaccounted for. I want to bring in the chopper and search the grounds."

"There's no time for that!" Mikhaylov countered. "From the sounds of it, you're going to have half the reservation showing up there any minute. Yes, bring in the chopper, but get on it and get out of there as fast as you can."

"Our men, the ones that were killed…"

"Leave them! We need to cut our losses on this!"

"But if they can be traced back to—"

"They have no identification on them!" Mikhaylov interrupted. "They won't be traced back here."

"How can you be sure?"

"I'll see to it!" Mikhaylov shouted into the phone. "That's all you need to know. Now get the hell out of there!"

The Butcher clicked off the connection and stabbed the cell phone back into his pocket. He was seething and his jaw was clenched so tightly it ached.

Idiots! Incompetents!

Mikhaylov's bottled rage came to a head moments later when a pair of eighty-pound male javelinas wandered into range of his headlights. The creatures froze in place and stared at the Russian with their small, myopic eyes. When they began rubbing their tusks together, giving off a chattering sound meant to ward off predators, Mikhaylov gave in to his wrath and pulled a PA-63 Makarov semiautomatic pistol from his coat pocket. He took aim and put a 9 mm slug through the skull of one of the beasts, dropping it into the mud. The second javelina bolted off into the darkness.

Mikhaylov glared at the downed creature, then got out of his cart and shouted to the underling standing by the still-opened gate.

"Get this pig on the cart and put it on ice for the night!" he commanded. "I have plans for it in the morning!"

The other man jogged forward and they crossed paths without exchanging words. Mikhaylov strode out of the pen and away from the barn. The last thing he was interested in at the moment was dealing with Tramelik and the items he'd stolen from Alan Orson. All those plans suddenly felt as if they'd been shoved to the back burner, their place taken by the seemingly never-ending matter of Franklin Colt.

Mikhaylov walked past the house, as well, seeking the sanctuary of the farm's onetime milk shed. Behind the converted weapons depot was a renovated space Mikhaylov had turned into his personal quarters. The room was outfitted with a space heater, and Mikhaylov turned it on high before sitting down at his cluttered desk and propping his feet on the blotter. He started up his notebook computer, then reached for a half-pint silver flask he always carried in his hip pocket. He sipped its contents slowly, letting the vodka warm him incrementally as he considered the best way to deal with the unsatisfactory results of Cherkow's assignment. It now seemed clear that, short of getting their hands on Walter Upshaw's second cell phone, interrogation would be the only way to find out what kind of information Colt had unearthed about GHC's covert operations on the reservation. That matter could wait until morning. More pressing seemed the matter of tending to the man who'd apparently survived Tijeras Arroyo and turned up at the reservation. If Cherkow had correctly identified the man, there was a chance that he, like Walter Upshaw, had been informed of Colt's findings. As such, he needed to be dealt with in the same manner as the Taos Governing Council president. He needed to be taken out, preferably without dispatching SVR agents back to the reservation.

By the time he'd emptied the flask and the room had heated up every bit as much as Mikhaylov's inebriated metabolism, the Butcher had figured out his next move and how best to undertake it.

Hopefully, it would only take one call.

CHAPTER FOURTEEN

Albuquerque, New Mexico

John Kissinger had rationed himself a few catnaps between calls to the Farm and the front desk at the El Dorado Hotel, but with dawn approaching he felt as if he hadn't slept at all. He was starving, as well, and tired of staring at the walls of his hotel room, so he decided to go down to lobby and wait for the restaurant to open for breakfast. Thankfully the hotel was upscale enough that there was a coffee urn in the reception area along with an assortment of fresh fruit and pastries. Kissinger poured himself a cup and took a croissant over to one of the sofa chairs facing the lobby fireplace. There was a flat-screen television mounted from the ceiling just to the right of the fireplace, and as he snacked on the pastry Kissinger idly watched a tight-sweatered woman stride back and forth in front of a display map of New Mexico pocked with temperature readings, cloud symbols and blinking icons indicating which of the state's major arterial highways were experiencing traffic problems. The sound was turned down, but the Stony Man armorer easily gathered that the previous night's storm had moved north to Colorado. Watching the screen, however, he found himself less interested in the weather than wondering where Franklin Colt may have been taken after his abduction. He had little to go on but a gut instinct that his friend was still somewhere in the immediate vicinity, likely within a fifty-mile radius of the airport. Similarly, he had a sense that the man was still alive, but given what'd he learned about the murders of Alan Orson and Walter Upshaw he wondered if he was deluding himself about Colt's fate.

Kissinger's thoughts had shifted to concerns about the welfare of Colt's family and the outcome of Bolan's stakeout when a woman in her early thirties made her way from the registration counter to the reception area.

"Excuse me," she told Kissinger, "but the man at the front desk said you've been asking about Alan Orson."

Kissinger glanced up at the woman. She was thin and plain looking, with her wavy auburn hair pulled back in a ponytail that trailed down the back of her teal-colored raincoat.

"You know him?" he asked.

The woman nodded and held out her hand. "I'm Leslie Helms. I'm here to help him run his booth at the NMT Expo."

Kissinger stood and shook her hand, producing his Justice Department ID and introducing himself as Special Agent John LaViellere. Leslie was taken aback.

"Is there a problem?" she asked.

"Have a seat," Kissinger told her, gesturing at the chair across from him. "Can I get you some coffee?"

Leslie shook her head as she sat down. "Orson and I are supposed to have breakfast here before we go to the expo," she said.

"I'm sorry, but that's not going to happen," Kissinger told her.

"Why not?"

Kissinger saw no point in trying to sugarcoat things. "Orson's been murdered," he told the woman. "Up at his place in Taos."

"Holy shit," Helms muttered. She could see that Kissinger hadn't been expecting the profanity and quickly apologized. "Pardon my French. What happened?"

Kissinger quickly informed the woman, keeping the details as brief as possible and avoiding any mention of the altercation at the airport involving Frankin Colt. Helms stopped him in midexplanation and reached into her raincoat.

"Before you go on," she said, "I wasn't totally up-front when I introduced myself."

The woman handed Kissinger a business card.

"'Private investigator,'" Kissinger read.

"Yes, I was going to be at his booth at the expo," she explained, "but it was more a security thing than helping out, and that's not the main reason he hired me."

"Let's have it, then," Kissinger suggested.

"Before I do, can I ask why you're involved?" Leslie asked. "If Orson was murdered, it seems like it'd be in homicide's court back in Taos."

"There are some other things going on that he was connected to," Kissinger replied.

Helms nodded knowingly. "GHC? Or Shiraldi?"

"I don't know what either of those mean," Kissinger confessed.

"Global Holdings Corporation runs Roaming Bison Resort for the Rosqui tribe," Helms said. "Same for the nuke dump there."

It was the first time the nuclear waste facility had come up on Kissinger's radar. He instantly suspected it was tied in somehow with everything that had gone down since he'd arrived in Albuquerque.

"Shiraldi Management was the outfit that ran things there before GHC," Helms went on. "Orson hired me to look into both companies, particularly with regards to their handling of the fuel rod inventory."

"What was he trying to find out?"

"He wouldn't say," Helms said. "I know he does a lot of work with depleted uranium, so I figured it had something to do with that."

"DU's a component of some tank armor he developed," Kissinger said, recalling his earlier research. "He was using it for a new generation of body armor, too."

Helms nodded. "Yeah, I got all that from him. I think he used a lighter version of the tank armor on a helicopter he's built, too."

"That's my understanding."

"My take was that he wanted to put in a bid for a uranium source once he cleared the patents on the suit and chopper. With the tank armor he sold the idea outright to DOD. This time around I think his idea was to produce at least the suits on his own so he could clear a bigger profit."

"That makes sense for the most part," Kissinger responded.

"What part doesn't?"

"Why have you looked into Shiraldi if they're out of the picture?"

"I was getting to that," Helms said. "The other thing he wanted me to look into was how Shiraldi wound up getting booted off the reservation so GHC could move in."

Helms started to go into detail about the graft charges that had been made against Shiraldi Management while it was still partnered up with the Rosqui Tribal Council. Much as he knew the information might help explain matters, Kissinger had trouble following the woman's explanation as he was distracted by a news segment airing on the television screen behind her. A male correspondent was reporting live from an outdoor location against a backdrop of police cars with their light bars flashing. What caught Kissinger's attention wasn't the Breaking News logo at the top of screen so much as the superimposed subtitles below the correspondent, which declared that he was reporting live from Rosqui Pueblo.

"I'm sorry, but excuse me a second," Kissinger interrupted. He got up and strode to the television set. The controls were within reach, so he turned up the volume. Helms joined him. Together they listened to the newscast. Although they'd missed the initial disclosure, by the time the correspondent finished his update and quickly recapped the situation, Kissinger had a pretty clear idea of what had happened.

"A bison stampede during the middle of a shootout?" Leslie said after Kissinger turned down the sound. "Sounds like something out of the Wild West."

"I'm sorry, but I need to cut this short," Kissinger told the woman.

Gesturing at the television, Helms asked, "Is that tied into what you're investigating?"

"I can't get into that, either, I'm afraid," Kissinger told her.

"No offense, but I've got a stake in this, too," Helms said. "If this is related to what Orson was paying me to—"

Kissinger interrupted, "Look, do what you have to, but I really have to go now." He pocketed the woman's business card then veered over to the serving table long enough to jot a phone number on a napkin. He handed the napkin to the woman. "We can touch base later and finish this. I think we might be able to help each other."

"Thanks," Helms replied, "but with Orson dead I'm out a client, not to mention the tab I'd been running."

"Stay on the case and we'll cover his tab," Kissinger offered. "If we can use what you come up with, we'll pay double."

Helms grinned. "Based on your word and a number on a cocktail napkin? I'd rather have some kind of contract."

"Triple what Orson was paying," Kissinger bartered. "Take it or leave it."

"Sold."

Kissinger excused himself and ventured outside, punching numbers into his cell phone. By the time he'd wandered clear of the doorman, he was in touch with Barbara Price back at Stony Man Farm. He got straight to the point.

"Have you picked up anything on a shootout at the reservation?" he asked.

"As a matter of fact, yes," Price told him.

"The report I just heard said there were no survivors," Kissinger said.

"No *known* survivors," Price corrected. "They're still trying to piece everything together and figure out what happened."

"Has Striker checked in?"

There was a pause on the line, then Price somberly replied, "No. No, he hasn't."

Cochiti Lake, New Mexico

CHRISTOPHER SHIRALDI HELD ON TO the edge of the large rattan gondola holding one of his balloon pilots as well as a honeymooning couple from Winona. Raising his voice to be heard above the roar of the balloon's twin propane burners, Shiraldi gave his standard spiel about safety concerns, then wished the couple bon voyage and stepped clear of the basket. The tether ropes had already been cleared and slowly the large bulb of inflated nylon lofted into the patchy blue skies overhead. Inscribed on its sides, appropriately, were the words *Just Married*. Twenty yards away, another crew was preparing yet another balloon for takeoff. The gondola was tipped on its side, cool air from a generator-powered fan slowly inflating the ripstop nylon envelope. The awaiting passengers, a family of three, were taking photos of the process and Shiraldi volunteered to take their pictures while they stood before the crew.

"I'm so excited!" the mother said as she posed for the camera.

"You should be," Shiraldi told the woman. "Right after a good rain's the best time to go up. You'll be able to see for miles."

"How many times have you been up in one of these things?" the father asked.

Shiraldi took a couple pictures then handed the camera back to the father, telling him, "I stopped keeping track after five hundred, and that was a while ago."

Ballooning had been a weekend pastime for Shiraldi since his early thirties. Now, in the wake of his fall from grace as senior partner of Shiraldi Management, the forty-nine-year-old Harvard Business School graduate had turned his hobby into a full-time job. The portly, bearded owner of Aerial Grand Adventures made only a fifth of what he'd been earning as President of Operations at the Roaming Bison, but Shiraldi had never been happier in his life and he often claimed the sorry debacle he'd been caught up in had turned out to be the best thing that ever happened to him.

"Call for you, boss," a young man in his early twenties called out from the doorway of the motor home that served as Shiraldi's base of operations. AGA was a nomadic business venture made up of the motor home and two semitrailers carrying Shiraldi's inventory of balloons, gondolas, propane and other gear. Shiraldi moved freely about the state throughout the year, usually setting up shop near public gatherings likely to draw the sort of well-heeled visitors most inclined to splurge on his services.

"I'll take it over here," Shiraldi called back, heading for the nearest of the two semis. His cell phone was in the front seat of the cab. As he picked up the unit he stared up at the newlyweds, who were already drifting their way over the easternmost edge of a nearby golf course.

"Aerial Grand Adventures," he said, reflexively launching into his company's slogan. "We're full of hot air and we like it that way."

"Mr. Shiraldi, it's Leslie Helms again. The private investigator?"

Shiraldi's peaceful expression quickly soured.

"I've already told you, Ms. Helms. I have no comment. Now if you'll excuse me, I—"

"Please don't hang up," Helms pleaded. "Something's come up. I need just a minute to explain."

Shiraldi was about to disconnect the call but caught himself. He sighed and told the investigator, "It's not likely to change anything, but go ahead."

"When you were charged with skimming profits from the casino, you counterfiled saying you were framed," Helms said, restating the crux of their earlier conversation a few days before. "Afterward the charges against you were dropped, and you dropped your countersuit as well."

"We've been through this," Shiraldi said impatiently.

"Let me finish. You don't have to answer this, but I'm guessing some kind of deal was made. You agreed not to fight for reinstatement in exchange for some kind of settlement that stipulated that you keep silent about anything related to the corruption charges."

"No comment," Shiraldi repeated. "Are we finished?"

"To a lot of people, you did the equivalent of copping *nolo contendere*," Shiraldi said. "Those people still think you were guilty."

"I don't care what some people might think," Shiraldi said. "As far as I'm concerned, that's all water over the dam."

"What about the people who framed you?" Helms asked. "You're content that they got away with it? At the expense of your reputation?"

"What did I just tell you?" Shiraldi snapped. "That's all over and done with as far as I'm concerned."

"I've just made contact with some people who are look-ing into things from another angle," Helms said. "With your input, they could nail whoever set you up without it looking like you had anything to do with it."

"What people?"

"They're with the Justice Department." Helms went out on a limb and bartered, "They're willing to guarantee you won't be connected."

"If they're going at it from another angle, why do they need me?" Shiraldi countered.

"The right information could speed up their investigation," Helms said. She was improvising, but she knew Shiraldi was going for the bait and wanted to make sure he bit. "Not only that, they'd be able to pursue things in a way that wouldn't tip anyone off. It'd be a shame if they got the people who screwed you over in their sights only to find out they'd fled the country."

Shiraldi was silent a moment. He could feel his stomach knotting the way it had during all those months of scandal. Damn her, he thought. He knew she was right; no matter how much he insisted that his ouster from Roaming Bison was in the past, he was lying. And the idea of payback? What he wouldn't give to see that happen.

"I'll have to think about this," he finally told the woman.

"Of course," Helms responded.

Shiraldi could detect the confidence in her voice; she knew she had him. Frustrated, he threw down the phone and drew in a deep breath, then shook his head miserably.

"Damn her," he repeated, this time whispering the words aloud.

CHAPTER FIFTEEN

Albuquerque, New Mexico

Jack Grimaldi paced the sodden ground twenty yards from the seething floodwaters of Tijeras Arroyo. There was a glimmer of morning light on the far horizon but it was still dark along the stretch off University Boulevard where the Stony Man pilot and his colleagues had gone into the channel a few hours before. Fending off the darkness were the harsh beams of two high-powered halogen lamps running off a generator half as loud as the Pratt & Whitney turboshafts powering a CH-54 Skycrane that hovered over the rain-soaked terrain like some disemboweled aerial predator. A handful of Albuquerque police officers shared Grimaldi's vigil near the water; another three were back up on the main road, where tattered remnants of crime-scene tape fluttered off gnarled sections of guardrail.

Soon a pair of Water Search and Rescue divers surfaced from the brackish water and quickly grabbed hold of a towline drawn tight across the channel to keep them from being swept along by the current. Each man held a large caliper affixed to a length of steel cable an inch thick. Up on the embankment, an officer next to Grimaldi switched on a flashlight and signaled to the Skycrane's pilot. Moments later, the ninety-foot-long chopper eased down closer to the water, feeding out its own hook-ended cable. Once the hook was within reach of the divers, they attached the two calipers and tested them to make certain they were secure, then gave the main line a quick tug. While the Skycrane slowly rose a few yards, taking up the slack in the feed lines, the divers used the towline to make their way to the embankment. There, Grimaldi and one of the other officers helped the divers out of the water and quickly untethered the towline.

As soon as the officer with the flashlight gave the Skycrane pilot another signal, the chopper continued its slow ascent. Grimaldi watched with morbid fascination as the submerged taxi was slowly pulled from the arroyo. Water spewed from the broken windows, and bits of debris clung to the muddied chassis, then fell free as the cab's weight shifted, tilting it slightly.

"That's one sorry sight," the cop next to Grimaldi observed.

Grimaldi said nothing. He knew that if the Reaper had decided to call in a few markers there could well have been three bodies inside the vehicle, including his own.

Within a few minutes, the taxi had been hauled clear of the flood channel and set down on the barren landscape near the men who'd watched its retrieval. Grimaldi silently went about the quick task of going through the vehicle and removing the tote bags belonging to him and his Stony Man cohorts. He was able to find his pistol as well as Kissinger's, but Bolan's Beretta was nowhere to be seen. Grimaldi didn't realize it was an omen until he stepped back from the car and saw David Lowe making his way down the slope from the main road. The homicide detective had just come from speaking to the widows of the two officers slain at the site earlier.

"I gotta tell ya," Lowe said, once he caught up with Grimaldi, "whoever the hell you are, you've got some friends in high places."

"How's that?" Grimaldi asked.

"I just got orders to hand you the keys to the Skycrane," the detective said. "Seems one of your buddies has gone missing."

Stony Man Farm, Virginia

"HEY, HEY, SCORE ONE FOR the Barbster!" Akira Tokaido called out from his work station in the Annex Computer Room. Huntington Wethers and Aaron Kurtzman glanced up from their computers. They were the only other ones in the room; Carmen Delahunt had clocked out already and Barbara Price was presumably still back at the main house having breakfast after taking a few hours off to sleep.

"You got hold of the phone records?" Kurtzman asked.

Tokaido nodded. "Both Colt's and Orson's."

"And the last time they spoke to each other was right before Orson's blog rant?" Wethers queried.

"Twelve minutes, give or take a few seconds," Tokaido said. "Considering Orson lives out in the boonies, that's not enough time for him to have gone running errands."

"Sounds right to me," Kurtzman said.

"Actually, it depends," Wethers countered. "I've checked, and there are a few shops near the airport just down the road from his place. If Orson went there to run errands instead of into town, he could've gone and made it back during that twelve-minute window."

"Nice, Hunt," Tokaido muttered. "I give Barb some props and you rain on the parade. What's up with that?"

"I'm just saying we can't positively rule out that Orson wrote the blog before he was killed."

"Okay, then, answer me this," Kurtzman challenged, eyeing his computer screen. He'd secured authorization to tap into computerized updates from the Taos officers investigating Orson's murder, and the latest dispatch had just come in.

"Some forensics geeks went through Orson's computer to check on timeprints. Turns out somebody flash-drived all his files right after the blog was written."

"That could still have been Orson," Wethers replied. "It fits his profile to be a little paranoid. And if he was just robbed, it makes sense that he'd make a copy, no matter how upset he was."

"Gotcha!" Kurtzman said.

Wethers frowned. "What do you mean?"

"Think about it," Kurtzman said. "Better yet, put yourself in the perp's shoes. You sneak into Orson's place, whack the guy and his dog and decide to make off with everything worthwhile. Why not the computer?"

Wethers nodded thoughtfully, then asked, "Was it a desktop by any chance? Maybe locked or anchored somehow?"

"Negative on both counts," Kurtzman said. "It was a laptop, no strings attached, so to speak."

"I think he's got you, Hunt," Tokaido said. "If they took the computer, there'd be no way to make it look like Orson wrote the blog, 'cause he wouldn't have had anything to write it on. And you gotta figure they knew there'd be valuable stuff on the hard drive, so there's no reason for them to leave it behind except to plant the blog."

"No apparent reason," Wethers corrected.

"I'm with Akira on this one," Kurtzman said. "I'm saying the perp wrote the blog and then flash-drived the computer so he could leave it behind."

"Who are we talking about, then?" Wethers said. "Going by your theory, it can't be Donny Upshaw. There's no reason he'd do this and then write a blog pointing a finger at himself."

"No apparent reason," Tokaido said. He grinned at Wethers. "Sorry. Couldn't resist."

Wethers smiled blandly. *"Touché,"* he conceded. "Now, assuming you and Bear are right, the obvious—"

"Hang on," Kurtzman interrupted, his eyes drawn back to his computer screen. "There's still more coming in."

"Nice to know we aren't the only people who work around the clock," Tokaido said.

A troubled expression came over Kurtzman as he read the update. "We've got oursevles a double whammy."

"They found Upshaw?" Wethers asked.

"Yeah," Kurtzman said, "but not Donny. His old man. He just turned up dead behind the wheel in his driveway on the reservation. Shot to the head at close range."

"Ouch," Tokaido said. "That's not where I saw this going."

"What caliber?" Wethers asked.

"It's a .25," Kurtzman said, skimming back over the dispatch. "Same casing as the ones they found next to Orson."

Tokaido whistled. "Man, this throws everything off."

"His father was head of the Pueblo, right?" Wethers recalled.

Kurtzman nodded. "And I don't know what kind of relationship he had with Donny, but you're right. We need to reconsider things. His kid might be the perp after all."

"What else did they come up with?" Tokaido asked.

"That's the second part of the double whammy," Kurtzman explained. "Remember when you were talking earlier about Donny having a drug relapse? Well, the cops there just did a second pass on the guesthouse where he was staying. They came across a loose floorboard and found a kilo of heroin tucked in the crawl space beneath, along with a fix kit. The stuff hasn't been cut and the kit had been used."

"Sounds like he sampled the wares," Weathers said.

"Wait. An uncut kilo?" Tokaido said. "We're talking more than a hundred grand. Where'd he get that kind of money?"

"Not mowing lawns," Kurtzman said. "I'll tell you that much."

"The inventions and Orson's backup data," Wethers said.

"That's gotta be it," Kurtzman responded. "My guess is they're worth at least that much. Probably a hell of a lot more to the right people."

"This is getting crazier all the time," Tokaido said.

"I was thinking just the opposite," Kurtzman said. "To me it's starting to fit."

"Yeah, maybe some of it," Tokaido admitted, "but come on, we're talking some major loopholes here."

"Such as?"

"Just look at what we've got. Donny goes off the wagon and scores a kilo from somebody who'll take Orson's gizmos as payment. Okay, no problem. I get that. Same with him whacking Orson and the dog, especially if he's strung out and they're in the way. So far, so good. But what does he do right after he whacks them? Does he hightail it out of there and get the goods to his dealer ASAP? No. We've got him hunkering down at Orson's computer, taking the time to log on to Orson's blogsite, then writing a tirade that makes it looks like Orson's fingered him as the killer. Um, somehow I don't think so. And if that's not loony tunes enough, what does he do next? *Now* does he get Orson's loot to this dealer—a dealer who's already given him a hundred grand worth of powder without being paid up front?"

"You're right," Kurtzman said. "It never works that way."

"It could be he delivered the inventions first, then got the heroin and brought it back so he could hide it," Wethers suggested. "Maybe that's when he killed Orson."

"Nice try, but it doesn't fit the time line," Tokaido reminded his colleague. "Orson had his stuff with him when he talked to Colt. The blog's written twelve minutes later. No time to go visit the friendly neighborhood drug dealer."

Wethers thought it over, then nodded to himself.

"What if the dealer was there the whole time?" he theorized. "What if he helped Donny kill Orson and the dog, loaded Orson's inventions into the pickup and *then* handed over the heroin?"

Kurtzman grinned at his counterpart. "Not bad, Hunt."

"That's still not it, though," Tokaido insisted. "It doesn't explain the blog, for starters."

"How about this?" Wethers suggested. "As soon as Donny gets the smack he goes off to hide it. All along the dealer's been thinking of a way to avoid being connected with Orson's murder, so while Donny's away he sees an opportunity and goes with it."

"He writes the blog blaming Donny and then leaves," Kurtzman said.

"That or maybe he doubled back once he saw Donny heading for the guesthouse," Wethers said. "Either way, he's there within that twelve-minute time frame."

Kurtzman turned to Tokaido. "What do you think?"

"I think we're damn close," the young hacker conceded. "Now we just need to get a time of death for Donny's old man so we can try to figure out where that fits in with all this. And I don't know if it's just because I love an underdog, but I'm still thinking there's gotta be a way to see this in terms of Donny being framed."

"I'm with you on that," Wethers said, "mostly because of what happened in Albuquerque. There has to be some kind of connection that would account for someone wanting to make him the fall guy."

"I've got a two-way comp-link with Taos," Kurtzman said, turning back to his keyboard. "Let me see if they've come up with anything else we can work with."

"You might want to have them check to see if Orson's speed chopper's still accounted for," Tokaido said. "I remember reading that it's stored at the airport there."

"Will do."

Kurtzman had just begun typing his query when Barbara Price strode into the room, wrapping up a long-distance cell call to Jack Grimaldi.

"I already checked with the hotel and they have a heliport on the roof," she was telling the Stony Man pilot. "Cowboy will be waiting for you. Let me know as soon as you find out anything. Either way."

As Price clicked off, she saw the three men watching her intently. Despite the intensity of the brainstorming session they'd just put themselves through, from the look on the mission controller's face they knew their possible breakthrough on the Taos case had just lost its urgency.

"We have a situation at the reservation," she said matter-of-factly. "It involves Striker."

CHAPTER SIXTEEN

Antwerp, Belgium

"It's your mess." Evgenii Danilov stared out the window of his high-rise office suite overlooking the sluggish churning of the River Scheldt as he spoke to Frederik Mikhaylov. "Don't make me have to clean it up for you."

Danilov tapped his cell phone and ended the transcontinental call without giving Mikhaylov a chance to respond. The buoyant optimism he'd felt a few short hours ago had long faded, replaced by a sense of foreboding. This had been the second time he'd spoken to Mikhaylov since preparing for what he'd thought would be a good night's sleep. The call had only underscored what he'd concluded after the first one: the situation in New Mexico, after so many months of running with a steady precision, was in danger of spiraling out of control. Something had to be done. He'd already made a call of his own to that effect.

Outside it was bitterly cold and had begun to snow again, the kind of snowfall where the flakes were so large and weightless it almost seemed as if they were floating upward. One of the larger flakes landed against the window and the elderly

Russian watched as it slowly lost its shape and dissolved into a tearlike droplet that trailed down the tinted glass and was quickly absorbed by a growing puddle on the windowsill.

That's all it takes, Danilov mused darkly. One wrong move and you're nothing.

Slipping his phone into the pocket of his tailored coat, the silver-haired CEO of Global Holdings Corporation strode past his antique mahogany desk to a matching wet bar and poured a healthy portion of Hennessy Ellipse cognac into a crystal snifter. At five thousand dollars a bottle, the cognac was meant to be slowly savored and Danilov usually observed the proper ritual of letting it warm in the glass to release its aroma, but after speaking to Mikhaylov he was in no mood for ceremony. He swirled the amber liquid briefly and indulged in a perfunctory sniff, then layered his palate and let the liqueur linger there as he walked back to his desk. The cognac's warm glow radiated through him, and he was grateful for the way it seemed to blunt the rage that had been building up inside him. He needed to calm himself in preparation for the unpleasant task that lay before him. He was about to, as some of his unsavory American business associates sometimes put it, "eat crow."

Danilov spent the next few minutes affixing his signature to a handful of documents his secretary had delivered to him earlier. Those few scrawls would put into motion over four and a half billion dollars' worth of business transactions, most of them hostile takeovers of EU corporations whose weakened underbellies had been exposed during the recent global downturn. In most respects, those dealings far dwarfed GHC's financial stake in the Roaming Bison Casino and the other, more covert, enterprise taking place at the reservation's nuclear waste facility. But the latter situation, with its combination of intrigue and mayhem, bore a far greater sense of immediacy and crowded Danilov's thoughts, so much so that he was startled when his intercom bleated and his secretary informed him that Alek Repin had arrived.

"Send him in," Danilov said.

Moments later, a stodgy middle-aged man wearing a rumpled, ill-fitting suit hobbled into the room, using a cane to favor the prosthetic right leg that had replaced the one claimed by a land mine during his military service twenty years ago in the mountains of Afghanistan. Alek Repin was still in many ways haunted by the stigma of the failed Russian occupation, and though he'd managed to exonerate himself of any responsibility for that debacle, he went through life guarded against the possibility of having to repeat the dishonorable means by which he'd done so. As deputy director of Vympel, the Special Operations Branch of SVR's Directorate S, Repin was notorious for choosing his battles based on the greatest likelihood of success, and his track record in terms of his dealings on behalf of Global Holdings was thus far impeccable. The incidents of the previous night in New Mexico were no exception; they, after all, had been carried out by Mikhaylov, whom Danilov had chosen as his point man over Repin's objections. As such, there was the faintest trace of mirth in the man's eyes as he eased himself into the tooled leather chair facing Danilov's desk. The look wasn't lost on Danilov.

"You've heard about what's happened in the States, I take it," he said.

Repin shrugged. "When you said it was urgent that I see you, I took an educated guess and made a few inquiries."

Danilov saw no sense in putting off his concession.

"You were right about Mikhaylov," he said. "I overestimated him."

Repin fumbled through his coat pocket and took out a gold-plated cigarette case. He popped it open and held it out to Danilov, who he knew despised smoking with a passion. Danilov shook his head and restrained his contempt as he calmly searched his desk for something to serve as an ashtray. He settled on an onyx paperweight carved in the shape of a turtle. He turned it over, exposing the hollowed underside, and handed it to Repin. Repin nodded his appreciation and took his time lighting one of the hand-rolled cigarettes. He was clearly enjoying the moment every bit as much as Danilov would normally have enjoyed his cognac. It was only after he'd fouled the office with his first exhalation of smoke that he responded to Danilov's initial mea culpa.

"As they say," he intoned, "there are two different meanings to the word 'butcher.'"

"He may need to be replaced," Danilov said. "Is Vishnevsky available?"

Repin looked puzzled. He frowned as he tapped ash into the turtle's belly, then leaned back slightly in the chair and blew a smoke ring, watching it drift up toward the unmoving propellors of the ceiling fan directly above him.

"Ah, you mean Dmitri Vishnevsky," he said, as if it were some long-forgotten name. "My first choice for that particular job."

"I know you assigned him to Mikhaylov's former position in Bolivia," Danilov said coldly. "But I suspect he's as impatient to move up as this blundering moron I chose instead."

Repin couldn't help but smile at hearing Mikhaylov so soundly denigrated, especially when it was Danilov making the denunciation. Still, he was in no rush to accommodate the other man.

"What about Diaz?" he suggested.

"Diaz is strictly a tech person," Danilov said. "Besides, he's not one of us."

"But I thought there were already plans to fly him into the States."

"That's still the plan," Danilov said, "but he's only coming to look over the inventions and do the job Orson wouldn't."

"Help with uranium processing."

"Exactly. Technical matters only. We need Vishnevsky to help bring the situation there under control."

"Help?" Repin seemed incredulous. "Work alongside Mikhaylov? With their history?"

"He'd take over operations in Taos to begin with," Danilov said. "That's far enough away from Santa Fe that he wouldn't have to be in the same room with Mikhaylov. If he keeps us from being linked to what happened last night and can get us access to the uranium mines, he'll take over the whole operation."

"Oh, so this would be an audition, as it were," Repin said. "You're not just offering him the job up front?"

"If he's gotten more of a backbone, as you claim, Taos should be no problem for him," Danilov challenged.

"Dmitri's always had a backbone," Repin countered. "He just has a tendency to be more discreet than Mikhaylov. He's more of a surgeon than a butcher, if you will."

"Sometimes you need to be both."

Repin smiled. "Funny you should mention that," he said. "Do you remember how Mikhaylov earned his job as a pit boss back in Moscow?"

"He killed the head of an outfit Dolgoprudnenskaya was having problems with."

Repin nodded. "What if I told you Vishnevsky is about to do the same thing in Bolivia, only on a much larger scale?"

He wants me to eat still more crow, Danilov thought to himself as he listened to Repin describe the specifics of Vishnevsky's assignment on behalf of the Andean Splendor. Despite himself, he was impressed by the magnitude of the undertaking.

"If he succeeds," Danilov conceded afterward, "I'd say it proves you've been right about him all along. Still, given the situation, at this point I can only offer him Taos."

"A minor hurdle," Repin said.

"Well, then?" the financier replied. "Is he available or not?"

"I guess that would depend," Repin countered.

"You want to know what's in it for you."

Repin shrugged again and held his hands out expansively. "We live in a selfish world, Evgenii."

"What's your price?" Danilov asked, fighting his impatience.

Repin looked down at his rumpled suit and flicked off some ash that had fallen on it. "I'm a simple man," he replied. "I have all I need."

"You just said this is a selfish world," Danilov said, "so let's dispense with the humility. And I'm in no mood for haggling. What's your price?"

Repin took another puff, then stubbed out his cigarette and turned his attention to his cane, an oaken staff knobbed with the ivory likeness of a perched eagle.

"Thanks to the Butcher," he said, "in New Mexico you have not just one can of worms to deal with, but three. Taos, the reservation and that little incident at the airport in Albuquerque. It's not the sort of goulash I care to stick my fork in, if you catch my meaning."

Danilov was expecting reticence from Repin. He knew there was no sense in holding back his trump card. He pushed back from his desk and silently returned to the wet bar. Moments later, he handed Repin a snifter of the cognac. He'd splashed more of it into his own glass. This time he was prepared to give the liquid a chance to warm.

"There is talk that Grigoriev is stepping down next year," Danilov said offhandedly on the way back to his chair. As he sat down he eyed Repin directly. "Like Mikhaylov, he will need to be replaced, too."

Stanislov Grigoriev was the SVR director, Repin's immediate superior as well as the only obstacle standing in the way of the one-legged man's ultimate ambition as a member of Russia's Foreign Intelligence Service.

Repin tried to remain blank-faced, but a flickering spark of desire in his eyes gave him away.

Danilov knew they had a deal.

CHAPTER SEVENTEEN

Rosqui Pueblo, New Mexico

The sun had yet to rise but in the predawn light police Captain Tina Brown stood solemnly before a makeshift podium erected in the middle of the service road fifty yards from the gateway leading to Franklin Colt's property. The road was closed and the gateway was cordoned off to allow a forensics team to collect blood samples and other evidence from the driveway area. Past the gate, out on the rolling hills that blocked the media's view of Colt's house, several other similar teams were at work at the locations where known victims of the previous night's skirmish had fallen, some slain by gunfire, others trampled by bison. Three paramedic vans were parked along the lengthy stretch, their crews awaiting confirmation that it was all right to start retrieving bodies. Elsewhere on the grounds a handful of volunteers from the reservation were engaged in the tedious chore of herding the few remaining stray bison across the property toward the break in the fence they'd knocked down during their wild stampede. Overhead, taking it all in, was a handful of news choppers, their collective drone echoing across the hills.

Brown was a slight woman, slim and barely regulation height, but she carried her fifty-six years with an air of self-assuredness and resolve that had served her well during her rise through the ranks of the Rosqui Tribal Police Force. She stared out at the assembled reporters and news cameras with a measured calm, her craggy face a dispassionate mask that belied the alertness in her obsidian eyes. Several reporters were already hounding her with questions that she had no intention of addressing at the moment. She would handle this press conference on her terms and her terms alone. She stalled a few minutes longer, letting the media stew in its collective juices while she busied herself conferring with fellow officers who were helping her to coordinate what was shaping up to be the largest-scale criminal investigation on the reservation since the Shiraldi Management scandal a few years prior.

It was only after the sun had crested the lofty peak of Mt. McCray that Brown launched into her remarks, taking private satisfaction in the way she'd orchestrated matters so that her back would be turned to the sun, leaving the media to contend with its blinding rays.

Brown introduced herself then stated, "As I'm sure you've already gathered, insofar as last night's incident occurred on tribal land, the investigation has fallen under my jurisdiction as head of the police force here. An investigatory agent from the Bureau of Indian Affairs will be here shortly, and his input will be both welcome and appreciated."

"What about the off-reservation law enforcement?" one reporter asked. "Our understanding is this incident is likely tied in with Colt's abduction at Albuquerque International last night. It seems like that would make this the business of the—"

"Excuse me," Brown interrupted, "but I have to ask you all to kindly refrain from questions until I've finished my statement."

The reporter fell silent but look unappeased.

"I will tell you, however," Brown conceded, "that of course all other relevant agencies will be apprised of our findings once we have a clearer idea of what exactly happened here.

"At this point I can tell you this much—at approximately three forty-five Central Time this morning there was an altercation on the property of tribal member Franklin Colt involving four of our officers, four other residents of the reservation and at least five individuals whose identities have yet to be determined. At some point during the exchange of gunfire, a large portion of our bison colony was apparently startled enough to breach a fence separating their grazing land from Colt's property and stampede the site. To the best of our estimation, the altercation ended shortly afterward.

"I must regretfully inform you that all four of our officers involved in the incident were killed, three as a result of gunshot wounds and another as a result of being caught in the path of the stampede. One of the perpetrators was similarly killed by the bison while the others are apparent gunshot victims. We have no information at this point regarding the other members of the reservation."

"Can we have some names?" one reporter called out.

"What about Colt's wife and son?" another interjected, cupping one hand over his brow to deflect the morning sun.

Brown glared at the questioners. "I made my opening remarks in plain English in hopes they would be understood without the need for a translator," she said. "If you'll allow me to finish without any further interruptions, most likely the majority of your questions will be answered."

There was a subdued murmuring among some members of the media. As Brown waited for it to subside, Daniel Walsh, a younger member of the force, made his way around the media ensemble driving a Yamaha Rhino ATV similar to the ones still parked behind Colt's gristmill. As he neared Brown, Walsh nodded and held up a manila envelope for the police chief to see. Brown nodded back and gestured for the officer to park next to one of the RTPF's unmarked sedans, where a middle-aged Native American in a plain brown suit stood solemnly watching the proceedings.

Brown turned back to the media and was about to resume her remarks when she caught herself, noticing, for the first time, a woman with dark hair standing at the rear of the throng, dressed in a long teal jacket and a matching rain hat. The hat's wide brim partially obscured her features, but Brown got enough of a look at her to sense she'd seen the woman before. It quickly came to her. The woman had been detained at the reservation a few days earlier after taking photos near the nuclear waste plant, which was off-limits to visitors. She'd claimed to have gotten lost while hiking on authorized trails on the other side of the mountains surrounding the facility. Similar incidents happened every few months and the woman, like the other trespassers, had been released with a warning after the photos had been deleted from her digital camera. It was only later that Brown had learned that prior to her hike the same woman had been in the casino asking a few bartenders about Christopher Shiraldi, claiming she was an old friend passing through town.

When told Shiraldi no longer worked there, the woman had apparently asked a few pointed questions about the circumstances behind his leaving. And now here she was, back on the reservation, far from the nearest hiking trail, attending a press conference that, like the waste facility, wasn't open to the public. This time Captain Brown wasn't about to just let the woman walk away. First, however, she had to wrap things up with the media.

"Gwenyth Colt and her two-year-old son, Franklin Jr., were apparently not present at the time of the shootout," she went on. "Their whereabouts at this time is unknown, but we're making inquiries and hope to have some answers shortly.

"Also unknown at this time is the motive for the altercation. Yes, we're aware of Mr. Colt's alleged abuction, and that's one of the reasons we had officers dispatched here last night to his residence. Whether they were followed here or if the gunmen they exchanged fire with were already here lying in wait is something we hope to determine upon further investigation."

"Last night in Taos there was another incident involving a friend of Franklin Colt's named Alan Orson," yet another reporter called out. "You'd have to think there's a link between the two."

Brown stared hard at the reporter and shook her head the way an elementary school teacher would when dealing with a wayward five-year-old. She'd had enough.

"All right, listen, all of you," she snapped indignantly. "I watch my share of news conferences on television, most of them involving the same members of the press I'm looking at now. In all those instances, I don't recall the official giving the conference being bombarded with questions until after he's had a chance to make his opening remarks. I don't know if it's because I'm a woman or a Native American or both, but I have to tell you I find the disrespect being shown here is not just inexcusable, it's also unacceptable. Given that one of my officers has just arrived with pertinent information on a case that gets colder with each passing second, I'm disinclined at this point to shirk my duties any further to accommodate what I see as little more than a media feeding frenzy. Ladies and gentlemen, this press conference is over."

There were instantaneous cries of protest from the press corps. Captain Brown raised her voice slightly and drowned them out. "Furthermore, I need to advise you that on the chance that other perpetrators in this incident are still at large on the property, we will be doing a routine search of all media vehicles as they leave this area. And, insofar as you're on tribal land, I'm now officially asking you to vacate the premises so we can do our job."

Brown turned her back on the media and continued to ignore their renewed onslaught of questions. Over where Officer Walsh had parked the Rhino ATV, the man in the brown suit, RTPF's Chief Investigative Officer Russell Combs, leaned against his unmarked Camaro as he inspected the contents of Officer Walsh's manila envelope. As Brown approached the two men she waved over two other uniformed officers loitering near the forensics crew surveying the property gateway.

"Way to give them hell, Captain," Officer Walsh told Brown.

"They were asking for it." Brown turned to Combs, her closest confidant on the force. Combs was wearing his omnipresent dark-tinted glasses, not as a surveillance ploy so much as to conceal a genetic palsy defect that had left him cross-eyed. "Any chance you have a bug or homing device on you?"

"Both," Combs said. "Not on me, but in the glove compartment."

"Good." Gesturing at the arriving uniformed officers, she told Combs, "Take Hayes and Leyva and handle the vehicle searches. Try to get to the lot before everyone starts pulling away."

"This is about more than just pissing them off some more," Combs said matter-of-factly. "Who gets the bug?"

"A woman with a greenish hat and raincoat," Brown said. "She was lurking in the back. She's the one I told you about the other day."

"The hiker?"

Brown nodded. "If you can swing it, follow her, even if you make the plant."

"Got it." Combs handed her the photocopies he'd taken from the manila envelope. "These should work."

Combs got in his Camaro along with the two other officers. As they screeched off and raced along the shoulder past the retreating press throng, Brown stayed behind with Walsh and turned her attention to the photocopies. They were all the same, a blown-up freeze frame taken from one of the surveillance cameras mounted outside the Albuquerque International baggage-claim area.

"Nice job," she told Walsh.

"No problem, Captain," the officer replied. "I ought to tell you, though. Somebody else was asking about footage from the same time frame."

Brown furrowed her brow. "APD?"

"I don't think so. They said it was classified. I only found out by accident. They wanted footage from the parking lot cams, too."

Brown considered the possibilities. If it'd been BIA she would have heard about it already. Most likely, she figured, it had to be the FBI, since Colt's abduction was officially on the books as a federal offense—kidnapping. In the same thought, it occurred to her that the woman she'd just seen might be with the Feds, working undercover. If that was the case, she didn't even want to try to fathom the implications. She could only hope she was wrong. Until she found out for sure, however, she knew it was imperative to get as much done here as she could in as quick a time as possible.

Brown thanked Walsh again, then ventured past the forensics crew to another pair of officers watching from just inside the gate to Colt's property. One of them echoed Walsh's praise about the way she'd put the media in its place then added, "You didn't tell them the Feds had somebody here during the shootout."

"Must have slipped my mind," Brown said. She ignored the officer's knowing smirk and went on. "I have reason to believe one of the shooters is still on the property somewhere. He might be wounded or maybe he's just hiding out waiting for a chance to make a run for it."

"Which is why you're having their cars searched," the other officer guessed.

Brown nodded. "That's a long shot, though, so we need to search the grounds."

"Is that him?" the first cop said, gesturing at the photocopies.

Captain Brown nodded again and handed over the copies. "Track down Romano and Covina to help you. Nobody else. Start at Colt's place and work your way outward. Cover the whole reservation if you have to. Take this guy alive if you can, but we've already lost four men today, so if it seems necessary, don't hestitate to take him out."

"How'd you find out about him?" the other cop asked.

"An informant," the police chief said.

Captain Brown's informant was Frederik "the Butcher" Mikhaylov.

The slightly blurred photos were of Mack Bolan.

CHAPTER EIGHTEEN

Stony Man Farm, Virginia

Eager to distract themselves from dwelling on Bolan's uncertain fate, the assembled cybercrew was firing on all cylinders at the Annex Computer Room. Although the Taos Police Department as well as the local County Sheriff's Department had declared Donny Upshaw the prime suspect in the murders of his father and Alan Orson, Kurtzman's team had decided to more thoroughly explore the theory that the missing groundskeeper had been framed, likely by whomever had supplied him with the heroin found in his guest quarters. Their primary focus was a search for possible links between the Taos murders and the incidents to the south stemming from Franklin Colt's abduction.

In hopes of making a connection, Akira Tokaido had taken up Barbara Price's directive to follow the money and was culling through databases for more details on Alan Orson's business dealings, especially with recent clients who may have been privy to information about the inventions he'd been planning to bring to the New Military Technologies Expo. Carmen Delahunt had returned to the Farm and was working the heroin angle, checking with law-enforcement agencies throughout New Mexico in hopes she could track down an active trafficking network that might have recently moved a large shipment of smack through the upper part of the state. Huntington Wethers, meanwhile, was looking into Franklin Colt's life during the years he and John Kissinger had drifted apart. He'd already come across references to Colt's antidrug speaking engagements, which raised obvious questions about what role he might have played in Alan Orson's decision to invite Donny Upshaw to live on his property. He'd yet to find out how Colt and Orson knew each other, but there was a brief item on Rosqui Pueblo's Web site about Colt's wedding three years ago and Orson had been listed as best man at the ceremony. Colt's name had come up elsewhere on the site, where three separate times he'd been named the Roaming Bison Casino's Employee of the Month.

Barbara Price had just received confirmation that Jack Grimaldi had picked up John Kissinger in the borrowed Skycrane and was en route to the reservation with Detective Lowe and another APD officer to begin searching for Bolan. Resigned that there was nothing more she could do on that front, she was now simultaneously monitoring pertinent police investigations in Taos and Albuquerque as well as fielding an update from Carl Lyons on Able Team's mission in upstate Washington.

That left Kurtzman.

The former Rand Corporation brainstormer was combing through the airport surveillance footage he'd accessed shortly before RTPF's Officer Walsh had shown up at Albuquerque International seeking the same on the men Colt had met with just prior to his abduction. Unlike Captain Brown, however, Kurtzman was less concerned with photo images of Bolan and his Stony Man colleagues. His initial hope had been that one of the airport cameras had captured Colt's abduction. Unfortunately, the parking lot surveillance cameras were not fixed but rather swivel-mounted, panning back and forth at regular intervals. The skirmish between Colt and his captors had taken place out-of-frame, and by the time the camera had panned its way to Colt's Nova, the panel truck was already pulling away.

"Damn," Kurtzman swore in frustration. He let the footage continue to play out as he finished his cup of coffee. He was setting down the cup when his spirits suddenly spiked. The camera had just panned back to the Nova, capturing the moment when the Chevy muscle car had backed into the luxury SUV whose driver was about to become the first known fatality linked to the kidnapping. Kurtzman wasn't able to get a clear look at the man driving the Nova, but the fleeting glimpse prompted him to cue up footage from yet another surveillance camera: the one mounted at the pay station. It proved to be an inspired hunch, as a few minutes later Kurtzman had footage of both the panel truck and the Nova as they were speeding through the checkpoint. In the case of the panel truck, its tinted windows prevented Kurtzman from getting a look at its occupants, but when the Nova came barreling down on the parking attendant moments later, the camera clearly captured the man behind the wheel.

"Yes!" Kurtzman cried out. When the others looked up, he apprised them of the breakthrough, adding, "I'll have to go back and check the footage from outside the baggage area, but I'm pretty sure this same guy's lurking in the background while Colt's talking with our guys. He must've hightailed it to the Nova once all hell broke loose."

"Nice going, Aaron," Price said, glancing up from the unassigned computer station where she was multitasking. "How clear is the footage?"

"I'll need to do a little photo-enhancing," Kurtzman confessed, "but I think if I tweak the clearest freeze frame I'll have something to run through Profiler."

"Good idea."

The Farm's high-tech answer to police station Indenti-Kits, Profiler was a wide-range software program capable of doctoring facial images with alternative appearances and then running all the variants through existing databases from more than a dozen worldwide law-enforcement agencies in search of potential matches. The program was far from foolproof, but countless times in the past it had, in a matter of seconds, produced results that, years before, would have required days or even weeks of legwork and bureaucratic wrangling.

Kurtzman was retracing the surveillance camera footage frame by frame when Sensitive Operations Director Hal Brognola strode into the Computer Room. He nodded to the cyberteam members as he made his way to Price.

"Still no word from Striker?" he asked.

Price glanced up and shook her head, then pointed at her headset to indicate she was in the middle of a call. As he waited for her to finish, Brognola took off his trench coat and draped it over a nearby chair. When she wrapped up her call, he was tempted to offer some kind of encouragement but knew the words would ring hollow. Instead, he gave her the first option to respond.

"That was Carl," she said. "Able Team just took down the Takoma operation. Four killed, two arrested and one's already looking to plea bargain."

"And our side?"

"Pol and Gadgets were banged up, but it doesn't sound serious," Price reported. Rosario "the Politician" Blancanales and Hermann "Gadgets" Schwarz were Carl Lyons's Able Team colleagues. "They've been admitted at Takoma GH and Ironman says Pol might wind up being kept overnight for observation on a possible concussion."

"But Lyons is good to go?"

"There might be some loose ends to tie up with the authorities, but other than that I think so."

"Good," Brognola said. He stared across the room momentarily, his gaze falling on the far-wall monitors. Their images were lost on him, however, as his mind was elsewhere. The situation in New Mexico was now a Farm priority, and much as the big Fed had faith in both Jack Grimaldi and John

Kissinger as interim field agents, with Bolan still missing, Brognola had to consider the possibility that he was either incapacitated or, worse yet, that his War Everlasting had come to a permanent end. In either case, a clear chain of command needed to be maintained so long as the mission was active. With Phoenix Force entrenched halfway around the world, there were too many time constraints to even consider flying one of that team's members back to the States to fill in for Bolan. That left only one feasible option. Much as Brognola was loath to give Price cause to fear the worst, he turned to her and passed along his decision.

"Get back to Carl," he told Price, "and see how fast you can get him on a plane to New Mexico."

CHAPTER NINETEEN

Rosqui Pueblo, New Mexico

Once the morning sun cast its first ray into the craggy depths of Healer's Ravine, Mack Bolan stirred. He opened his eyes briefly, then shut them to block out the bright light. He was disoriented and feverish, his body wet and shaking beneath what felt like some sort of damp blanket. Weakened, as well, he drifted back into a fitful sleep. When he awoke a few minutes later, he began to remember where he was and how he'd gotten there.

Thinking back, he recalled clinging to a section of the battered gristmill waterwheel once it had bobbed back to the surface after knocking him into the icy river running past Franklin Colt's property. He'd been too dazed to do much but hold on and keep his head above the frothing water as it carried him along its winding course.

A seeming eternity had passed before the he'd come to a sharp bend near the ravine and the waterwheel had snagged itself amid other debris trapped by a long-dead tree that had toppled into the river. Bolan had abandoned his makeshift raft and used the tree to drag himself ashore, where he'd collapsed, exhausted. Once he'd gathered his strength, he'd ventured deeper into the ravine and found it cluttered with old, rain-soaked mattresses, rusting appliances and other household items apparently dumped from the edge of the precipice far above him. Shivering, he'd begun to roam through the trash, hoping to make some sort of lean-to to help shield himself from the cold. The likeliest prospect was a discarded cast-iron bathtub resting on its side near an old bicycle missing its front tire.

Bolan was scraping mud out of the tub when he'd heard a stirring in the brush growing up around the heaps of refuse just off to his left. Drawing his borrowed 9 mm Browning pistol, he'd ventured forth and discovered a large male bison lying on its side, blood trailing from its mouth. Bolan figured the beast had to have strayed from the herd during the stampede and tumbled over the precipice. Beyond its obvious internal injuries, the bison had broken at least two of its legs in the fall and was clearly near death. Bolan had tried to put the creature out of its misery with his pistol, but his downriver sojourn had left the gun inoperable. Bolan had backtracked to the trash heap, where he'd recalled seeing an old steel-legged chair as well as a rusty, long-discarded tree saw. He'd broken off one of the chair legs and brought it back along with the saw. The chair leg had been sharp enough where he'd snapped it free that, with considerable effort, he'd been able to pierce the bison's hide and gouge through its chest until he reached its heart. He'd twisted his crude tool until the beast stopped moving, then had cast the chair leg aside in favor of the saw, using the last of his strength to partially skin the animal. The last thing he remembered was dropping alongside the bison, leaning into the still-warm carcass and drawing a section of the skinned hide over him.

Now, hours later, the beast's flesh had gone cold but Bolan realized the scavenged hide had likely saved his life.

As his senses slowly came back to him, Bolan smelled smoke and could hear the distinctive crackle of a nearby fire. On his guard, the Executioner slowly rolled away from the carcass and reached for his web holster, only to find it empty.

A long shadow suddenly fell across him, blocking the sun from his eyes.

"Looking for this?"

Bolan blinked and stared up at the man looming over him. He was middle-aged and dressed in rags, his long, bedraggled black hair streaked with gray. Judging from his ruddy features and dark eyes, Bolan figured he was from the reservation. In one hand the man was holding Bolan's handgun. In the other he clutched a gleaming bowie knife with a nine-inch blade.

"Morning," the man said calmly. "I figured it was time to come say howdy. Name's Rafe."

The man flipped the Browning in his hand, then held it by the barrel and extended it to Bolan.

"I let it dry by the fire but no guarantee it's working."

"Thanks," Bolan managed to whisper.

"No problem," Rafe said. "We got plenty of our own. Here, let me help you up."

Bolan took the other man's hand and grimaced as he cast off his improvised blanket and slowly stood. He was wobbly on his feet and still shivering, so Rafe took him by the arm and guided him over to a nearby cable spool and helped him sit down.

"Go ahead and rest up a second while I get our breakfast."

Bolan watched on as the transient crouched before the slain bison and used the bowie knife to begin carving away at the beast's right hip.

"Good call helping send this poor guy to his Maker," Rafe called back to Bolan. "We usually offer up some kind of prayer to make things right. You?"

Bolan shook his head. "I just didn't want to see it suffer."

"Close enough." When Rafe finished his carving he was holding a slice of bloodied red meat the size of a catcher's mitt.

"Sirloin," he told Bolan. "Doesn't get much better than that."

"Whereabouts am I?" Bolan asked.

"About dead center on the reservation, I'd say," Rafe told him. "This here's Healer's Ravine, though I guess you'd say these days most folks call it the town dump. You up to walking? Got a campfire going just a ways over."

Bolan drew in a deep breath and struggled back to his feet. He could tell that he'd reinjured his shoulder and his thigh was bruised from where he'd been struck by the bison near the gristmill but other than that and a mild fever he felt thankfully intact.

"When'd you show up here?" Rafe asked as they threaded their way through the debris. Bolan limped slightly, favoring the bruised hip.

"A few hours ago probably," he guessed.

"Sorry we didn't hear you or we would've come got you out of the cold," Rafe said. "We got a decent place up there in the caves."

Bolan glanced where Rafe was pointing and saw a series of small openings in the side of the ravine, each one reachable by a well-camouflaged rope ladder.

"You keep saying 'we,'" said Bolan.

"Yeah, that would be me, Leonard and Astro," Rafe said. "The Three Rosquiteers. They're right over here."

Up ahead Bolan saw smoke rising up from behind a haphazard row of tall bushes. Rafe led him around the plants to a small clearing where two other men, both considerably younger but similarly dressed, sat on a log near a fire pit, warming their hands over the flames. Rafe introduced them. Astro was the youngest of the three. Bolan assumed he'd gotten his nickname from the *Jetsons* cartoon dog tattooed on his right biceps.

"You ask him who he is?" Astro asked Rafe.

"Not yet," Rafe confessed. "I figure he'll get around to telling us."

"Nicolas Hayes," Bolan said, using his Justice Department alias.

There was an old crate across from where the other two men were sitting. When Rafe gestured at it and nodded, the Executioner sat down, welcoming the warmth put off by the fire.

"He's honest, I'll give him that," Leonard said, reaching into his pocket. He pulled out Bolan's Justice Department ID and held it out to him along with his cell phone. "We took it along with your gun. For safekeeping, y'know?"

As Bolan flipped open the cell phone, Astro told him, "Don't bother. Sucker's deader than a doornail."

Sure enough, the cell phone's miniscreen refused to light up. Bolan stuffed the ID into his still-drenched shirt pocket. Remembering his exchange with Kissinger the previous night, he pried open the cell phone to get at its battery and SIM card. Even if he could get the phone working after they dried out, he knew there still was a chance he'd be beyond range of a signal.

"You look a little flushed for a white man," Rafe told him. "I'm guessing you got a fever to go with whatever gave you that limp," Rafe told him. "Lucky for you Leonard here's something of a herbalist."

Leonard nodded. "Back in the day this used to be where the medicine men planted their herbs."

"Healer's Ravine," Bolan murmured.

"Yeah, that's what it's named for," Leonard said. "You gotta sift around the trash, but a lot of it's still growing. I'll fix you up with some cayenne and willow bark. It'll clear your head right up. Throw in some arnica anywhere you've got some kinda bruise or inflammation and you'll be a new man."

"A change of clothes wouldn't hurt, either," Astro suggested. "You're about my size. I can loan you something if you don't mind a little BO."

"I'd appreciate that," Bolan said.

"No problem," Astro said. "We go by the Golden Rule here. 'Do unto others unlike what the government do unto you.'"

"Speaking of the government," Leonard said, "what brings a federal agent to the res?"

"Official business," Bolan said. "I was caught up in a shootout and wound up in the river."

"Shootout with who?"

"I can't go into that," Bolan told the men. Much as he was grateful for their having befriended him, he had a mission to get back to. He glanced out at the sheer walls of the ravine, then asked, "What's the best way out of here?"

"What's your hurry?" Rafe said. He'd already skewered the bison meat with two thin metal skewers. There were makeshift brackets on either side of the fire and when Rafe set the skewers on them, the meat rested six inches above the flames and quickly began to sizzle. "We'll get you in some dry clothes and conduct a little herbal therapy, then you can have some breakfast and rest up a little. After that maybe we can talk a little bit about the going rate when it comes to rewarding Good Samaritans."

CHAPTER TWENTY

Santa Cruz, Bolivia

The day after Frederik Mikhaylov had throttled Dmitri Vishnevsky with his bare hands in the employee lounge of Moscow's Regal Splendor, the then-scrawny card counter had begun to work out with a personal trainer at the casino's health facility. In the three years since that humiliation, Vishnevsky had added almost forty pounds to his six-foot frame, nearly all of it toned muscle. A regimen of steroids and human growth hormones had supplemented the workouts, pocking the intellectual's face with acne and diminishing what had already been a thin crop of hair atop his boxlike head, but for Dmitri this had been an acceptable price to pay. When he'd moved to Bolivia to replace Mikhaylov at the Andean Splendor, Vishnevsky had tracked down the nearest boxing gymnasium and placed himself under the tutelage of a former South American heavyweight champion whose most-oft used words of encouragement when the two men sparred together in the ring were, "Pretend I'm the Butcher."

Vishnevsky had just finished going three rounds with the former champion and was making the three-block walk to work. His stride was boastful and he hummed to himself as he made his way down Avenue Independencia, navigating past slower-moving pedestrians as well as a phalanx of sidewalk vendors hawking everything from fresh produce to sweatshop garments and bootleg DVDs. The Russian had a welt on his cheekbone where he'd been met with a fierce jab, but he was oblivious to the lingering pain, so exultant was he over the way he'd stood up to the blow and countered with a right cross that, for the first time in four months of grueling face-offs, had sent his mentor reeling to the canvas. It was an omen, Vishnevsky figured, a sign that all would go well on this, the day he would prove that he had what it took to take the next step up the ladder in the casino's hierarchy.

THERE WAS AN AIR of festivity throughout Santa Cruz. In addition to a fleet of small trucks blasting celebratory music through rooftop speakers from one side of town to the other, thousands upon thousands of brightly colored helium balloons had been released at regular intervals into the hazy morning air, bound for the heavens where several small, vintage biplanes maneuvered in intricate patterns, releasing puffs of smoke to spell out the reason for the widespread fanfare.

"Grand Opening Today!" one of the planes wrote across the sky.

Another declared: "Loose Slots! Win! Win! Win!"

The new gaming hall, located adjacent from the main tourist center two miles from El Trompillo Airport, was about to open its doors as Santa Cruz's second-largest gambling enterprise, surpassed only by the Andean Splendor, which loomed three blocks away as the tallest structure in the entire downtown area. Traffic was being diverted for a block-long stretch along the street that dead-ended at the casino's main entrance, where a growing throng of expectant gamblers, rich and poor alike, crowded either side of the roped-off entrance to the casino, waiting for the doors to open so they could claim one of countless prizes being offered for the first few thousand patrons.

Inside the roped-off area, a seven-piece band was wrapping up a half-hour set with "Treasure for All," a song commissioned specifically for the opening by the casino's owner, flamboyant industrialist Alfredo Cavour. The crowd embraced the upbeat, feel-happy tune and, as much as possible considering the extent to which they were packed close together, they danced in place and sang along to the rousing chorus.

HALFWAY DOWN THE BLOCK, Andres Favre observed the celebration from the opened fourth-story window of his rented room at the Hotel Aymara. Favre had registered under a false name and tipped heavily to secure his room, which not only afforded the best view of the casino's entrance but also had ready access to the exterior fire escape by which he planned to make his escape once he'd completed his assignment. That moment was nearly at hand, and Favre was a picture of dispassionate calm as he raised his assembled Parker-Hale M-82 sniper rifle and peered through its Unertl 10-power scope.

As the band finished its set in front of the casino, a handful of employees hastily removed the webbed netting over two decorated canvas bins situated on either side of a speaker's stand. Another two hundred helium balloons rose from the bins, tethered by twelve-foot lengths of heavy string so that they formed a bobbing, multicolored canopy over the podium. Seconds later, a raucous cheer rose from the crowd as one of the main doors opened and out stepped Cavour, resplendent in a sharkskin suit studded with diamonds only slightly smaller than the ones mounted on the rings he wore on all of his fingers. Hair gelled back and his beaming face tanned several shades darker than his normal olive complexion, the sixty-four-year-old Santa Cruz native looked more like a cross between a Hollywood mogul and a Vegas entertainer than a financier. He waved and blew kisses to the crowd as he strode to the podium, soaking in the adulation.

"Treasure for all!" he shouted into the microphone, gesturing for the crowd to repeat the phrase. They responded in unison, their combined voices so loud that no one heard the shot that streaked through their midst and burrowed into Cavour's heart.

THE SNIPER'S TWENTY-EIGHT-YEAR-OLD nephew, Julio Favre, witnessed Cavour's assassination from behind the wheel of one of the casino's advertising trucks parked at the intersection just beyond where the street leading to the Inca Treasure had been cordoned off. He'd carjacked the vehicle hours before and its original driver lay dead in the enclosed rear bed, surrounded by more than eleven hundred pounds of high explosives rigged to a detonator Julio held clenched between his right palm and the steering wheel.

The moment Cavour slumped behind the podium, Julio started up the truck. As soon as security officers manning the sawhorse barricades abandoned their posts and raced toward the erupting bedlam outside the casino, Julio shifted into gear and bore down on the accelerator. The truck quickly gained speed as it pulled away from the curb and crossed the intersection, smashing through the sawhorses. Julio's heart raced both with terror and exhilaration as he put the pedal to the floor, his eyes fixed on the podium and the main doors directly behind it. In a matter of seconds he knew his life would be over, but he comforted himself with his uncle's assurances that his name would live on for years to come whenever fellow members of the National Liberation Army recalled the greatest martyrs to their cause.

One of the security officers stopped in his tracks when he heard the truck roaring down the boulevard toward the casino. By the time he drew his gun and turned to face Julio, the truck had already caught up with him. Struck head-on, the officer bounded into the air as if he were weightless and fell clear of the truck, which continued to zero in on its target.

"Viva la revolución!" Julio Favre screamed at the top of his lungs, tears streaming down his cheeks as he prepared to press the detonator. *"Viva la revolución!"*

DMITRI VISHNEVSKY HAD reached the Andean Splendor and taken a private elevator up to his penthouse suite on the seventeenth floor. Standing out on a balcony that overlooked the city, he held his cell phone in one hand as he watched the rival casino's opening ceremony on a small portable television. When he saw Alfredo Cavour go down, the acne-faced Russian smiled with satisfaction and turned from the television to his view of the Inca Treasure. Raising the cell phone, he focused on the faux Incan ruins that adorned the other casino's six-story rooftop. The phone was equipped with a built-in video camera, and as Vishnevsky filmed away, a loud explosion suddenly reverberated through the city, sending out shock waves that faintly trembled the concrete beneath his feet. A black cloud of smoke rose up from the rival casino and within seconds the gambling hall and its attached hotel facilities began to collapse, bringing down the rooftop ruins. Vishnevsky suspected the devastation wouldn't be as complete as the controlled implosions that flattened obsolete casinos in Las Vegas, but he was certain that it would be some time before the Treasure would reopen, if ever.

As the smoke thickened and the din of the explosion was replaced by howling sirens, Vishnevsky left the balcony and entered the living room of his penthouse suite. He quickly saved the video file and then used the cell phone's miniaturized keyboard to log online and e-mail the film clip into cyberspace. Once he'd completed the task, the Russian sauntered into the kitchen and looked through the refrigerator for a snack, settling on a cup of flavored yogurt. He scooped it into a bowl and was adding granola when his cell phone bleated.

It was SVR Deputy Director Alek Repin.

"I just saw your movie," Repin said. "It looks like you pulled it off, Dmitri."

"A piece of cake," Vishnevsky said nonchalantly as he stirred the granola into the yogurt. "Within the hour ELN will put out an announcement taking responsibility for the bombing. I, of course, will offer my condolences to the Cavour family and condemn the terrorists."

"And offer a reward."

"Yes, that will be part of my statement," Vishnevsky replied. "I was thinking it might go over even better if I double the amount we discussed."

"Not a problem," Repin replied. "Offer whatever you wish. No one is going to collect it."

"My feeling exactly."

"You've done well, Dmitri," Repin told his longtime associate, "but I think it would be best if you leave the country for a while. Just to be safe."

Vishnevsky's pallid face took on a sudden tint as he blushed with anger. "What are you talking about?" he demanded. "Our agreement was that once this was done I would be promoted here."

"I realize that," said Repin, "but something has come up."

"You can't retract that offer!" Vishnevsky snapped. "We had an understanding! I had your promise!"

"Relax, Dmitri." Repin chuckled. "You've jumped to the wrong conclusion entirely. You're still being promoted. It's just that another job has opened up that I thought might interest you more."

"Unless it's the one in the States I was passed over for, I'm not interested," Vishnevsky said. "That's final!"

Repin's chuckle broadened into full-out laughter.

"Dmitri, my friend," he finally managed to say, "you need to follow the advice of the late Mr. Cavour and believe in good fortune."

CHAPTER TWENTY-ONE

Santa Fe, New Mexico

Driving south on Interstate 25 toward the state capital, Leslie Helms was still thinking about the press conference back at the reservation, particularly the way Captain Brown had brought things to such an abrupt end and announced that all media vehicles would be searched on their way off the property. Something seemed off. To Helms, the searches had seemed pointless, as most of the press corps, like her, had parked in plain sight along the shoulder of the service road leading to Franklin Colt's property. Brown herself had had a clear view down the road while she was making her remarks. If someone had tried to break into one of the vehicles, she likely would have seen it. Yes, there was a chance the captain had ordered the searches out of spite, but Helms doubted the other woman could have been so petty. There had to be another reason. Maybe, she thought, it had had something to do with the officer who'd pulled up in the ATV during the middle of the briefing.

Once she reached the outskirts of Santa Fe, the private investigator veered onto Veteran's Memorial Highway, the relief route circumventing the city. Off in the distance she saw a hot air balloon floating lazily above the foothills. She knew it wasn't one of Christopher Shiraldi's, but the sight of it was enough to derail her obsession over the press conference. She wondered how long it would be before Shiraldi broke down and called her back. If she could get his cooperation and come up with something worth feeding the Justice Department agent she'd met back in Albuquerque, it'd be the best break she'd had all year.

Helms was debating whether to make the hour-long drive to Shiraldi's temporary site in Cochiti Lake when she did a slow double take in the rearview mirror. A few hundred yards behind her, a car had briefly pulled out into the far lane, then eased back behind the UPS truck ahead of it instead of passing. She'd seen someone execute the same maneuver a couple of times back on the main highway, but she couldn't tell if it was the same car.

Helms was driving 60 mph in a 55 mph zone. When she passed the next sign posting the speed limit, she used it as a pretense to slow. By the time she reached the La Cuchara intersection, she'd been passed by the delivery truck and could get a better look at the car that had been behind it. It was a late-model Camaro the same color as the one driven by a plainclothes tribal officer who'd nearly run over a couple reporters back at the reservation while racing to set up a search point for the media vehicles.

"Holy shit," Helms cursed. Suddenly it all made sense. The way the press conference had ended and the subsequent search—it had to have been because she'd been recognized from her ill-fated visit to the reservation earlier in the week.

"Next time try a better disguise, girlfriend," Helms chastised herself.

Helms was less than three miles from her apartment but there was no way she was about to lead her pursuer to her front door. Instead, she exited two ramps earlier, putting herself on Camino la Tierra. Moments later, as she'd cloverleafed under the relief route, the Camaro was still tailing her.

Helms had a lightweight Kimber Ultra Carry .45 in her purse but wasn't inclined to provoke a firefight. Nor did she like her chances of outrunning the Camaro with her four-cylinder Volkswagen. Her best bet, she decided, was to make her way into the city. If she couldn't shake the Chevy along the crowded side streets, she knew she'd at least cut down on the risk its driver would decide to take a potshot at her.

Taking a quick left onto Buckman Road, Helms headed north, parallel to the relief route she'd just gotten off. Behind her, the Camaro's driver followed suit but dropped back, letting a couple cars move in between him and her Jetta.

"It's a little late for lying low, pal," Helms said, still eyeing Russell Combs in her rearview mirror. "I'm onto you."

"SHE LIKES TO TALK to herself a lot, I'll say that much," Combs told RTPF Captain Tina Brown as he continued to follow Helms's bugged Jetta along the road leading into Santa Fe. The chief investigatory officer was using a speakerphone attachment clipped to his windshield visor, leaving both hands free on the steering wheel on the chance he would have to make a sudden turn to stay on Helms's tail. Brown was still back at Franklin Colt's property and while she hadn't come out and said it, Combs suspected the captain was having problems with the BIA agent assigned to investigate the shootout.

"She hasn't called anyone?" Brown asked.

"Negative."

"Do you think she's made you?"

"I doubt it," Combs lied. He suspected Helms had wised up to him back on the relief road, but he didn't see any need to get on the wrong side of Brown's foul mood. "I already ran her plate through DMV and have her address, so if you want I can pull back and set up a stakeout. Her place is here in Santa Fe."

"You can do that later," Brown told him. "Stay on her for now. If she's meeting someone and gets out of the car, I want you to be able to at least see who's in on this with her."

"Will do," Combs responded.

"And remember you're off the home field," the captain said. "Use lethal force only as an absolute last resort. I don't need another fire to have to put out."

"I hear you, Captain."

"Get back to me as soon as you have something."

"Of course."

Once Brown clicked off, Combs glowered out at the world around him, in far less than a pleasant mood himself. He'd known Cecil Farris as well as the other three tribal officers killed during the previous night's shootout and it weighed on him that they'd wound up as collateral damage in what had become an increasingly desperate effort to conceal the extent to which members of the RTPF, including himself and the captain, had fallen into collusion with the man he knew as Freddy McHale. It infuriated Combs to realize how readily he'd allowed himself be led astray, not only by McHale but also countless others who over the years had tempted him to step outside the law. Succumbing to corruption, after all, had been the last thing on his mind when he'd first joined the department. And yet now here he was, years after accepting what he'd told himself would be a one-time-only bribe, compromised into becoming little more than part of a badged goon squad at the beck and call of Global Holdings Corporation. It wasn't supposed to be this way.

Combs followed Helms past the vast sprawl of Frank S. Ortiz Park to where Buckman Road merged with Camino de las Crucitas. The speed limit dropped to 30 mph, and the officer began to feel as if he were part of a slow parade as he tried to keep three cars back from the Jetta. After passing through a couple of subdivisions, the charade finally came to an end when Helms pulled into a drive-through car wash and fed her credit card to the automated pay caddy. Combs drove past the facility and pulled over to the curb, then glanced back, just in time to see the Jetta roll into the enclosed wash building. There was nothing coming over the bug's FM frequency in terms of Helms speaking to anyone about her sudden need to clean her car.

"What the hell is she up to?" he wondered.

ONCE THE SPRAY JETS began to noisily pelt the Jetta with soapy water, Helms unclicked her seat belt and leaned across the front passenger seat. The far door had been opened back at the reservation when it had been her turn to be searched and she recalled that the man who was now following her had made a point to tilt the passenger seat forward to get a better look into the back. It had seemed a pointless gesture at the time, as he could have merely glanced through the windows and seen there was nothing in the backseat other than some dry cleaning Helms had picked up on the way to the press conference. The Jetta wobbled in place as mechanical arms dragged a series of rumbling, soft-bristled rollers across the car's exterior, further masking Helms's movements as she crawled over the seat to more thoroughly search for the dime-size bug she finally found stuck to the base of the post separating the front door from the back.

Nice try, she thought to herself, prying the small microphone loose and setting it on the dashboard.

She wasn't finished.

Her trunk had been searched, as well, and once the washing cycle was completed, Helms quietly exited the vehicle and braved the blasts of hot air drying the Jetta from all sides. Squatting behind the car, she ran her hand along the underside of the rear bumper and came across a homing device twice the size of the bug. As with the bug, the backside of the homing transmitter was embedded in a soft, puttylike adhesive. Helms pried the device free, along with the adhesive, then stood, smirking to herself. Behind her, a Jeep Wrangler with a roof rack had pulled up to the payout caddy. Helms ventured out of the washing enclosure, patting down her mussed hair as she approached the Jeep's driver, a man in his forties wearing a Sante Fe Opera T-shirt. Helms got him to roll down his window and pretended she was lost.

"I'm not sure how to get back to the freeway," she told the man, nonchalantly placing one hand on the Jeep's roof. By the time the man had given her directions, Helms had planted the homing device onto one of the roof rack's brackets.

She thanked the man and hurried back to her car, slipping behind the wheel and quietly drawing the door closed. A green light flashed above the opening that led out of the wash building. Helms drove out and immediately pulled over and parked. Off to her left she could see the Camaro parked by the curb, some fifty yards away. The driver was looking away from her, but Helms suspected he'd probably tilted the side-view mirror to keep her car in sight.

You want to hear something juicy, do you? Leslie thought to herself. I've got just the thing.

While she waited for the Wrangler to go through the car wash, the private eye fished through her purse for both her cell phone and her gun. She slipped the gun in her coat pocket, then punched in the number for her Aunt Marge in Los Alamos. All Helms had to do was ask how the older woman was doing, and Marge launched into an uninterrupted litany of her various physical ailments and her dissatisfaction with the medical attention she was receiving for them. It was the same spiel, more or less, that Helms had been hearing for the past twenty years and she was able to easily tune it out. She doubted that the man eavesdropping would be able to do the same. Hopefully, he was hanging on every word, trying to decipher some possible code Marge was imparting.

When she heard the Jeep going through its drying cycle, Helms quickly wrapped up the call, promising to come visit her aunt sometime soon. She then opened the dashboard's swing-down ashtray and pressed the cigarette lighter. By the time the lighter popped up, she'd retrieved the bug from the top of the dash. As she'd hoped, its diameter was slightly smaller than the glowing orange tip of the lighter. Holding the bug by its adhesive backing, she pressed it against the lighter and smiled as she heard the popping of blown circuits. The bug gave off a smell of burned plastic as she dumped it in the ashtray.

Once the Wrangler drove past, Helms waved to the driver, then began to follow him. As she'd anticipated, the Camaro was quick to follow suit. After another four blocks, Helms got the opportunity she was looking for and gunned her accelerator to race through the next intersection just as the light was changing to red. Behind her, cross traffic lurched forward, preventing the Camaro from continuing its pursuit. Helms had nearly rear-ended the Jeep but the ploy had worked and she quickly turned down the nearest side street while the Wrangler kept going straight. If the Camaro's driver relied on the homing device, by the time he caught up and realized he was following the wrong car, Helms would be long gone in the other direction. Just to be safe, she planned to ditch her Jetta at the nearest mall and switch to a rental car. It was an expense she planned to put on the tab she figured she would soon be presenting to the Justice Department agent who'd left his phone number on the cocktail napkin tucked in her wallet. Once she got the other car, she would call the man. Maybe she hadn't secured any new information from Christopher Shiraldi, but she was hoping that her revelation about being followed from the reservation would count as proof that she was still on the case with the meter running.

CHAPTER TWENTY-TWO

Carl Lyons had the rearmost window seat on the Dassault Falcon 7X Barbara Price had secured for his trip from Seattle to New Mexico. One of the fastest private jets on the market, the Falcon was due to reach Santa Fe in less than a half hour. The blond-haired, square-jawed Able Team leader wasn't the only passenger. To get Lyons in the air as quickly as possible, Price had gone down Hal Brognola's master list of Seattle businesses the Justice Department had ongoing relationships with and pulled strings to delay the takeoff of the St. Louis–bound Falcon, which belonged to a giant in the software industry. The four sales executives already booked on the flight had been amenable to the delay as well as the detour to New Mexico. They could use the time to fine-tune their presentation to their client.

Lyons dozed off an hour into the flight only to be awakened soon after by a call routed to the custom-installed in-flight telephone nestled in a compartment next to his leather armrest. Lyons knew it had to be the Farm calling, and he hoped it was news that Bolan had turned up alive and well.

"No word on that front yet," Barbara Price informed him once he'd picked up, "but we're wondering if you can wrangle your way into being dropped in Taos instead of Santa Fe."

"I can try," Lyons said. "What's the latest there?"

"They just found Donny Upshaw's body."

Once Price had filled him in on the details, Lyons clicked off and ventured to the front of the cabin. There was no objection to switching his drop-off point, and the head of the sales team passed along instructions to the pilot while Lyons went to the galley and poured himself some coffee. He was still stiff from the beating his body had taken during the Takoma takedown, and between sips he paced the rear of the cabin to loosen up. It wasn't long before the jet began its descent and the pilot advised all passengers to be buckle up in preparation for landing. Once back in his seat, Lyons peered out the window. As the jet closed in on Taos Municipal Airport, he got a bird's-eye view of the police activity he would soon be monitoring.

Within a radius of less than two miles, Lyons detected no fewer than eight black-and-white units at three different locations. Two of the cruisers were parked at Alan Orson's estate, where officers and a forensics team were continuing to investigate the inventor's murder and the theft of valuables from the converted horse stables. A mile to the north, another two squad cars were parked at the entrance gate where Walter Upshaw had been gunned down. A tow truck was in the process of readying Upshaw's car for transport to the police impound yard. The rest of the vehicles were at the third site, just up Route 64, where Donny Upshaw's Buick LeSabre had been found parked beneath a cottonwood less than fifty yards from the Rio Grande Gorge Bridge, a canti-lever truss structure rising more than six hundred feet above the river. Since the bridge's construction in 1965 several hundred lost souls had chosen to end their lives by plunging over the waist-high railing and, by all appearances, Donny Upshaw had just joined their ranks.

In addition to police cars, an ambulance and a handful of other vehicles were parked on the shoulder on either side of the bridge, which had been temporarily closed. Two small groups of curiosity-seekers were mingling as close as they could get to the crime-scene tape, hoping for a glimpse of the body, which a local Search and Rescue team had climbed down to a few minutes before. The media was on hand, as well, represented by teams from three different camera trucks as well as four news choppers hovering high above the gorge like so many circling vultures. A fifth chopper, belonging to the Taos Police Department, was holding a steady position deeper into the ravine, a cable extended downward from its underbelly to the SRT crew, which was carefully placing Upshaw's body onto a gurney so that it could be airlifted to the ambulance. Price had told Lyons that a Raven Arms MP-25 found near the body was missing three bullets from its 6-round magazine.

The grim three-site tableau lingered in Lyons's mind even after the jet had touched down and begun to taxi its way closer to the terminal. From his vantage point he'd gotten a clear idea of how the police would likely view the course of events that had rocked the small tourist town over the past few hours. Everything pointed to Upshaw having killed Orson at the inventor's estate, then driven up the road to lie in wait for his father before continuing on to the bridge and committing suicide. It would be a hard scenario to dismiss, especially if Donny's prints were on the gun and an autopsy were to turn up signs of heroin in the man's bloodstream. The only thing left unexplained was the whereabouts of Orson's pickup truck and the missing items taken from his workplace. Price had told Lyons that despite the mounting evidence, she and the Farm's cyberteam were still looking into the possibility that a third party was behind the killings and had framed Donny. If that was the case, Lyons felt they were up against a formidable enemy indeed.

Once the jet came to a stop, Lyons thanked the salesmen and disembarked to the tarmac. As he made his way into the terminal and tracked down the car rental facility where Price had already lined him up a Chevy Impala, Lyons couldn't shake the image of Upshaw's body being placed on the gurney. The image left him unsettled, but the discomfort had little to do with the assignment that lay ahead for him. Rather, Lyons was still troubled by the notion that an hour's drive south of Taos a similar recovery might soon be taking place should it come to light that his longtime friend and colleague Mack Bolan had, like Donny Upshaw, met an untimely end.

Glorieta, New Mexico

"It's MY DAY OFF!" Frederik Mikhaylov barked into his cell phone. "None of that is a casino matter, and it has nothing to do with the treatment plant, so there's no reason for me to drive all the way there just to hold hands with you!"

The Russian was on the phone with Charles Stuart, the short-tempered seventy-year-old governor of Rosqui Pueblo. Stuart was up in arms about the previous night's shootout at Franklin Colt's place as well as the subsequent encounter involving his tribal police at Healer's Ravine. The governor had already given Captain Brown a thorough tongue-lashing but was clearly not through venting his displeasure over the negative publicity the reservation was receiving. He'd rung Mikhaylov on his private number just as the Russian was about to leave his quarters at the javelina farm's converted milk shed to interrogate Franklin Colt. Stuart, of course, assumed the Russian was at his condominium in Santa Fe, only a twenty-minute drive from the reservation.

"If we start to lose customers because of all this, that falls under casino business," Stuart countered. "I want some help coming up with a way to spin this that doesn't make us look like Crime Central."

"Then contact Penbrooks at Public Relations!" Mikhaylov said. "I still say this is none of our concern, but I can tell her to expect your call and offer our full cooperation. That should give you what you want."

"What I want is this whole mess swept under the rug as quickly as possible so things around here can get back to normal."

"Trust me, Governor, I know the feeling," Mikhaylov replied, thinking of his own dire predicament. He softened his tone slightly before he went on, figuring it would be better to defuse Stuart's wrath than antagonize him further. "Let me do this. I'll call Penbrooks and tell her to look over the situation with her people, then get back to you with some ideas."

There was a pause on the line, then Stuart grumbled, "I suppose that might help."

"She's a wizard at this," Mikhaylov assured the governor. "It's just a matter of putting the focus elsewhere until everything blows over. Spin control, just like you were saying."

"How soon can I expect to hear from her?"

"I'll tell her to drop what she's doing and have something for you first thing after lunch," Mikhaylov offered. "If you want some input before then, I'll tell her you're coming by and you can sit in while they're brainstorming."

"I like that idea better."

"Then we're all set," Mikhaylov said. "I'll call her right now."

The Russian quickly wrapped up the call, then clicked off and spewed a flurry of epithets as he stormed across the small room and unearthed a fresh bottle of vodka from the case stashed in the bottom of a closet built into the north wall. He cracked the seal and guzzled a few shots' worth, then refilled his flask before putting the bottle back. He hadn't eaten breakfast yet, and his body was quick to respond to the alcohol as it raced through him, partially quelling an anxiety that gnawed at him.

Just before speaking with Stuart he'd gotten a troubled call from Captain Brown not only about the rescue of the federal agent involved in the confrontation at Colt's place but also her concern that some woman who'd been sniffing around the reservation might be an undercover government agent, as well.

Troubling as those disclosures had been, they paled compared to his third wake-up call of the morning: word from Evgenii Danilov that none other than Dmitri Vishnevsky would be accompanying Melido Diaz to the States to "assist" with the situation in New Mexico. Danilov had assured the Butcher that it would only be a temporary arrangement, but Mikhaylov knew the man was lying. He felt betrayed. The son of a bitch hadn't even given him a chance to bring things under control before deciding on another option. That he'd turned to Vishnevsky of all people had only added insult to injury.

Mikhaylov booted up his laptop as he quickly dispensed with his call to Roaming Bison's Public Relations Director Elizabeth Penbrooks. Penbrooks was in the middle of putting together the next month's casino promotions and balked at gathering the work aside to deal with Stuart, but Mikhaylov stressed the urgency and secured her promise that she'd tend to matters. By the time he'd hung up, Mikhaylov's computer was up and running and he'd already navigated to his mailbox, where Danilov had forwarded the cell-phone video footage Vishnevsky had earlier sent to both him and SVR Deputy Director Alex Repin. Danilov had already described the bloodbath Vishnevsky had just orchestrated in Bolivia, but as Mikhaylov watched the footage of the collapsing Inca Treasure casino, he could feel still more salt being poured onto his wounded pride.

He watched the footage twice, then switched to a search engine and typed the words *Santa Cruz casino bombing* as well as *Dominic Fishciel,* the name Vishnevsky went by at the Andean Splendor. There were already dozens of Web site stories about the bombing, most of which stated that Bolivia's renegade National Liberation Army had claimed responsibility, citing Alfredo Cavour's long-standing opposition to the group as the reason for their attack. The few times Vishnevsky's alias showed up in the same articles was in the context of his denouncing the incident and offering a two-million-dollar reward for the arrest and conviction of those behind it.

"Nice touch," Mikhaylov muttered bitterly. He next switched to the search engine's option to seek out visual images of "Dominic Fishciel" and was stunned to see how Vishnevsky had transformed himself from an anemic scarecrow into a what looked like a muscle-bound freak of nature with bad skin and a vanishing hairline. The only thing that hadn't changed was the haughty gleam in Vishnevsky's slate-gray eyes.

Thrown, Mikhaylov felt his anxiety battling back against the alcohol. He pushed away from his desk and was halfway back to his closet when he heard someone enter the milk shed and head toward the inside door to his quarters. He veered from the locker and grabbed his jacket, then called out as he stabbed his arms through the sleeves.

"Who is it?"

"Tramelik."

Mikhaylov relaxed slightly and opened the door, waving his colleague in.

"I'm just on my way to tend to Colt," Mikhaylov said.

"I have some news first," Tramelik said.

"Cherkow's been taken care of?"

"He will be soon enough," Tramelik replied. "He and Hedeon left a few minutes ago."

It had been Tramelik's suggestion to not only set up Cherkow as a fall guy for the attack at Colt's property, but to also link him as the dealer who'd sold Donny Upshaw heroin in exchange for Alan Orson's hoard of inventions. Mikhaylov had jumped at the idea and ordered Cherkow to accompany Hedeon Barad when the mechanic drove Orson's repainted pickup to Santa Fe to buy bumper stickers and a camper shell. A side trip had been added to that particular mission. After further disguising the pickup, the men were to stop by an abandoned motel near Algodones, a half hour south of the capital, supposedly to close a deal for seven kilos of heroin earmarked for SVR's street suppliers throughout the state. In truth, Tramelik had placed an order for only two kilos, which both he and Mikhaylov had agreed would be an acceptable sacrifice to make for having Cherkow killed in what two of Captain Brown's undercover officers would make appear to be a drug deal gone wrong. One of their Colombian suppliers would have to be killed in the process but, again, it was deemed to be a necessary trade-off. Of course, the whereabouts of Orson's inventions would remain a mystery, but evidence planted at the scene would lend credence to the theory that Cherkow had quickly turned around and sold the contraband on the black market in exchange for the money for the two kilos, in effect doubling the profit on the smack he'd purportedly bartered to Upshaw.

"What else has happened, then?" Mikhaylov said warily. "And let me forewarn you—I've had enough bad news dumped on my plate this morning to last a lifetime."

Tramelik grinned. "I think you'll make room on your plate for this," he stated.

"Try me."

"For starters," Tramelik said, "up in Taos they just found the Indian's body where I dumped it off the bridge. They found the gun, too, and everyone's already decided he jumped after killing Orson and his father."

"If that holds up, it would definitely qualify as good news," Mikhaylov admitted. "Probably not enough to change matters, but it couldn't hurt."

"Change what matters?" Tramelik wondered.

Mikhaylov answered with a question. "What do you think of Dmitri Vishnevsky?"

Tramelik turned his head and pretended to spit.

"Good," Mikhaylov said. "Once I tell you what that bastard has arranged behind our backs, I think you'll agree that it'll be worthwhile for you to head back to Taos and help Vladik with another assignment."

"You can tell me in a minute," Tramelik responded. "First let me finish."

"Is it really that important? This business with Vishnevsky is urgent."

"So is this." Tramelik reached into his pocket and pulled out a cell phone. "It won't be necessary to have Vladik try to get to Upshaw's other phone. I found the one Colt used to talk with him."

When Tramelik handed him the device, Mikhaylov stared at it, dumbstruck. "Where did you find it?"

"I couldn't sleep so I decided to go for a little drive," Tramelik said. "To Albuquerque."

"The impound yard."

Tramelik nodded. "It's a lot larger and busier than the one in Taos. You'd think they'd have better security."

"I told you to wait on that."

"You said to wait until Cherkow checked on Colt's house," Tramelik reminded the other man. "When he came up empty-handed, I thought back to Colt's last conversation with Upshaw. The one I overheard yesterday morning."

"About him wanting to run his evidence by someone with the government?"

Tramelik nodded again. "Remember? It's the whole reason we had him followed to the airport in the first place. I figured if he didn't have the phone on him and it wasn't at his house, the only other place it could be was in his car. He had it tucked in a cavity beneath the dashboard."

"How ironic," Mikhaylov mused.

"How's that?"

"Cherkow told me he wanted to search the car more thoroughly after he knocked that taxi off the road," Mikhaylov said. "The others talked him out of it."

"Too bad he listened to them."

"A fatal mistake as it turns out." Rather than dwell on Cherkow's pending demise, Mikhaylov turned his attention back to Colt's cell phone.

"Let me guess," he said. "Like everyone else, Colt never bothered to set a PIN code."

"No, he didn't," Tramelik said, flipping the phone open. It quickly booted and lit up, going straight to a menu screen. He thumbed the keypad as he told Mikhaylov, "There aren't any text messages, but the only calls are to Upshaw, all over the past two weeks."

"Then we were right," Mikhaylov said. "They each had a separate phone just for this."

Tramelik nodded. "Now take a look at these."

Mikhaylov stared at the phone screen as, one after the other, Tramelik uploaded a series of photos taken at night, half of them showing freight trucks bound along the service road leading to the reservation's nuclear waste plant. The rest were taken from various vantage points behind the facility, where the trucks had parked while their cargo was transferred to the mountain bunkers by way of a tunnel whose entryway was normally camouflaged by large shrubs set in movable planters disguised to look like weed-covered mounds. Shown in sequence, the photos revealed, step-by-step, how centrifuges and other equipment for Operation Zenta was being delivered in the dead of night to the clandestine destination where they would be put to use in the making of nuclear warheads.

"Colt's 'smoking gun,'" Mikhaylov said. "When were these taken?"

"The night before last," Tramelik said.

"One of Colt's nights off."

"It turns out he came to work after all," Tramelik said. "Just not for us."

CHAPTER TWENTY-THREE

Rosqui Pueblo, New Mexico

With more than fifty-three square miles of reservation land to search, more than two hours had passed before Rosqui Tribal Police Officers Joseph Romano and Ryan Covina had made their way to Healer's Ravine. They were up on the ridgeline trailing down from Mt. McCray, more than a hundred feet above the fast-moving river, riding side by side in one of the department's Yahama ATVs. Romano was at the wheel while Covina scouted both sides of the mountain for any trace of the man depicted in the photocopy they'd been given back near Franklin Colt's home. Covina had a Savage 110FP sniper rifle at the ready, and both men were additionally armed with police-issue 9 mm H&K pistols sheathed at their waists in black leather holsters.

After another twenty yards the ridgeline sloped down to a broad plateau, one section of which backtracked by way of a long, grassy incline to the river as well as grazing land for the reservation's bison herd. The plateau itself was a patchwork of mesquite, prairie grass and raw earth turned to mud by the previous night's rains. There were hoofprints in the mud left by bison that had strayed uphill during the stampede, but no manmade tracks. Up ahead, however, just beyond where the plateau dropped precipitously to the base of the ravine, the two officers spotted a wisp of smoke rising up from the gorge.

"Has to be those transients," Covina murmured.

Romano slowed the Yamaha to a stop and killed the engine. "We might as well check it out."

Covina readied the sniper rifle and Romano drew his pistol as they approached the precipice. Overhead, one of the news choppers began to drift toward them.

"Assholes," Romano muttered. He glanced up and gestured angrily for the pilot to back off. The pilot partially obliged, pulling away but then rising into a holding position on the other side of the river, some two hundred yards away.

"I'd like to put a stray shot through that moron's forehead," Covina complained.

"I'd cover for you," Romano replied, only half joking.

Covina turned his attention back to the plateau. He pointed out a set of hoofprints heading straight to the edge of the cliff. "Looks like one of the bison tried to pull an Evel Knievel."

"My guess is he didn't make it," Romano said.

Once within a few yards of the drop-off, the men crouched low and flattened themselves atop the rain-soaked grass, preferring wet uniforms to the idea of crawling through mud. They wormed their way to a spot where a clump of mesquite helped conceal them while affording a view down into the refuse-littered ravine. A hundred feet directly below them, lying on its side, was the slain bison. Forty yards away, past the scattered trash and dumped appliances, four men huddled around the dying remnants of a campfire.

"What'd I tell ya?" Covina whispered. "Hobo jungle."

"I don't know," Romano said, looking closely at the men. "The one on the far right looks like he's been to a barber this century. Check him out."

Covina reached for the minizoom binoculars clipped to his holster. He cupped the viewers in his palm to keep the sun from reflecting off its lenses, then peered through the mesquite, focusing on the man Romano had pointed out.

"Bingo," he whispered. "He's changed clothes, but that's him all right."

"Keep an eye on him," Romano said, backing away from the ridge. "I'll see if we've got men on the other side of the ravine so we can cover him from both sides."

"Why don't I just shoot him and be done with it?" Covina asked.

"We've got the eye-in-sky, remember?" Romano told him. "You wanna have to explain yourself on the six-o'clock news?"

Covina glanced back at the distant news chopper. "Assholes."

"WELL, WHAT DO YA THINK?" Leonard asked Mack Bolan.

The Executioner extended his right leg and flexed it near the campfire. Beneath his borrowed jeans he'd wrapped gauze around an herb-soaked poultice pressed against the thigh bruise left by the bison that had struck him. The pain had lessened dramatically, as had the tightness.

"Feels fine," he said. "Same with my shoulder."

"What'd I tell ya?" Rafe said. "Leonard's a one-man E.R."

It wasn't only Bolan's thigh and shoulder that had improved. His fever was gone and, with it, the chills that had been rattling through him from the moment he'd awoken. His share of the bison had satisfied his hunger, as well.

"How about some dessert?" Astro suggested, holding out a clear plastic bag filled with doughnuts and muffins. "Take your pick."

Bolan helped himself to what looked like an oatmeal muffin. "Somehow I didn't think there was a bakery around here," he said before biting into the snack.

"Every few days we go Dumpster diving behind the casino," Rafe explained. "You won't believe the stuff they throw out. Same with the cafeteria at the nuke plant."

Bolan glanced at Rafe. "Nuke plant?"

"Correction," Rafe said. "Nuclear *waste* plant. It's just over the mountain. You didn't know about it?"

Bolan shook his head, intrigued. He was about to ask more about the facility when he noticed the news copter hovering in the distance just beyond the river.

"All right if I build up the fire a little?" he asked. "I want to try to get that chopper's attention."

"What, you're tired of our company?" Rafe teased.

"I owe you guys, all right?" Bolan told them. "I know that, but I've got things to take care of."

"Well, go ahead with the fire," Rafe told him, "but it's not likely to do you much good. They're gonna think you're just another bum. No story there."

"If that's the case, why haven't they moved on?" Bolan countered, tossing the muffin wrapper into the flames and then adding another couple branches of mesquite.

"You might have something there, Nick," Astro said. He sat upright and stretched his arms a moment, then turned his head from one side to another as if trying to work out a kink in his neck. When he lowered his arms, he set aside the pastry bag and let his hand drift to his right leg. Pulling up his pant leg, he slowly reached for a small Smith & Wesson .32 wedged in an ankle holster.

"Nobody make any quick moves or anything," he whispered, "but we've got ourselves a party crasher."

As he finished his muffin, Bolan slowly diverted his gaze and caught a glimpse of someone downhill through the thick overgrowth blanketing the steep slope.

"Looks like he's packing," he told the others. He was reaching for his pistol when a shot rang out, striking Astro in the upper arm.

"Son of a bitch!" Astro howled, dropping his gun and then quickly picking it up with his other hand.

Bolan and the others were already on the move, diving clear of the fire. Another shot whistled past the Executioner's ear as he scrambled for the cover of the clawfoot bathtub he'd briefly considered spending the night in. Rafe and Leonard had made it to a cluster of boulders and had pulled out their own concealed weapons, both Ruger P90s. Astro, meanwhile, planted himself behind a rust-covered oven and returned fire, shouting, "Back the hell off! We aren't bothering anyone!"

Astro was answered by a slug that clanged off the oven's range top.

"Tribal police!" came a shout from the upper reaches of the ravine. "Toss your guns out where we can see them and then come out with your hands up!"

"Sorry, but I forgot to take my stupid pill this morning!" Astro shouted back. He glanced at the blood streaming down his wounded arm, just below his tattoo. Furious, he fired another round from his Smith & Wesson. "If you're the cops, let's see a badge!"

"Not stupid here, either!"

There was a lull in the firing. Bolan had his gun out. He had his doubts that they were being fired at by the tribal police, but he wasn't about to shoot to kill until he was sure. He took aim uphill at an outcropping near where the gunman was crouched. When he tried to get off a warning shot, nothing happened. Frustrated, he jammed the gun back in his holster and called out to Rafe, "I need another piece."

"Here, take mine!" Astro called back, flinging the .32 "Terrier" Bolan's way. "I got a little leak here to deal with."

Bolan was grabbing the S&W when another shot zinged nearby, clanging off the side of the cast-iron tub. The Executioner was forced to roll away from the tub, as the second shot had come at him from behind. He squirmed behind a large, termite-infested wooden desk. Seconds later an incoming round from yet another direction left a fresh hole in the butcher-block desktop.

"We have you surrounded!" someone shouted from atop the opposite edge of the ravine.

"No shit," Rafe murmured from behind the rock pile. He changed position and fired up at the latter gunman. Leonard followed suit.

Bolan held his fire and shouted, "I'm with the Justice Department! Hold your fire!"

Two different gunmen responded by rattling off shots from two different directions, driving Bolan beneath the desk.

"I don't think they're buying it," Rafe called out to him. "Might be a good time to start firing back."

"I need to make sure they're not law enforcement," Bolan said.

Two shots fired in quick succession scarred the rocks Rafe and Leonard crouched behind.

"You might wanna rethink that, Nick, buddy," Rafe shouted to Bolan, "'cause we're goddamn fish in a barrel here and these guys seem to think we're their dinner!"

STILL POSITIONED AT THE lip of the southern precipice, Officer Covina had thus far held his fire, waiting while Romano and two other tribal cops triangulated their fire at the men below. There was no avenue for escape and the men had returned fire, which for Covina was a green light to put his Savage 10FP to use and bring things to a close without having to worry about possible furor from whoever was doing the play-by-play from the media chopper.

The rifle was bolt-operated, and Covina wanted to make sure each shot counted so he took his time, squinting through the scope as he scanned the maze of rocks and trash, finally spotting his target half-burrowed beneath an old desk.

"Nighty night," he murmured to himself, his finger on the trigger.

Covina was aligning the scope's dot reticule on the back of Bolan's head when a volley of incoming rounds danced through the mud to his immediate right. One of them caught up with him and bored through his calf. Covina dropped his weapon and jerked in place, cursing. When he spun and grabbed his leg, he heard a growing drone and glanced skyward to where an S-64 Skycrane had just risen into view above the ridgeline. Covina knew at once it wasn't the media.

JOHN KISSINGER LEANED OUT the passenger window of the Skycrane's front cab, brandishing the assault rifle that had thwarted Covina's attempt to kill Bolan. Slung around Kissinger's neck was a pair of high-powered binoculars. Behind him, Detective David Lowe leaned forward and squeezed a bullhorn through his opened window.

"This is the Albuquerque Police!" Lowe shouted over Kissinger's shoulder.

"This is our jurisdiction!" Covina shouted back. His words were drowned out by the chopper, but apparently Lowe was good at reading lips.

"Take potshots at a federal agent and jurisdiction goes out the window!" he retorted.

Covina had made no effort to retrieve his rifle, but Kissinger spotted another officer in the brush just below the precipice raising his handgun. When the Stony Man armorer cut loose a few warning rounds, the second officer lowered his weapon. The badged gunmen on the other side of the ravine held their fire, as well.

"That's more like it," Kissinger murmured.

"Brace yourself, kiddies," Jack Grimaldi called out from behind the controls. "It's a tight squeeze, but I'm gonna try to take us down for a pickup."

In addition to the three men in the Skycrane's front cab, one of Lowe's APD counterparts was posted in the chopper's rear-facing compartment. Like Kissinger, he was armed with an M-4 A-1 carbine, which helped keep the tribal force at bay while the chopper slowly lowered into the craggy maw of Healer's Ravine. Down below, Bolan and his three companions cautiously made their way into the open.

"That's the goddamn ugliest helicopter I've ever seen," Leonard said. "Sucker looks like it went in for liposuction and the doc didn't know when to quit."

"Like I said, I have some unfinished business," Bolan responded. "I guess they want to make sure I get a chance to finish it."

As the chopper drew lower, the roar of its power plant amplified off the ravine walls. Dislodged by the rotor wash, old wrappers and other bits of loose debris began to to hop and swirl about the rescuees. Bolan gestured in greeting to a clearly relieved Kissinger then glanced over at Astro, who had made his way back to the campfire and sat down for a better look at his gunshot wound.

"I think there's room for at least one more," Bolan told Astro. "Let's get you airlifted to a hospital."

Astro shook his head. "I'm a little behind on my insurance premiums," he said. "Leonard'll fix me up."

"Not so fast," Leonard said. The herbalist strode over and inspected Astro's wound, then shook his head. "Sorry, amigo. You're gonna need a little bit more than some willow bark for that thing."

"Well, I'm not going to leave you to those numbnuts up there," Astro countered, giving a finger to the tribal police. "You think they're gonna just mosey outta here after they've been shown up? No way."

"He's right," Bolan said. The Executioner looked up and shouted to Kissinger. "Does that thing have a cable lift?"

"It's good to see you, too!" Kissinger shouted back. "Yeah, we've got a line. Why?"

"We're all coming," Bolan shouted back. "We just need to rig up something for a couple of us to ride in."

"You're joking, right?"

"I owe them!" Bolan yelled.

Kissinger shook his head and grinned down at his colleague. "Well, make it quick! That posse up there's not going to stand pat forever."

Bolan flashed him a thumbs-up, then glanced at the strewed refuse, looking for a suitable riding carriage.

"I don't know about you, Nick," Rafe said, "but I'm thinking the bathtub."

CHAPTER TWENTY-FOUR

At the same time Petenka Tramelik was driving back to Taos to deal with the anticipated arrival of Dmitri Vishnevsky, the man behind the bombing of the Inca Treasure was aboard his casino's Cessna Citation X jet. The Cessna was bound for Mexico City, where it would quickly refuel before continuing on to Santa Fe Municipal Airport. There, Vishnevsky's other passenger would disembark prior the final leg of the Russian's impromptu flight.

"While I go on to Taos," Vishnevsky told Melido Diaz, "you'll take a rental car to the safe house where Tramelik brought Orson's inventions. I know you've already gone over the schematics, but seeing everything firsthand will give you a better idea how we can best proceed in terms of mass production, especially with the armored suit."

"Thermal armored suit," Diaz amended. "And I already spoke with Mikhaylov about it. He called me just before I left for the airport."

Vishnevsky stopped eating and stared at the Bolivian inventor, a short, myopic man whose large, dark eyes appeared almost cartoonishly oversize behind the lenses of his round, black-rimmed glasses. "What did he want to know?"

"How to make sure it was operational," Diaz said.

"What's to know?" Vishnevsky laughed so loud the attractive young flight attendant sitting in the rear of the cabin glanced up from her fashion magazine. The Russian winked at her, then turned back to Diaz. "You put it on and activate the solar panels. What, he doesn't know how to turn a switch?"

"He also asked about the helicopter. They have the schematics and a model Orson was going to bring to some convention, but the actual aircraft is still in storage back in Taos."

"I know," Vishnevsky said. "At the airport there. It's on my list of things to do when I get there."

"He was concerned the police might impound it and was wondering if I'd be able to oversee the building of a new prototype based on the plans."

"And?"

"Orson was meticulous about all his data," Diaz said. "I haven't looked over everything but I'm sure I can manage it."

"I think he already knew that," Vishnesvky said. "I think he was calling more to get a read on you. He's concerned where your loyalties will lie."

"My thoughts exactly."

"You told him we're flying to the States together?"

"He already knew." Diaz shifted uncomfortably in the large leather seat that dwarfed him nearly as much as the gargantuan dimensions of the man sitting across from him. Vishnevsky took a small brown bottle from his shirt pocket and used its built-in dropper to add an amberish liquid to his mineral water. Diaz suspected it was some sort of illegal bodybuilding compound but wasn't about to press for details.

"I'm a little wary of having to deal with Mikhaylov on my own," the Bolivian said. "Is it really necessary for you to fly to Taos immediately?"

"Absolutely," Vishnevsky said. "There's more to be done than just trying to get to the helicopter. I need to work on securing the rights to those uranium mines."

"I realize that," Diaz said. "But what difference would another day or two make?"

"You worry too much, Melido," Vishnevsky said. "What, are you afraid of Mikhaylov or something?"

Diaz's silence gave him away.

"Look," the Russian went on, "that sorry bastard is on the ropes, and he knows it. He needs your help to save face, not to mention his neck. If anything, he'll be glad to see you."

Diaz wasn't convinced. "I know about the bad blood between you. And he knows that you and I have a history. He could make things hard for me as a way of getting back at you."

Vishnevsky laughed again. "Melido, my friend, I'm not sure which is worse, your paranoia or your imagination. Trust me, everything will go smoothly."

"Suppose you're wrong," Diaz challenged. "What if I show up and find he hasn't laid out the red carpet?"

"Well, if it comes to that, you have three choices," Vishnevsky told the shorter man. "You can let him bully you around, you can stand up to him, or you can bad-mouth me behind my back and ingratiate yourself into his corner."

"If I did that he'd know I was lying."

"Not if you're convincing enough," Vishnevsky insisted. "I can even tell you about a few minor indiscretions you can pass as proof that you'd betray me if he were to make it worth your while. For him *that* would be a far better way of getting back at me."

Diaz looked suddenly squeamish. "You want me to be a double agent."

Vishnevsky raised an eyebrow suggestively. "An exciting prospect, wouldn't you say?"

"I think I can do without that kind of excitement."

"I'm sure if you give it some more thought you'll reconsider. You just need to be more sure of yourself, Melido. I think we need to work on your self-confidence a little."

Glancing over Diaz's shoulder, the Russian gestured to the flight attendant. The young woman smiled and set aside the magazine, revealing her long, shapely legs as she stood up and made her way to the two men. She was Scandinavian, a blond-haired former beauty queen now earning upward of two million dollars with an elite escort agency catering exclusively to high rollers at the Andean Splendor. The Russian's decision to bring her along on the flight had more to do with her sexual prowess than her marginal skills as a flight attendant.

"Can I get you something?" she asked Vishnevsky, speaking in Diaz's native Spanish. Glancing her way, the Bolivian couldn't help but notice her uniform blouse was partially unbuttoned, revealing a faint glimpse of two of the reasons she'd been voted Miss Helsinki.

"I'm going to have a little chat with the pilot, but first I wanted to apologize for not introducing you to my colleague," Vishnevsky said. Nodding at Diaz, he said, "Vanya, this is the famous secret agent James Bond."

Vanya smiled brightly at Diaz. As she bent over to pick up Vishnevsky's tray, Diaz tried to avoid staring at the exposed gleam of the woman's black satin bra. It was, at best, a meager effort.

"It's a pleasure to meet you, Mr. Bond." Vanya balanced the tray with relative ease and dropped to a crouch, riding the hemline of her already short skirt higher up her well-toned thighs. Diaz suddenly found reason to distract himself from the woman's cleavage.

The Bolivian finally stammered, "That's not really my name."

"Of course, how silly of me," Vanya said. "You're on an assignment and using an alias."

Vishnevsky winked at Diaz, then rose from his chair and headed toward the cockpit. Vanya removed Diaz's tray and set it down along with Vishnevsky's on one of the empty seats across the aisle. She took the cloth napkin from Diaz's lap, touching his inner thigh as she did so, and wiped off the table so that she could sit on the edge of it, facing him. She brushed her leg against his and smiled invitingly.

"I've heard so much about you, Mr. Bond," she purred, letting her manicured fingers drop lightly onto the Bolivian's knee, "but I have to confess there's one thing I haven't been able to find out."

Diaz swallowed hard. His skin, head to toe, felt as if it were lined with goose bumps and he shifted once more in his seat to better conceal another part of his anatomy that had reached a heightened state of arousal.

"What's that?" he asked.

As Vanya's fingers crept their way farther up Diaz's knee, she asked him, "I was wondering if you've been initiated into the Mile High Club yet."

CHAPTER TWENTY-FIVE

Glorieta, New Mexico

Franklin Colt had been up the entire night.

When his captors had brought his wife and son to him in the cramped room where he was being held prisoner, they'd also cut him free and replaced the chair he'd been tied to with a musty queen-size mattress and a single coarse, woolen blanket. As a precaution against any notions of escape, the inside shutters had been removed and an inch-thick sheet of plywood had been drilled into place over the lone window. The door had been dead-bolted, and a guard had been posted in the hallway just outside the room. In the near total darkness Colt had huddled close to Gwen beneath the blanket, her back to his chest, his arms reaching around her to help comfort young Frankie.

Once the boy had been lulled to sleep, he and his wife had spoken in whispers. Gwen had tearfully recounted their abduction, filling Colt with grief, fury and no small measure of guilt over the way Jeffrey and Leeland Eppard had been shot and dumped in the Camry's trunk as if they were nothing more than luggage. When Gwen had asked why all this was happening, Colt had been straightforward. He'd told her about

his findings at the reservation and how he'd been in touch
with Walter Upshaw at the Taos Pueblo to warn him against
dealing with Freddy McHale or anyone associated with Global
Holdings. He also confessed to lying to her when he'd said
he was playing poker the previous night. In fact, he'd gone
to the reservation and stolen his way to the rear of the waste
plant, taking photos with his cell phone as evidence of GHC's
secret building of a bunker facility in the mountainside.

In light of what had come to pass the past few hours, he'd
told his wife he now wished he'd never gotten involved, but
Gwen had assured him that he'd done the right thing and
that she would never have expected anything less from the
man she'd chosen to marry. They'd spoken of other things,
including the dire straits they now found themselves in, then
they'd both wept and held each other close, fending off the
cold. Colt had stroked Gwen's hair and hummed to her until
she'd finally drifted off to sleep.

For a long time after that Colt had lain still in the darkness,
listening to his loved ones breathe and feeling their warmth
against him. Although he knew there was a good chance they
might never spend another night together, having Gwen and
Frankie so close had led him to forsake any notion of forcing
their captors to kill him rather than subject himself to a torturous interrogation. Now, if anything, he was determined to do
whatever was humanly possible to save his family, and he was
equally determined to do it without sacrificing his own life.
And so, just as he had during the ride to the javelina farm,
for the next few hours Colt had focused intently on his surroundings, using his senses to seek out any information that
might somehow help him devise a way out of the nightmare
he'd been sucked into.

Gwen had given her husband a sketchy description of the
farm and Colt tried to associate the sounds in relation to the
buildings she'd described. There had been little activity on
the grounds until the past half hour, when he'd heard voices
outside the barn and the clatter of the gate leading to the

javelina pen. Soon after that a car had started up and headed away from the farm. Two men had talked their way to the farmhouse, then one of them had come inside while the other had strode past the boarded window, heading for what Gwen had described as a milk shed.

There were at least two men in the house now in addition to the guard posted outside the door, who, as near as Colt could tell, had carried out his vigil sitting in the chair he had been tied to earlier. Someone was cooking breakfast, and his stomach grumbled as the smell of coffee and bacon permeated the house, competing with the scent of the javelinas. Little of this information seemed to offer much for Colt to work with. Instead, he'd found his greatest encouragement from the sound of the trains passing near the property. While some of them had barreled past at full speed, others had slowed and even stopped briefly, suggesting that they were near a train yard. If there was a way to get away from the house while one of the trains was idling, Colt felt there was a chance his family could clamber aboard and ride their way to freedom. It was a long shot with countless obstacles to surmount, but with few other options, Colt dared to hope that somehow he would be able to do the impossible.

Now, as the morning sunlight tried to pry its way through gaps in the plywood slab blocking the window, Gwen and Frankie both stirred and began to awaken. Colt kissed the back of his wife's head and tousled his son's hair.

"Good morning," he whispered to them. "I'm glad you both got some sleep."

"What about you?" Gwen asked.

"I rested my eyes," Colt said.

"Does that mean you didn't sleep?" Frankie said.

Before Colt could respond, he heard footsteps in the outer hallway. The chair creaked and dragged slightly across the hardwood floor as the guard bolted to his feet. There was an exchange of words as Colt heard a key slide into the deadbolt lock and turn. Colt sat up as the door was pulled open.

Zhenya Ilyin stood in the doorway. He ignored Colt's gaze and stared at Gwen, who'd pulled the blanket around herself as well as her son.

"You and your boy can eat in a few minutes," he told the woman.

"What about my husband?"

"He's coming with me." Ilyin turned to Colt. "We have plans for you."

Outskirts of Santa Fe, New Mexico

AFTER BEING RESCUED FROM Healer's Ravine, Mack Bolan and his former ravine companions had been airlifted to an urgent care facility located just off the highway a half-mile south of the entrance to the reservation. Homicide Detective David Lowe had arranged to have a smaller APD police chopper flown to the facility so that he and the Stony Man crew could swap the bulky Skycrane for something more maneuverable. While they awaited the arrival of the replacement helicopter, Bolan's team had split up to deal with the transients. Jack Grimaldi had accompanied Astro into the clinic and, with Aaron Kurtzman's long-distance assistance, was making the necessary financial arrangements to have the homeless man treated for his bullet wound. Kissinger was similarly befriending Rafe and Leonard, securing registration for them at a franchise hotel across the street. Bolan, meanwhile, leaned against the side of the discarded bathtub that had served as a precarious shuttle cab for him and the transients during the airlift. The Executioner had borrowed Grimaldi's cell phone so that he could touch base with Barbara Price back at the Farm.

"You need to cut down on the water sports out there, soldier," Price told Bolan once he'd accounted for the long hours he'd been missing.

"Gladly."

"Hal sends his regards and apologizes for calling in Carl."

"No apology needed," Bolan replied. "It was the right call. Besides, with everything going on here we'll take all the backup we can get."

Price quickly filled in Bolan on the latest developments, both in Taos and at the reservation. Bolan was intrigued by the news that Alan Orson had been killed in what the local police were convinced was a murder-suicide rampage carried out by Donny Upshaw. Hearing that Cecil Farris had been killed along with the other tribal police officers during the shootout at Franklin Colt's property left the Executioner every bit as unsettled as learning that Gwenyth Colt and her son were missing along with the two men who'd taken responsibility for driving them to safety. The way Price described the forensics team activity near the gateway leading to the property, Bolan feared the foursome had run into foul play, likely care of the same men responsible for the attack he'd barely managed to survive.

When told that Captain Brown had failed to identify him as a federal agent during her aborted press conference, Bolan said, "I guess that would explain why they came gunning for me."

"Maybe," Price said, "but I don't see how she could've made that kind of slipup. It's not like you barged onto the reservation unannounced."

"You're right. I'd like to hear her explanation."

"You're not the only one," Price told him. "Apparently she's getting the third degree by somebody from BIA even as we speak."

"What about this whole thing with the nuclear waste plant here?" Bolan asked. In addition to Rafe's mention of the facility, Kissinger had also told the Executioner about his run-in with a female private investigator Alan Orson had hired to look into possible illegal activity at the site as well as the casino.

"The cyberteam just started in on that," Price informed him. "So far they haven't turned up any red flags other than a laundering scandal at the casino a few years ago."

"Shiraldi Management?"

"Yes," Price said. "We're looking at them as well as the outfit that took over things. Global Holdings. Like I said, nothing's turned up yet but it's still early."

"How about something we can run with?" Bolan asked. "We should be ready to roll within the hour."

"We've had a breakthrough of sorts as far as what happened at the airport," Price said. "Bear went through surveillance camera footage and used Profiler to get a possible ID on the guy who drove you off the road in Colt's Nova."

"Good job."

"His name is Viktor Cherkow," Price said. "He showed up in Interpol's database as a member of Dolgoprudnenskaya."

"Russian Mob," Bolan said. "Moscow, right?"

"That's right," Price said. "He started out running drugs for them but apparently got some kind of promotion when they got into the gambling racket."

"That fits if you consider Colt works at a casino," said Bolan. "New Mexico's a long way from Moscow, though."

"We're still trying to connect the dots on that front," Price told him. "There's nothing on Cherkow after the Russian goverment clamped down on casinos, so it's all speculation for the moment, but we're working on the theory he got himself a forged visa and came stateside to ply his trade."

"And Colt somehow found out about it?"

"Like you said, it fits," Price replied. "Because of the drug angle, we're also looking to see if he can be linked to the heroin they found at Upshaw's place in Taos. For that matter, we're not ruling out that he had a hand in the murders there and framed Donny Upshaw."

"I don't know about that," Bolan said. "It sounds like Up-shaw's father was killed around the same time Colt was abducted in Albuquerque. Cherkow couldn't have been in two places at once."

"Our theory is that he didn't come to the States alone," Price said. "He probably brought a crew with him."

Bolan flashed back to the sequence of events at Albuquerque International as well as his fleeting glimpse of the only shooter he'd encountered during the altercation at Colt's place. It felt like the pieces were beginning to fall into place.

"What does Cherkow look like?" he asked.

Price gave Bolan a quick description based on the surveillance camera still frame Kurtzman had run through Profiler.

"You're right about him having a crew," Bolan told her afterward. "Cherkow was in on my shootout. He nearly put a slug through me right after the bison showed up."

"We thought that might be the case," Price said. "I have to tell you, though. We leaned on BIA for a description of the shooters who were killed there. Cherkow wasn't one of them."

"He got away."

"It looks that way," Price said. "And I don't know about you, but I'm a little wary of seeing 'Russian mobsters' and 'nuclear waste plant' in the same sentence."

Santa Fe, New Mexico

"HE GOT IT WRONG," Viktor Cherkow told Hedeon Barad as he drove Alan Orson's repainted Chevy Silverado along the bowlegged stretch of Interstate 25 running between Glorieta and the state capital. The Russian's face and forearms were bandaged where he'd taken glass and shrapnel hits the previous night. His cracked ribs were taped, and he was wearing a knee brace that extended all the way up to the dressing that had been applied to the hip wound he'd received from Cecil Farris before gunning down the officer. The cumulative pain had been dulled somewhat thanks to the drugs he'd taken before setting out from the javelina farm. The painkillers also filled him with a sense of calm not shared by Hedeon, who was concerned about the way they'd disobeyed Mikhaylov's order that they drive the back roads to dirty up the vehicle before driving into Santa Fe.

"Wrong or not, that's the way he wanted things done," the mechanic protested.

"Think about it," Cherkow reasoned. "If we took the back roads and splashed through every mud puddle along the way, we'd have to clean off the bumpers before we could put on the stickers, right? They'd stand out like sore thumbs. The same with the camper shell. What makes sense is to buy everything first and go on ahead to Algodones. That way any dirt we pick up will spread around evenly."

Hedeon had no ready comeback and rode silently a ways. Cherkow got off at the Old Pecos Road exit and started north toward Quail Run golf course.

"Besides," he finally went on, "it's not like he's following us to make sure things get done his way. If we come back with the heroin and the truck looks the way he expected, that's all he'll care about."

"Let's hope you're right," Hedeon said.

"I'll take bets if you want," Cherkow offered. "Ten to one."

Hedeon had no interest in taking Cherkow up on the wager. He stared quietly out at the golf course, allowing Cherkow some time alone with his thoughts.

Cherkow was glad for the opportunity to make the run to Algodones after tending to the Silverado. Drug deals, after all, were his strong suit, something he had experience at going back to his mobster days in Moscow. Kidnapping and home invasions were matters he'd rather leave to others, especially in wake of the past night's debacles. He hoped Mikhaylov had learned his lesson and would now leave him to concentrate on what he did best.

After a few miles, Cherkow pulled into a suburban strip mall anchored by a used auto parts store boasting the widest selection in all of New Mexico. When they went inside, Hedeon brought along the attaché case containing the money for the heroin. Cherkow led the way, limping slightly as they roamed the aisles, finally tracking down three different camper shells compatible with the pickup. Cherkow opted for the one with the most wear. When he pointed out a nearby spinner rack loaded with bumper stickers, Hedeon brought up Mikhaylov's insistence that they make that purchase at a separate store. Cherkow rolled his eyes and glanced around the store.

"Funny, I don't see him anywhere," he scoffed. "What, you think he's going to ask for receipts? I'll give you twenty-to-one odds on that."

Again Hedeon balked at taking the bet.

Cherkow paid for the shell in advance, arranging to have it installed while he and Hedeon skimmed through the sticker selection. They settled on a University of New Mexico sticker, one reading Support Your Local Police and another featuring an American flag emblazoned with the words Don't Tread On Me. Afterward, they walked to a Mexican restaurant at the far end of the strip mall and ordered breakfast to go. By the time they returned to the Silverado, one of the store employees had just finished securing the camper shell to the pickup's rear bed.

"You're all set," he told them.

"Any problems?" Cherkow asked.

The employee, a Hispanic man in his fifties with the name Ozzie stitched on his shirt pocket, shook his head.

"Nope. It fits like a glove."

When the worker stayed put looking the men over, Cherkow sighed and fished a wadded-up dollar bill from his pants.

"Here," he said. "Good job."

"Thanks."

Ozzie headed off. Cherkow and Hedeon got in the Silverado. Cherkow rolled his eyes as he started the engine.

"Guy expects a tip for doing his job?" he wisecracked. "What's he think this is, a casino?"

Hedeon indulged Cherkow with some token laughter as backed out of their parking spot.

"Guess what?" Cherkow told him. "Just for you, I'm going to follow the boss's orders and drive a few blocks before we put on the stickers."

OSWALDO GONZALEZ PEERED out from inside the store as the Silverado pulled away, then took out his cell phone as he beelined down a long aisle stacked on either side with used hubcaps. By the time he reached the employee lounge, he'd dialled 9-1-1 and gotten through to a dispatcher.

"My name is Ozzie Gonzalez," he said, "I work at the Value Auto Part store on Riddoch Road, and I was just installing a camper shell on a 2008 Chevy Silverado some men bought here. It's dark green, but it looks like a new paint job. By accident I nicked off a little paint and underneath it's white."

"What's the reason for your call?" the dispatcher asked with the tired voice of someone who'd long lost patience with callers seemingly unaware that 911 was to be dialed only in the case of extreme emergencies.

"I read in the paper about some murders up in Taos last night," Ozzie said. "There was something about a missing white Silverado."

CHAPTER TWENTY-SIX

Rosqui Pueblo, New Mexico

Police Captain Tina Brown paced angrily inside her office on the second story of RTPF's headquarters, located adjacent to the Roaming Bison Casino. From her window she could see the casino's main entrance as well as its half-filled, three-acre parking area. Just across road, safely off the reservation, much of the media throng she had addressed earlier had reassembled along the shoulder. Several new crews from the major networks had arrived, as well, and at least two reporters were giving live updates, backs turned to the road so that the casino would feature prominently in the background while they rehashed the events of the past few hours. Brown was certain that included somewhere in the reports would be sound bites from her press conference as well as a few veiled digs at the way she'd abruptly ended her remarks and ordered everyone's vehicles searched as they were leaving the property.

The media circus, however, was only a minor aggravation compared to the heat Brown was receiving on other fronts. Pueblo Governor Charles Stuart had accused the captain of antagonizing the press for no good reason and demanded that she make some sort of conciliatory gesture. The sentiment had been echoed by Michael Fisk, the BIA Supervisory Criminal Investigator who'd heard the press conference on his car radio while en route to the reservation. In addition to insinuating himself into the investigation of the shootout at Franklin Colt's estate, Fisk had informed Brown that there would be also be an inquiry into the abbreviated skirmish at Healer's Ravine insofar as it involved a federal agent Brown had misidentified as a suspected perpetrator. After all, Fisk had reasoned, the agent had received security clearance before entering the reservation and had been accompanied to Colt's residence by several of Brown's own officers.

Brown had defended herself on the latter issue, claiming that she'd been off duty at the time and that proper protocols hadn't been followed when the agent had received his clearance. Neither Brown nor Fisk had yet been able to question the agent, though they'd managed to catch a fleeting glimpse of him as he was being airlifted from the ravine along with three transients involved in the confrontation.

And then there was Frederik Mikhaylov, who'd pressured Brown to dispatch two of her undercover officers to Algodones to help set up one of his own men as the supposed mastermind behind the attack at Colt's home. With Russell Combs already off the reservation tailing the mystery woman Brown had spotted during the press conference, that meant she now had three officers taking the law into their own hands outside the pueblo's jurisdiction.

And soon I'll be the fourth, Brown thought to herself.

The woman was still staring out the window when one of her officers showed up with the file she'd been waiting for. She dismissed the officer, sat down at her desk and began to go through the file, which contained documentation on all drug-related arrests Franklin Colt had made at the casino over the past six years. Setting aside those involving patrons caught smoking marijuana, she was left with only three arrests involving other substances. Of those, two involved heroin. One of the arrestees was still doing time at the state penintentary.

The other, Marcus Walker, had been released less than two months ago, having had his sentence reduced for cooperating with authorities in an unrelated investigation. His parole forms listed his current residence as a halfway house in a run-down neighborhood on the outskirts Pueblo Santo Domingo, less than thirty miles away off the highway leading to Albuquerque. Brown managed a half smile when she turned to the offender's booking mug shot. Marcus Walker was black.

"Perfect," she whispered to herself.

Brown unlocked her desk file drawer and pulled out a photo of Viktor Cherkow she'd earlier downloaded and printed from a file sent to her by Mikhaylov. She paper-clipped Cherkow's photo to Walker's and slipped them into her purse, then pulled out a dog-eared, palm-size address book filled with various contacts she'd cultivated over her years on the police force. She thumbed through the book for the number of Buddy Carman, a freewheeling entrepreneur who ran a series of roadside stands near Pueblo Santo Domingo. Carman didn't pick up when she called, so she left a message for him to get back to her as soon as possible. She stressed that it was urgent.

There was still one piece of unfinished business for Brown to attend to. On her laptop the captain had already composed a press release in which she'd buried a halfhearted apology to the media amid news that no new evidence had been found at Colt's property, and that Missing Persons reports had been filed for both Gwenyth Colt and the family's two-year-old son, Franklin Jr. She'd additionally mentioned a joint resolution just drawn by Stuart and Roaming Bison's Public Relations Director Elizabeth Penbrooks offering a two-million-dollar reward for the safe return of all three Colt family members and an additional million for information leading to the arrest of those responsible for Colt's abduction at Albuquerque International and the subsequent shootout on his property.

Once she'd proofread the statement and softened her mea culpa even further, Brown printed out the document. She would have copies run off downstairs and then passed out to the reporters across the street in lieu of her holding another press conference. She wasn't about to make that mistake again.

Brown was shutting down her computer when her cell phone rang. It was Buddy Carman.

"What's up, Captain?"

"I'm glad you called back," Brown told him. "I was just heading out your way and wondered if we could meet. It's important."

"With you it's always something important," Carman chuckled. "How about a social call now and then?"

"I'm saving that for a special occasion."

Carman laughed again, then told Brown, "I'm where I always am this time of day. Come on down."

"I'll be there in about an hour."

"What's so important this time?"

"I'll tell you more when I get there," Brown told the man, glancing over the reward offer in her press release, "but it's a way to make some easy money."

CHAPTER TWENTY-SEVEN

Stony Man Farm, Virgina

"I don't know about you," Hal Brognola told Barbara Price as he huddled with her at the workstation she'd appropriated in the Annex Computer Room, "but I'm starting to think Striker must've been a cat in a former life."

Price managed a smile. "More like a litter of cats," she said. "I think he's used up a few more than nine lives."

"Let's try not to keep track." The big Fed gave his mission controller a reassuring pat on the shoulder then turned his focus to the cybercrew.

"How are we coming, gang?"

"I just finished running a check on the Rosqui waste facility," Huntington Wethers reported. "It's been up and running almost ten years now. There's been the usual political controversy, but its record's clean. In fact, most of those years they've gotten higher inspection ratings than any other plant in the country."

"How up-to-date are the ratings?" Brognola asked. "Do they cover this new outfit?"

Wethers nodded. "DOE and the Nuclear Safety Commission stepped in for a few months during the transition, then turned things over to Global Holdings. Same clean record the past six quarters."

"What about GHC?" Brognola asked Carmen Delahunt. "Do you have a lowdown on them yet?"

"I can give you the once-over-lightly if that'll help," Delahunt offered.

"That'd be a start."

Brognola raided his trench coat for a cigar tube. He'd long given up smoking cigars but rolling one between his fingers or chewing on one remained a benign way to work off stress.

"They're headquartered in Antwerp," Delahunt reported, "and most of the Board of Directors is made up of EU heavyweights. Top dog there is Evgenii Danilov. He's Russian-born but has been out of the country for years. He's got six homes, none of them anywhere you'd associate with Moscow."

"All the same," Brognola said, "if he's got any motherland in his blood, it's worth seeing if we can tie him somehow to this Cherkow fellow."

"I think I'm already there," Aaron Kurtzman called out from his wheelchair. He was poised before his computer, coffee cup in one hand, mouse trapped beneath the other. "I was scanning headlines while waiting on a download and saw something about that casino attack in Bolivia."

"Alfredo Cavour's place?" Brognola asked.

"Yeah, the Inca Treasure," Kurtzman said. "ELN has taken credit and it fits their agenda."

"Not to mention their M.O.," Akira Tokaido ventured.

"What's this have to do with Danilov or Cherkow?" Brognola wanted to know.

"I'm getting to that," Kurtzman said. "Seeing as I already had casinos on the brain, I did a little digging to see if there's been a Russian influx in South America there since the Russian clampdown. Check out what I came up with. Screen eight."

The assembled Stony Man team directed its attention to the far wall where, for the second time in as many hours, Kurtzman called up a mug shot from one of his international crime databases. The man on screen eight was gaunt in the face with a full head of dark brown hair.

"Dmitri Vishnevsky," Kurtzman said. "This is an old shot from a few years ago when he was blackballed at several casinos in Moscow for counting cards at blackjack."

"Nerd City," Tokaido said. "All he's missing is a pocket protector."

"That's probably how he wanted people to see him back then," Kurtzman said. "At any rate, there's intel on him cleaning out these other casinos while he was on payroll at the Regal Splendor."

"The same casino Cherkow worked at?" Delahunt queried.

Kurtzman nodded. "Yeah. And we have a present-day photo."

"Hardly even looks like the same guy," Brognola observed.

"He's now going by the name Dominic Fishciel," Kurtzman explained. "He helps run the biggest casino in Santa Cruz and has offered a reward for bringing in whoever masterminded the attack on the Inca treasure."

"Okay, I'm following you so far," said Brognola. "You're saying Dolgoprudnenskaya has its fingers in this other casino?"

"I'm just about to look into that," Kurtzman replied. "Obviously, if they're invested there it'll be under the table so I'll need to dig deep."

"Go for it," Brognola said. "You might as well check to see if GHC's hiding in the woodwork while you're at it."

"If you're looking for a shortcut," Wethers suggested, "Bolivia probably has some sort of gaming commission that'll have photo IDs of all casino employees. You could cross-reference with the databases where you got the shot of Cherkow and see if it turns up any of his people."

Kurtzman gave Wethers a thumbs-up. "Good thinking, Hunt."

"I'll rattle a few cages with CIA and Interpol down in Santa Cruz," Brognola said. "If they don't have something on Vishnevsky already, I'll see if they can divert someone over from the bombing investigation."

"You think the Russians might've had a hand in the attack?" Delahunt asked.

"Can't rule it out," Brognola said. "It's their M.O. as much as ELN's."

"Well," Delahunt replied, "if we're right about them being in on this whole New Mexico business, it's pretty clear they don't mind killing a few innocents."

"True," Price said, "and that doesn't take into account the people we've still got missing out there." She was speaking about the Colt family as well as Jeffrey and Leeland Eppard.

"You got that right," Tokaido said. "And I hate to say it, but the longer we go without a ransom demand or some kind of contact, the less I'm liking their chances."

Glorieta, New Mexico

AFTER ALL THE HOURS he'd been held captive in the boarded-up room, it took a while for Franklin Colt's eyes to adjust to the bright New Mexico morning. Only a few wispy clouds marred the clear blue sky, and the sun beat down on him as he sat on a tree trunk gouged from its use as a chopping block for the pile of firewood neatly stacked a few yards to his right. There was an ax propped next to the woodpile, but one of Frederik Mikhaylov's men was standing next to it, armed with a considerably more potent Bizon 2 submachine gun. Even if the man hadn't been there, Colt's hands had once again been duct-taped behind his back and his ankles were similarly bound, as well. They were in the narrow clearing that separated the farmhouse from the barn, and moments ago Zhenya Ilyin and another of Mikhaylov's underlings, Yuri Reinhart, had emerged from the nearby walk-in freezer lugging the large javelina Mikhaylov had put a bullet through the night before. Long dead and half-frozen, the javelina still gave off its trademark stench, turning Colt's stomach as he watched the two Russians set the beast down at the base of a well-used engine hoist. Two large meat hooks had been affixed to the crane's boom. Once Reinhart had lowered them to the ground, he and Ilyin skewered the javelina's hindquarters, then used a hand crank to raise the creature off the ground. They stopped cranking once the javelina was fully suspended so that it swayed slightly on the boom, upside down, its snout facing the ground.

"You wouldn't believe it from their smell," Reinhart told Colt when he noticed the prisoner's discomfort, "but if you barbecue them just right they don't taste half-bad."

Colt presumed the barbecuing was done in the large pit that lay between the hoist and the woodpile. The pit was surrounded by small boulders and nearly a dozen thick chunks of mesquite had been stacked in the center atop a layer of muddied ash from previous fires.

"They just need a little tenderizing," Ilyin quipped.

"And you're in luck," Reinhart told Colt. "Today we're going to try out a new way to do the tenderizing."

The two Russians shared a laugh and the man guarding Colt joined in. Colt didn't understand the joke. For that matter, he was unclear what the men had in store for him. He hadn't been questioned on the way from the farmhouse and while the men had bound him they'd contented themselves to converse in their native Russian.

Colt was still pondering his fate when Frederik Mikhaylov stepped out of the barn and slowly strode toward them across the dirt parking area.

"Did you tell him what we have in store for him?" Mikhaylov asked his counterparts.

Reinhart shook his head. "We thought he'd enjoy being surprised."

"I'm sure you're right."

The Russian circled the woodpile and disappeared for a moment behind the large walk-in freezer. When he returned he was carrying what appeared to be a bulky wet suit layered with thin strips of what looked like black plastic. Colt had seen the outfit before; it was the prototype for Alan Orson's thermal body armor.

"Recognize this?" Mikhaylov said.

Colt glared at Mikhaylov. "Where's Orson?"

"You're just like your lovely wife," the Russian responded. "You seem to think you're here to ask questions instead of answering them."

"I've already told your men," Colt said. "I have no idea what it is you think I'm supposed to tell you."

"Maybe I'll help you out in a few minutes," Mikhaylov said. "In the meantime, excuse me, but we want to see what kind of job your friend did with this monkey suit of his."

Mikhaylov turned his back to Colt. With Reinhart's help, he draped the armored suit around the javelina and guided the dead beast's front hooves through the suit's pant legs. Thick, flat strips of wiring dangled from the pant leg cuffs to a pair of thin, rubberized-looking boots. Similarly, a set of gloves were attached to the upper sleeves, which the Russians allowed to dangle freely rather than try to fit around the meat hooks. The suit had Velcro straps as well as a zippered front. The javelina's girth was too wide for them to zip the suit up so they made do with the straps. When they were finished, the men held the swine until it was still, then took a step back and surveyed their handiwork.

"It looks like a dead superhero," Ilyin observed. "A dead, fat superhero."

"Porky the Wonder Swine," Mikhaylov deadpanned. "Doesn't have much of a ring to it."

Reinhart gestured at Colt and told Mikhaylov, "He's already heard the tenderizer jokes."

"I see," Mikhaylov said. "Then we might as well get to the punch line."

The Russian gestured for the guard's submachine gun, then took a few more steps back and leveled the weapon at the javelina. When he pulled the trigger, gunshots echoed across the farm and the slain pig resumed swaying as the Bizon's 79 mm rounds slammed into the armored suit drawn tightly around its underbelly. Colt finally understood the tenderizing jokes and found himself even further despising his captors.

Mikhaylov returned the subgun and followed Reinhart and Ilyin back to the engine hoist. They murmured to one another as they looked over the armored suit and ran their fingers over the plating. Colt's view was blocked, and it wasn't until they'd undone the straps and pulled the suit open that he was able to see that while the javelina's exposed underbelly showed signs of discoloration where it'd been shot, none of the rounds had penetrated the armor.

"I'm impressed," Mikhaylov told Colt. "Your friend was obviously very talented."

Colt's heart sank at hearing Orson referred to in the past tense. He stared at Mikhaylov but said nothing.

Reinhart and Ilyin began to peel the suit off the javelina. Mikhaylov gestured at the guard, who stepped forward and flicked open a switchblade, using its sharp edge to cut away the duct tape binding Colt's wrists and ankles. All the while he kept the subgun trained on Colt's head. As an added precaution, Mikhaylov drew his Makarov and pointed it at the prisoner.

"Don't get too comfortable," Mikhaylov told Colt. "You'll be bound up again once you change into the suit."

"You just saw that it works," Colt countered. "What's the point in testing it on me?"

"We still need to test its thermal capacity," Mikhaylov responded.

Reinhart brought the suit over and handed it to Colt, grinning. "Sorry about the smell."

Once the guard had pulled off Colt's boots, Mikhaylov told the man, "Go ahead and put it on. I have a little more work to do with our friend Porky."

The Russian holstered his pistol and reached for a sheath strapped to his thigh, pulling out a short-bladed skinning knife.

"Years ago I worked in a slaughterhouse," he told Colt. "I haven't lost my touch, but I like to keep in practice now and then."

As Colt slowly fitted himself into the armored suit, he watched with horrified fascination while Mikhaylov took his knife to the javelina. With swift ease, the Russian made a series of strategic incisions, each time dragging the razor-sharp blade in a neat line. In less than forty-five seconds, he'd deftly skinned the swine's hide and pulled it free of the carcass.

"Need a new wallet?" the Russian asked Colt. "Or a belt maybe?"

Colt ignored the wisecracks. "I still don't know why you're holding me," he said, doing his best to sound reasonable. "Why don't you just let us go?"

"For starters, you haven't tested the suit yet," Mikhaylov said. "Now zip up and put on the booties. The gloves, too."

Colt slowly drew the chest zipper closed. "What kind of themal test can you do here? It's not even cold out."

"No, but it's a bit cooler in the freezer," Mikhaylov said. "We have it set to minus five degrees Fahrenheit. Not quite as cold as Siberia in the dead of winter, but it will do. We have a lot of meat stored, but you'll have room to be comfortable.

And we left the suit out in the sun an hour longer than the minimum needed for the thermal lines. You'll be—how do you say it?—toasty."

Colt pulled the suit's hood over his head. It fit snugly and, like the suit itself, had an exoskeleton made of armored panels comprised of depleted uranium, ceramic and a few other compounds Orson had made a point never to disclose to him. The hood's inside lining contained a number of shoestring-thin tubes that Colt guessed were conduits for the heat put out by solar generators built into the suit's four-inch-wide belt.

"It looks better on him than the pig," Ilyin commented once Colt had finished suiting up.

Mikhaylov handed the javelina skin to Ilyin then told Colt, "Before we send you off to our little Gulag, I meant to ask you—how much do you figure your wife weighs?"

"Why do you want to know?"

"I'm guessing maybe a hundred pounds," Mikhaylov said. "About the same as Porky here."

With that, the Butcher calmly thrust his knife into the javelina, just below the beast's loins. He made a lateral cut from one leg to the other, then bent over and made a similar incision just below the creature's throat. Then, midway across the latter cut, he planted the knife and drew it upward back to where he'd started, creating two near-identical flaps. When he pulled the flaps aside, half the javelina's entrails spilled out and tumbled into the mud at Mikhaylov's feet. His demonstration completed, he turned back to Colt, no longer smiling.

"Once you come out of the icebox," he said, "it will be your wife on the hoist. She'll still be alive. For how long will depend on what you've decided to tell us. A good place to start would be with this…."

Reaching into his pocket, Mikhaylov withdrew the prepaid cell phone Colt had used to send his incriminating evidence to the late Walter Upshaw.

"The time for playing dumb has passed, my friend," Mikhaylov told Colt. "We're onto you. All that's left is for you to fill in a few of the blanks."

CHAPTER TWENTY-EIGHT

Outskirts of Santa Fe, New Mexico

"'Didn't follow protocol'?" Jack Grimaldi said, referring to Captain Brown's explanation for having sent her men to track down Bolan as a possible instigator of the shootout at Franklin Colt's property. "That's the best she could come up with?"

The Stony Man pilot had just finished checking Astro into the emergency clinic and returned to the parking lot, where Bolan was being briefed by BIA investigator Michael Fisk, an overweight, dough-faced man in his midthirties who looked as if he spent far too much of his workday behind a desk. Kissinger was still at the hotel across the street and Detective Lowe had moved to the other side of the parking lot with the APD officer who'd helped rescue Bolan from Healer's Ravine. They were turning over the Skycrane to the pilot who'd just arrived with one of the department's Bell 206 JetRangers.

"That's almost verbatim what I told her," Fisk told Grimaldi. "She's sticking to it, though. She wants me to cut her some slack, too, because she had a lot of info coming at her from all directions."

"And she was erring on the side of caution," Bolan said.

"That's her story at any rate."

"What else did you turn up at Colt's place?" Grimaldi wanted to know.

"Not much, really," Fisk confessed, "though we're pretty sure there was a carjacking at the main gate. We've got an ABP out for the car. It's a 2006 Camry."

Detective Lowe had made his way back to the group in time to overhear the last exchange.

"Speaking of APBs," he said, raising his voice to be heard over the drone of the Skycrane, which was lifting off for the return flight back to Albuquerque, "we might've just caught a break on Orson's pickup."

"It's turned up?" Bolan asked.

"Right down the road, provided it's the right truck." Lowe quickly related the dispatch call that had come in while he was handling the copter switch, concluding, "The license number the guy gave us doesn't match up with Orson's, but you gotta figure if they went to the trouble of repainting the thing they probably swapped plates, too."

"They haven't been taken in yet?" Grimaldi said.

Lowe shook his head. "SFPD has all units on alert and they're looking to set up checkpoints at all the highway ramps. Unless you guys have other plans, I figured we'd take the bird up and do a little aerial surveillance."

"Let's do it," Bolan said.

He turned to Fisk. "We've got a guy taking care of some business across the street. Any chance you can fill him in when he gets back?'

"As long as he shows up before I finish the report I need to send out," Fisk said. "Once that's done I still have that mess up in Taos to deal with."

"He should be here any minute," Bolan said. "Just have him wait for us."

"Done."

Bolan and Grimaldi followed Lowe to the JetRanger. The other cop had already caught a ride back on the Skycrane.

"I take it you've flown one of these before," Lowe said to Grimaldi.

"If it has wings, I've flown it," Grimaldi replied.

As the men piled into the chopper, Bolan asked, "Did the guy who called nine-one-one give a description of the men in the truck?"

"Sure did," Lowe replied, taking a seat in back so Bolan could ride alongside Grimaldi. Once he'd described the suspect who'd tipped the auto parts employee for installing the camper shell, the two Stony Men exchanged a look. Grimaldi said what they were both thinking.

"Sounds like our boy Cherkow."

Santa Fe, New Mexico

MELIDO DIAZ WAS STILL beaming as he entered the terminal after disembarking from Dmitri Vishnevsky's company jet at Santa Fe Municipal Airport. Gone was his usual hunch-shouldered tentativeness and his face was plastered with the sort of sly, confident smile he found befitting of a world-class secret agent. To his left, through the tall windows of the terminal, he could see the airfield he'd just departed, and as he watched the Citation X loft itself from the runway, Diaz's smile widened at the memory of his mile-high romp with the lovely Vanya, whose perfume still clung to him like some magical talisman. So lost was the Bolivian in his rapture that he paid little heed to the pair of uniformed officers striding briskly past him with an air of decided urgency. As they headed toward the gate through which he'd just entered the terminal, Diaz resumed sauntering the other way.

There were two people already lined up at the rental counter, a situation that would have normally filled Diaz with impatience and frustration. But the inventor's ebullient mood carried the day and he calmly waited his turn, reflecting on an advertising poster for eye surgery taking up much of the wall to his immediate right. The procedure was one he'd long frowned upon as vain and gratuitous, but he now found it to be an inviting prospect. Yes, he thought to himself, getting rid of his glasses would be a good thing. And exercise. Yes, he would have to definitely make exercise a part of his daily regimen once he settled into his new life as a valued consultant for Russia's SVR. It would be yet another part of his anticipated makeover, a transformation that he felt would ensure that the next time he chose to visit a casino and try his luck at roulette, beautiful women would flock to his side, just like they did with James Bond.

Having unleashed these and other fantasies of his bygone adolescence, it was little wonder that when the Bolivian finally made his way to the counter he found reason to take issue with the Honda Civic that had been reserved for him by Vishnevsky's personal secretary.

"This won't do," Diaz said calmly, eyeing the young woman across the counter as if considering her as a possible consort. "What do you have in the way of sports cars?"

"I'm sorry, sir," the woman told him, "but your reservation is for only a compact."

"Then I guess we'll just have to change the reservation, won't we?" Diaz replied. "It's a nice day for a convertible, don't you think?"

Before the woman could respond, Diaz felt a hand on his shoulder. He turned to find the two officers standing before him. One of them was hovering his hand just above the pistol dangling from his waist holster.

"We need to have a word with you, sir," one of the men told him. With a jerk of his head he indicated the hallway branching off from the terminal's main walkway. "If you'll come with us, please?"

"What's the meaning of this?" Diaz asked. Already his elaborate facade was beginning to crumble.

"Just come along, if you would," the other officer replied. "And I'd advise against any sudden moves."

With each wavering step Diaz took away from the rental counter, his illusions of grandeur diminished exponentially. By the time he'd been led to the hallway and asked to spread-eagle himself against the nearest wall, gone was any pretense of bravado. In its place, the Bolivian found himself trembling with fear and a wariness that he was about to void his bladder.

"The jet you just got off," the first officer asked. "According to its manifest, it's bound for Colorado Springs. Is that really where it's headed?"

Diaz tried to rally himself and think of some snappy comeback, but even as he was grasping for lies he found himself blurting, "No, he's heading for Taos."

CHAPTER TWENTY-NINE

Taos, New Mexico

Carl Lyons was wrapping up the first leg of his tour of the crime scenes he'd viewed earlier from the air while flying in to Taos's Municipal Airport. Conferring with the investigatory team at Alan Orson's estate, the Able Team leader had just been apprised that there were no new developments at the site and that everything continued to support the notion that Donny Upshaw, either alone or with help, had killed both Orson and his dog and stolen the bulk of the inventor's work. As far as both the Taos police and county sheriff's department were concerned, at this point the only thing in need of verification was the sequence of events. The hope was that an autopsy would be able to establish that the terrier had been killed during the time that, according to Orson's blog, he'd been off running errands. If Orson's own death could be pinpointed as having occurred more than twelve minutes later, after the time of the blog entry, the authorities figured it would refute the idea that the blog had been forged by someone attempting to frame the inventor's groundskeeper.

"You can't be serious," Lyons told county sheriff's Officer Eric Gibson, a dimple-chinned, beefy man with retro sideburns. The two men were standing in Orson's driveway between Gibson's police cruiser and Lyons's rental Impala. "Narrow down a time of death to within twelve minutes? Hell, without witnesses you're lucky if you can pin it down to within a few hours."

"You're probably right," Gibson conceded, "but if you ask me, it's still pretty open-shut that Donny's our guy."

"What about the computer?" Lyons said, launching into the alternative theory the cyberteam back at the Farm was working on. "If Donny cleaned out the place of everything worthwhile, why'd he leave behind the computer?"

"Beats me," Gibson said. "The guy was on smack, right? Who knows, maybe he wasn't thinking straight. Maybe he had a one-track mind and was only thinking about the inventions. If that's what he was pawning for the heroin, it kinda makes sense, don't you think?"

"I've heard better," Lyons said. "And speaking of witnesses, have you talked to all the shop owners within a ten-minute drive of here? Did any of them see Orson out running errands like the blog says?"

"We're working on it," Gibson said. "Canvassing can take a while."

"Good luck with that," Lyons said.

"Look, don't get me wrong here," Gibson said. "It's not like we're trying to railroad the guy or anything. It's just that we cops have a saying—if it looks like a duck, walks like a duck and sounds like a duck, it's probably a duck."

"Actually, I used to be a cop myself in L.A.," Lyons replied. "We had the same saying. The thing is, we dealt with enough cases in Hollywood to know that sometimes what passes for a duck is either a prop or special effects, so it pays to look beyond the obvious."

"Tell ya what, then," Gibson countered. "Give us another suspect and we'll start looking for him."

Lyons had yet to hear that Viktor Cherkow had possibly been spotted in Santa Fe, but he'd already received clearance from the Farm to divulge any findings that might help get to the truth of matters, so he quickly laid out the notion of a possible link between the previous night's events and clandestine activity taking place at Rosqui Pueblo. Gibson listened intently. By the time Lyons finished, the police officer's initial skepticism had been overcome by a sense of intrigue.

"It's all pretty damn convoluted," he said, "but in a screwy way it all kinda fits."

"A few more breaks and hopefully it'll tie up a little neater."

"Wish I could help," Gibson said, "but I gotta be honest, if we've got some Russian mobsters hiding out in Taos, they're doing a damn good job of it."

THE SVR SAFE HOUSE IN Taos was far more inauspicious than the javelina farm serving as Frederik Mikhaylov's base of operations in Glorieta. Located on a weed-choked quarter acre at the end of a dirt road, the two-story, four-bedroom log cabin was shared by Vladik Barad and the two other agents who'd lent a hand cleaning out Alan Orson's workshop after the inventor's murder. Their Dodge Caravan was parked in front of the cabin along with a nondescript Saturn. The surrounding lot was bordered, like many properties throughout the city, with a fence made of seven-foot-high cedar latillas tethered with bailing wire. The original owners had erected the fence to keep out coyotes but Barad and the others found it did an equally good job of keeping their two Rottweilers from getting loose and terrorizing the neighbors.

The three men were in the cabin's upstairs all-purpose room, smoking cigarettes as they sat around a slab of drywall laid across a snooker table, playing a card game. Two large picture windows flooded the room with light and gave the men a near-panoramic view of the surrounding neighborhood as well as the wide, open field that stretched northward toward the Rio Grande. Told to forgo any attempts to raid the police impound lot and wait for Petenka Tramelik's return, the men were in the grips of boredom.

"I say we should just close down here and join everyone else down south," Franz Khartyr complained. "More is bound to be happening there."

"Like getting killed?" scoffed Bertrand Gustavo. "Me, I can do without being run over by a hundred buffalo."

"They're called bison," Barad said, dispensing with the last of his cards, leaving it to his colleagues to determine who would be left holding a hand.

Gustavo laughed. "That's America for you. You have to be politically correct even when you talk about their fucking animals!"

"We need to stay here and help this Vishnevsky idiot try to talk the Indians out of their uranium mines," Barad reminded Khartyr. He glanced at his watch, then went on, "Once Tramelik gets here we're supposed to head to the airport and pick him up so we can show him the lay of the land. We also need to see if Orson's helicopter is still being stored there."

"Why didn't they just put Tramelik in charge?" Khartyr made a face as he was forced to draw more cards. "He already knows his way around. Why bring in some stranger?"

"Vishnevsky just blew up a casino in Bolivia so suddenly he's a big shot," Gustavo guessed. "We only killed a couple guys so that makes us amateurs by comparison. This is how they think back in Moscow."

"I still don't see why we need access to the mines here, anyway," said Khartyr as he replenished his drink. "There's plenty of uranium in all those fuel rods at the waste plant. Why not just use those?"

"Because the regulatory agencies keep track of the fuel rods," Barad stated. "You think we can just siphon them off and replace them with colored sticks without them noticing?"

"If we start hauling uranium out of the mines they'll be regulating that, too, won't they?"

"Not on-site," Barad reasoned. "We'd do our own accounting. For every hundred pounds of uranium we take out, we'd only report the fifty pounds that goes straight to the waste plant. The rest gets diverted to the bunkers they're building."

"And there it gets processed into plutonium," Gustavo reminded Khartyr, playing a few cards without having to draw from the pile. "And the plutonium winds up in warheads that we'll use to blow up more than just some casino. How many vodka gimlets did you drink when we went over all this our first week here?"

Khartyr grinned as he raised his effervescent cocktail. "I take this only for medicinal purposes on orders from my doctor."

Gustavo laughed. "Would that be Dr. Smirnoff or Dr. Popov?"

Khartyr shook his head. "Dr. Absolut. He is the Vishnevsky of doctors when it comes to my condition."

Gustavo and Barad smirked at each other. Khartyr, meanwhile, was forced once again to go to the pile and add to his playing hand. When it was Gustavo's turn, he quickly played out the last of his cards.

"How appropriate," he said, ending the game. "You are the Fool, Khartyr. The Fool!"

Khartyr swore and guzzled down his drink. Out in the yard, the two Rottweilers began yelping and charged past the Saturn to where another car had pulled up to the gate blocking the driveway. Barad stood and peered down, barely able to glimpse the man behind the wheel of a familiar-looking Land Rover.

"It's Tramelik," he told the others. "Get your things so we can go meet our new czar."

IT TOOK LYONS LESS THAN ten minutes to drive from Alan Orson's estate to the gateway where Walter Upshaw had been gunned down while retrieving his mail. Gibson had followed the Able Team leader in his squad car. The county sheriff's department had a cooperative relationship with the Taos tribal police, and Lyons's security clearance consisted of little more than being introduced by Gibson, showing his Justice Department ID and shaking hands with PTPD's Lieutenant Andrew Zimmer, a handsome, well-groomed man in his early forties who, with the help of two fellow officers, was wrapping up his investigation of the site.

"Quick question, Eric," Zimmer said to Gibson as he handed back Lyons's ID. "Did you guys happen to find a computer or cell phone in Donny's car?"

"Not that I know of," Gibson replied.

"Could you check?" Zimmer asked. "Walt's place was broken into at some point before we got there, and so far that's all we can figure is missing."

"The bridge was going to be my next stop," Gibson said. "I'll head out and give you a holler back if need be."

"That'd be great. Thanks."

"I'll catch up with you there," Lyons told Gibson.

Gibson nodded and headed back to his cruiser, leaving Lyons to trade intel with Zimmer. The lieutenant had known both Upshaws and was still trying to make sense of the men's deaths. As such, he was relieved to hear that Lyons had doubts about Donny's guilt.

"I know how it looks," Zimmer told Lyons, "and everybody knows there were hard feelings between him and his old man. But killing him? I don't know, I just don't see it. Especially after checking out Walt's place."

"Why's that?" Lyons wondered.

Zimmer pointed at the driveway extending past the gateway. "It's nearly a mile and a half from here up to the house, and I can tell you for a fact that Walt always had this gate shut and locked when he was off the property. I'm just as sure

Donny didn't have a key card, so there's no way he could've driven up there beforehand. And I don't see him hopping the gate and hiking all the way up there in the rain, even if it turns out he wasn't on smack. It's a hell of a walk."

"I'm with you," Lyons said, "but just to play devil's advocate, could Donny have driven up after he killed his father? The gate was open then."

"Not likely, I'd say," Zimmer replied. "The driveway dead-ends at the house. The only way out would've been to come back down the same way. With his dad here dead in a wrecked car the whole time, it would've been too risky. Anybody driving by could've seen the car while he was up there and called us."

"I've been getting a lot of 'guys on smack don't think straight,'" Lyons said.

"I wouldn't argue that, but still, I don't think Donny did it," Zimmer said. "Here, let me show you something else."

Zimmer led Lyons to his black-and-white and reached into the front seat, where several pieces of evidence had been placed in plastic bags. The lieutenant showed Lyons the one containing the mail Upshaw had dropped after being shot.

"A boot print," Lyons said, noting a muddy tread mark on one of the larger envelopes.

"When Donny went over the bridge he was wearing moccasins," Zimmer said.

"No treads."

Zimmer nodded. "I know there's a chance somebody else might've left the print, but I'm guessing it's the perp."

Lyons shifted his gaze from the evidence to the mailbox and the shrubs that lay beyond it. "Did you check around the bushes for more prints?"

"If there were prints, the rain got to them," Zimmer said. "There are a few snapped branches where he was probably lying in wait, but it's nothing to go on."

Lyons was on his way to take a closer look when his cell phone bleated. He excused himself and moved away from Zimmer to take the call.

It was Aaron Kurtzman, calling from the Farm.

By the time Lyons had received the latest update and hung up, Eric Gibson had pulled into the driveway, having doubled back before making it to the main road.

"Just got a call from the station," he reported as he got out of his squad car. "I figured you'd want to hear about it."

"Vishnevsky?" Lyons said, slipping his phone back in his pocket.

"Who?" Gibson said.

"A Russian agent," Lyons said. "He's supposedly on a plane headed here from Santa Fe."

"When it rains, it pours," Gibson said. "That's the first I've heard about that. I got called about something else."

"What'd you find out?" Zimmer asked.

"We got hold of Walt's cell phone. At least one of them."

"In Donny's Buick?" Lyons said.

Gibson shook his head. "Forensics found it going through Walt's car. Thing is, all of the calls are to the same number."

"Colt," Lyons guessed.

Gibson nodded. "All within the last three weeks."

"Any text messages?" Lyons asked. "Photo files?"

"No," Gibson said. "But there's one more thing, and it supports your theory a whole lot more than it does ours."

"Well?"

"It's Donny's autopsy," Gibson said. "The M.E. doing it says he found a fresh scalp wound that likely wasn't the cause of death."

"I'm not sure what that means," Zimmer interjected. "He struck his head on something?"

"More like the other way around," Gibson reported. "Apparently there are some faint stitch marks along the abrasion. The M.E.'s guessing somebody got to him with a sap."

CHAPTER THIRTY

Outskirts of Santa Fe, New Mexico

John Kissinger knew something was up the moment he left the Rosqui Sushine Suites Hotel and saw Michael Fisk standing alone in the parking lot of the urgent-care facility across the highway. Rather than wait for an explanation, he put through a call to Stony Man Farm while taking the pedestrian overpass spanning the six-lane thoroughfare. He was amazed to find out just how much had transpired, not only in Santa Fe but also up in Taos, while he was checking Rafe and Leonard into the hotel.

Once he caught up with the BIA agent, Kissinger explained that he'd already received the lowdown on his cohorts' aerial pursuit of Viktor Cherkow.

"Sorry to hold you up," he said afterward, "but I had to do some arm-twisting with the check-in clerk and then I got waylaid by a call from a P.I. tied into what's going on at the reservation."

"Seems like everybody and their uncle's thrown themselves into the mix over there," Fisk replied.

"Actually, she was involved before the rest of us."

Kissinger quickly related how Leslie Helms was drawn into the investigation by way of Alan Orson and then described how the woman was followed into Santa Fe after leaving Captain Brown's press conference.

"Not too bright of her showing her face there after they'd already caught her snooping around," Fisk said.

"I don't think it's a mistake she'll make again," Kissinger said. "At any rate, after she shook the guy tailing her she tried to turn the tables and get behind him but there was too much traffic."

"Probably just as well for her," Fisk said.

"I don't want to keep you any longer," Kissinger stated. "She's on her way by to pick me up, then we'll try to join in looking for that Silverado."

"Any chance she drives a white Lexus?" Fisk said, glancing over Kissinger's shoulder.

The Stony Man armorer turned and saw Helms pull into the medical facility in the car she'd rented in place of her Jetta. He shook hands with Fisk, then jogged over to the Lexus.

"Ready for a little more adventure?" he asked her as he got in.

"Always," Helms said, "but if it's all right with you, I want to change the itinerary just a little."

"I don't know about that," Kissinger said. "Tracking down Cherkow is top priority."

"I think I can trump that," Helms said. "I just got off the phone with Christopher Shiraldi. He's ready to talk about how GHC convinced him to walk away from his countersuit over being canned from the casino. I want to get to him before he changes his mind."

Kissinger weighed the news and reached for his cell phone.

"You're right," he said. "Let me tell my crew we're taking a detour. How far away is Shiraldi?"

"He's at a place called Cochiti Lake," Helms said. "It's south about an hour from here…."

Cochiti Lake, New Mexico

"I'M SORRY, BUT IT'S A private matter," Christopher Shiraldi said, speaking on the phone to the last of five customers whose afternoon appointments he'd just canceled. "I'll give you a call about rescheduling if you're still interested."

The former Roaming Bison executive was inside his Coachmen Mirada motor home. He'd already paid his staff for the day and given them each an extra fifty dollars to blow at Casino Hollywood, the nearest gambling mecca located some ten miles away on the other side of the main highway. Outside the motor home, he'd posted a handmade sign over his AGA sandwich board reading No Balloon Tours Today—Family Emergency. One of the balloons was still inflated and ready to take off, however, having been prepped shortly before an unexpected visitor had arrived and convinced Shiraldi to close for the day.

As he set down the phone, Shiraldi's hand was trembling.

"That's everyone?" Russell Combs asked.

The undercover tribal officer was standing alongside Shiraldi, the lethal snout of his .357 SIG P-266 pressed against the other man's ribs. It hadn't been long after Leslie Helms had given him the slip that Combs had recalled how the woman had been asking bartenders back at the casino about Shiraldi. He'd been keeping periodic tabs on the man ever since the lawsuits over GHC's takeover, so it'd been easy enough for him to track Shiraldi to Cochiti Lake and use him to lure Helms back into his sights. He was looking forward to having the last laugh on the private investigator.

"Yes," Shiraldi replied hoarsely. "At least everyone with reservations. We occasionally get walk-ins."

"Hopefully they'll read the closed signs and move on," Combs said.

"What are you going to do with us when she gets here?" Shiraldi asked.

"It'll be all fun and games, I promise," Combs replied. "But while we're waiting, how about if we sit down and have a little chat about that gag clause you agreed to when you were paid off to drop your lawsuit."

CHAPTER THIRTY-ONE

Algodones, New Mexico

Enterprising town locals had high aspirations when they'd renamed a section of El Camino Real linking Algodones with Bernalillo the Pan-American Central Highway. The short four-mile, two-lane stretch paralleling Interstate 25 ran through largely barren land once touted as a potential boomtown due to its proximity to Santa Ana Pueblo's casino and several upscale golf courses. The boom never materialized, however, dooming the lone commercial venture that sprung up along the roadway to a quick and certain demise. For the past dozen years, the Happy Trails Motel and its adjacent eighteen-hole miniature golf course had been left to the elements as well as an endless parade of transients, vandals and graffiti scrawlers who, like vampires, tended to come out only at night.

And then there were times, like this day, when financial transactions made at the site far surpassed the wildest dreams of its former owners. It was here, more often than anywhere else in the state, that Viktor Cherkow usually made his high-volume drug buys from Colombian dealers that, ironically, trafficked most of their wares along various points of the original Pan-American Highway in Central and South America.

Cherkow had gotten onto the interstate a few minutes before the SFPD dragnet had been set up at the highway's entrance ramps, and the twenty-mile drive had gone by without incident. Less than five minutes after taking the Algodones exit, Cherkow turned into the cracked asphalt driveway leading to the motel. Hedeon Barad rode beside him in the front seat of Alan Orson's stolen Silverado, still holding the well-worn attaché case filled with unmarked currency skimmed from the Roaming Bison Casino's counting rooms. Barad had already raided the valise for his CZ 75 SP-01 Phantom pistol, and Cherkow had strapped on his shoulder holster for easy access to his gun, an MP-446 Viking.

"There's Jaime's pimp mobile," Cherkow said, spotting his Colombian contact's tricked-up, cherry-red 2009 Mustang parked behind the abandoned hotel's registration office.

"You'd think he'd get something more discreet for when he's doing business," Barad said.

Cherkow laughed. "That's what I told him last time. Know what he said? 'This *is* discreet. You should see the car I show off in.'"

"Must be nice to be rich."

"I hear you, my friend. One of these days we'll have to cut loose from Mikhaylov and go into business for ourselves, eh?" Cherkow pulled to a stop and killed the engine. "I don't know about you, but I get tired of doing all the dirty work while he gets all the glory."

"Let's get this dirty work done, then."

Barad opened his door and was stepping out when he suddenly retreated back inside the cab and thumbed the Phantom's safety.

"What's wrong?" Cherkow asked.

"Next door. Behind the concession stand," Barad murmured.

Cherkow glanced to his right and stared past the deteriorating assortment of obstacles adorning the weed-choked miniature golf course next door. The abandoned refreshment stand was a little more than sixty yards away. Parked behind it, but not enough that Cherkow couldn't see its front end, was what looked to be a late-model sedan. Even as the Russian's radar was going up, he was alerted by a growing drone overhead. Peering up through the sunroof, he sighted a clearly marked Albuquerque Police Department JetRanger drifting lazily into view.

"Son of a bitch!" Cherkow roared, keying the ignition. "It's a setup!"

Cherkow was shifting into Reverse when the rabid *brrraaatttt* of a Chilean-made FAMAE SAF submachine gun sounded from the long-shattered front window of the hotel registration office. The noise was almost simultaneously joined by the shattering of the Silverado's windshield under the force of incoming 9 mm Parabellum rounds.

INSIDE THE REGISTRATION OFFICE, Rosqui Tribal Police Officer Argenis Gordon stared past the barrel of his submachine gun, looking for signs of life inside the Silverado. The bodies of Colombian drug dealer Jaime Elmira and his two bodyguards lay on the floor nearby, next to a blue canvas duffel bag containing the heroin they'd planned to sell to Viktor Cherkow. Elmira and the others had been shot multiple times with handguns identical to those carried by Cherkow and Hedeon Barad. Once he was certain the Russians had been killed, Gordon planned to swap their guns with the murder weapons and arrange all five bodies to make it look as if the men had killed each other in a brief shootout the local police would be likely to write off as a botched drug deal.

"Did you get 'em?" asked Gordon's partner, fellow RTPF Officer Paul Boggs. Boggs was behind the registration counter, armed with another SAF appropriated from the slain

Colombians. Like Gordon, he wore cotton lab gloves to keep his fingerprints off the weapon. Also like Gordon, he was out of uniform, wearing jeans and a flak jacket over his drab flannel shirt.

"I think so," Gordon replied. "The guy riding shotgun is definitely out, but I can't see the driver."

"He's probably slumped over," Boggs replied, "but stay put and I'll circle around on them from back."

"Do it!"

CHERKOW WAS COVERED with blood but most of it was Barad's. His bandaged face had been nicked by flying glass and a fresh slug buried in his left shoulder burned every bit as much as the one he'd taken in the hip a few hours before, but he was anything but dead. Enraged, he leaned over his slain partner and threw open Barad's door, then stuffed the dead man's Phantom into his holster for backup and crawled out. He dropped to the ground and left the door open, leaning close to the vehicle. One of the aspens drooped low over the Chevy, blocking his view of the chopper. He hoped those in the bird would have the same trouble spotting him. He wanted payback with those who'd fired at him, and he got his chance a few seconds later when Boggs bolted into view from behind the registration office. The officer was trying to reach a carport on the other side of the driveway but made it only halfway across before Cherkow brought him down with his Viking. The Russian stared at his victim, startled to see that the man was not Colombian but rather Native American.

"A tribal cop?" the Russian muttered. The idea that Captain Brown was possibly behind the ambush infuriated him still further. Cherkow took out his fury on Boggs, pumped another two rounds into the downed officer to make sure he was dead.

The Russian's volley was quickly answered by Boggs's partner and Cherkow was forced to duck low when a fresh torrent of 9 mm rounds raked the Silverado's front end. Cherkow wasn't sure how many gunmen he was up against in addition to those in the helicopter, which was shifting position overhead, most likely so its occupants could get him back in their sights. He had to make some kind of move. Cherkow looked around and decided his best course was through the aspens to his right. He gathered his strength, then broke clear of the truck, ignoring his wound and the pain in his hip as he dashed from tree to tree to an overgrown beltway of unmowed grass that separated the motel grounds from the miniature golf course. He hurdled a collapsed wood rail fence that bordered the course and by the time his enemies were onto him, Cherkow had reached the thirteenth hole, which featured a windmill and a high-arched footbridge. Rainwater had collected in a small, narrow channel beneath the bridge, and Cherkow splashed his way through it until he reached cover. A few shots thumped into the nearby windmill and another glanced off the bridge railing, but for the moment Cherkow was safely out of range.

"TRY TO HOLD IT STEADY!" Bolan called out as Jack Grimaldi guided the JetRanger wide of the aspens for a clearer view of the motel driveway as well as the registration office. The Executioner was armed with one of the M-4 A-1s that had been transferred earlier from the Skycrane. Detective Lowe had the other carbine and was using it to keep Cherkow pinned beneath the minicourse footbridge.

"How's this?" Grimaldi replied, hovering the chopper in place.

"Good enough."

Bolan squinted through the rifle's scope and focused on the front window of the motel registration office. When Argenis Gordon came into view, the Executioner fired a stream of

5.56 mm rounds. Vibration within the JetRanger thwarted his aim, but he managed to ravage the window frame and drive Gordon back before the rogue cop could line up a shot.

"Any luck?"

"I don't think so," Bolan confessed. "I'll try the launcher."

The M-4 was equipped with a submounted M-203 grenade launcher. Bolan switched his grip to the carbine's forward trigger, then took aim once again, this time through the launcher's leaf sight. He figured he'd have a better chance at a kill shot firing through the window, but he and the others had already discussed trying to take their quarry alive in hopes of getting some answers. He wasn't sure how the shooter in the building fit into the puzzle, but on the chance he'd be worth talking to, Bolan drew bead on the office's low-angled wood shingle roof. The carbine bucked sharply into his shoulder as the M-203's 40 mm grenade whooshed from the barrel. Seconds later, the decrepit roof partially disintegrated, raining debris down into the office area.

"That should give him something to think about," Lowe said, surveying the damage as he reloaded his own carbine.

Bolan waited a moment. When there was no sign of activity within the building, he told Grimaldi, "Swing over to the golf park and set me down, then come back and double-check on things."

"Gotcha," Grimaldi said.

CHERKOW GRIMACED AS HE pressed his fingers against his shoulder wound, trying to ease the flow of blood. The bullet hadn't hit an artery but he was still concerned about bleeding out to the point where he'd lose consciousness. He knew he couldn't stay put beneath the bridge. Somehow he had to escape. The Silverado had taken too many hits to be of any use, which left Jaime's Mustang and the sedan behind the concession stand as possible getaway vehicles. It seemed more likely that he'd find keys in the Ford's ignition, so he braced himself for a run back to the motel. He was about to bolt from cover when the JetRanger's shadow drifted across the bridge and an M-4 chipped away at the bridge. Bits of shrapnel pelted Cherkow's legs and waist.

"Bastards!" the Russian seethed. His frustration increased when he saw the chopper drop into the clearing between the aspens and the golf park, blocking his way back to the motel. Worse yet, when the JetRanger's passenger door opened, Cherkow found himself staring at the same dark-haired, blue-eyed warrior he'd failed to kill three times already.

When Bolan the man leaped from the chopper and landed in the knee-high grass just outside the minicourse, Cherkow snapped. He switched the Viking to his left hand and drew Hedeon Barad's 9 mm Phantom with his right, then lurched to his feet and staggered into the open, firing both weapons. Bolan had already dropped from view below the grass line, allowing the fallen fence to intercept any rounds headed his way. Several of Cherkow's slugs, however, pounded the side of the chopper and one pierced the back window, boring its way into Lowe's side. In response, Grimaldi brought the chopper up and pulled away.

Cherkow saw a window of opportunity and seized it, reversing course and plunging deeper into the golf course. He veered past a dwarfed skyscraper and kicked his way through a service gate leading to a hole whose main feature was a mold-covered hard plastic replica of Mt. Rushmore. He dropped behind the facade, weakened and winded. He'd made it halfway to the concession stand and figured that between the two handguns he still had at least a dozen shots left.

"Hang in there, Viktor," he whispered to himself. "You'll get out of this yet."

ONCE HE'D CRAWLED AS far as the fallen fence, Bolan steeled himself and broke from cover, leaping over the rotted wood and entering the minicourse. He's lost sight of

Cherkow, but the Russian had left spatters of blood in his wake and the Executioner was able to follow the trail into the maze of cheaply constructed props standing between him and the concession stand where he assumed Cherkow was headed. A faint wind had picked up, filling the course with the sound of flapping banners as well as the scraping of overgrown bushes against woodwork and the clatter of litter being blown across concrete. The noise worked for and against Bolan, masking his advance but also making it difficult to detect Cherkow's movements. There came a point, as he neared the Mt. Rushmore hazard, that Bolan began to wonder if perhaps the Russian had either passed out or died from his wounds.

To his left, the course's seventh hole consisted primarily of a twenty-foot length of partially buried sewer pipe. There was a three-foot clearance, and Bolan took the risk of detouring into the conduit in hopes that when he came out the other side he'd be at a point from which he could spot Cherkow. Crawling across a ragged, timeworn length of artificial turf, at several points Bolan encountered holes through which errant golf balls were intended to be diverted to other hazards. The ground had apparently shifted over the years, however, and the previous night's rain had sent several muck-blackened balls rolling back to the base of one of the holes. After he came across the second such hole, Bolan began to collect the balls. By the time he reached the opposite end of the pipe, he'd gathered up four of them.

Inching back out into the open, Bolan crept to the cover of a nearby concrete bench. He glanced around him, M-4 at the ready, but there was still no sign of Cherkow. If the man was still alive, Bolan decided it was time to flush him into the open. Clutching all four golf balls in one hand, Bolan drew his arm back, then sent them flying into the air. As he'd hoped, the balls quickly split off in different directions, bounding off props and concrete alike with enough racket to be heard above the other noise.

The stratagem paid off. When he rose to a crouch and peered over the top of the bench, Bolan saw Cherkow stagger away from the Mt. Rushmore monument, whirling one way, then the other, still clutching his two handguns. Bolan waited until the Russian was looking the other way, then rose and shouted, "Drop the guns!"

Cherkow froze a moment. Bolan had long lost track of the number of times an enemy had reached this same turning point, and he could tell in an instant that Cherkow was among those who had no intention of disarming themselves. Unlike most of that lot, however, Cherkow didn't resort to spinning and trying to draw bead. Instead, back still turned to Bolan, he suddenly swung back both arms until the Phantom and Viking were both aimed in Bolan's general direction. The weapons were upside down when Cherkow fired. Their trajectories were off and did little more than decimate the hardscape before the Executioner's return fire pummeled through the Russian's back, piercing his spine and then his heart. Dead on his feet, Cherkow teetered forward, overturned a bird feeder, then crashed face-first to the Mt. Rushmore putting green, just inches from the nearest hole.

Bolan slowly moved forward, keeping his carbine trained on the Russian. Something troubled him. According to all available intel, he'd just brought down the mastermind behind the mayhem of the past twelve hours, but as he stared down at Cherkow, Bolan felt a glimmer of doubt. He still was unclear as to the circumstances behind the ambush he'd just stumbled upon, but to him it smacked of goon work, much like the earlier purchase of a camper shell and bumper stickers that had led to Cherkow's being identified. If the Russian had truly been in charge, assignments of this sort would have been delegated to underlings.

An eruption of gunfire near the motel confirmed Bolan's misgivings that things were a long way from being over.

INSIDE THE MOTEL REGISTRATION office, Argenis Gordon
had emerged bloodied and battered from the debris that had
come crashing down on him after Bolan's grenade attack.
Snatching up the canvas tote bag containing the heroin,
he straggled through the ruins, hoping to put the Mustang
to the same use Viktor Cherkow had earlier considered.
When he bolted out the rear door of the office, however,
he saw the APD JetRanger landing in the central courtyard
just beyond the souped-up Ford. Detective Lowe was in
bad shape from the round he'd caught near the minicourse
but he was still able to trade shots with Gordon. The tribal
cop's rounds missed their mark, but Lowe managed to put
two slugs through Gordon's right leg, dropping him to the
ground a few yards shy of his would-be getaway car.

"Tribal police!" Gordon roared, casting aside the subgun
as well as the satchel. Kneeling in the dirt, he raised his
hands in surrender. "My badge is in my shirt pocket!"

Grimaldi kept the chopper running as Lowe slowly
disembarked. The effort was too much for him and he
pitched to one side, falling to the courtyard, unconscious.
Gordon took advantage of the situation and reached out
for his Bizon, only to be driven back by a warning shot
from Bolan, who'd just cleared the minicourse and was
charging past the spot where Cherkow had brought down
Officer Boggs earlier. Up close, the Executioner recognized Gordon as one of the tribal officers he'd met near
the casino the previous night before heading to Franklin
Colt's house.

"You're a little far off your beat," Bolan told Gordon.

"We had a last-minute tip," Gordon lied, lowering his
hands so that he could grip his wounded leg. "We were
told someone was about to bring a load of heroin onto
the reservation."

"You're still out of your jurisdiction."

"We wanted to be preemptive."

Bolan eyed Gordon skeptically, then glanced over at Grimaldi, who'd bounded from the chopper to check on Lowe.

"He's still alive, but it looks pretty serious," Grimaldi reported.

"Call in an ambulance," Bolan told the pilot.

"I think we'll need more than one," Grimaldi said. "And as if we don't have our hands full, Cowboy just called. He's heading out with that P.I. to meet the guy with some dirt on GHC's takeover of Roaming Bison."

"Shiraldi?"

Grimaldi nodded. "He's up at Cochiti Lake, just a puddle jump from here."

"Let's wrap this up first." Bolan turned back to Gordon. "Do you always wear cotton gloves when you go undercover?"

"We didn't want to disturb any evidence," Gordon insisted.

"I think you were more interested in planting evidence than disturbing it," Bolan countered.

Off in the distance several police sirens howled to life as a pair of Bernalillo County Sheriff's cruisers sped toward the unlikely battlefield. Bolan unzipped the duffel bag and eyed the heroin, then stared back at Gordon.

"Looking to give yourself a little bonus?"

"I've already explained what happened," Gordon said.

"Every lie only digs you in deeper," Bolan advised the officer. "If I were you, I'd come clean and start thinking about ways to cut a deal."

Gordon's gaze hardened. "We're through talking," he said. "I'll wait for my lawyer."

"Suit yourself," Bolan said, "but we both know you're not the brains behind this. Captain Brown sent you here, didn't she? And it had nothing to do with keeping drugs off the reservation."

When Gordon glanced away, Bolan knew he had his answer.

CHAPTER THIRTY-TWO

Santo Domingo Pueblo, New Mexico

Captain Tina Brown exited the southbound interstate twelve miles before Algodones and took Route 22 north to Santo Domingo Pueblo, one of the few reservations in New Mexico that had resisted the urge to jump on the Indian casino bandwagon. Located near the ancient Cerrillos turquoise mines, the impoverished tribe made much of its income from the tourist trade, peddling jewelry and other craft works as well as fresh farm produce from roadside stands strategically located around the settlement's periphery. Buddy Carman ran one of the larger operations, with a dozen adjacent booths taking up a prime stretch of the main street leading to the pueblo. In addition to the usual wares, Carman offered picnic seating around a well-stocked catering truck featuring standard fare along with a few local specialties. While merchandise and food sales accounted for much of Carman's income, he also dabbled in a few gray areas, such as bootleg CDs, forged driver's licenses and nickel/dime loan-sharking. He was discreet about such practices but had been twice caught in the act and evaded criminal charges only through the intervention of Captain Brown, who'd made use of Carman several times as an informant in dealing with casino-related crimes. Brown had needed to call in markers with the local D.A. to ensure Carman's clean record, and now, she figured, it was time for the man to return the favor.

When the captain reached the roadside emporium she parked her Nissan Altima near the picnic area, where Carman was regaling a few tourists with an embellished tale of his days as a prospector in the surrounding mountains. When he spotted Brown, Carman abbreviated his anecdote and gave the tourists a discount coupon, then ambled over to the far picnic table where his benefactor had taken a seat. Carman's lifelong love affair with tequila had left him with a bulbous nose several shades redder than his native complexion, and he walked with a slight limp due to a degenerating hip condition.

"Looks like you're overdue for that replacement surgery, Buddy," Brown told him as he winced from the ordeal of sitting.

"Sure am," Carman said. "And from the sounds of it, you've come up with a way for me to pay for it."

"If you can spin this yarn as well as you do the others, you'll be all set," Brown assured him.

"Lay it on me," Carman said.

"I assume you've heard about the shootout we had at the reservation last night," Brown said.

"Sure did," Carman told her. "Complete with a bison stampede. Damn, I wish I'd had a ringside seat for that one."

"Well, there's a reward out for information on whoever was behind it," the captain said. "I'm giving you first crack at it."

Carman frowned. "I'm smelling a little perjury here."

"It's a chance you're going to take," Brown told him. "You owe me, Buddy. Do we understand each other?"

Carman was silent a moment. He had with him a can of soda pop half-filled with tequila. He drained what was left of it, then stifled a belch and nodded.

"Loud and clear, Captain," he said. "What do you have in mind?"

Brown took out the mug shots she'd put clipped together back in her office. She referred to them as she laid things out for him.

"Around closing time a few nights ago you overheard a conversation here," Brown said. "Probably right at this table. This guy here is an ex-con named Marcus Walker. He lives just down the road and he came by to eat and wound up talking trash about a security officer at the casino named Franklin Colt."

"The guy who just got kidnapped?"

"That's him," Brown said. "Colt nabbed Walker for heroin possession at the casino a few years back, and the kid wound up doing time. He just got out of the pen, and I figure he was looking for payback. This is the guy you overheard him talking to. His name's Viktor Cherkow."

Carman glanced at the photo of Cherkow. "And why was Walker blabbing to him?"

"Cherkow's a drug dealer," Brown said. "Let's say they did business in the past and somewhere along the line Walker helped Cherkow out of a jam. Sort of like I've done with you."

"Got it," Carman said. "And I overheard Cherkow agree to take care of not only Colt, but the rest of his family."

"I knew you'd be able to figure it out," Brown said. "Commit these faces to memory, then I'll give you a few hours to flesh out your story. Call me back once you're ready and we'll take it from there."

"One problem," Carman said. "These two guys obviously are going to call me a liar."

"I have a feeling Cherkow's not going to be around to give you any problems," Brown assured him. "As for Walker, he's an ex-con, and you're supposedly a respectable member of the community. Who do you think people are going to believe?"

"Good point."

"We're all set, then?"

"Just in case somebody asks, what do these guys sound like?" Carman wanted to know.

"I assume Walker talks gangsta, but I'll try to get hold of some court transcripts to make sure," Brown said. "As for Cherkow, just say he had some kind of foreign accent you couldn't put a finger on. Don't say Russian but steer things there as best you can."

"I think that about covers it, then," Carman said.

"Good." Brown put the photos away and stood up. "Put on your thinking cap and make this your coup de grâce."

"Coodie who?"

Brown smiled. "Three hours tops, then I want to hear from you."

The captain returned to her sedan, glad to have the task out of the way. Before she started the car she double-checked her cell phone to make sure the ringer was on. She'd expected to hear back from Gordon and Boggs by now with confirmation that they'd handled matters in Algodones. There were no messages, however. The captain felt a faint twinge of apprehension as she turned her Nissan for the drive back to the reservation. She'd only gone a little way when the phone rang. She pulled over to answer it.

"Combs here."

"Have you heard from Gordon or Boggs?" Brown asked him.

"No," Combs told her. "I've been busy."

"Where'd you track the woman to?"

"I've gone one better," Combs informed her. "I'm about to have both her and Chris Shiraldi at my disposal so we can find out what they've been up to."

"Where are you?" Brown asked.

"Cochiti Lake," Combs said. "Shiraldi's got his balloon gig set up there."

"I'm just over in Santo Domingo," Brown told her. "I want to hear this firsthand."

"No problem," Combs said. "We'll keep the party on hold until you get here."

Stony Man Farm, Virginia

"THE GUY WHO WAS FLYING with Vishnevsky is Bolivian," Barbara Price told the cybercrew once she had fielded an update from the authorities at Santa Fe Municipal Airport. "The IDs they found on him say his name is Guillermo Guerrero, but he's probably using an alias like everyone else he's mixed up with."

"Maybe they could send us a photo so Bear could run it through Profiler," Huntington Wethers suggested.

"They're doing that as we speak," Price said.

"Did they get him to talk?" Hal Brognola wanted to know. He'd worn out the cigar he'd been fiddling with and was making do with a pencil.

"Nothing besides copping that Vishnevsky was bound for Taos," Price said, "and there's still a chance he tossed that out as a red herring."

"If he didn't, Carl should be in position there when he lands," Akira Tokaido reported.

Brognola's mind was still on the events transpiring in Santa Fe. "So we have no idea where this guy was headed?"

Price shook her head. "He's holding out for a plea bargain."

"Just our luck," Brognola groused.

Carmen Delahunt had been fielding a call at her workstation but quickly joined in once she tapped off on her headset.

"I just got the latest from Striker," she announced. Quickly she related Bolan's account of the altercation in Algodones along with the Executioner's suspicion that Viktor Cherkow hadn't been the prime strategist behind Colt's abduction or what had taken place in Taos.

"If he's right, I think I may have found a couple likelier suspects," Kurtzman called out. The others turned to him. "I followed Hunt's tip and ran a check through the Bolivian Gambling Commission's database. I skimmed through ID photos and came across more than a dozen guys that I could cross-link back to Russia. From there I went by rap sheets for what looks like the two biggest players. If you're up for a little more show-and-tell, I'll throw them up on the screen."

"By all means," Brognola told Kurtzman.

While Kurtzman typed the necessary commands, Delahunt interjected, "Back to Striker. He's flying out with Jack Grimaldi to meet with Cowboy, who's apparently tracked down the head honcho for the outfit that got bounced from Roaming Bison before GHC moved in."

"That would be great," Brognola said. "The sooner we come up with enough to get that nuke plant put under the microscope the better."

"Funny you should mention GHC," Kurtzman said once he'd posted two ID photos on one of the far-wall monitors, "because that's where both these guys wound up after logging a few months in Bolivia. These shots are actually from the New Mexico Gaming Control Board.

"The guy with the red hair on the left is Petenka Tramelik, aka Pete Trammell. Next to him's Frederik Mikhaylov, who goes by Freddy McHale at the Bison. They go back together to the same casino in Moscow that turned out Vishnevsky. Mikhaylov's been higher in the food chain the whole time, so he gets my vote for the brains behind whatever they're trying to pull here in the States. Tramelik comes across as more of the trusty sidekick type."

"Good work, Bear," Brognola told him.

"It's all in the keystrokes," Kurtzman said with a shrug. "Unfortunately, my guess is that they don't have Colt and his family holed up at the casino, so we're still out in the cold on that front."

"I might be able to do something there." Brognola turned to Price. "Get back in touch with whoever's sitting on this Bolivian back in Santa Fe. Once his lawyer shows up, I want to cut through a few middlemen and broker the plea bargain myself. I want that bastard to help us get to the Colts while they're still alive."

"That's assuming they still are," Delahunt murmured.

CHAPTER THIRTY-THREE

Antwerp, Belgium

"I can't get through to him," SVR Deputy Director Alek Repin told Evgenii Danilov as he lowered his cell phone.

"Maybe he's already landed," the Russian financier suggested.

Repin shook his head. "Tramelik is at the airport. Vishnevsky hasn't shown up yet. He says it looks like the authorities have, however."

"That's the last thing we need."

The two men had reconvened in Danilov's office at GHC's Antwerp headquarters. There was no sipping of cognac this time around. Both men were struggling to maintain their composure in the wake of the grim news they'd been receiving from New Mexico. Cherkow was dead, Melido Diaz was in custody and it now appeared Vishnevsky was about to blindly wander into some kind of trap in Taos. Hopefully Tramelik's crew could help prevent the latter setback and there was word that Christopher Shiraldi and some private investigator were about to be silenced before they could shed light on Global's subversive takeover of the facilities at Roaming Bison, but Repin and Danilov both had the sense that bandages were being applied to a hemorrhage. In a matter of less than twelve hours, Operation Zenta had turned from a viable means to compromise the United States on its own turf into something more akin to an operatic farce.

"How could things have deteriorated so quickly?" Danilov wondered.

Repin's first instinct was to lay the blame on Mikhaylov's ineptitude, but with his own favorite son suddenly incommunicado he'd lost some of his righteous leverage. Besides, he felt there was little to be gained in pointing fingers. He'd just learned that investigatory agents, most likely from the U.S., were sniffing around not only GHC's business dealings but also those of the SVR, looking for links between the two entities and the Russian Mob organization Dolgoprudnenskaya. If Washington were to succeed in verifying the troika's grand plans in New Mexico, the political fallout would be every bit as widespread and damaging as the drifting of a nuclear cloud across the American Southwest. Repin's hopes of replacing Grigoriev atop the SVR pecking order would not only be dashed, most likely the director would see to it that he, Repin, was first in line for reprisal.

Danilov was beset by his own equivalent broodings as he wandered back to the window overlooking the city. The unseasonable snowfall had picked up, blanketing the rooftops of lower buildings as well as the steeples of the nearby cathedral. The bleak pall depressed him still further, but it also yielded a possible course of action for dealing with his rapidly compromised situation.

"I've been meaning to spend some time at my villa in the Caribbean," he told Repin once he'd turned from the window. "Perhaps it's time I followed through."

"I assume you're speaking about your villa on Isle St. Louise."

Danilov nodded. "It's the best time to be there. The weather is perfect, and all the island flowers are in bloom."

"And then, of course, there's the matter of their nonextradition status."

Danilov smiled. "A fortunate coincidence. Are you interested?"

Repin didn't need to be asked twice. "How soon could it be arranged?"

Danilov shrugged. "How soon can you pack?"

Taos, New Mexico

TAOS MUNICIPAL AIRPORT WAS easily the smallest of New Mexico's public airport facilities. No major carrier provided service to the town and the entire main terminal could have fit within the confines of the local high school's gymnasium. As such, Carl Lyons and a combined response team made up of members of all three local law-enforcement agencies had been hard-pressed to be discreet in their efforts to lie in wait for Dmitri Vishnevksy's Cessna Citation. The black-and-white units had already taken the precaution of parking down the road beneath a carport at Olquin's Sawmill, after which the ten officers had crammed into Lyons's rental car as well as a KIA Sedona minivan they'd borrowed from the mill owner. After the short ride to the airport, the men had conferred with TMA's manager as well as the four uniformed officers providing security at the terminal.

Now, less than ten minutes later, Lyons was out on the tarmac dressed in coveralls and an orange reflective vest, seated at the controls of a small luggage cart. Sheriff Officer Gibson and TPPD Lieutenant Zimmer were similarly attired, stationed alongside a maintenance truck. Three other members of the strike team lingered just inside the doorway leading from the terminal to the runway. One was disguised as a ticket agent while two plainclothes officers passed themselves off as locals awaiting the arrival of loved ones on other flights. The other four officers were still in the parking lot, two in Lyons's Impala and two in the minivan.

Both vehicles were parked wide of the terminal, allowing an unobstructed view of the runway. There were no fences or other obstacles between the parking lot and the tarmac; on Lyons's signal, should it come to that, the drivers would race out to the runway to provide backup. On the other hand, were there a need to deal with matters from afar, one officer in each vehicle was equipped with a high-powered sniper rifle.

"I think we've got it covered," Gibson called to Lyons. "If anything, we're on overkill."

"Given who we're dealing with, I'll take overkill," Lyons countered.

As they waited for Vishnevsky's arrival, Lyons scanned the nearby holding area, where a handful of Piper Cubs and other small planes rested on the tarmac near a newly constructed maintenance hangar. Inside the hangar was a strange-looking helicopter with stacked coaxial rotors and pair of large propellers mounted perpendicularly to the tail assembly.

"I take it that's Orson's speed chopper."

"Yeah. AirFox I," Gibson told Lyons. "We had a big turnout last week when he had the sucker out for a test flight. Two hundred and ninety-three miles per hour, if you can believe that."

"That's even faster than that X2 Sikorsky's working on," Lyons said.

"I think that was the idea," Gibson said. "Throw in the armor plating and he figured to go to the head of the line for one of those bazillion-dollar Defense contracts."

"Well, at least the commies didn't get their hands on it along with everything else."

"I think they would've had a little trouble loading it onto the Silverado," Gibson joked.

"Incoming," Zimmer interrupted, glancing up into the clearing skies overhead. Lyons tracked the tribal officer's gaze and saw the Cessna Citation come into view, taking the same approach by which he'd arrived at the airport a few hours earlier. As the jet began its descent, Lyons reached for the borrowed com-link transceiver clipped to his vest collar.

"On your toes, everyone," he said. "It's showtime."

"STAY DOWN," PETENKA TRAMELIK told Franz Khartyr and Bertrand Gustavo, who were hunched low in the rear of his Land Rover. Vladik Barad was sitting up front beside him. They were parked just off the access road that led to the airport, their vehicle partially concealed alongside the framework of a half-built convenience store three months away from its grand opening. They'd pulled into the lot after spotting Lyons and a handful of others pile out of the Impala and KIA minivan that had arrived at the airfield moments ahead of them. Wary of the implications, they weren't about to show themselves at the terminal. If it turned out to be a false alarm, they would arrange to have Vishnevsky walk down the road and meet them once he'd disembarked from his Cessna, which was just now making its landing approach.

There was one small problem with the contingency plan.

"The idiot still isn't answering," Barad complained, glaring at his cell phone.

"Keep trying," Tramelik told him.

The four men were each armed with automatic handguns, but Tramelik was beginning to wonder if they might soon be in need of more firepower. Glancing in his rearview mirror he told Gustavo, "If you can do it without too much commotion, reach behind you. Beneath the tarp there are a few extra weapons I brought up from the farm. Track down the launcher and carbines."

"I knew this Vishnevsky would mean trouble," Gustavo said as he lowered the middle seat and reached beneath a canvas coverlet draping the weapons cache. He had no problem identifying each item by touch and, one by one, he retrieved three Russian-made Bizon 2 submachine guns as well as an RPG-7 grenade launcher and stacked the weapons on the floor in front of him. "What about the hand grenades?" he asked.

"We might as well have them ready," Tramelik said.

Moments later, the Russian Vymper agent saw the Citation touch down on the runway and roll past the terminal. Beside him, Vladik Barad had finally gotten through to Vishnevsky aboard the jet.

"There you are! Why the hell didn't you pick up earlier?"

"I was busy and I just turned on my phone. I had to return a call to Repin," Vishnevsky replied tersely. "He told me about Diaz being picked up in Santa Fe."

"Well, brace yourself," Barad told the other man, "because you're next on their list."

BY THE TIME VISHNEVSKY had finished speaking with Barad, the Cessna had rolled to a stop in front of the terminal. The ground forces reacted quickly. Officer Gibson pulled the maintenance truck forward, blocking the jet from moving any farther. Lyons, meanwhile, veered the luggage cart around to the rear, boxing the Citation in. Vishnevsky had a clear view of both maneuvers.

"Keep the engines running," Vishnevsky told his pilot as he finished buttoning his shirt. He and Vanya had indulged in a lovefest during the fight and both had hurriedly dressed. The woman looked frightened as she stared out a portal window and saw two uniformed officers exit a Chevy Impala and KIA minivan parked behind the terminal, each brandishing a sniper rifle.

"My God!" she gasped. "They're going to shoot us!"

"Not if I can help it," Vishnevsky assured the woman.

"But what can we do?" Vanya was trembling. Vishnevsky moved to her, placing his hands on her shoulders.

"Vanya, you're always telling me how you want to be an actress," he told her calmly. "This is your chance."

CHAPTER THIRTY-FOUR

"Rifle up!" Tramelik shouted to Gustavo and Khartyr from behind the wheel of his Land Rover. "Vladik, get the RPG and be ready to clear that truck away from the jet!"

Gustavo and Khartyr armed themselves with the Bizon subguns. Tramelik reached behind him for the remaining carbine. Barad, meanwhile, fed a single-stage HEAT round into the launcher.

Tramelik had spotted the police snipers the moment they emerged from their vehicles in the airport parking lot. They were drawing bead on the Citation, but he couldn't tell if they were targeting the cockpit or the jet's doorway, which had yet to open. At this point, it didn't much matter. He was determined to take both shooters out of the mix.

"Gustavo, you've got the sniper near the minivan," he ordered. "Khartyr, take the other. I'll try to shake things up around the terminal."

The way they were parked, Barad and Gustavo were both able to roll down their windows and take aim from inside the vehicle. Khartyr slipped outside and crept past Tramelik before raising his Bizon and extending the barrel across the front hood. Tramelik stayed put for the moment but had his left hand on the door handle, ready to throw it open.

"Start firing on my signal," he advised the others.

Two seconds later the Citation's cabin doorway began to open.

VANYA'S ACTING EXPERIENCE was limited to sexual antics, but she played well the role of a terrified hostage when she opened the cabin door and found no less than a half-dozen weapons aimed her way, not counting the Russian-made GSh-18 pistol Vishnevsky held pressed to her head as he used her for a human shield.

"Get the truck out of our way!" he shouted at Zimmer, the closest gunman he could see. The tribal officer was crouched behind the maintenance vehicle, his LAR Grizzly pistol aimed at the doorway.

"Let the woman go and surrender!" Zimmer retorted.

"Wrong answer!" Vishnevsky yelled back. "Do what I ask and nobody will be hurt!"

"I don't want to die!" Vanya cried out. "Do what he says!"

Vishnevsky leaned close to the woman and whispered, "Well done, Vanya."

Zimmer held his fire and signaled for the others to do the same. He did his best to avoid shifting his gaze to Lyons, who'd abandoned the luggage cart and dropped to his knees so that he could crawl beneath the idling jet. The Able Team leader was armed with his weapon of choice, a .357 Magnum Colt Python. Some considered revolvers obsolete in this age of automatics, but the handgun had served him well in the past and he hoped for a chance to prove its worth again. He couldn't see his target at this point, but from what he'd just overheard it seemed clear that Vishnevsky wouldn't be an open target. Lyons was counting on the element of surprise and the slight chance that from beneath the doorway he would find enough clearance between the Russian and his hostage to get off a close-range kill shot. He knew the odds were against him, but there seemed little likelihood of otherwise ending the standoff without allowing Vishnevsky to get away.

As Zimmer continued to barter with the Russian, Lyons inched closer to his destination. That's it, keep him distracted, Lyons thought. He had only another five yards to go.

TAOS P.D. OFFICER ROBERT Puckett was the first member of Lyons's team to realize Vishnevsky had ground support. Standing alongside the KIA Sedona, the SWAT-trained sniper had been lining up a shot on the Cessna's cockpit when he'd detected movement far off to his left. More than a hundred yards away, a carbine-armed gunman had just gotten out of a Land Rover parked next to a partially constructed commercial building and was taking aim at Puckett's fellow sniper, Sheriff Officer Kevin Yount.

"Get down!" Puckett shouted to Yount as he shifted position and leveled his vintage Springfield M1903-A4 at Franz Khartyr.

Puckett rushed his shot and only managed to take out one of the Rover's front headlights. His warning saved Yount's life, however, as Khartyr's return fire laced over the Impala's front hood and through the vacated space where the officer had been standing.

Fast on the heel of Khartyr's rounds, a 9 mm burst fired from inside the Rover caught Puckett just below his right cheekbone. Killed instantly, the police sniper slumped against the minivan and dropped to the asphalt.

"Son of a bitch!" Puckett's partner, TPD Sergeant George Fernandez, bolted from the minivan and crouched beside Puckett long enough to see the man was beyond help. Enraged, he snatched up the fallen Springfield and charged forward to the raised concrete base support for one of the parking lot's light fixtures. Behind him, Yount was advancing, as well, dodging another incoming round before taking cover behind an airport shuttle van.

Fernandez was drawing bead on the Rover when a cloud of smoke erupted inside the enemy SUV. The officer was just beginning to realize the smoke was discharge from a grenade launcher when he heard a resounding explosion out on the airport runway.

VLADIK BARAD'S AIM HAD been as true as Franz Khartyr's but with far better results.

No one had been in a position to warn Officer Gibson that his maintenance truck was in the crosshairs of the Russian's grenade launcher. Gibson knew something was wrong when he'd heard an exchange of gunfire out in the airport parking lot, but before he had a chance to react, the RPG-7 HEAT round fired from down the road had homed in on his truck, a far more vulnerable target than the armor-plated tanks the warhead was designed to penetrate. In an instant, the six-ton truck was turned into a shrapnel-spitting mass of twisted metal. Gibson was killed the moment the driver's cab disintegrated and Zimmer, still standing behind the vehicle, was knocked to the asphalt seconds later by flaming shards of steel. His right arm severed and a gnarled shiv embedded in his chest. The tribal officer's last rememberance was seeing Dmitri Vishnevsky jerk his hostage back inside the Cessna's passenger cabin and slam the door shut, even as it was being pelted by hasty rounds fired by panicked officers standing just outside the terminal.

SHOCK WAVES FROM THE explosion had knocked Lyons off balance just as he was about to dodge out from beneath the jet and try to get a shot off at Vishnevsky. He was lying flat on the tarmac when officers near the terminal fired over his head, inflicting minimal damage to the cabin door. Shrapnel had glanced off the jet's nose assembly and cracked the cockpit window, but the pilot had apparently determined that the craft was still airworthy. Lyons had to roll to one side to avoid being crushed by a landing wheel when the jet began to move forward. The truck in front of it had been sufficiently flattened to allow the pilot to negotiate past its smoldering remains and head down the approach lane leading back to the runway.

"Damn it!" Lyons shouted, scrambling to his feet. He gave chase as the jet began to pull away from him. Once he was close enough he leaped forward, planting himself on the Cessna's right wing. Smoke from the destroyed truck wafted past him as he slowly began to crawl toward the fuselage, still clutching his revolver. The Cessna veered slightly, picking up speed and angling toward turnaround at the end of the taxi lane. Lyons wasn't sure what he could do to prevent the jet from taking off, but he was hell-bent on trying.

He wasn't alone thinking along the same lines.

Moments later, Lyons's rental Impala rolled onto the tarmac and headed after the rolling luxury jet. As best he could, Lyons waved one arm and signaled toward the runway. He knew the driver couldn't hear him but shouted nonetheless, "Try to get in its way!"

The Impala responded by shifting course. Instead of chasing the jet to where it would make its turnaround, the Chevy ventured the other way, heading for the runway itself. Lyons, meanwhile, continued to inch toward the passenger cabin. By the time he reached it, the jet was making its turn. The Stony Man warrior rose to a crouch and peered in through one of the portals. Vishnevsky and the flight attendant were standing near the cockpit. The Russian had put away his gun and the woman gave no indication that she feared for her life.

She's in on it, Lyons thought.

Suddenly the wing shuddered beneath Lyons and he was half-deafened by the overhead roar of the jet's twin turbofans. He dropped back to his knees, then was forced to lie flat again as the jet lurched forward down the runway, preparing for takeoff. Up ahead, Lyons saw the Impala turn and face the oncoming jet. Once it had lined itself up, the Chevy accelerated, trying to get to the Cessna before it could leave the ground. Lyons could see that it was going to be close. He also realized there was little more he could do, so he eased backward, then relinquished his grip on the vibrating wing. He landed hard on the tarmac but rolled on impact to minimize the pain.

Moments later, as he slowly staggered to his feet, Lyons watched helplessly as the Cessna lifted off. Its landing gear retracted a split second before the front wheel would have otherwise clipped the Impala's roof. Thwarted, the officer behind the wheel slammed on his brakes and bounded out, swearing. Lyons jogged over to him and they both watched the jet streak away from them.

"One more second!" Sheriff Officer Willie Matte moaned angrily. "Another second and I would've had them!"

"You tried. No use beating yourself up."

"Maybe not," Matte said. "Better we take it out on those bastards still here."

"Did you get a look at who nailed the truck?"

Matte nodded and pointed past the far end of the runway. Petenka Tramelik was pulling away from the commercial building farther down the road. "There's at least two snipers along with the guy who fired the launcher."

"Let's get them," Lyons said, breaking for the Impala. "I'll drive."

The Stony Man warrior ducked into the driver's seat. As soon as Officer Matte got in the other side, Lyons gunned the engine. The quickest route to the main road was diagonally across the runway, which took the men in the direction of the terminal. When they reached the officers huddled around the ravaged truck and the body of Officer Zimmer, Lyons slowed to a stop alongside them.

"Find somebody who knows how to fly Orson's chopper and follow us!" he told them. "We're going to make sure somebody pays for this!"

CHAPTER THIRTY-FIVE

Tramelik knew there was still police activity on the Rio Grande Gorge Bridge, so once he'd pulled back on the main road he backtracked as far as the nearest junction and then turned left on Route 522, heading north out of Taos. The Impala following in pursuit took the same turn and slowly began to gain on the Vympel op's Land Rover.

"Drop down!" Vladik Barad shouted to Gustavo and Khartyr as he shoved another HEAT warhead into his RPG-7. "I'll fire through the back window and take them out!"

"No!" Tramelik screamed at his colleague. "The smoke will blind me and you could blow us all up instead. Use the sunroof!"

"Much better idea." Barad reached for the controls, and the tinted sunroof slowly eased open. As Barad began to stand up in his seat, Tramelik bore down on the accelerator. Within two miles they'd left behind the nearest housing and were out on the open highway, flanked on either side by raw, undulating terrain gashed by deep trenches and aspiring canyons.

"Wait a second!" Gustavo called out to Barad, reaching into the rear storage area. "Let me give you a little diversion before you show yourself!"

Gustavo fetched one of the RGD-5 frag grenades Tramelik had brought from Glorieta. His window was already down, and once he'd pulled the pin he leaned out of the SUV and heaved the projectile. The grenade hit the median well shy of the Impala, but its 110 g TNT payload gouged the roadway and added flying asphalt to its frag load. A puff of smoke given off by the grenade further screened Barad as he rose up through the sunroof and prepared to fire at their pursuers.

LYONS AND MATTE FLINCHED when incoming shrapnel bombarded the Impala. The windshield took nearly a dozen hits, all leaving dime-size craters connecting to one another by way of jagged cracks. Amazingly, the glass held in place but Lyon's visibility, already impaired by smoke in the road, was further compromised. He had no choice but to let off on the gas and lean forward in hopes of spotting the road damage he would need to steer around. He sped over a large chunk of dislodged asphalt, which thumped against the undercarriage with a clamor that frayed his nerves still further.

"Hang on!"

Lyons swerved sharply in hopes of avoiding the divot Gustavo had put in the road. He half succeeded, but when the Impala's left front tire dropped into the cavity, the car jerked to one side and began to spin out. Lyons clawed at the steering wheel, but the road was still slick from the previous night's rain and the Impala lurched off the road. A billboard saved him from vaulting the shoulder into an erosion ditch, but Lyons had clipped one of the wooden supports with enough force to activate Matte's air bag, which lashed out with the might of an oversize boxing glove. Matte was KO'd and slumped across his seat, unconscious, nudging into Lyons, who finally brought the Chevy to a halt on a muddy slope extending down from the road's shoulder. He was dazed himself but quickly shook it off. The Impala was aimed diagonally at the shoulder, and he wasn't able to see the road. His window was down, though, and he could hear the distinctive sound of a car backing up toward him.

"That's it," Lyons murmured, unsheathing his Colt Python. "Try to come and get me."

The Stony Man warrior quietly eased out of the vehicle and crouched behind his opened door. Beside him, Matte stirred, his face whitened with powder from the air bag.

"Stay down!" Lyons whispered to him without taking his eyes off the road. Soon he was presented with two targets. Franz Khartyr had left the Land Rover and advanced to the shoulder clutching his Bizon 2 subgun. A few yards ahead of him, the Land Rover itself was rolling into view. Barad was still propped up through the sunroof, readying his grenade launcher. He hadn't spotted Lyons yet, so the Stony Man warrior took aim at Khartyr and fired two quick rounds. One slug glanced off the subgun's barrel, but the other nailed Khartyr just below the neck. The Russian dropped the gun and keeled forward.

Lyons didn't wait to see if the man was dead. He whirled toward the advancing Land Rover. Barad had the RPG-7 braced to his shoulder and was drawing bead when Lyons beat him to the trigger, this time getting the job done with one shot. Struck in the chest, Barad unleashed an errant shot that pulverized the billboard before slumping across the SUV's roof. The RPG fell from his lifeless fingers and when Tramelik veered away from the shoulder, the launcher clattered across the roof and landed butt-first on the roadway.

Lyons stayed put a moment longer, scanning ahead up the road. No other shooters had left the vehicle. The Land Rover had moved out of view but once he heard its tires squeal, Lyons knew that its driver was about to resume his attempted getaway.

Lyons climbed back in the Impala. Matta had pulled himself upright, still trying to clear his head.

"I'm all right," he told Lyons in a thick-tongued voice that suggested otherwise.

"Seat belt," Lyons advised him. "We need to get back into the hunt."

When he found himself stuck in the mud, Lyons cursed and jockeyed the steering column back and forth, shifting into Reverse momentarily, then putting the transmission back into Drive. He had to rock back and forth several times before he gained some traction and was able to drive back up to the roadway. For the first time, however, Lyons noticed steam seeping up through the hood vents. Glancing at the dashboard controls, he saw the engine's temperature gauge inching toward the red.

"Shrapnel must've got to the radiator," Matta said.

"One way or another," Lyons replied, "it looks like we're in for a short chase."

"THEY'RE AFTER US!" Gustavo called out, peering out the back of the Land Rover. They'd just driven past Khartyr, but Gustavo's warning squelched any notion Tramelik might have had of stopping to retrieve the body.

"Grab Barad before he topples onto me," the red-haired op told his lone-remaining cohort.

Gustavo leaned forward and grabbed Barad by the belt, dragging the slain warrior down through the sunroof and guiding him away from Tramelik. The corpse crumpled into the front passenger seat, one arm flopping out the window. Tramelik picked up more speed and raced down the empty straightaway. Glancing in his rearview mirror, he took heart at the sight of steam rising up from the engine compartment of the frag-riddled Impala. With any luck, the Chevy would overheat and have to abandon its pursuit.

Tramelik had never ventured this far north of Taos and knew little about where they were headed other than the fact they were five miles from the nearest town. If they could lose the Impala by then, Tramelik figured they could venture into Arroyo Hondo and ditch the Land Rover for another vehicle. Beyond that, they'd have to play it by ear.

Tramelik's optimism was soon dashed when an elongated shadow swept over the Land Rover and continued to drift forward until he was able to trace it to Alan Orson's experimental AirFox I. The chopper dropped closer to the roadway as it sped ahead of the Land Rover, giving Tramelik a good look at its twin rear propellers. They, along with the main coaxial rotors, gave the aircraft a deceptively clumsy appearance. If anything, it appeared to Tramelik that the prototype was as advanced in terms of maneuverability as it was in speed. Suddenly the copter did an about-face and lowered itself to within a few feet of the highway.

"Roadblock!" Gustavo shouted, eyes on the aircraft hovering directly before them.

"No kidding."

Slowing, Tramelik surveyed the uninviting landscape on either side of the highway. The terrain looked formidable, but less so than the prospect of trying to negotiate around the AirFox. He veered right, first leaving the road, then the shoulder. By the time he'd guided the vehicle down a steep incline, he'd activated the SUV's four-wheel drive, a feature he knew wasn't part of the Impala's skill set. Out before him lay nothing of promise in terms of being able to elude the helicopter, but he saw no other choice than to forge ahead and hope for the best.

"That thing has armored plating," he told Gustavo as he negotiated around the first of what he knew would be many shallow crevasses, "but if we can get to a point where we can make a stand, I'm trusting you to find its Achilles' heel."

"I'll do my best," Gustavo promised, grasping his subgun. "Just make sure you get us in a position where I have time to take aim."

THE AIRFOX WAS ABOUT to head after the Land Rover when Lyons brought the Impala to a stop and leaned on his horn.

"I'll take it from here," he told Matte, bounding out of the Chevy. He waved frantically through the billowing steam to make sure he'd gotten the chopper's attention. The AirFox lifted away from the roadway and banked slightly, then drifted toward Lyons. The Stony Man warrior ran clear of the Impala, meeting the copter halfway. At the controls was a short, solidly built African-American. Beside him was one of the plainclothes officers who'd been part of the standoff back at the airfield.

"Phil Ramon," the pilot introduced himself once he'd powered down his window. "I run a flight school at Muni and did the test runs for this sucker."

"Glad you were around," Lyons said. "Let's try to wrap this up."

"Only room for two here," Ramon countered.

"It's a nice day," Lyons said, climbing onto one of the AirFox's landing skids. "How about if I hitch a ride outside?"

"Okay by me," Ramon said. "Orson didn't get around to arming this, so we could use a little firepower."

"Speaking of little firepower," the other man said. "You wanna upgrade that Python to something with a little more oomph?"

Lyons saw that the man was holding a 32-round 9 mm Colt submachine. He'd gone through nearly all of the Python's ammo and firing on the fly would likely require a lot more rounds to hit his target, so he relented and stabbed the revolver in his waistband.

"Well, it *is* a Colt," he said philosophically as he took hold of the subgun.

"Damn straight," said the other man.

TRAMELIK HAD GAINED nearly a quarter mile on the AirFox before the speed chopper left the highway and headed their way. He knew they were running out of time. He drove as fast as he could along the sodden terrain, sticking to a stretch of flatland between two twenty-foot-high hillocks stretching for at least another few hundred yards. Other than a few random clumps of tumbleweed, there was nothing in the way of cover.

"This isn't going to work," he told Gustavo, yanking on the steering wheel. He turned toward the hillock on his right, and the vehicle groaned up the steep-pitched slope. When they reached the crest, the Russians found themselves facing another, deeper trough thirty yards wide and glimmering with a few inches of collected rainwater. The next ridge consisted largely of rock, and halfway along its hundred-yard stretch the dark maw of a cave beckoned as a possible hiding place.

"If we can reach it before they're on us, we might have a chance," Tramelik said.

"It's worth a try," Gustavo told him. He reloaded his Bizon 2, readying the carbine for what he saw as an inevitable last stand.

Tramelik powered his way downhill and through the shallow water. They were halfway to the cave when Gustavo saw the AirFox clear the ridge they'd just driven down. For the first time, he noticed someone standing outside the aircraft atop one of its skids.

"Keep going!" he told Tramelik as he moved to the front of the SUV and began to wriggle his way up through the sunroof. "I'll pick up where Barad left off."

AS THEY BORE DOWN on the retreating Land Rover, Lyons was glad he'd swapped weapons. Another shooter had just sprung up through the sunroof armed with an assault rifle.

"Throw it down!" Lyons shouted over the collective drone of the AirFox's powerplants.

The gunman either hadn't heard the command or chose to ignore it, and when he saw the Russian's carbine angling his way, Lyons took aim and opted for the Colt's full-auto mode. He decorated the Rover's rooftop with a half-dozen rounds before the the bullets blasted into Gustavo. The Russian twitched as the slugs hammered into him, then began to sag from view, rattling off a few errant rounds. Bullets plinked off the AirFox's armored plating just to Lyons's right, stinging him slightly with slug frag. He ignored the superficial wounds, determined to put an end to things.

As the AirFox drew still closer, he strafed the waterline just below the Land Rover's chassis, taking out both tires on the right side. The SUV tilted at a slight angle as Tramelik tried to compensate for the blown tires and continue toward the nearby cave. It was a futile effort, though, as soon the exposed wheel rims bit into the mud and slowed the vehicle to a halt. Tramelik quickly abandoned the driver's seat and crawled into the back, then opened the far rear door, hoping to reach the cave on foot. He had one of the Bizon subguns and fired blindly behind him as he slogged through the shallow water.

Lyons was nowhere near the line of fire and he braced himself on the skid, then put the Colt back to work, directing a fusillade at the fleeing Russian's legs. Tramelik spun as the shots struck him, then fell into the water and tried crawling the last few yards to the cave.

The AirFox circled the abandoned SUV and soon faced Frederik Mikhaylov's right-hand man square on, just as it had back on the road.

"It's over," Lyons shouted to the man. "Give it up already!"

As he closed in on the cave, Tramelik saw there was only a shallow recess in the rock wall. His attempt to reach the opening had been a fool's errand. He cursed in his native Russian and stared down at his bleeding legs.

"The hell with it," he muttered, resigned to his fate. Unwilling to let himself be taken into custody, Tramelik glared at Lyons and raised his subgun, inviting the rounds that soon bored into him. With his dying breath, he shouted back at Lyons, "I hope they're all dead by the time you get to them!"

Lyons gestured for Ramon to drop a little lower, then jumped clear of the AirFox and cautiously approached Tramelik. The Russian was dead before he could get to him, but Lyons couldn't help asking the man for answers. He knew Tramelik had been speaking about the Colt family.

"Where the hell are you hiding them?" he said.

CHAPTER THIRTY-SIX

Cochiti Lake, New Mexico

Christopher Shiraldi had been right about getting walk-in business at his mobile AGA operation. Three times within the past twenty minutes passersby had stopped and come knocking at the door to Shiraldi's motor home, ignoring the closed sign he'd posted out near the street as well as on the door itself. In all three cases, the would-be customers had presumed that since one of the hot-air balloons was inflated and ready for liftoff Shiraldi had merely forgotten to take down the signs.

After the fourth such interruption, Russell Combs had had enough.

"Okay, that's it," the cop said after Shiraldi had, as with the others, sent the fourth visitor away with a handwritten rain check guaranteeing twenty-five percent off the regular rate on a future ride. "Let's go take that goddamn balloon down!"

The two men ventured out of the motor home, Shiraldi leading the way with Combs following behind, his SIG P-266 aimed at the former Roaming Bison executive from within the confines of his suit coat pocket. Even with the gun concealed

Combs felt conspicuous and less in control of his prisoner, but he wasn't about to court yet another intrusion while he waited for Captain Brown and Leslie Helms to show up.

"Try anything and the first slug goes through your spine," he warned Shiraldi.

"I'm not going to try anything!"

Shiraldi was as furious as he was despondent. He'd already assured Combs that he hadn't divulged any information to Helms, but the cop refused to believe him, having already concluded that the private eye wouldn't have come nosing around the reservation unless Shiraldi had at least aroused her suspicions. Shiraldi had insisted that Helms was working for someone else, but Combs wasn't buying that explanation either. Shiraldi had no idea how things would play out once the others arrived, but he felt trapped in a no-win situation. One way or another, it seemed as if the scandal he'd hoped to put behind him had come back, not just to haunt him, but ruin the new life he'd made for himself.

Or worse…

"THERE'S ONE OF HIS balloons," Leslie Helms said, guiding her rental Lexus up a winding mountain road leading to the Pueblo de Cochiti Golf Course. She and Kissinger had already passed a handful of signs touting the New Mexico Invitational along with another of Shiraldi's sandwich-board advertisements for his Aerial Grand Adventures.

"Let's hope you're right about him coming clean," Kissinger said.

"If he made a deal under the table to keep quiet about how he was framed he might be looking for some kind of immunity," Helms forewarned.

"I'm sure that's negotiable."

Shiraldi's temporary accommodations were located a mile from the golf course just off the main road on an undeveloped patch of land surrounded by piñon pines. As they drew closer,

Kissinger could read AGA's Full of Hot Air motto stenciled on the side of the balloon, a traditional inverted teardrop with multicolored nylon panels. The two semis and Shiraldi's motor home blocked their view of the balloon's gondola and it wasn't until they'd parked and circled around that they realized Shiraldi wasn't alone. The proprietor had just gotten into the rattan riding carriage and was reaching for the propane controls while a man in a brown suit stood nearby, one hand in his pocket, the other on one of the balloon's tether lines. Even before the man turned around, Helms recognized him and uttered her all-purpose mantra.

"Holy shit!"

As much as Helms was taken aback to find herself facing the man who'd tailed her after she'd left Captain Brown's press conference, Combs was equally startled to see that the woman hadn't come alone. When the man with her reached inside his coat, the tribal officer acted on instinct and yanked out his gun.

"Freeze!" he shouted.

Combs had the drop on Kissinger, and the Stony Man operative knew it. His hand was clenched around a 9 mm Browning similar to the loaner Mack Bolan had been given to replace the Beretta lost in Tijeras Arroyo, but Combs's SIG pointed at Helms, and Kissinger wasn't about to risk having the woman shot.

He was releasing his grip on the weapon and pulling his hand when a car pulled around the rear of the nearest semi and braked to a halt.

"You heard him!" Captain Brown shouted as she bounded from her Nissan Altima, drawing her service pistol. "Hands in the air! Both of you!"

"This isn't what I had in mind," Helms murmured to Kissinger as they obeyed the captain's command. "Sorry about that."

"I guess this'll teach me not to pass out my number on cocktail napkins."

Brown moved forward, her gun still trained on Kissinger. Once she was close enough, she reached inside his coat and helped herself to the Browning. Combs, meanwhile, warned Shiraldi to stay put and advanced on Helms, quickly frisking her and then going through her purse, where he unearthed the woman's Kimber Ultra Carry .45.

"Nice piece," he told her.

"Don't get fresh, asshole," Helms told him. With a smirk she added, "Trailed any good Wranglers lately?"

"That was pretty clever of you," Combs conceded. "Too bad I can't take a joke."

ONCE IT WAS CLEAR to him that Combs's attention was divided, Shiraldi decided this was as close as he was apt to get to escaping his nightmare. He slowly lowered his hand from the propane controls, leaving the valves open, and reached for the closer of the two tether ropes anchoring the gondola. The man with Helms had apparently seen what he was up to, and he subtly shifted position as he began to argue with the two cops. Back turned to the balloon, Kissinger moved until he'd partially blocked both Combs's and Brown's view of Shiraldi.

By the time Combs realized Kissinger was running interference, Shiraldi had yanked on the slip knots of both tether lines. Instantly the balloon began to ascend.

"No way!" Combs roared, lunging to one side and shoving Kissinger away from him so he could have a clear shot at Shiraldi. Brown had seen the balloon lift off, as well, and she fired in unison with her colleague.

Shiraldi had ducked from view and flattened himself against the base of the gondola, but as the incoming rounds chewed through the rattan, two of them caught up with him.

One grazed his skull; another plowed through his shirt just below the right armpit. Shiraldi groaned and rolled over, his vision already clouding. He tried to get up, but his body refused to cooperate. Collapsing back onto the rattan, he passed out. His blood seeped through the coarsely woven material and began to fall like droplets of crimson rain to the ground below.

WHEN COMBS AND BROWN turned from Kissinger to fire at the ascending balloon, he fell back on instinct with a vengeance. The moment he regained his balance after Combs shoved him, Kissinger crouched slightly and dived back toward the cop, driving his shoulder into Combs's side and clawing at the cop's gun as if it were a football he was trying to force into a fumble.

Kissinger had two inches and fifty pounds on Combs and the other man buckled under the tackle, losing hold of not only his gun but Helms's. The Stony Man armorer ignored the weapons for the moment and stayed on Combs, pounding him at close quarters with a combination of fist jabs and judo chops. He brought his right knee into play, as well, slamming it into the cop's abdomen. Combs cursed and fought back as best he could, but he was outmatched from the onset and his wild punches did little to counter Kissinger's throttling.

A few yards away, Helms had taken the offensive, as well, twisting to one side and paying off six years of weekly karate lessons with a sweeping kick that caught Tina Brown squarely behind her left knee, throwing the police captain off balance. The round she'd intended to put through the private eye instead zinged wildly off-target and vanished into the neighboring piñons.

"Close but no cigar." Helms seized the shorter woman by the wrist and torqued herself yet again, this time slamming her hip into Brown's right thigh and then throwing the captain over her shoulder. Disarmed, Brown did an involuntary half somersault before landing on the ground. Before she could scramble to any of the fallen weapons, Helms let loose with another kick that clipped her opponent beneath the chin. Dazed, Brown slumped backward, the fight gone out of her. Helms quickly retrieved her pistol as well as the other guns, handing Kissinger the Browning once the man rose to his feet alongside his immobile counterpart.

In all, it had taken fewer than twenty seconds for Kissinger and Helms to turn the tables on their would-be captors.

"That was almost too easy," Helms panted, still trying to catch her breath.

"Let's save the gloating for later." Kissinger turned to Brown and Combs, who were both still on the ground, sullen about their sudden reversal of fortune. "My guess is you're both lawyering up, so I won't bother asking you to explain yourselves."

"I have my share of clout off the reservation," Brown retorted, rubbing her jaw where she'd been kicked. "This isn't over."

"I wouldn't count on it."

"We've got one major loose end," Helms reminded Kissinger as she glanced skyward.

Kissinger looked up. The errant balloon was continuing to rise as it drifted past the piñons toward the nearby golf course. Shiraldi had yet to reappear inside the gondola.

"Keep an eye on them," Cowboy said, stuffing Brown's pistol in his waistband so he could have a hand free for his cell phone. "Hopefully my guys are close enough to go into the search-and-rescue business."

CHAPTER THIRTY-SEVEN

"We see it," Bolan told Kissinger, cell phone pressed to his ear as he stared out the JetRanger's windshield at the distant balloon. He was riding up front in the chopper alongside Jack Grimaldi. From Algodones they'd followed a course along the Rio Grande, passing over Pueblo Santo Domingo and Plena Blanca as far as the dam at Cochiti Lake before veering northwest in response to Kissinger's distress call. "We're probably at least a mile away."

"I'm not sure what you'll be able to do other than ride alongside it," Kissinger said.

"We'll figure out something," Bolan said.

"If there's anything we can do to help, give a holler," the Stony Man armorer said.

"Will do," the Executioner replied. "And keep an eye on Brown. We ran into some of her goons while we were tracking Cherkow, and one of them fingered Brown as being in league with the Russians."

"Somehow that doesn't surprise me," Kissinger said. "How'd it play out with Cherkow?"

"He's dead along with a cohort and one of the tribal cops," Bolan reported. "I'll give you the details later."

"Fair en— Hey, I just spotted you," Kissinger said. "Check down to your right, around four o'clock. Two semis and a motor home."

Bolan shifted his view from the runaway balloon and spotted Shiraldi's makeshift launch site. Kissinger waved to him. He was standing alongside Leslie Helms, who'd just finished using Combs's and Brown's own handcuffs to secure the rogue cops to one of the steep hoop rings Shiraldi used for his tether lines. The lengths of rope lay sprawled across the ground nearby like long white snakes. Staring at them, Bolan saw a way to possibly rescue Shiraldi.

"Take us down for a second," he told Grimaldi.

"No problem."

Bolan went back to his phone and told Kissinger, "Look, do me a favor and gather up the tether ropes and tie them end to end, then see if there are any gloves lying around, the sturdier the better. A parachute and first-aid kit, too, if you can find them."

There was a pause, then Kissinger looked up at the descending chopper and shook his head.

"I know what you're thinking and you're crazy," he told Bolan. "It'll never work. Not in a million years."

"You got a better idea?"

"No," Kissinger replied, "but you can sure as hell bet I'm going to try to think of one."

CHRISTOPHER SHIRALDI STIRRED at the base of the gondola, his face slathered with blood, the rattan weavework imprinted on his right cheek. He groaned, wincing not only from his wounds but from the throbbing pain inside his skull, made worse by the roar of propane jets continuing to feed hot air into the balloon hauling him deeper into the New Mexico morning sky. With monumental effort he shifted onto his side and drew a hand to his side. In seconds his trembling fingers were red.

Get up, he told himself.

Shiraldi struggled to raise one arm, elevating it as far as the twin propane tanks feeding the burners. He held on to one of the tank's carrier rings a moment while he gathered more strength, then reached a little higher and cupped his fingers over the gondola's upper rim. When he tried to pull himself up, he felt himself faint again and let go, falling back onto the thin pad slick with his blood. As darkness began to once more sweep over him, he tried to take comfort in the thought that if he was going to die, there was no way he'd rather go out than airborne in one of his own balloons.

I've got a head start to heaven, he thought to himself.

"LOOKS LIKE HE'S STILL ALIVE," Grimaldi said, holding the JetRanger on a steady course fifty yards from the balloon.

"That settles it, then." Bolan donned the thick flame-resistance gloves Kissinger had handed him along with a first-aid kit when Grimaldi had brought the chopper down to the launch site. The Executioner had also picked up the knotted lengths of tether rope and fashioned a loop at one end. The other end was tied around one of the Ranger's skids. He'd already tucked the first-aid kit inside his shirt.

"I still say there's got to be a better way to do this," Grimaldi said.

"If there is, we didn't come up with it." Bolan put one hand through the loop and opened his door. "Ready?"

"As ready as I'll ever be."

"Then let's do it."

Bolan crawled out of the chopper and planted his feet on the skid. They were more than a thousand feet in the air, and from his perspective the sprawling golf course below looked like a board game. Taking in the view, Bolan found himself wishing Kissinger had been able to track down a parachute.

STANDING WITH HER PARENTS as part of the crowded gallery watching the board leader tee off at the fifth hole, four-year-old Darlene Crews glanced skyward and pointed. "Lookie!"

Darlene's mother and father looked up and saw Bolan crouched on the skid of the JetRanger, hovering near the seemingly unattended balloon.

"What the hell?"

"Matthew, please," Darlene's mother scolded her husband. "Watch your language."

Soon half the gallery was staring up at the strange aerial tableau. There was ample murmuring among the spectators, some wondering why nobody'd announced that there'd be an air show, others questioning why the people running the invitational had scheduled a performance that would obviously distract golfers competing for the million-dollar purse. Much of the chattering gave way to gasps when Bolan suddenly leaped clear of the skid and began to free-fall, clutching the tether rope. Once the line had drawn taut, the Executioner's momentum brought him swinging beneath the chopper toward the balloon.

"It's Tarzan!" Darlene marveled.

"Tarzan sticks a little closer to the ground, sweetie," Matthew Crews told his daughter.

Matthew's wife stared spellbound as Bolan closed in on the balloon, but a sense of dread led her to reach down and cover Darlene's eyes, not wanting the child to see what a part of her feared was about to happen.

"I don't think this is a stunt," she whispered to her husband.

BOLAN WAS COMING IN high of his mark.

Instead of swinging within range of the gondola, he found himself bound instead for the balloon's skirt, a band of fire-resistant fabric thicker than the inflated nylon panels of the balloon itself. With only a split second to deal with the miscalculation, the Executioner decided against deflecting off the skirt and making another attempt. Instead, the moment he made contact, Bolan released the tether rope. Most of the impact was absorbed by his sore shoulder, which he'd already reinjured when the line had gone taut shortly after his leap and briefly jerked him upward. The skirt gave a little under his weight, drawing him briefly into its embrace before gravity began to drag him downward.

As he slid past the open collar, Bolan ignored the sudden heat of the propane burners. His full focus was on the nearest suspension line linking the balloon with the gondola. He grabbed at the line and closed his fingers around it. Even with the heavy gloves he could feel the friction heat as his hand slid down the line. When his palm slammed against the gondola's upper rim, Bolan's fall was brought to a sudden halt. His body swung to one side and he went with the momentum, kicking upward and grabbing at the rim with his other hand. When his leg cleared, he immediately hooked it and shifted his weight so that he was partially straddling the gondola. Straining, he pulled himself farther up until he was able to pivot his other leg into the basket. Finally he reached a point where he was seated on the rim able to peer down at Shiraldi, who'd come to and stared up at him in bleary-eyed amazement.

"I thought the next person I'd see would be an angel," he said weakly.

"You'll have to make do with me."

As he caught his breath, Bolan glanced over his shoulder and gave an equally incredulous Grimaldi a thumbs-up. Then he turned back to the balloonist and carefully stepped down into the basket, withdrawing the first-aid kit from inside his shirt.

"Hang in there," Bolan told Shiraldi as he crouched beside the man and cracked open the kit. "I'm going need a few pointers on how to bring this thing in for a landing."

CHAPTER THIRTY-EIGHT

Airspace above Santa Fe National Forest, New Mexico

Bolan may not have been able to get his hands on a parachute, but there were a handful of them in Vishnevsky's Citation X. The Russian was the only one with plans to use one, however.

"Still no sign we're being followed?" he asked the pilot as he secured the pack and adjusted its straps to accommodate his bulky frame.

"There's nothing on the radar," the pilot assured him. "There was nothing on that runway fast enough to catch up with us."

"No, but if they called down to Santa Fe someone could be coming at us from the west."

"They'd show up on the radar," the pilot said. "Don't worry, you'll be out and on the ground before anyone gets to us."

"I hope you're right," Vishnevsky said. "When we close in, bring it down to a few thousand feet. I'm not interested in taking time to enjoy the scenery."

"Understood," the pilot responded. "I'm already close to that."

With nothing left to do but wait, Vishnevsky paced the passenger cabin, ignoring Vanya, who stood before the galley, apparently fortifying herself with a drink after her ordeal back in Taos. They'd been back in the air only a short while but were already halfway across the mountainous greenery of Santa Fe National Forest. Vishnevsky didn't have precise coordinates for the javelina farm but he'd gone over maps of the area enough times to know that if they overshot their mark, once they cleared the forest they could follow either the train line or interstate to Glorieta.

The Russian had already contacted Mikhaylov to advise him of his pending arrival and ask that one of his men pick him up once he landed. It had been a strained conversation, due not only to their mutual animosity but also the fact that news accounts coming out of Taos had confirmed Mikhaylov's suspicion that Petenka Tramelik had been killed along with four other SVR agents after facilitating Vishnevsky's escape from the airfield. This on the heels of word that Melido Diaz had been taken into custody had left Mikhaylov convinced that Vishnevksy's arrival, rather than reversing the string of setbacks to Operation Zenta, had only served to accelerate the plan's unraveling. Things had come to a head when Vishnevsky had been advised to kill both Vanya and the pilot before he jumped. Vishnevsky himself had considered the option but, sensing a power play on Mikhaylov's part, he'd balked, countering with concerns that the pilotless jet might crash prematurely near the farm, tipping off its location to the authorities. He'd dismissed Mikhaylov's argument that the jet could fly indefinitely on autopilot, insisting it would better serve their needs if the pilot were to change course once he'd jumped and lead any pursuing aircraft on a wild-goose chase. Mikhaylov had accused him of being too soft to kill his own people when necessary and hung up, leaving Vishnevsky to wonder if, in fact, someone would be sent to meet him once he'd touched down.

When he felt the plane descending, Vishnevsky ventured to the nearest portal and glanced out at the verdant landscape below. They'd just passed over the headwaters of the Rio Pecos, and the pilot had begun to veer westward. Ahead in the distance the Russian could see signs of development in a scalloped flatland just beyond the forest. It had to be Pecos, Vishnevsky thought, which would put them just five miles east of their target.

Almost there, the Russian thought.

"I've been thinking about your offer," Vanya interrupted. She'd put down her drink and moved away from the galley to within a few feet of Vishnevsky. Gone was her sense of playful mirth, replaced by a look Vishnevsky immediately recognized as naked greed.

"What about it?" Vishnevsky said. He'd offered Vanya and the pilot each half a million dollars to carry out a diversion once he'd jumped, assuring them they'd be able to collect it even if they were arrested because he'd secure them a lawyer capable of having any charges dropped on the grounds they'd been hostages during the standoff in Taos.

"We wouldn't have gotten away if I hadn't bought us enough time for your men to knock that truck out of our way," Vanya contended.

Vishnevsky stared at the woman whose passions he'd shared less than an hour ago. Now that she'd served her purpose he was in no mood for theatrics.

"What do you want, an acting award to go along with the half million?" he said.

Vanya smiled. "Well, it was quite a performance, if I have to say so myself. The same with what happened before we landed."

Vishnevsky bristled but before he could respond the pilot interjected, "Get ready, we're nearly there."

"I'm ready," Vishnevsky told him.

He turned back to Vanya. "I'm not sure what you're getting at, but I don't have time for this."

Vanya cut to the chase. "I think I deserve a whole million, not just half."

"Oh, do you?" Vishnevsky retorted. "Here, let me get my checkbook."

Vishnevsky reached past his parachute straps and quickly drew the GSh-18 pistol from his web holster. Before Vanya could react he calmly put a bullet through the woman's heart, then brusquely shoved her to one side when she fell toward him. Holstering the weapon, he headed for the cabin door and called over his shoulder to the pilot.

"Now your story will be more convincing," he told the other man. "And if you do what I told you, you can have her share."

Glorieta, New Mexico

FRANKLIN COLT HAD BEEN in the walk-in freezer for just over an hour, but it seemed forever since he'd left his wife's side. He was seated in the middle of the frigid storage space, which was half the size of the room where he'd been held captive earlier. Like then, he was bound to a chair, this time not with rope but duct tape. Every ten minutes, Yuri Reinhart had entered from outside, armed with his subgun, and parted the dangling strips of thick plastic separating the main freezer compartment from a smaller, slightly warmer antechamber. The Russian was checking to make sure the battery charge operating Colt's thermal armor was still holding up. Each time Reinhart had felt compelled to make some lame joke about Colt's being used as a human guinea pig to test how long the suit could effectively ward off subfreezing temperatures, and the next time he entered was no exception.

"You haven't turned into a Popsicle yet, I see."

"I have an idea," Colt told the man. "I'm not gagged, so why don't I just call out to you when the suit gives out and I start to freeze to death?"

"What, you don't enjoy my visits?"

"I've already said I'm willing to talk about what I know," Colt said.

Reinhart smiled. "Yes, but you were a little late with that. Besides, the part about letting your family go free first was what we call a deal breaker."

"Those are my terms," Colt said.

"Suit yourself," Reinhart told him. "Actually, I think our boss fancies the notion of seeing your wife put on the hoist whether you talk or not."

Enraged, Colt tried to bolt from his chair but managed to only send himself teetering sideways into a waist-high stack of cardboard boxes filled with shrink-wrapped javelina cuts. Reinhart stepped forward and righted Colt, shaking his head disapprovingly.

"You know what they say," he joked, "'You break it, you bought it.'"

"Go to hell," Colt seethed.

"I'll bet it's a little warmer there than here."

Reinhart turned and passed back through the plastic curtain, leaving Colt alone to resume his icy confinement. For all his anger, Colt was amazed at how effective his friend's suit had been in warding off the cold. Except for his nose and cheeks, he felt, head to toe, every bit as warm as he'd been back in the farmhouse. No wonder the Russians were so interested in the armor. What better means to give its infantry a decisive edge should they stage a winter offensive against an enemy less equipped to deal with the cold.

As he sat in the cold recalling Reinhart's taunt about Mikhaylov placing his wife on the same hoist he'd used to carve the javelina, Colt's frustration mounted and once again he began what had been a long and futile attempt to wrestle free of the duct tape. It had been twenty minutes since his last effort and he fully expected it to be another wasted exercise, but in that time the protracted exposure to the cold had produced a result neither he nor his captors had anticipated. The normally malleable duct tape had not only hardened in places where it wasn't in direct contact with the thermal suit, it had also turned brittle enough to give way under Colt's continued wriggling.

First he'd freed his right hand, then his left, and soon Colt had also managed to break loose the tape securing his ankles to the chair legs. Dumbfounded, he flexed his limbs and quietly stood, pondering his next move. He'd taken a step toward the thick curtain when he checked himself and stopped, staring through it at the outer door. As he turned and stared at the boxes he'd crashed into moments before, a plan took shape in his mind. He thought it through, then slowly stepped back and lowered himself onto the chair, assuming the same position as before he'd broken free.

Reinhart would be returning in less than ten minutes to check on him. For once, Colt was looking forward to the visit.

Stony Man Farm, Virginia

AARON KURTZMAN'S COMP-LINK access to the Taos Police Department had kept him first in line for news on the aftermath of the standoff at the town's Municipal Airport. Once he'd procured a description of the men who'd been killed fleeing the scene, he knew that his short list of likely masterminds behind the Russian machinations in New Mexico had just been cut by half.

"Petenka Tramelik was the last to go down," he told his fellow cybermates, who'd already been briefed as to Lyons's role in the pursuit. They were all still entrenched at their Annex facility battle stations. Price was on hand, as well, fielding another call on her headset, while Brognola had gone to a private room down the hall to arrange for his long-distance bartering session with the Bolivian detainee in Santa Fe, whose true identity had just been revealed as Melido Diaz.

"The Land Rover's in his name with a Taos address," Kurtzman wrapped up, "so I'm guessing he was point man there, answering to Mikhaylov."

"I assume that address will turn out to be their safe house," Huntington Wethers ventured.

"Safe guess, but we'll know any minute," Kurtzman replied. "There's a SWAT team en route with aerial backup."

"What about Carl?" Tokaido asked.

"He's up in Orson's speed bird chasing Vishnevsky," Kurtzman said. "The Citation has a head start and is twice as fast, though, so he's got his work cut out."

Price had just gotten off the phone. "If we've got a radar track on the Cessna," she interjected. "Grimaldi's free to help with an intercept."

"Perfect," Kurtzman said. "Let me get their position."

"Striker got the balloon down?" Carmen Delahunt asked.

Price nodded. "Shiraldi's being airlifted to the same facility where they're treating Lowe. It sounds touch-and-go for both of them."

"And this Captain Brown?"

"Jail-bound along with the cop who was with her. Russell Combs."

"They'll get a different cell from the goon who's ratting on them, I take it," Tokaido said.

"I would hope so." Price changed the subject. "I managed to reach Fisk before he headed for Taos. He's decided to stay put and ask BIA to put Roaming Bison into receivership while Global Holdings goes under investigation."

"Let's hope they bring some bloodhounds to sniff around the nuke plant," Delahunt said as she nodded a greeting to Brognola, who'd just rejoined the group.

"I'm sure that'll be top priority," Price said, "That along with tracking down Mikhaylov."

"I have a prettty good idea where to find him," Brognola said.

All eyes turned to the SOG director.

"You look like the cat that ate the canary," Delahunt told him. "You got Diaz to spill?"

Brognola nodded. "He was on his way to report to Mikhaylov just outside some town called Glorieta."

CHAPTER THIRTY-NINE

Glorieta, New Mexico

When Frederik Mikhaylov had claimed the back room of the milk shed as his personal quarters, the only thing he'd left unchanged was the east wall, which a previous owner had adorned with a collection of New Mexico state license plates. There had originally been only eighteen, but thanks to his access to the GHC-run salvage yard in Santa Fe, Mikhaylov had nearly tripled the collection to fifty-two. All but a handful of the plates contained the state's nickname, and as the Butcher stared at the repeated phrase he let out a sudden laugh that was steeped far more in rage and irony than any sense of amusement.

Hoisting his hip flask, Mikhaylov toasted the collection.

"To the Land of Enchantment!"

Mikhaylov drained the small container, then hurled it across the room, knocking down several of the license plates. The Russian had forgone all discretion and dragged his vodka supply from the closet to his desk. He reached down and grabbed the nearest bottle, then sat back and cracked the seal.

He raised the bottle to his lips and began to guzzle, intent on drinking as much as it would take to blot out the sense that he was as marked for doom as the operation.

The brief euphoria Mikhaylov had felt when Tramelik had come by earlier with Colt's telltale cell phone had been long shattered by the steady bombardment of grim news from nearly every other quarter. So much had gone wrong in just the past hour he had difficulty keeping track of it all. Evgenii Danilov and Alek Repin conspiring against him; Melido Diaz in custody, no doubt ready to turn on his benefactors in exchange for leniency; Petenka Tramelik—his right-hand man and the nearest to a friend he'd ever known—slain in the process of allowing that scumbag Vishnevsky a chance to lay claim to all Mikhaylov had spend the past few years working toward. Those were only the first things that came to mind, the tip of an iceberg the Russian feared would soon include confirmation that something had gone awry with the plan to execute Cherkow in Algodones and scapegoat him for at least a portion of the violent maelstrom that over the past few hours had turned The Land of Enchantment into a veritable war zone.

Mikhaylov had swilled nearly a third of the bottle when someone knocked on the outer door.

"It's open," Mikhaylov said, his voice slurred. He set the bottle on the desk rather than make any attempt to conceal it.

Cheslav Abramowicz, the only agent besides Cherkow to survive the reservation shootout, opened the door and did his best to ignore the alcoholic fumes that greeted him.

"You wanted to be notified once Colt had been on ice for over an hour."

"He's still alive, I take it." Mikhaylov stared at Abramowicz as if daring the sniper to comment on his inebriation.

"The suit's still working," the other man replied. "Reinhart wants to know if we should test it awhile longer."

"That won't be necessary," Mikhaylov said. "Get Colt out of the suit. I'll be there shortly."

"Yes, sir." Abramowicz allowed his gaze to drift briefly to the vodka-filled case at Mikhaylov's feet, then turned and left, gently closing the door behind him.

"You'd have a drink or two if you were in my position!" Mikhaylov snapped once the other man was beyond earshot.

The Butcher took two more long swallows, then tossed the half-emptied bottle in with the others and slowly rose to his feet. He felt calm and composed, a burden lifted from his shoulders. He was no longer interested in interrogating his prisoner. To him, it no longer mattered who else the Indian might have gone to with the information he'd collected on his cell phone. None of it mattered anymore. All Mikhaylov was interested in now was seeing to it that Colt paid for triggering the chain reaction that had undermined the Russian's best-laid plans and sown the seeds for his downfall.

Before leaving his quarters, Mikhaylov holstered his Makarov pistol, then sheathed the skinning knife he'd used earlier on the javelina. He figured he'd start with Colt's wife, and then his son, gutting them both on the hoist while the Indian watched. They'd both be alive when the knife first went in, and when it came Colt's turn, he'd be alive as well, forced to stare into the Butcher's eyes as he was subjected to the same grisly fate.

AFTER SPEAKING WITH Abramowicz, Yuri Reinhart once more entered the walk-in freezer, clutching his Bizon 2 submachine gun, glad this was the last time he'd have to subject himself to the sudden drop in temperature. As he approached the dangling curtains he stopped a moment. It appeared the test may have gone on a few minutes too long. Colt was slumped in the chair, his head bowed limply to one side, not moving.

"It's just as well," Reinhart mumbled, parting the curtains. "I'm out of jokes."

Colt suddenly sprang to life and flicked his right wrist out from behind his back, letting fly the frozen javelina steak he'd taken from one of the storage boxes. The rock-hard slab caught Reinhart above the bridge of his nose, striking with enough force to knock the man out. Colt lunged from the chair and caught his tormentor as he teetered forward, then eased him to the floor and grabbed the fallen subgun. Untethered, the prisoner passed through the curtains and paused before the closed door leading to the outside world. He had no idea what would await him when he threw the door open, but one way or another he was determined to rescue his family and flee their captors or die trying.

DESPITE MIKHAYLOV'S LONG-STANDING tolerance for vodka, the Russian's system was ill-equipped to handle the volume he'd just ingested. He'd only made it as far as his Hummer, parked a few yards from the milk shed, when he was forced to lean against the vehicle to catch his bearings. His head was swimming and his legs felt as if they'd turned to rubber. Before him, the farm grounds swayed and wavered in the brutal sunlight like some uncertain mirage. He saw two Camrys parked outside the barn, two Abramowiczses standing near the walk-in freezer, two skinned javelinas roasting on spits near twin engine hoists. Mikhaylov blinked but was still seeing double so he closed his eyes a moment and leaned across the Hummer's front hood, drawing in a deep breath. He felt an urge to sleep and was giving in to it when his insides rebelled against the alcohol and he abruptly reeled away from the SUV, dropping to his knees as the vodka came up on him.

This is a good thing, he thought drunkenly as he vomited onto the ground before him. In all, he was racked by three such convulsions before the purge ran its course. Weakened, his stomach aching, Mikhaylov eased back and sat beside the Hummer, his back to the front quarterpanel. He was feeling much better.

A flurry of shouts sounded across the grounds, followed by the excruciating sound of gunfire. Mikhaylov glanced up, his vision cleared, and saw Franklin Colt standing outside the walk-in freezer in the thermal suit, a submachine gun in his hands. He'd already downed Abramowicz and was trading shots with two armed men rushing out of the nearby barn. It looked to Mikhaylov as if both men had nailed Colt in the chest, and it was only when the Indian returned fire, clearly unscathed, that the Russian recalled the suit's amored capacities.

Colt was making his way to the repainted Camry when Mikhaylov mustered a semblance of sobriety and stood up, drawing his Makarov. By then, his would-be prisoner had reached the car and was about to climb in. Before he did so, Colt turned toward the farmhouse and screamed at the top of his lungs. For once, the tables were turned on Mikhaylov and the other Russians scrambling to prevent his escape, because Colt's cry was in a language they'd never heard before.

"Hokahey!" Colt roared. *"Hokahey!"*

AFTER BEING SERVED BREAKFAST, Gwen had been ordered, at gunpoint, to clean the farmhouse kitchen, a chore clearly shunned by the SVR agents to the point where the sink and half the counter space had been cluttered with an assortment of piled dishes, unwashed pans and food-encrusted silverware. Gwen had undertaken the denigrating task without complaint, grateful in some respects to have something to do other than pace the locked bedroom worrying about what her captors might be doing to her husband. She was thankful, too, that their son had become engrossed enough watching television so as to not create a disturbance. She could see Frankie while she worked; he was curled up in blankets on the overstuffed sofa in the adjacent room, which was separated from the kitchen by a counter where Zhenya Ilyin sat on a bar stool, a Bizon 2 straddling his lap as he supervised Gwen's efforts between sips of coffee.

"Where do you want the pans?" Gwen asked Iylin.

"The cupboard over the stove," he told her gruffly. "Clean the shelves first."

"I can barely reach them."

"Use the step stool," Ilyin said, pointing. "It's right next to the refrigerator."

Gwen withdrew the stool and was unfolding it when the first shots were fired outside the farmhouse. The only window in the kitchen faced away from the direction of the gunfire, and Gwen's heart sank with fear, thinking her husband had been the target. However, when the blasts were followed by a chorus of shouts and Ilyin rose to his feet, readying his carbine, she realized there had to be another reason for the outburst. Across the room, Frankie screamed and bolted from the sofa, running past Ilyin into the kitchen. He clasped himself to his mother's leg and bawled into her hip.

"Shut him up!" Ilyin shouted, moving to the screen door. He peered out, then suddenly kicked the door open and fired out into the clearing between the farmhouse and the javelina pen.

Gwen patted Frankie's head and pulled him away, then crouched to his level and held him by the shoulders. She was about to plead with him to stop crying when, during a lull between gunshots, she heard her husband cry out.

"Hokahey! Hokahey!"

It was a prearranged signal, one they'd discussed the previous night while Frankie was asleep, inspired by the Sioux warrior Crazy Horse, who'd spurred his warriors on to victory with the same incantation during the Battle of the Little Bighorn. Some took the phrase to mean "It's a good day to die!" Others translated it more simply as "Let's roll!" Either way the war cry galvanized Colt's wife.

Without hesitation Gwen coaxed her son aside and grabbed the unfolded step stool by one of its lower legs. Clutching it the way she'd hold a bat, she charged past the counter and was halfway to Ilyin before he turned from the doorway and whirled his carbine her way. He fired wildly, missing both Gwen and Frankie before the top edge of the metal stool crashed into his right cheek. Gwen had swung the makeshift weapon with all her might and the blow dislocated Ilyin's jaw while shattering his cheekbone. He let out a muffled howl and reeled off balance, lowering the Bizon 2. Gwen stayed on him and moved in closer, plowing her knee into the man's groin and butting his wrist with the stool's base. The subgun fell clear and Ilyin went down, doubled over in pain.

Gwen cast aside the stool and snatched up the submachine gun. She hadn't gone hunting with her husband since Frankie was born but there was little to forget when it came to firing a rifle and with unflinching certainty she took aim at the downed Russian and put a bullet through his head.

Frankie had gone silent in the kitchen and when Gwen looked back at him she could see that he was in shock, standing before the stove as if frozen in place, his eyes wide. Still clutching the Bizon, she rushed to her son and scooped him up in her other arm and held him tight as she charged back toward the doorway.

"It's going to be all right, Frankie," she whispered to him. "Everything's going to be all right."

As COLT HAD HOPED, the keys had been left in the Camry. Tossing the subgun on the seat beside him, Colt started the engine and shoved the gears into Reverse, then turned in his seat and looked behind him as he pressed on the accelerator, speeding backward toward the farmhouse. He veered around the body of Yuri Reinhart and flinched when someone fired a slug through the rear windshield, missing him by inches. Through the shattered glass he saw Mikhaylov standing alongside his Humvee, readying his Makarov for another shot. Colt jostled the steering wheel and swerved slightly as he neared the house. Mikhaylov's next round glanced off the trunk. Colt pulled to a stop in front of the house and grabbed the Bizon 2, driving Mikhaylov to the ground with an autoburst. When he saw the screen door swing open, Colt swung the weapon around but held his fire. It was Gwen, rushing out with Frankie in her arms. She yanked open the car door and hurriedly eased Frankie into the backseat, then slid in beside him, exchanging a look with her husband that spoke all at once of pride, love and desparation.

"Stay down," Colt told her. Gwen nodded and dropped low in the seat, pulling Frankie down with her. Staring up at his father, the boy snapped out of his catatonia.

"Paparoni looks like Batman!" he cried out.

CHAPTER FORTY

Dmitri Vishnevsky had just deployed his parachute when the gun battle had erupted at the javelina farm. He was unaware of the skirmish, and by the time he'd stabilized himself enough to survey the terrain below him, he'd drifted considerably west of his target and was concerned primarily with finding a safe place to land. It was only after he'd guided himself toward an open field that he glanced back toward his intended destination. He saw two vehicles pull away from the compound, one a Camry, the other a Hummer SUV. They were both speeding his way, heading down the same road he was about to land next to. Vishnevsky was heartened; it seemed that Mikhaylov had decided to send men to pick him up after all. He hoped it was a sign that he would be treated with more respect than the other man had shown him during their phone call. Things would go much easier if they could put aside their differences long enough to ride out a few setbacks and put Operation Zenta back on track. Once that was done, hopefully Mikhaylov would wise up and bow out gracefully so he could take full rein over the territory without a fight. If Mikhaylov resisted, Vishnevsky hoped that fight would be man-to-man like it'd been back in Moscow at the Royal Splendor. This time he'd be the one beating his adversary to a pulp.

MIKHAYLOV FELT HE WAS sober enough to keep the Hummer on the road as he barreled past his minions in pursuit of the fleeing Camry. There was no way he was about to be denied the vengeance he had in store for Colt and his family.

The Toyota had a sizable lead. Mikhaylov tried to gain ground by cutting the first corner he came to but was slow to compensate and overshot the bend, drifting across lanes to the far shoulder and almost plowing into a drainage ditch that ran parallel to the road. He corrected course and the Hummer rumbled back onto the wet asphalt. He'd managed to close the gap despite his blundering, but the Camry was still a good fifty yards ahead. In Mikhaylov's favor, Colt was unfamiliar with the road while the Russian had traveled it numerous times since. There would be other opportunities to overtake the Camry before it reached the highway.

It was when Mikhaylov rounded the next corner that he caught his first glimpse of Vishnevsky's parachute. The Russian's archrival was closing in on an open field a quarter mile away. Mikhaylov had all but forgotten about the man and he soon found himself at cross-purposes. He knew the sensible thing would be to pull over and pick up the bastard, as having a gunman on board would give him an extra means by which to prevent Colt's getaway. On the other hand, stopping would lose him what little ground he'd gained. And, too, there was the matter of not wanting to indebt himself to Vishnevsky by drawing on the man's help.

As he drew near, Mikhaylov realized the point was moot, as Vishnevsky's parachute had been slow to collapse after he'd landed and had taken on wind, dragging him far from the road. By the time he'd wrestled free of his harness, Vishnevsky was eighty yards from the passing Camry. He waved frantically, trying to get Colt's attention. When that failed, he turned toward the Hummer and began gesturing at Mikhaylov.

Mikhaylov ignored his rival and kept his eyes trained on the road. As he passed the spot where he most likely would have stopped to wait for the other Russian, Mikhaylov muttered, "If you're so brilliant, why couldn't you land a little closer to your mark?"

SOMEONE HAD DONE A reasonably good job of cleaning the interior of the Camry before painting the body, but there were remnants of Jeffrey Eppard's blood on both the dashboard display and steering column. Colt finally noticed them as he continued to speed along the back road, keeping a safe distance ahead of the pursuing Humvee.

"What'd they do with Jeff and Leeland?" he asked Gwen as he rounded another bend and came to a long straightaway. A mile up the road he could see a railroad crossing and, beyond that, a short stretch leading to the highway and the increased likelihood of escaping from the hell that had been the javelina farm.

Mindful of Frankie, Gwen told her husband, "We can talk about that later."

A few miles back Colt had asked Gwen to remove the hood of his armored suit, as its weak link was the extent to which it muted the sound of his surroundings, particularly in the distance. Now, freed of that restraint, he had little trouble hearing the sonorous blare of the train engine that soon appeared to his left, heading toward the same crossing Colt needed to pass to reach the highway.

"Are you buckled up?" he called back to his wife.

"As best as we can without a car seat," Gwen told him. Frankie was too small for a seat belt, so she'd put the boy on her lap and drawn the strap across his shoulder as well as hers. She'd heard it was unsafe, especially in the event of an accident, but it seemed a better option than leaving him without any kind of harness.

"Well, hang on," Colt warned her, "because there's a chance we're going to be cutting things a little close."

Colt tightened his grip on the steering wheel and eased down on the accelerator, racing toward the railroad crossing. The train was picking up speed as well as it pulled away from the Glorieta train yard. How ironic, Colt thought. It hadn't been that long ago that he'd hoped that riding the rails might somehow prove to be their ticket to freedom. Now, as he glanced in his rearview mirror and saw the Hummer keeping pace with him, he wondered if it might turn out that a train would thwart his escape and place him back at the mercy of his captors.

MIKHAYLOV SAW THE TRAIN, TOO. He was also familiar with its running schedule and always avoided the road at this time of morning because it was common to have trains running in both directions, often with loads more than a hundred boxcars long. He smiled faintly as he saw the long procession of cars trailing behind the engine as it rolled toward the warning lights flanking either side of the road where it intersected with the rail line. He knew Colt would never beat the train past the crossing. In fact, the Camry was a good thirty yards from the light fixtures when the adjacent swing arm wavered from its perpendicular position and slowly dropped to a point where it blocked the road.

"Thank you," Mikhaylov murmured, reaching across his seat. He popped open the glove compartment and pulled out a spare ammo cartridge for the Makarov. Once the Camry was forced to stop, he'd pull up behind it and put the gun to use. Yes, it would be a little more impersonal to have to gun down Colt and his family rather than carve them open with his skinning knife, but sometimes one had to be flexible.

HAD HE BEEN THE ONLY one in the car, Colt knew what he'd do. But as he saw the wooden barrier begin to lower, he suddenly balked at the prospect of having his wife and child crushed by the oncoming engine. His foot was still on the gas and he could see that the Hummer was still hot on his tail. There might still be time to slam on the brakes and hope he could stop in time to avoid the train and take his chances going up against Mikhaylov with however few rounds were left in the Bizon 2. He knew he had to make a decision, but he was still conflicted.

"What do I do?" he cried out to his wife.

Gwen could see Colt in the rearview mirror. In his eyes there was fear and uncertainty. It hadn't been fear and uncertainty that had gotten them this far.

"Hokahey!" she shouted back at him.

Frankie Jr., oblvious to what was going on around him, smiled and took on the cry. *"Hokahey,* Paparoni!"

Colt held his breath and pressed the accelerator until it touched the floorboard. Seconds later, there was a splintering snap as he crashed through the barrier. Gwen glanced to her left and saw the engine bearing down on them. She held Frankie tight and closed her eyes, thankful that at least they would die quickly. And free...

CHAPTER FORTY-ONE

Mikhaylov pulled to a stop well short of the passing train. Littered on the road before him were the splintered remains of the barrier Colt had just crashed through. Gun in hand, he slowly strode forward, his head throbbing from the vodka still left in his system. The deafening rumble of the passing boxcars made the pain worse, but he did his best to ignore it and moved still closer to the tracks, inspecting the rail bed for remains of the Camry and its occupants. All he could see was a scattering of weeds and litter. There was a lone hubcap lying in the gravel of the rail bed, but when he moved closer he saw that it was layered with rust and bore no resemblance to the caps on the Camry.

Standing this close to the rails, Mikhaylov could feel the boxcars rolling past, and the noise made it feel as if his skull had been placed in a slowly closing vise. The Russian holstered his weapon and put his hands to his ears as he crouched and tried to stare past the ever-moving wheels. It was like watching an old silent movie where the projector was out of sync, flashing not only images but also the glimpses of the lines between each frame.

Less than twenty yards away, just off the road on the other side of the tracks, Mikhaylov saw the Camry. It rested almost perpendicular to the road and seemed totally intact except for the right rear end, far behind the backseat, which had been partially sheared off and partially crushed on impact with the engine's cowcatcher. From his compromised perspective, it was hard for him to tell if anyone was still in the vehicle, alive or dead.

Mikhaylov roared with frustration and staggered away from the rail bed, his hands still clamped over his ears. When he reached the Hummer he glanced eastward, hoping to glimpse the train's caboose. All he could see were more boxcars, dozens of them, stretching all the way back to the bend leading to the train yard. The Russian retreated inside his Hummer and slammed the door, welcoming the relative quiet. He stared numbly out the windshield, watching boxcar after boxcar clatter by, barring his way to the other side of the road. There was nothing for him to do but wait for them to roll by. It would take more than a mile to come to a stop after the accident, if indeed it came to a stop at all.

Lulled by the rhythmic clatter, Mikhaylov licked his lips and shook his head, struggling to remain awake.

"I need a drink," he said.

FRANKIE WAS THE FIRST to come to.

Miraculously, he was still strapped in place, his mother's arms around him. His shoulder ached where the strap had bit into him during the collision and he whimpered slightly as he turned and looked up at Gwen.

"Mommy?"

After Frankie had called to her a second time, Gwen stirred and opened her eyes. She instinctively hugged her son as she looked around her, trying to make sense of what had just happened. She could see the train still rumbling past but realized they were on the other side of the crossing. Looking over her shoulder, she saw the mangled rear end.

"Mommy, my shoulder hurts."

"I'm sorry, sweetheart," Gwen whispered. She grimaced as she unclasped her seat belt, then kissed Frankie's shoulder and gently moved him off her lap onto the seat. "We'll take a look at it in a minute, okay?"

"Okay."

Gwen leaned forward, waving away the faint, whitish cloud that had been unleashed when the front air bags had deployed. Franklin was slumped to one side in the front seat and she lightly touched his neck, seeking out a pulse, already grateful his skin was warm to the touch. When she could feel his heartbeat she whispered, "Franklin? Franklin, honey?"

"Wake up, Paparoni!" Frankie called out.

Colt groaned faintly. Gwen leaned closer and kissed the back of his head, then whispered in his ear, "We made it, Franklin. You did it."

It took Colt a moment to orient himself and his surroundings. Once he did, he took Gwen's hand and kissed it, then unfastened his seat belt and pushed the sagging air bag out of his way so he could turn to his son.

"You okay, Frankie?"

Frankie nodded, repeating, "My shoulder hurts."

Colt suppressed a grin, knowing full well how much worse it could have been. "Next time we do this, I'll make sure you're wearing the armored suit."

Frankie shook his head. "I don't want to do this again."

"I like that idea better."

Colt reached for his door handle and told Gwen, "Stay put."

The Bizon 2 subgun had fallen to the floor in front of the passenger seat. Colt grabbed it, then got out of the car. He glanced back at the ravaged rear end, then looked toward the train, which was still passing. A few pieces of the Camry lay scattered in between him and the tracks. He had the same shifting view of the other side of the road Mikhaylov had had, and when he saw the Hummer idling near the barrier he'd crashed through, Colt realized it wasn't over yet. He looked the Toyota over again. Both rear tires were flat. Even if they hadn't been, he doubted that the car was drivable. There was no other traffic on the road and it was a long walk to the highway, with little in between in terms of places to try to hide once the train passed and Mikhaylov resumed his pursuit.

"So close," he muttered.

Colt was about to check the magazine on his assault rifle when he heard the unmistakable drone of an approaching helicopter. Turning, he saw the chopper dropping toward the road. Recalling Mikhaylov's arrival the previous night, he assumed the worst and called out to his wife.

"Get down!"

Colt circled to the front of the Camry and crouched behind the front grille. The sun was behind the copter, making it difficult for him to distinguish its make. There was no doubt, however, that it was closing in on him. He had readied the rifle and taken aim when he saw someone lean out the passenger window. They weren't holding a weapon, however, but rather a bullhorn. The voice that boomed out at him seconds later was slightly distorted, but he was able to recognize it.

"Is that any way to greet an old friend?" John Kissinger called out to him.

MIKHAYLOV SAW THE HELICOPTER, as well. He knew it wasn't one of his.

To the east, at long last, he finally spotted the train's caboose. There were still at least twenty boxcars between it and the crossing. The Russian was suddenly in no hurry for the train to pass by.

Placing the Makarov on his lap, Mikhaylov put the Hummer into Reverse, backing up just far enough that he could make a U-turn without running over the shattered crossarm. Once he was facing the farm, he pressed the accelerator and sped off. Other than retreating, before he turned from pursuer to prey, he had no idea what his next move should be and could only hope it would come to him by the time he rejoined his men. He figured he would have at least twenty of them at his disposal and enough firepower to fend off an initial assault. If they could put down an undermanned force, there might still be time to flee the area and regroup elsewhere.

Mikhaylov continued to rally himself as he cleared the straightaway and negotiated the first turn in the soon-to-be winding road. Two turns later, the Russian ceased his plotting, brought back to the moment by the sight of Dmitri Vishnevsky. Mikhaylov's would-be successor had made it to the road and was walking along the shoulder, back turned to the Hummer. As Mikhaylov drew closer, however, Vishnevksy slowly turned to face him, reaching for his shoulder holster. Mikhaylov found himself in the similar quandary as before: should he pick up his hated rival in hopes another soldier might help ensure that he live to fight another day? Or should he bypass the man and leave him as an offering to the people who had rescued Colt and his damnable brood?

Mikhaylov was within twenty yards of the other man when Vishnevsky recognized him and drew his pistol, prompting the Butcher to consider a third option. He eased off the gas a fleeting second, then suddenly floored the accelerator and yanked on the steering wheel, veering onto the shoulder.

Caught flat-footed, Vishnevsky wildly raised his gun and put a shot through the windshield, but not before Mikhaylov had lined up the Hummer so that it would strike his nemesis the way he'd hoped the train engine would have struck the Camry: dead center.

"THAT'S FANTASTIC!" CARL Lyons said, speaking with Jack Grimaldi by way of AirFox I's cockpit transceiver. Phil Ramon was at the controls, guiding Alan Orson's speed chopper over a course due west of the route taken by Vishnevsky's Cessna Citation before the Russian had parachuted from the jet. They'd been called off chasing the Cessna and advised instead to rendezvous with the JetRanger in preparation for storming the SVR's Glorieta compound. Lyons had just been informed that the rendezvous point had been changed to a rail crossing near the Glorieta train yards, where Bolan, Kissinger and Grimaldi had just tracked down the missing Colt family.

"They're safe and in one piece," Grimaldi reported, "but they were in one royal fender bender and Colt wants his wife and kid airlifted somewhere so they can get checked out."

Lyons glanced at Ramon. The test pilot nodded and told him, "No problem."

"We'll be there shortly and they can hitch a ride on the AirFox," Lyons told Grimaldi. "What about Colt?"

"He says he's fine," Grimaldi said. "He's wearing Orson's armored suit so he figures he's suddenly indestructible."

"Which means he wants to stick around and go back there?"

"Yep. He says he has a score to settle."

As Lyons clicked off, he saw a trio of SFPD police choppers heading eastward toward what he assumed was the SVR hideout. Lyons had been told that APD was sending aerial units, as well, and out to their right on Interstate 25 there were at least two dozen black-and-whites bound for the Glorieta exit from both directions, rooftop beacons flashing.

"We usually like to wrap these things up on our own," Lyons told Ramon, "but I guess the locals must've felt they were missing out on all the excitement."

"That'll probably be the case again," Ramon said, shifting course slightly to align himself with a back road leading to their rendezvous point. "A show of force like this and my guess is there's going to be a quick surrender."

"That or a massacre," Lyons said. "Let's hope they're not that stupid."

The AirFox was flying toward one of the final turns in the side road when Lyons glanced down and spotted an untended parachute sprawled across an open field.

"What do you think?" he asked Ramon. "Vishnevsky?"

"If it is, it doesn't look like he got very far."

Lyons looked where Ramon was pointing and saw a man lying by the side of the road. Judging from his contorted position, Lyons guessed he hadn't just dropped dead in his tracks.

"Let's take a quick look," he said.

As they drew closer, the men spotted a late-model Hummer half-submerged in a drainage ditch just off the road twenty yards from the body. Ramon veered toward the SUV and brought the AirFox down to where they could see through what was left of the front windshield. The driver was still behind the wheel. He wasn't moving. His face was smeared with blood, but not enough that Lyons wasn't able to recognize him from several descriptions he'd received over the past hour from Aaron Kurtzman back at SOG headquarters.

"Mikhaylov," he said.

"He's their ringleader, right?" Ramon said.

Lyons replied, "Not anymore."

EPILOGUE

Antwerp, Belgium

Once Evgenii Danilov's chauffeur reached Antwerp International Airport and passed through the necessary checkpoints, he drove the financier's Lincoln Town Car down the small access road leading to a private hangar. The building was shared by GHC and a handful of other large corporations, and in addition to Danilov's Learjet 31 there were three other luxury aircraft lined up and being readied to board passengers.

"I suspect they're all bound for business meetings and not running off somewhere with their tails between their legs," said Alek Repin, who sat beside Danilov in the backseat of the Lincoln.

Danilov sighed philosophically. "If they're in business long enough, they'll all have reason to make a strategic retreat at some point or another."

"Maybe so," Repin said, "but I'll bet you whatever mess they leave behind won't match ours."

"You'd be surprised."

The Lincoln finally pulled to a stop along a curb already lined with two limousines and another Town Car. While Danilov waited for the chauffeur to circle the vehicle and open the door for him, he revisited his regret over having invited

Repin to fly with him to Isle St. Louise. The SVR deputy director had been obsessing nonstop about the travails that had befallen Operation Zenta back in New Mexico.

Inwardly, Danilov was every bit as devastated by the news that Roaming Bison and its nuclear waste facility had been snatched from his grasp by American bureaucrats hiding behind badges, and the idea that most of his corporation holdings were about to follow suit was equally troubling. But he knew that what happened couldn't be changed or reversed, and therefore he was determined to go into exile with the notion that, like another of his military heroes, the great Napoleon Bonaparte, he would one day return to glory. In the meantime, at least he was free, which was more than could be said for Mikhaylov's underlings in Glorieta, who'd meekly surrendered.

When his door was opened for him, the silver-haired financier grabbed the small briefcase containing his more valuable papers and stepped out onto the curb, only to find himself facing, not his chauffeur, but rather a pale-faced man who'd somehow managed to appropriate the uniform of Danilov's personal pilot. The chauffeur had been intercepted behind the Town Car and was being placed in handcuffs, as was Alek Repin on the other side of the vehicle. The arresting officers wore the uniforms of the AIA security force, but Danilov had a feeling they were no more legitimate than the man who was just now slapping a set of cuffs on his own wrists.

"Sorry, sir," Phoenix Force leader David McCarter told Danilov as he produced another set of handcuffs. "Your flight's ready for boarding but I'm afraid there's been a slight change of itinerary."

Stony Man Farm, Virginia

"WHAT CAN I SAY?" Hal Brognola said with a shrug. "After I convinced Diaz to turn stoolie on Mikhaylov, I figured I was on a roll and decided to go after the top banana."

The SOG chief was sitting with Barbara Price in the dining alcove down the hall from the Annex Computer Room. They were both sipping coffee from cups they just used to toast the success of SOG's inadvertent mission in New Mexico as well as news that Danilov and Repin had just been apprehended by McCarter and PF commandos Gary Manning and Rafael Encizo at the GHC honcho's private hangar in Antwerp.

"Let me guess," Price said. "You dusted off your Geography 101 and figured since Belgium was just a couple airfields away from Germany you'd have Phoenix hop over and play errand boys for Interpol."

"Well, actually, I only used half the team," Brognola said. "The others stayed behind and kept the ball rolling on the missile front. They'll all be back together in time to do whatever's needed next."

"I suppose I should be upset," Price teased. "Moving our people around usually falls under the category of mission controller."

"I won't let it happen again," Brognola promised. "Besides, if I remember correctly, you were up to your elbows in chess pieces at the time."

"True," Price admitted. "Speaking of which, I better get back to it."

"And I'm due back in Washington," Brognola said. "When you talk to Striker, tell him to pass around some high fives for me. He and the crew there did one hell of a job."

"I'll do that," Price promised. "Right now, though, I think he's out of phone range."

Rosqui Pueblo, New Mexico

"AH, HOME SWEET HOME," Rafe said as he climbed out of the JetRanger and set foot amid the squalor of Healer's Ravine. Leonard and Astro had already disembarked from the chopper.

Bolan and Grimaldi remained aboard the aircraft and would soon be heading back to pick up Kissinger at the Santa Fe hospital where the Colt family was being treated for the minor injuries they'd sustained during their ordeal of the past twelve hours. Lyons had already boarded a flight back to Takoma so he could meet back up with his Able Team partners.

"You're sure you're okay with this?" Bolan asked. "I've got a few more strings I can pull for you."

"No, thanks," Leonard said. "I had some lousy room service and there's nothing good on TV out there, so why bother? We like it better here."

"And once they weed out the tribal Gestapo, I won't have to worry about being used for target practice again," Astro piped in. He patted the bandage around his upper arm and added, "I'm gonna need a new tattoo to disguise that bullet hole, though. You could spring for that if you want."

"Done," Bolan said. "And I'll put in a word with Governor Stuart about having some of the trash hauled out of here so you'll have room to plant more herbs."

"I could go for that," Leonard confessed.

"I guess that's it, then," Bolan told them. "Unless you want your clothes back after I change."

"Nah, you keep them," Astro said. "Seems like they brought you good luck."

Bolan thought back over the gauntlet of adversity he'd just come through and realized that, sure enough, the moment he'd donned the transient's clothes had been a turning point in his quest to make sense of Franklin Colt's kidnapping and see to his safe return.

"You're right," he told Astro.

"Maybe you should think about making it your official uniform," Rafe suggested.

Bolan grinned at the men and shook his head. "I don't think I'd go quite that far."

JAMES AXLER

DEATH LANDS®

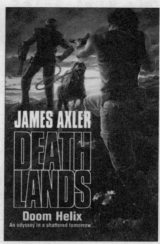

JAMES AXLER

DEATH LANDS

Doom Helix

An odyssey in a shattered tomorrow...

Doom Helix

A new battle for Deathlands has begun...

The Deathlands feudal system may be hell on earth but it must be protected from invaders from Shadow Earth, a parallel world stripped clean of its resources by the ruling conglomerate and its white coats. Ryan and his band had a near-fatal encounter with them once before and now these superhuman predators are back, ready to topple the hellscape's baronies one by one.

Available September wherever books are sold.

TAKE 'EM FREE

2 action-packed novels plus a mystery bonus

NO RISK

NO OBLIGATION TO BUY

GE10

James Axler
Outlanders®

OBLIVION STONE

A shocking gambit by a lethal foe intensifies the war to claim planet Earth…

In the wilds of Saskatchewan, a genetically engineered Annunaki prince returns after 4,500 years in solitary confinement to seek vengeance against the father who betrayed him. And his personal mission to harness Earth's citizens to build his city and his army appears unstoppable.…

Available August wherever books are sold.

GOLD EAGLE®

www.readgoldeagle.blogspot.com

GOUT54